StarFire Dragons

Book One of the Dragon Spawn Chronicles

By Dawn Ross

“It's been my experience that the prejudices people feel about each other disappear when they get to know each other.”
– James T. Kirk (“Elaan of Troyius”)

StarFire Dragons

Book One of the Dragon Spawn Chronicles
Updated

by Dawn Ross

Cover
Dragon art by Dmitrii Brigidov, purchased under the standard license agreement through istockphoto.com in 2017. Spaceship purchased from Waldemar Schmies under the standard license agreement through Depositphotos Inc. Eclipse image and starry background from NASA. Images combined by germancreative on fiverr.com.

Special Thanks

I'd like to extend a special thanks to all the beta readers and editors who helped me make this novel shine. And additional thanks to my final editor, Grace Bridges, who has been instrumental in helping me with content and line edits as well as with pointing out opportunities for story improvement.

"A thoughtful novel that owes a debt to
Star Trek but works on its own terms."
—Kirkus Reviews

"A subtle space opera that explores the ethical
conundrums of intergalactic relations with main
characters who are worth rooting for."
—Becca Saffier, *Reedsy Discovery*

"Fans of epic sci-fi that look for realistic characters and complex
yet believable settings will find *Starfire Dragons*
a powerful introductory story that promises more, yet
nicely concludes its immediate dilemmas."
—D. Donovan, Senior Reviewer, *Midwest Book Review*

StarFire Dragons

Book One of the Dragon Spawn Chronicles

by Dawn Ross

1
The Blue Blight

3790:256:02:22. Year 3790, day 256, 02:22 hours, Prontaean time as per the last sync.

A rising vibration hummed through J.D. Hapker's body as he phased from the space vessel onto the planet. The phasing sensation dissipated and a chill from this world's atmosphere enveloped him. Regret sank in for not wearing a helmet, as the tips of his ears and nose turned raw from the cold. The air filtered by his nosepiece filled his lungs and radiated throughout him like a morning frost.

His form-fitting enviro-suit quickly adjusted to the temperature but it took a moment longer for him to regain his bearings. He rested his hands on his hips and ignored the team of working scientists to scan the distant horizon instead. The lines between the slate-blue land, ocean, and sky merged seamlessly into a vast heavy blanket of twilight fog.

Only stunted plants grew, yet it was more than what had been here a few decades ago when the terraforming experiment had started. Back then, the planet contained only microbial organisms hidden beneath an infinite bleakness of pale-blue ice. No wonder they nicknamed it the Blue Blight.

A heaviness settled over him that had nothing to do with the planet's strong gravitational force. How had his life come to this? His parents had been so proud when he began the same career path as his father, grandfather, and great-grandfather before him.

It wasn't enough—not for him, anyway. The time he'd spent vacationing with his family in the forests of his homeworld inspired him to explore further. So in a decision his dad had said was rash and irresponsible, Hapker left home for a career in space.

This should have been a new adventure, but his expectations fell short. The decisions were harder, the ethics fuzzier, and his superiors less forgiving. One incident gone awry and now his life had taken a turn as cheerless as this land.

If this second chance didn't work out, he'd return home an utter failure and face the perpetual disappointment of his father.

Hapker pushed down a rising sense of gloom and plodded over to the scientists. Gravity made his trek slow and arduous. No dust billowed from under his feet. He left no marks on this dense terrain. He was like an elephant tromping on stone.

Excited banter reached him as he arrived within earshot of the terra-team. A science officer tapped his finger on the viewscreen with apparent glee. Hapker watched with envy. It had been a long time since he'd been so passionate about his own job.

All conversation cut off at his approach. "Doctor Canthidius." He smiled at the lead science officer.

The man looked up but didn't return the greeting. Doctor Holgarth Canthidius' features were more extreme than any Hapker had encountered in his travels thus far. The man's eyes reminded him of a tropical fish. His skin was grey with a hint of blue and his mouth puckered.

Since Canthidius came from the nearly all-ocean planet of Nomare, his resemblance to a fish seemed a cosmic joke. Hapker would have thought the man was a space alien if he didn't already know such beings beyond a few lower-life forms hadn't been discovered yet. As a human, Canthidius was much the same as every other person in the galaxy. However, the passing generations of people spread over a wide variety of ecosystems had diversified their characteristics.

"Did you find something interesting?" Hapker asked.

"Nothing that would interest *you*, Commander," Canthidius said.

Hapker clenched his jaw. He was the Vice Executive Commander of the *Odyssey*, the largest and most advanced science and service vessel of the Prontaean Colonial Cooperative. It was his job to monitor the progress of his crew, even if he didn't understand all of what they were doing.

Canthidius had a right to resent him. Hapker had little in common with his new crew. Early in his adult life, he'd served as a Pholatian Protector like his father. Later, he became a high-ranking military officer with the Prontaean Galactic Force. Though he never fit in with the PG-Force's hard-core attitudes, his combat and strategic skills meant he resembled them more than these scientists and engineers.

"Give me an abbreviated version anyway," Hapker said brusquely.

Canthidius droned on with a long explanation full of technical terms, no doubt talking over his head on purpose.

Hapker suppressed a frown. His lack of understanding sent his mind wandering as the man rattled on. When the comm beeped in his ear, he readily raised his hand to stop the doctor. He pressed the lower part of the comm-strip taped below his earlobe. "Hapker here. Go ahead."

"Commander, we have a situation," Captain Arden said. "I need everyone to return to the ship immediately."

Hapker shifted into high alert. He saw no immediate threat, but his training didn't allow him to take this as anything less than serious. "Yes, Sir."

He released the comm and addressed the scientists. "The captain wants us all back on the *Odyssey*, now."

"What? Why?" Canthidius replied with a look of consternation.

"No time for questions, Doctor. If you want to know the reason, you can ask the captain yourself, *after* we return to the ship."

Canthidius pursed his fishlike lips in apparent reluctance. Captain Silas Arden had never served in the military, but his crew respected him in the same way *everyone* respected a general.

2
The Cougar and the Serpent

3790:256:02:43. A flush of heat swept through J.D. Hapker's body as he phased back to the reasonable temperature inside the *Odyssey*. He nodded a thanks to the transport officer as he passed and exited into the corridor. He set a brisk pace, dodging civilians and officers alike. Service and maintenance bots veered around or waited for him to pass. A smaller machine whirred as it cleaned the floor. The larger one operated on a door panel, making an audible and visible zap.

Traffic diminished as he turned into the unremarkable hall leading to the bridge. While colored panels hid much of the ship's dull framework, the walls here were white. Only an occasional emergency toolbox broke the monotony.

Hapker stopped at the entrance and straightened his shoulders. He was the captain's new vice executive commander and if he expected his career with the PCC to last much longer, he'd best look less like an owl at sunrise and more like a sparrowhawk at dawn.

Captain Arden sat in the central chair with an iron composure and a solemn expression. His piercing eyes met Hapker's but the man neither spoke nor gestured.

Hapker had served under harsh leaders before, but this man gripped his career by its heart.

"Should I change from my enviro-suit, Sir?" After three months of serving with Captain Arden, he still had no idea what the man expected of him.

The captain flicked his hand toward the secondary central chair. "Have a seat. We have two unidentified ships headed to the planet. No information yet."

Hapker sat. While encountering vessels wasn't unusual, unauthorized visitors to a planet in the terraforming process was.

The console at his chair showed them too far from the short-range sensors. The large viewscreen at the front of the bridge displayed an expansive stretch of deep black dotted with an array of shimmering constellations. Hapker was awed by the universe—empty, yet so full at the same time.

In a strange way, the vastness of space resembled the forests of his homeworld. Behind every tree, around every star, a new adventure awaited. The semblance ended there, though. Back home, the trees brought serenity. Nothing but discord awaited here.

He pushed down the hollowness rising within. Once upon a time, the prospect of visiting different worlds sent his heart soaring. Although every human-inhabited planet had been cultivated with flora and fauna from Earth, each had developed its own distinctive aspects. A range of unique landscapes promised a lifetime of adventure, allowing human cultures to evolve, or devolve, into new and fascinating facets of living.

The Kimpke incident had changed his perspective. The exuberance of his youth faded and was replaced with a disillusionment as depressing as the blackness that surrounded him.

Several officers operated the stations organized in a half-moon section at the front of the bridge. As usual, they seemed indifferent to his presence. He probably imagined the weight of their judgment regarding Kimpke. One would think his actions might find favor with non-military personnel, but innocent people had still died.

It had been a mistake coming here. He should have declined the commission to serve on the *Odyssey*. Dad had been right. The galaxy wasn't ready for the enlightened view of a Pholatian Protector.

"Sir." The comm officer's tone struck through the lull of the starship bridge. "I'm receiving a distress signal."

Hapker's pensiveness cleared away as though emerging from the gloominess of a dark forest. He focused on the information scrolling across the bottom of the front viewscreen.

After thirty days of sitting around a mundane planet, he could use some action.

Officer Brenson tilted his half-bald head and pressed the earpiece into his uniquely shaped ears. "The signal is Tredon, Sir."

Hapker's skin turned cold. The Tredons—or more accurately, the Toradons. Most people used the term Tredon for this race with the mentality of the ancient Earth Huns. It derived from their inclination to *tread on* and dominate.

"Major Bracht, to the bridge," the captain called into the comm.

Hapker flinched. The *Odyssey* was no military ship, but it still had weaponry and a small military presence. The captain and commander had ultimate authority here but, protocol or not, calling the Rabnoshk warrior to join them was like using a photon torpedo when only a phaser was needed.

Brenson turned to Captain Arden with a tilted head and wrinkled brow. "Sir, they say they're being pursued by Grapnes."

Hapker blinked. "Grapnes? Are you sure?"

Brenson nodded. "Yes, Sir."

Hapker leaned forward. His mouth fell slack as he read the transcript Brenson posted on the viewscreen. This had to be a first. The galaxy's fiercest warriors being chased by space vultures? It had to be a trick.

Captain Arden's dark bushy brows twitched downward over his stark blue eyes as he tapped his thick bearded chin. "Can your scanners verify?"

The operations officer reviewed his console. "I can only detect a ship is following them, Sir. I can't yet tell if it's a Grapne ship."

The hulking form of the defense chief entered the bridge. His firm jaw and unruly blond hair enhanced his savage look. Hapker's chest hardened as Major Bracht stomped to the tactical station on the captain's other side. He'd never met a Tredon before, but god help them all if they were anything like the Rabnoshk warriors.

Bracht seemed to embody every unpleasant Rabnoshk stereotype he'd ever heard—loud and abrasive, confrontational, limbs like tree trunks, and most unsettling, front teeth filed to reveal a carnivorous snarl.

The viewscreen switched from the displayed data to a digitized image of two dots speeding toward the planet. Hapker thumped his fingers on the arm of his chair, adding to the faint sounds of mechanical beeps and the tapping on consoles.

Things had been uneventful for too long, making this situation as captivating as a volcanic lightning storm. A quick glance at the crew led him to believe they felt the same way. Bracht watched the screen with a fierce focus. Chandly hovered over his station. Brenson kept his hand to his earpiece and a hawkish gaze fixed on his console.

Captain Silas Arden seemed as cool as ever. The man sat back in his chair with his hands relaxed on the armrests. His face always held a scowl, but perhaps it was because of his prominent brows. Even with his reputation as a peacemaker, one could only guess at how many enemies he'd dealt with in his career. The Tredons were merely another variation.

"Both ships are now within primary SRS," Chandly said of the short-range sensors. "The Tredon ship is only a small Serpent. The other is an Angolan Cougar."

Hapker nodded to himself. This explained the fleeing Tredons. The smallness of their ship compared like a mouse to the Grapne ship's namesake. Those ships, however, were dwarfed by the *Odyssey*. Even as a civilian-run Expedition-class starship, the *Odyssey* carried more firepower too.

Hapker absently rubbed his jaw, still unused to its clean-shaven smoothness. Knowing the types of ships involved illuminated part of the situation, but it didn't explain why the Grapnes would risk attacking such a dangerous warrior race. No one purposely messed with the Tredons.

"We have a full visual, Captain," another bridge officer announced.

The captain flicked his hand, and the officer flipped the screen to an up-close view of the Serpent.

The ship resembled a black cottonmouth snake with its flat head and narrowing tail. Its sleek design was admirable, even if it belonged to a notorious race of warriors.

The Cougar didn't share its elegance. The only thing cougarish about this clam-shaped ship was its color, yet the yellow was different than on the real live cougar Hapker had seen during a safari on his homeworld. This was dirtier, bespeckled like an aged pear.

He inched forward as the ships raced onward, exchanging rapid fire. The spread of the dissipating energy from their shields indicated an even match, but the Serpent would eventually succumb.

“Open a channel to both ships,” Captain Arden said.

The comm officer tapped his console. “Open, Sir.”

“This is Captain Silas Arden of the Prontaean Colonial Cooperative. You are in Cooperative territory in violation of the Ornman Treaty and committing a criminal act by using your weapons. Stand down immediately or we’ll fire.”

The strength of the captain’s gruff tone penetrated Hapker’s core. The man seldom spoke, but when he did it was direct and to the point.

Brenson waited, hand to earpiece, but no response came in.

“They will be within firing range in twenty thousand clicks.” Bracht’s voice boomed. The ends of his long mustache stabbed down like daggers with each word. “I’ve targeted the Serpent.”

Hapker frowned at the Rabnoshk warrior. “The Serpent? The Cougar is the aggressor.”

Bracht scowled back. “Probably for good reason.”

“A small ship like that likely means they’re pirates,” another officer added.

It was a credible point, but not enough justification. “We don’t have all the facts yet.”

Bracht’s frown deepened. “They’re Tredons. That’s all we need to know.”

Hapker returned the look. “Target *both* ships, Major.”

Bracht’s expression didn’t change, but he followed orders. “Yes, Sir.”

Hapker glanced at Captain Arden to see if he’d overstepped. To his relief, the captain made a slight nod.

The ships neared.

Chandly interrupted the quiet tension. “The Cougar is called *Virtuous Dealings*.”

A few officers tittered. Hapker suppressed an eye-roll. Although Grapnes had a reputation opposite of virtuous, he didn’t appreciate the crew’s unprofessional reaction.

“The Serpent is called *StarFire*.”

Hapker’s mouth curled as a sour taste arose. Bracht might be right. A Tredon ship named after a deadly weapon probably meant pirates—or worse—slave hunters. “Do we have any records on this vessel?”

“Nothing, Commander.”

"They have now entered firing range." Bracht's glittering eyes hinted at his eagerness. "Should I fire, Sir?"

The captain glanced at Brenson.

"Still no reply, Sir," the communications officer replied.

"And they're still shooting at one another," Chandly added.

"Two warning shots," Captain Arden said. "One for each ship."

Bracht fired. Neither ship reacted. The *StarFire* sped to the Blue Blight as though intending to dive into it, and the Grapnes pursued.

"What are they doing?" Hapker asked as the Tredons charged into the atmosphere at neck-breaking speed. "They're not attempting suicide, are they? I thought the Tredons were more of the *die fighting* type."

"They might be trying a skimming maneuver," the helmsman said.

Hapker shook his head. "They'd better be excellent pilots." He'd only seen it performed in simulation. In the few times it had worked, the intentional combustion of the upper atmosphere blinded pursuers and allowed the fleeing vessel to disappear onto the other side of the planet. In the foolishness of his youth, he'd daydreamed about trying this amazing feat. However, most simulations ended in the destruction of the very ship that had deployed it.

He couldn't tear his eyes away from the Serpent as it dived. A bright cloud burst over a section of the atmosphere and rolled out in a gigantic wave. He reflexively pulled back. The fire rippled in waves of orange to yellow to brown and he lost sight of the ship. "Where's the Serpent?"

"Got it!" an officer said.

Hapker's heart jumped. The viewscreen blinked into focus on the *StarFire* as it flew away from the inferno. He leaned forward in amazement while other crew members mumbled their disappointment. Few had any liking for the Grapnes, but they undoubtedly hated the Tredons more.

The Cougar probably couldn't see the *StarFire* from their position but continued to fire.

"Major," the captain said. "Launch torpedoes at the Cougar, now."

Hapker felt the slight jolt of the *Odyssey* as weapon turrets fired, but the action came too late. As the Cougar's defense system destroyed the torpedoes, a random shot of their own penetrated the Serpent's shields and blasted its tail. Hapker's stomach twinged while the ship spiraled out of control, leaving a tail of flames as it fell through the atmosphere.

The shape of Captain Arden's brows matched Bracht's, but he suspected the captain held anger for a different reason. "Hold fire but maintain your target. Open the comm to the Cougar."

A distinct but subtle beep from the officer's console indicated the opened comm.

"Cougar ship! You will fall back at once!" The captain's knuckles whitened as his hands gripped the armrests of his chair.

"The *StarFire*'s about to crash," an officer said in an elated tone.

The screen focused on the Tredon ship as it continued its fiery descent. Hapker swallowed the lump in his throat. Whatever he thought he knew about the Tredons, it was still tragic to watch them go down after such an incredible feat.

"The Cougar is no longer firing," Bracht said.

"Keep your weapons ready." Captain Arden's hands wrapped into fists. "If you see one more burst come from that ship, Major, you are to open fire."

Hapker's heart thumped at the anticipation of battle, but he displayed an outward calm.

"Wait!" Brenson's high-pitched tone stabbed into his eardrum. "The Cougar is hailing us. A Captain Seth."

"They've disengaged their weapons," Chandly added.

Captain Arden gave Bracht a look. Hapker suspected it meant he should keep their weapons armed and ready. Bracht glowered but nodded respectfully.

The captain flexed his hands. "Open the channel."

The viewscreen changed to the image of a Grapne. The man's thin and wiry frame was typical of his race. He had a sly mien about him, like that of the eel Hapker had caught once while fishing with his dad.

"Captain Arden here," he said just as the Grapne opened his mouth to speak. "What in the *hell* are you doing firing your weapons in Cooperative space?"

"Captain Arden, we are ssso sssorry for the intrusion," Captain Seth replied in the typical Grapne hissing accent. He tipped his head down like a groveling dog. "We were in pursuit of these thieves and didn't have the opportunity to seek permission."

A brief flicker of smugness crossed the Rabnoshk warrior's face. Hapker clenched his jaw. Bracht might be right about the circumstances but targeting only the fleeing ship was still wrong.

"I do not have any reports of thieves, Captain Seth," the captain replied tersely. "Protocol states you are to report such things to the proper authorities. You didn't even do this much. I can only assume you are here for a personal vendetta rather than an ordinary pursuit of a thief."

"I assure you, Captain, my intentions are honorable."

"I doubt that," Hapker muttered. Captain Arden glanced at him with reproof. His gut twisted and the uncertainty of his new position threatened to well up again.

"Nevertheless," the captain said to the Grapne, "you will stand down and await disciplinary action. Is that understood?"

"Yes, Captain Arden." The meek tone made Hapker think of a devious little snake.

The viewscreen switched back to the full view of the planet. It was deceptively calm and undisturbed. The fire in its atmosphere had dissipated, leaving the blue-grey ball looking as gloomy as ever.

"The *StarFire* has crashed," the operations officer reported before anyone could ask.

"Survivors?" The captain's brows remained down but seemed more troubled than angry.

"Unknown, Sir. The ship's debris is interfering with our scans."

Captain Arden turned to Hapker. "Commander, take a team of medical personnel down to the surface. A squad of security as well."

Despite his surprise at the captain's consideration for the Tredons, Hapker almost jumped out of his chair. "Yes, Sir."

This must be a test. As security chief, Bracht generally led high-risk operations. Since Hapker had once been a PG-Force officer, he was also qualified—except he had failed in that position.

He glanced at Bracht to see if the man resented his going instead. The warrior frowned, but no more than usual.

"Commander!" Chandly's sharp tone stopped Hapker short. "It looks like the Grapnes are sending a team down as well."

"Make it two squads," the captain replied regarding security.

Hapker nodded. *This can't be good.* He left the bridge with haste. His heart raced in anticipation. Whatever was going on, he'd better be at his best. The last thing he needed was to get on the wrong side of another commanding officer.

3
The Unexpected Enemy

3790:256:03:28. J.D. Hapker phased onto the gloomy planet for the second time today. This time with defensive gear, an open-faced helmet with a tactical display, plus security and rescue teams—and with a rising anxiety.

He blinked away the flutter of disorientation that always accompanied this method of travel. The Blight's chill came and went as waves of searing heat swept in. The tang of burning metal tickled his nose.

Even at this distance, the black mass of the Serpent-class starship dominated his sight. Pockets of red flame billowed into a thick haze. Charcoal puffs rolled upward into the grey sky or drifted across the drab blue land.

A flash burst like lightning within the thundercloud of smoke that engulfed the *StarFire*. The beam of phaser fire escaped from the cloud and into a small group of approaching Grapnes, sending one to the ground.

Despite the carnage of the wrecked ship, it seemed at least one Tredon was up for a fight.

The remaining Grapnes returned fire. Three of the four in their tan suits shot wildly at a single black-garbed Tredon hunkered down behind a large bit of mangled debris.

Hapker peered through the smoky haze. A ribbon of clarity wafted by when the Tredon stood and fired again. He eye-clicked a feature on his visor to zoom in and scan.

The data came in. He frowned and rechecked it. Both the Tredon's height and build were all wrong. Tredon warriors tended to be tall and muscular.

A chill ran down his spine. This Tredon was only a boy.

Two Grapnes remained standing now, both firing relentlessly.

"Deflectors up." Lieutenant Sharkey's voice sounded nasal with the filtering apparatus fitted into her nostrils.

Hapker pinched the sides of the device hanging from his belt. An electric buzz indicated the activation of his invisible body shield. "Medics, wait for my call." He turned to the security officers. "With me. Weapons on stun and fire only if fired upon."

A copper haired officer stepped in front of him. "We got this, Sir," Sergeant Siven Addams said pointedly.

Hapker excused the man's initiative. Many PCC commanders, who generally didn't have much military training, allowed their PG-Force teams to handle direct conflicts.

"It's my prerogative to take charge, Sergeant," he replied, ignoring the skittering sense of doubt that popped up, "and that's what I'm doing."

Addams opened his mouth to speak. Hapker forestalled him with a raised hand. "Let's go. Now."

The sergeant glanced at Lieutenant Sharkey. She dipped her head. Hapker didn't need her assent but was glad to have it.

Phaser ready, he ran hard over the slate-blue land toward the action. The planet's stronger gravity made it feel like trudging through deep water. His feet pounded solidly on the flat dry surface. Even with the air filter, every breath took in smoke, which compounded his effort.

Some members of the team grumbled about the distance. He mentally shook his head. The transport chief had no way of knowing the extent of damage from the crashed *StarFire*. Any closer and they could have been deposited in the middle of burning wreckage.

His heart drummed in his ears. A point of decision fast approached. He must pick a side, but which one?

The Tredons were their enemies but the Grapnes appeared to be the aggressors. Two armed men fought against a mere boy. Tredon or not, he was still a child.

His lungs burned from the exertion as he led onward. "Security." He panted. "Take aim. Don't fire."

He touched the trigger as they approached shouting distance. "Stand down! In the name of the Prontaean Cooperative, stand down!"

The Grapnes paid him no mind. He opened his mouth to repeat the order when another blast from the Tredon's weapon sent a third Grapne into a heap on the ground.

Hapker recovered from his surprise and signaled one squad in the boy's direction while he and the others headed toward the remaining aggressor. "Stand down, all of you!"

Another quick shot from the Tredon boy felled the last Grapne.

"All teams halt!" Hapker said.

Did that boy just single-handedly take out all the Grapnes? Everything happened so fast, but he thought the boy had only fired four times. Four Grapnes, four shots. Despite his own skill in marksmanship, he doubted he'd be able to hit his targets so quickly and accurately.

A stillness settled. The roaring flames of the ship coincided with the throbbing in his ears. If the young Tredon remained standing, he might be weighing his chances against them.

Hapker shuddered. He reunited the two security teams and headed cautiously toward the boy's hiding place. "Lower your weapons but be ready." The last thing he wanted was to appear either threatening or vulnerable.

The black-haired youth stepped out from behind a chunk of wreckage, aiming with a small hand-held weapon. Hapker froze as the muzzle and two dark piercing eyes targeted him. A sinking feeling filled his gut. He might have to kill a child—or a child might kill him. His instinct told him to take aim, but he couldn't bring himself to threaten a boy.

The roundness of the boy's face marked him as about ten years old, maybe older considering his height. Even in his youth, he looked every inch a soldier in his black uniform. The boy had a well-balanced stance, poised both defensively and offensively and at an angle that presented a smaller target. The hateful look in his dark eyes along with the way he gripped his weapon indicated he was not only ready, but willing to fight.

Hapker's pulse quickened. The boy held a solid and direct glower as if daring him to make the first move. Hapker maintained eye contact but left his posture open and nonconfrontational.

"We're here to help," he said. Adrenaline flushed through his body, yet he kept his voice calm. Without taking his eyes off the boy, he flipped up his visor and holstered his phaser. It was stupid, but he had to defuse the situation somehow, and his deflector shield would protect him.

He pointed to the personnel further behind him. "I have three medical officers with me. Do you or your crew members need medical attention?"

The boy didn't respond.

Perhaps he didn't speak the universal language. Hapker used his visor to remote-open an application on the MM computer tablet secured around his wrist. The device repeated what he'd said in the Tredon language.

The boy remained silent.

Hapker resisted the urge to swallow down the saliva building in his mouth. The youth obviously needed aid. He had blood on his forehead and his other arm hung at an odd angle. He showed no sign of being in pain, though. If anything, he looked ready to spit fire.

"We're not here to harm you. I promise." The MM repeated the translation.

The boy neither moved nor spoke. Hapker remained still as well, as tension built.

The Tredon boy lowered his phaser, revealing a soot-blackened face with even more blood on his cheek and down his jawline. Hapker exhaled but didn't let go of his vigilance.

Without a word, the boy turned and walked away.

Hapker followed him deeper into the remains of the crashed ship. Waves of heat buffeted him, and hot acrid air entered his lungs, making him hack. Smoldering debris littered the ground. Fire burned in several places and the smoke thickened.

Bodies lay inside the gaping wound of the *StarFire*. Twisted limbs, blood, pieces of tissue, and the scent of burning flesh assaulted his senses. That anyone had survived this crash at all was surprising.

The boy led him and the squads to a damaged crash pod. Hapker set his nervousness aside and peered in at another youth—this one older and his body so mangled that he must be dead.

He blinked open a med-scanner in his visor anyway. A wave of lines popped up. He bent closer to the body to make sure it picked up the right signal. *I'll be darned.* This young man had a pulse.

He called for the medics.

Doctor Jerom arrived first, stepping through the debris with a hand-held scanner. After waving it over the body, a dozen different readings popped up on the larger device. "We must get him to the medic bay immediately." The greying man jutted his cleft chin in a way that brooked no argument.

"Of course." Hapker turned to the younger boy. The youth's dark eyes hardened, but he thought he saw concern in them too. "We can help him on our ship," he said. "We can help you both, but please trust me and put your phaser down."

"Trust you?" The boy snarled the words but spoke the universal language perfectly.

Hapker's eyebrows shot up. So, he understood him. "Trust me." His body still burned from the adrenaline rush, but he kept his voice calm. "Hand me your weapon, and we'll get you both some medical attention. I promise."

The boy's demeanor didn't change. Hapker held his breath. The youth glanced back and forth from him to the young man in the pod. Despite the dry heat from the wreckage, sweat formed on Hapker's brow.

His tension broke as the boy's glower softened and he handed over the phaser.

Hapker exhaled and grasped it, then almost dropped it. A starfire phaser had no stun setting, only a powerful kill one. If the Grapnes didn't have the same top-of-the-line body shields as the Cooperative officers, they weren't just stunned. They were dead, shot in self-defense—but killed by a child.

He swallowed, trying not to think of the implications. He shook off his unease and removed two bio-readers from a pocket in his jumpsuit. "These are so our ship can beam you aboard," he said. The boy didn't reply but took the chips and placed one on the other youth. "The doctor will go with you to our medical facility."

The boy still didn't speak. His stiff posture no longer looked ready to fight, but he seemed as alert as any full-grown soldier would be.

"You three." Hapker pointed to the nearest security personnel. "Escort them with the doctor." He tapped his comm to open a channel to his ship above. "Six to beam up, two for immediate medical attention."

Unease whirled in his gut as he watched the small group disintegrate. What were Tredon children doing here and why were the Grapnes after them?

He stood for a moment longer, thinking. His lungs burned with the heat of the burning ship and smoke stung his eyes. He coughed again and collected himself before making his way to clearer air.

"Commander," Lieutenant Sharkey said. She flipped up her visor to wipe away the tears created by the fumes. A black smudge accentuated the sharpness of her cheekbones and squareness of her masculine jaw.

"Yes, Lieutenant," he replied.

"We haven't found any other survivors, Sir."

"Were any of the other passengers children?"

"I don't think so, Sir. The dead were all adults as far as we could tell."

Great. What would they do with two orphaned warrior boys capable of killing and who'd probably been taught to hate them since birth?

"How many?" he asked.

"We've counted seven so far. There may be a few more."

He nodded. There might be two to three more bodies in a ship this size. "Any indication of why the Grapnes were chasing them? Slaves? Precious cargo?"

"We're still checking, Sir, but it's hard to tell."

"What about the Grapnes?" he asked as he flicked his hand toward the area where they had attacked.

"All dead, Sir," she replied.

Hapker's stomach knotted, but not from surprise. The Tredons had a way of getting the best weapons while the Grapnes got the universe's leftovers. "Thank you, Lieutenant. Keep looking over the wreckage."

"Yes, Sir."

He returned to his own survey of the rubble. The ship looked like a giant dead carcass with its side slashed open and its guts exposed. The entire rear was demolished. All the energy and unstable elements from the engine hull had created a mighty explosion. From what he recalled from his studies, some ships like the Serpent had long bodies to help protect the crew in front from such blasts. In this case, it blew all the way through the cargo hold and into the living area. The cockpit remained intact, but only on the outside. The inside reminded him of the pit of a dying campfire—black with some glowing embers, and nothing resembling what had existed before.

He shook his head. There couldn't possibly be anything of value left, so what the heck did the Grapnes hope to find? Whatever it was, it must have been worth risking their lives for. Four Grapnes dead, just like that. He hoped he hadn't made a mistake bringing the Tredon boys onto his ship.

4
Secrets

3790:256:03:47. Jori's head swam. The view of the planet distorted into the interior of the enemy ship. His skin tingled at the sensation of his molecules being reintegrated. The process didn't hurt, nor was it considered dangerous. However, the thought of every fiber of his existence being taken apart and put back together turned his stomach. What if the machine malfunctioned? Would he be the same person? Would he even know if he wasn't?

The prickling of his skin quickly dissipated, and his vision sharpened. He stood on a transport platform, making his short stature reach eye-level with a half-dozen enemies.

"Chusho," he cursed under his breath as several rushed forth. His heart skipped a beat when a skinny man with red hair shoved something at his chest. He slapped it away and swung back around with a fist. A firm hand at the crook of his arm halted his forward momentum.

"Take it easy, young man," a big-nosed Cooperative guard beside him said. The silver streaks in the man's dark hair indicated he was older than the others, but still very much a warrior with his hard expression and broad shoulders.

Another guard clamped Jori's injured shoulder in an iron grip. He gritted his teeth against the hot flush of pain bursting through him. He wrenched against his captors, but it didn't work.

His heart pounded. "No! You promised! Let me go!"

They tricked him. No one here would help him. He was their prisoner. He struggled harder but to no avail. If only he weren't so small—and if only he wasn't injured.

"Get that gurney over here!" a woman said.

Both she and the grey-haired doctor with the butt chin leaned over his unconscious brother. The doctor reached into the drawer of a contraption lingering beside him. This med bot resembled both a cabinet and computer.

When the doctor pulled something metallic out and moved to use it on his defenseless brother, Jori's heart leapt to his throat. "Don't hurt him!" He jerked and a flash of searing white blasted through his body followed by a wave of blackness. His legs fell beneath him, but the guards held him up.

His shoulder burned like molten steel and felt as heavy. He growled through the agony and regained his feet. The guards spoke but their words didn't register. He had to protect his brother.

He paused and breathed in deeply to recover his bearings. The pain abated to a small degree, enough to clear his head.

His captors eased their grip. With a slight twist and a swift movement, he slipped out and leapt from the transport platform.

"Don't hurt him!" He skidded to the doctor's side. A chop to the man's forearm sent the device in his hand tumbling down.

A pair of stout arms from behind coiled around Jori like the cords of an iron bola weapon. The pressure on his shoulder blazed in an agony of fire. He squeezed his eyes shut and yowled. His yell turned into a roar as he desperately increased his struggle.

The guard's crushing embrace held him firm. His heart went wild.

"Yo, kid! Take it easy. It's alright."

Jori opened his eyes.

The grizzled guard with the big nose knelt on one knee and pointed at the device in the doctor's hand. "Listen, it's only a med-scanner."

Jori worked to suppress the intense emotions prickling through him while also weighing the truth of his words.

"It's alright. We're trying to help you."

Jori swallowed hard. Pain racked his body and his racing heart ached, but he sensed the truth of the man's words. *Stop panicking and think.*

The skinny red-haired man came forward again, this time hesitantly. The guard pointed at the device in his hand. "See. It's a scanner. He's a medic. He only wants to help you."

The medic held it upright. It looked a little different from the ones used at home, but it was definitely a med-scanner.

Even so. "Help me?" Jori's tone challenged. He glanced back and forth between the guard and the medic as the doctor tended his brother. He focused his sensing ability and let their emotions seep in. The medic's wariness and worry were like an intruder upon his own emotions, but his desire to help was real.

"Yes. Help you." A touch of irritation came through the guard's sincerity.

Jori allowed his ability to absorb the other sensations around him. Carefulness and focus were the primary emotions of the ones wearing pale blue who picked up his brother and placed him on a wheeled bed. Urgency filled them as they rushed him away.

Jori's body tensed. "Where are they taking him?"

The guard raised his hand. "They're getting him to sick bay where they can give him more help."

Jori eased in a controlled breath. He observed the surrounding strangers. Several wearing the same light blue uniform as the red-haired man stayed back. Their postures, although tense, were not poised to attack. Some held scanners. Others carried medical supplies.

The only ones armed were the guards in the steel-grey uniforms with epaulettes on their shoulders. The sensations from them bore vigilance but none had their weapons out. The only sensation of hostility arose from the one holding him. Jori's hypervigilance still gripped him, but the pressing need to fight abated.

"Let him go," the grizzled guard with the sergeant's epaulette said.

The one restraining him harrumphed. "Sir? All this little dreg knows is violence. I don't want him to attack another medic or doctor."

"Yeah," the third guard said. "You saw how he killed four people down on the planet."

Jori's face flushed. He had acted in defense. He'd certainly like to bloody the nose of the man holding him now. If they truly planned on helping his brother, though, it would be smarter to cooperate. At least for a while, until he had his full strength back.

He wore a wooden guise. "*Never let your enemy know what you're thinking*," Sensei Jeruko's words echoed in his head. *Emotion is weakness.*

The tactic gained him nothing. A sense of agreement came from the grizzled sergeant, and he called for another gurney. "We can strap him down."

Heat washed over Jori's face again. "I won't be tied down!"

The sergeant shook his head. "Look, kid. We've got to get you to sick bay, and we're not carrying you."

The thought of being carried made Jori grow hotter. "I will walk," he said through clenched teeth.

The man hesitated, then pulled something from a pouch on his belt. "Cuff him."

Jori eyed him with disgust as he passed the manacles to the third guard. He hated the humiliation of being a prisoner on an enemy ship. What choice did he have, though?

He didn't resist as the guard clamped the cold metal around his wrists—not that the man gave him an opportunity. Dizzying blackness threatened again as they twisted his other hand behind him. He winced at the pain but suppressed the urge to cry out. Sensei Jeruko would've been proud.

The red-haired medic came forward with his scanner. "May I?"

Jori glared at him but nodded his consent.

The man waved the device over his body. "No internal injuries, but you need to go to the medic bay for your injured shoulder. Um…" he flicked his gaze at the guards. "The restraints will need to come off."

The guard behind Jori huffed. "You saw what he did. We're not taking them off unless he wants to be strapped to gurney."

Jori tensed. "No!"

"Are you sure you want to walk?" the medic asked him.

"I'm sure," he replied in a hard tone. It was bad enough being surrounded by the enemy. He wasn't about to lie vulnerable for them too. He moved to step off the platform. The guards held him by the shoulders but let him go forward.

The medic's brow furrowed. "You really should get on the gurney."

Jori ignored him and followed the other medics down the corridor. He focused his ability ahead to see if he could feel anything from his brother. Generally, he could find Terkeshi anywhere, even from a great distance. Not this time, though.

Terk's weakened lifeforce made Jori's throat go dry. A coldness swept over him. His brother lived but he emitted no other sensations.

He clenched his jaw to keep the rising despair at bay. He couldn't cry here—not in front of his enemies. *You can't die, Terk. You just can't.*

They turned the corner into the infirmary. Jori froze. He was struck by a scent so clean that it burned his sinuses. The bright lights stung his eyes. He blinked and his vision adjusted.

The orderliness of this place would have shamed a Zraben munitions store. In chaotic contrast, a swarm of pale-blue and white-garbed people scurried around the body of his brother like a pack of hungry blackbeasts on a shika. Their charged voices rang out, not unlike the anxious yips of the beastly predators. A swelling urgency threatened to overwhelm Jori's senses. Some was his own but most belonged to the medical personnel.

Perhaps the things he'd heard regarding the Prontaean Cooperative were true. His father would have called their compassion for all humankind a weakness. However, this flaw meant his brother had a chance to survive. He clenched and unclenched his muscles, releasing the tensions that had knotted up inside him.

A man wearing white approached and knelt before him. His green eyes seemed warm somehow, as warm as the brown of his skin.

The guard gripped Jori's shoulder again. "Careful, Doc," he said. "He nearly rammed his fist into the nose of the last person who came up to him."

"I can hardly blame him," the doctor replied in a deep but smooth voice. "It looks like he's been to hell and back, and now he's surrounded by a dozen people he doesn't know. Isn't that right, young man?"

Jori hoped he kept his surprise at the man's insight from showing on his face.

"Let's get you to a room so I can take a look at you." The doctor placed his hand on Jori's uninjured shoulder. Unlike the guards, though, his touch was gentle, and a genuine kindness emanated from him. "We will do everything we can to help you."

"And my brother?" A pang struck Jori's gut. It could be a mistake letting them know Terk was his brother. He couldn't take it back, though, and they'd probably figure it out anyway. Other than Terk being three years older than him, they looked similar. *So long as they don't find out the rest of it.* They'd let them die if they knew.

The doctor nodded. "And your brother. I promise."

Jori sensed the man spoke truthfully. He kept his posture rigid and alert, but his anxiety abated. He surveyed his surroundings as he followed the doctor through the infirmary. The vast room shrank as they made their way down a corridor with several sectioned off areas. Lots of places to hide—if the need arose—and multiple exits, ones that didn't have anyone guarding them.

He could use this opportunity to get away, but that would be stupid. Let them heal him. If they tried to hurt him later, at least he'd be healthy enough to defend himself.

The doctor motioned for him to enter a small, curtained area. The room's starkness struck him. The white walls, partitions, floor, and cabinet doors gleamed with the same sterility of the surgical steel cabinets. With the lid of the healing bed closed, it looked like a giant silver bullet from an old-fashioned gun.

Jori almost gaped at the female medic standing by the bed. Her long, dark hair hung over her shoulder in a braid weaved with purple strands. Her body was tall and narrow like a chokuto sword and a rainbow of painted color rimmed her golden eyes.

He'd seen such exotic people on the vid, but this was like having a dragon statue come to life. The Prontaean Cooperative was truly a patchwork of various human cultures. His people, the Toradon Nohibito, had their own diversity, but nothing so extreme. No one here had the same shade of skin or hair color. Most had what he considered a traditional human look, but some—like this medic with her golden eyes—were weirder.

His gaze followed the woman's elongated fingers as they moved to press a white button on the healing bed. The bed hissed open to reveal a glowing interior and he almost let out a hiss himself.

Specialized electrical currents ran through the bed's jelly-like cushions, which triggered curative nanites swimming inside. The thought of recovering faster than his already fast-healing ability appealed to him, but what would those nanites do to his own internal nanite defenses?

Although Toradons had strict laws about biological nanite use, a race of cyborgs Father had conducted business with gave him a sample of bio-nanites with unprecedented capabilities. Before Jori and Terk left home, their father had injected them with the sample.

Since the Cooperative had strict regulatory protocols to protect against unauthorized nanite use, they equipped their transports and decon chambers with an indiscernible shock pulse that deactivated such technology.

However, what the Cooperative thought would shut nanites down, activated the advanced ones Jori carried. If it worked, the microscopic machines were currently replicating and organizing to create multiple unlawful functions.

These nanites resembled ordinary protein bundles but the cyborgs never said whether the healing bed nanites could discover and destroy them.

The doctor motioned for him to sit. Jori considered not allowing himself to be healed. However, since Terk also had the nanites, his refusal wouldn't prevent them from being discovered. Besides, he and his brother had much greater secrets to hide. If the bed's curative nanites happened to find and destroy his own, so what? He'd rather recover and trust his own capabilities than trust the tech inside him.

He sat on the healing bed.

"What's your name?" the doctor asked.

Jori said nothing. He eyed the sergeant who followed him in and kept his senses focused on the other two standing outside the partition. They may be helping, but they could have other motives.

"I'm Doctor Gregson and this is Medic Shera."

He still didn't reply.

The doctor gave a forgiving smile and turned to the guard. "I need to remove his uniform."

The sergeant hesitated a moment before stepping forward with an electronic key. "If you want that shoulder fixed, I suggest you not harm my friends."

If it had been the guard who had restrained him earlier, Jori would probably jam his elbow into his neck. "I'll cooperate."

The cuffs came loose, and his useless arm flopped down with a twinge. He bit down to hide how the igniting pain affected him.

When the feeling settled, he looked down at his charred clothing. Even now, the burns and rips of his uniform repaired themselves. The suit not only deflected various weaponry but also knitted tears to protect him from blood loss.

He pressed an inverted nodule on the inseam of his neck and the uniform fell open to his naval. The medic gently helped pull the clothing away and the doctor examined his wounds, giving extra attention to his shoulder.

"Well, young man," Doctor Gregson said as he picked up a hypospray. "I need to set this broken bone. This will make it so you won't feel a thing."

Jori jerked back. "No."

The sergeant moved forward, but the doctor waved him away. "It's only a numbing agent."

"No drugs." Being injured and at their mercy was hard enough. It'd be worse if they drugged him too.

"Are you sure?"

Jori locked eyes with the man. "Do it."

The doctor's face reflected his reluctance, but he pressed his hand against Jori's chest. "Alright now. Sit back."

Jori leaned against the open hood of the healing bed. Doctor Gregson and the medic got on either side and held him.

"Ready?"

He nodded.

The doctor pressed down on his shoulder, sending a sharp burning through his upper body. He gritted his teeth and grunted, but he didn't dare cry out. His head swam and nausea swirled in his gut as the sharpness dulled. He panted, but in a controlled way that helped him deal with the pain.

"Are you sure you don't want any anesthesia?"

"Just hurry, damn it!"

With a sudden snap, the doctor jerked the bone into place. The pain blinded him with a white heat. The room spun. His vision darkened as blackness closed in. He growled to keep conscious, but not loudly enough for it to count as crying.

Doctor Gregson's eyebrows rose. "You were very brave."

Jori scowled. *Brave?* What did bravery have to do with it?

The ache in his shoulder subsided into a heavy throb. The doctor and medic guided him down onto the healing bed where a warm gel enveloped him. He shut his eyes and let the warmth relax him. They placed an oxygen mask over his nose and mouth, allowing him to breathe. Then the lid closed, leaving him immersed in a sea of soft white light.

The bed hummed to life. Rather than sleep, Jori concentrated his senses on another part of the infirmary. The strongest emotions belonged to the numerous doctors and medics. He focused his ability and found the weak lifeforce of his brother again. A lump formed in his throat. He couldn't lose Terk. They had to save him. They *had* to.

*****

3790:256:07:12. J.D. Hapker sifted through the last remnant of charred debris in the Serpent's cargo hold. Protein bricks, exactly as the manifest stated. He didn't understand. This made little sense. The Grapnes claimed the Tredons stole from them but everything this ship held was accounted for.

Captain Arden had been trying to get more information from them, but the Grapnes wouldn't or couldn't give details. It didn't surprise him since these people had a reputation for dishonesty. They must be after something, yet nothing of apparent value had been found.

He inhaled, then gagged. Although his breathing apparatus filtered out the smoke, his nose stung with the odor of burnt debris.

He stepped from the Serpent's gored innards to its charred head. The cockpit didn't look as damaged but smelled worse. Though the bodies had been removed, the stench of cooked flesh lingered.

Footsteps reverberated behind him. "Sir," Sharkey said. "We've confirmed. There are nine dead, not including the four Grapnes. They're all Tredons, all male, all adults."

He pressed his lips together and frowned. No slaves. If one had been a Grapne prisoner, it might have explained the elusive theft they'd claimed. He didn't want to find any innocent victims on this ship, but it would've cleared up this mystery. At least he'd have something to report to the captain. So far, he had nothing.

"Thank you, Lieutenant." He entered the information on his MM and transmitted it to Captain Arden.

He stared blankly at his surroundings and cupped his chin. The bareness of it sent a heavy wave over him. Different face, different life.

He'd been given such a hard time about how one side of his mouth always turned upward that he once grew a beard to hide it. Turning thirty-five changed his self-consciousness about his looks. Becoming clean-shaven again had been a way of shedding his physical insecurities.

He'd accomplished a lot. From a Pholatian Protector at age twenty to defense chief for the Prontaean Galactic Force at age thirty-three.

Of course, his career with the PG-Force had ended. Somehow, another chance had saved him from having to return home in humiliation. As second-in-command of this Expedition-class starship for the PCC, his position remained tentative. If all went well, his probationary period would end with Captain Arden accepting him permanently.

He should be proud of himself, but the Kimpke incident had changed him. It rattled his confidence and turned him into an unremarkable man who tripped over every step.

Another wave of acrid smoke spiked him out of his thoughts. He shook his head and focused on the task at hand. "Have you been able to access any systems here?" he asked the officer working under a console, hoping the Tredons had information the Grapnes wanted.

"Not yet, Sir. These stations are too damaged. I might be able to get some data from the cad deck, but I must take this unit apart to reach it."

"Do it." Something more was going on here. The mystery of it compelled him onward. This sort of excitement had inspired him to join the Prontaean Cooperative to begin with. Captain Arden roused his unease, though. He knew how the PG-Force would treat the enemy, but what would this man do?

Please don't let this be another lose-lose situation.

5
Security Deliberation

3790:256:08:38. J.D. Hapker caught himself twiddling his thumbs and stopped. The silence of the conference room set his nerves on edge.

Captain Arden took a seat at the head of the rectangular table. Heavy brows hooded his eyes as he scanned the reports on his tablet. Director Jeyana Sengupta frowned as she browsed her MM. Both Major Bracht and Lieutenant Sharkey sat erect with eyes forward. Bracht held a sour expression while Sharkey's was placid.

The captain looked up and leaned back. His gaze locked with Hapker's.

He braced himself, expecting a torrent of disapproval for his handling of the situation. Should he have allowed the PG-Force officers to take charge? Did the captain think he endangered the crew by not engaging in the firefight?

The man met the faces of all the officers with the same stoic look. "It seems we have a potential security risk on our ship. Suggestions?"

Hapker silently let out the breath he hadn't realized he'd been holding.

"We must keep him in the brig." Bracht's deep voice reverberated through the small conference room.

Hapker winced at the defense chief's direct and bold tone. It sounded like a demand, but neither Captain Arden nor the others appeared bothered by it.

Sharkey tilted her head. "The brig? For a single child of only ten year-cycles, Sir?"

Thank you, Sharkey. She was an impressive officer. He'd known her since they attended the PG Institute together. She had a knack for all aspects of security yet retained a human touch that many other PG-Force officers lacked. He'd made the right call when he suggested she be a part of the captain's advisory team in this unusual situation.

The Rabnoshk warrior growled. "He killed four Grapnes!" When Captain Arden's eyebrow rose, he added more calmly, "Singlehandedly. Plus, he's a Tredon. Our enemy. He can't be trusted."

Hapker clenched his teeth at the man's bullish attitude.

"Enemies or not," Captain Arden said, "we are not currently at war with the Tredons. Nor do we wish to be. This means we shouldn't overreact without good reason. We must handle this situation with care."

Bracht's nostrils flared. "Killing four men isn't a good reason?"

"It was self-defense," Hapker snapped.

"We don't know that," the Rabnoshk warrior shot back. "The Grapnes said the Tredons attacked them and stole their cargo."

Hapker's muscles twitched at Bracht's single-mindedness. "There is no evidence of stolen cargo."

The major harrumphed.

"Besides," he continued, "we shouldn't hold him responsible for anything his crew did. He's only a boy."

Bracht's hairy blond brows drew together. "You saw what that so-called boy did with your own eyes. He's dangerous."

"But he didn't shoot at *us*," Hapker said. Men like Bracht gave the military a bad name. Whether he named himself a warrior, soldier, or security officer, his job should be to defend people, not treat everyone as an enemy and stomp on them with those gigantic boots of his.

The Rabnoshk and the Tredons had a lot in common. Perhaps this was why the major was so opposed to the boy.

"He threatened you," the major insisted.

"He was simply trying to determine if we were a threat."

Bracht's lips curled into a sneer, showing his sharp canines. "Obviously, you were no threat at all since I heard you surrendered to him."

Hapker bristled. "That *is* enough, Major." Perhaps he'd been foolish to approach an armed enemy, but it wasn't Bracht's place to criticize him.

The Rabnoshk warrior clamped his mouth shut and deepened his frown.

The captain glanced back and forth between them. His demeanor gave no indication of his thoughts. Hapker resisted the urge to fidget. Captain Arden's apparent indifference always made him feel like a fish in a bowl.

The captain leaned on the conference table and intertwined his fingers. "Director Sengupta?" he said, addressing the chief director of intelligence.

Jeyana Sengupta squared her shoulders. Her high cheekbones and thin arched eyebrows gave her a snobbish appearance. She certainly had pride in her job, but her personality never came across as arrogant. "I wouldn't underestimate these Tredons—or more properly, Toradon Nohibito—at any age. It's obvious this one is from the senshi, or warrior, caste." Her native dialect of the desert world Kochuru was rhythmic and flowing, but her accent in this universal language came out harsh and halting. "There's no telling when this boy began training… Or what sort of training he's had."

"So, you're recommending the brig as well?" Captain Arden said.

Sengupta's black wavy hair swished as she shook her head. "I'm not certain. In one barrel we have many reports of their viciousness, including the bloodbath found on a transport ship a month back."

Sengupta shivered. Hapker suppressed the urge to do the same. At least when a pack of wolves attacked a deer, they did it out of necessity.

"In another barrel," she continued, "he's just a child, and we have a good security team to keep eyes on him."

"Then our officers must be armed," Bracht said.

"The bio-sensors on our phasers will keep him from using one," Sharkey added. Bracht glowered at her as though offended by the implication that the boy could get a hold of a weapon, but she seemed not to notice.

"I recommend unarmed," Sengupta replied. "There are dignitaries aboard. They may be upset at seeing armed officers."

"Not if we tell them there are Tredons here," Bracht said.

"That would create unnecessary problems," Hapker added. "They're just boys and we're not even sure if one will live."

With an unreadable expression, the captain rested his chin on his steepled fingers. After a moment of silence, he pressed his hands flat on the table. "I won't treat them as criminals unless there's a clear-cut reason. The Tredons are our enemies, but we'll never make peace with them if we react so harshly to even their children."

"Does this mean we're not turning them over to a PG-Force ship?" Bracht said.

"Not without cause," the captain said sternly. "So far, the Grapnes' claims are unfounded."

"Should we contact them, at least?" Sengupta asked of the PG-Force.

"Unless the child has committed a crime," the captain replied, directing his stare at Bracht as though daring him to continue arguing, "the PCC has jurisdiction. As the foremost authority in this region, I call for arming security with stun weapons only. Assign a four-man detail to each child. Commander Hapker, you will speak to the younger one."

"Yes, Sir."

The captain turned to Bracht. "Major, organize security as best as you can without reducing protection elsewhere."

"Yes, Sir. I will restrict the boy from all the common areas as well."

Hapker shook his head. "You might as well be putting him in the brig—"

"I agree," the major said.

"That's not what I meant," Hapker replied. "Except for you and your team, the entire ship is essentially civilian." Less than a fifth of the people onboard were passengers or relatives of the crew members. The rest, not including the PG-Force security, were PCC personnel who lacked military training, which made them civilians in his eyes.

"There are children here!"

Hapker suppressed an exasperated groan. The major was like a dog with a bone. "Then we keep him away from the educational rooms and play areas, but not the other places."

"I concur," the captain said to Hapker. Turning to Bracht, he added, "I understand your concern, but I also have faith in your team."

Bracht seemed somewhat mollified by the captain's acknowledgement that the boy could be a security risk. "Yes, Sir."

Sharkey's brow furrowed. "Where will this child stay? Shouldn't he have adult supervision?"

"Isn't having security follow him around everywhere a form of supervision?" Hapker asked.

The captain tapped his lips. "Yes, but it might be useful to have someone act as a guardian to build relations with him—and to help deter trouble."

"Since he's from the warrior caste, it should be a person with authority," Sengupta said.

"They should have martial skills as well," Sharkey added.

"Which means a security officer." Hapker repressed making a face. "If our intent is to keep the peace, it can't be anyone who will treat him like a prisoner."

"Sir," Bracht said. "We can't seriously be considering letting the boy be alone with someone in their quarters."

"We can assign a security officer to stay in there with them," Sharkey replied.

Hapker shook his head. "We're leaning too close to him being treated like a prisoner again. If this boy were an adult, he'd have his own room and we wouldn't expect security to reside with him."

"But he's not an adult. We'd be endangering a crew member," Bracht said.

Hapker was inclined to agree, but it still didn't sit right. "There are two parts to the quarters. The boy could sleep on a cot in the living area while the officer sleeps in their bedroom. They have locks."

"The rooms of our high-ranking personnel have consoles that can access ship's data," Sengupta said.

"True," Hapker replied, "but those consoles require biometric authentication that is ten times stricter than those on our phasers. Any unauthorized use will lock it down and alert security."

Bracht growled. "There is still the safety of our people to consider. No one should be by themselves with that dangerous boy."

"We could place nanocams in the room." Sharkey's tone was hesitant.

"That's illegal," Sengupta replied.

"Only with the PCC," Bracht said. "The PG-Force can use security cameras."

"You are a PG-Force officer," the captain replied, "but this ship is a PCC vessel. The P-Cam Compromise prohibits surveillance except in high-risk areas."

"Having that boy shut in with another crew member is a high risk," Bracht said.

The captain shook his head. "I'm afraid that crosses the line, Major."

"If we only put cameras in the quarters, our privacy-sensitive passengers won't be violated." Bracht sounded both argumentative and disdainful. Likely he felt as strongly for surveillance as some societies felt against it.

"The Cooperative made the compromise for reasons other than privacy," the captain said. "I realize this makes security a little more of a challenge, but I know you can handle it."

Bracht looked unhappy but didn't press further.

"What if they wear a bio-reader?" Sharkey said. "It won't protect them if the boy tries something, but it will raise an alert if they get hurt."

"Or killed." Bracht's voice was low, almost a mumble.

Hapker agreed with Sharkey. "A bio-reader doesn't violate the rules."

Bracht huffed. "It's not enough."

"You've stated your case, Major." The captain's expression turned thoughtful. "You all have made good points. I like the idea of the child having someone who can establish relations and authority, so I will assign a guardian. On the matter of security, I approve the use of a bio-reader. Whether security officers reside in the quarters is up to the guardian."

"Are we taking him home?" Sharkey asked.

Captain Arden's brow turned down. "Not until we have more information. In the meantime, Doctor Canthidius and the others will coordinate their work on the planet, and we will continue to investigate the *StarFire*. The wreckage is being brought to docking bay four. Add a security detail there and on the planet as well."

Hapker tilted his head. “Do you expect trouble on the Blight?”

“With the Grapnes still here… Yes.”

“Who be the child’s guardian?” Sengupta asked.

The captain looked at Hapker. “Commander?”

He was about to suggest an officer, but the captain’s expression told him he asked something else. “Me?”

Captain Arden’s stoic features didn’t change. “Your arguments lead me to believe you don’t think the guardian should be a PG-Force officer. I agree. Technically, you are no longer one, yet your rank provides the authority this child may need. This makes you the best candidate.”

Hapker’s mouth fell open and he snapped it shut. This was another test… Or perhaps a punishment for bringing the boys onto the ship. Then again, he couldn't argue with the captain's logic.

Captain Arden flattened his hands on the table. “Now that we’ve discussed the matter of the child, let’s figure out what the Grapnes have to do with all this.”

“I’ll see what I can find out.” A knot tightened in Hapker’s stomach. He’d expected to be the one to talk to the boy but being directly responsible for him added an additional layer of potential complications. Perhaps he’d taken the wrong stance.

What have I gotten myself into?

6
Rough Terrain Ahead

3790:256:10:05. The gentle heat of the healing bed eased Jori's tensions. His pains ebbed away as his body mended. The relief did nothing to alleviate the invisible weight pressing on him. *This can't be happening. It just can't.*

He groped for Terk's weakened lifeforce, worried it might disappear altogether. If that happened, the weight would crush him.

The doctors had since pulled away. At first, he thought they had given up. Then he remembered a time when Sensei Jeruko had injuries that left him in a coma for several days. They couldn't do much for him until he woke. *It's all up to you now, Terk. Come on, you can fight this.*

Damned those koshinuke, cowards. Those Grapnes were the reason his brother hovered on the edge of death.

An ache swelled in his chest. No one else on his ship had survived. The memory of Bok's impaled body and Veda's crushed skull flashed in his mind. They died protecting him, protecting Terk mostly. Now it was just him… And hopefully Terk.

His eyes watered. Without them, and without his brother, he had to face the enemy alone.

He wanted to go home. He imagined his mother pacing her small room, wondering what kept them. If she knew what'd happened, if she learned they'd been captured, she'd be devastated. The thought of his own predicament as well as her despair made the tears push out.

He clenched his fists. *I am a senshi. I won't be afraid.* He would eventually need to fight these Cooperative weaklings, even if they outnumbered him, even if they outweighed him. Too much was at stake.

He'd lost a great deal already—his men, his ship—but he held onto small hopes. When Terk recovered, they'd take back the device acquired from the space station and escape. All he could do now, though, was bide his time. He forced his worries aside and let his body relax.

After a few hours, a shallow beep indicated the healing bed had completed its work. The lid opened and medic Shera smiled down at him with her yellow eyes. He barely glanced at her and flicked his gaze to the Cooperative officer standing behind her instead. The same man he'd seen on the planet, a commander by the epaulette on his uniform, stood in a readiness like that of a soldier's but perhaps a little more at ease. His hair was the color of the Vandoran sand dunes. He was tall and well-built when compared to the other Cooperative men Jori had seen, but not as muscular as a Toradon senshi.

The man had a cocky twist to his mouth. Jori clenched his jaw and scowled. *This chima thinks he's triumphed over me?*

He sat up quickly. The insult on his tongue died away as the room spun. He gripped the edge of the bed, waiting for the whirling in his head to subside.

"Are you alright?" the commander asked.

Jori's vision came back into focus. The commander stood beside him now. To have a stranger, especially an enemy stranger, dare to step within such familiar proximity was an affront. Jori clenched his fists and prepared to strike the man straight up into his nose. He could draw blood—but no. He should wait and assess his situation.

The insult returned to his head, but so did a sense of the man's emotions. The commander didn't feel cocky. Concern emanated from him. Jori focused on the sensation and found no hint of arrogance.

So, it wasn't a smirk after all. One side of the commander's mouth naturally turned up more than the other.

Medic Shera gently placed her hand on Jori's shoulder. "How are you feeling?"

"Well."

She smiled, but he sensed her unease as she checked his vitals. He ignored her again. She wasn't what concerned him in this place. The enemy had healed him, but they might have something else planned. He needed a way out, just in case.

He subtly mapped his surroundings, as Sensei Jeruko had taught him. Two armed officers stood here inside the room divider. He sensed two more on the other side. He searched further. Four others with the vigilant auras of guards lingered near Terk or the main exit. Then there was the commander himself.

At least five medical personnel worked nearby. These feeble men and women couldn't possibly be warriors too, but he shouldn't assume. Despite their weakness, they undoubtedly still surpassed him in strength.

Nothing he could use as a weapon lay within reach, not even any medical tools. Security must have had them cleared away. Smart. It's what he would've done. Well, except his prisoners would be in a prison. If injured, he might let them recover but they'd be restrained. These Cooperative people seemed more trusting, but not foolish.

The medic handed him clothes. He unfolded the jumpsuit. The black color and long sleeves resembled his uniform, but the similarity ended there. The ordinary material had no auto-fitting tech, no body temperature regulators, and no built-in armor to protect him. It had no adornments either. He frowned but kept his complaint to himself. At least they selected a dark tint.

"I bet you're hungry," the medic said. "Would you like something to eat?"

The hollowness of his stomach became apparent. "Yes."

She smiled. "Anything in particular? I believe our processor has some Tredon recipes."

His mouth watered at the thought of an almost rare guniku steak seasoned with yakume. His body needed replenishing, though. More importantly, his hidden nanites required fuel. Instead of naming a meal, he gave her a list of nutritional requirements. For some people, tasty food was a vice. He might not be physically strong yet, but his mental strength did not allow him to give into temptation. "I do not care what form it comes in or how it tastes."

Both the medic and the commander raised an eyebrow.

She inclined her head. "Very well."

As soon as she left, Jori stepped down off the healing bed and faced the man. He chastised himself for automatically presenting a militaristic at-ease stance. He reported to his instructors and his father this way as a sign of deference, so defiantly unclasped his hands.

"Hello." When the commander smiled, the crookedness of his mouth became even more pronounced. "I'm J.D… J.D. Hapker." He held out his hand in greeting.

Jori glanced at it with a frown. *A trick?* No. Oddly, the commander emitted genuineness. He considered not taking it. After all, this man was the enemy—but then he remembered Terk.

He tentatively performed the customary handshake of the Cooperative. "Jori."

His informal name wasn't well known. The name Terkeshi, however, might be familiar with these people. Even using the short version was dangerous. They couldn't find out about him or what he'd been up to. Whatever kindness this man presented wouldn't last if they discovered the truth.

*****

3790:256:13:45. J.D. Hapker widened his smile. Shaking hands had to be a good sign. "Nice to meet you, Jori."

His grin faltered when the boy's placid expression remained. Jori had narrow eyes, not in a way that conveyed suspiciousness or slyness. They were hard and piercing, and they fixed on him like a predator on the hunt, making his neck prickle.

Jori's apparent youthfulness contrasted with the assured manner he carried himself. He held a rigid posture but seemed ready to spring into action at the same time. Wary eyes showed no sign of nervousness. They studied him with the vigilance of a soldier.

A strained silence settled.

Hapker cleared his throat. "Although our people aren't on the best terms, you don't need to be concerned. We're going to help you."

The boy's jaw twitched. "Are you helping my brother as well?"

So the other boy is his brother. It made sense. They shared similar features. "Yes. Our doctors are doing everything they can. He's stable now, but in terrible shape. He's in a status we call critical cond—"

"I'm familiar with the term," Jori said.

"So, you understand it's not as simple as putting him in a healing bed," he replied with sympathy.

The boy scowled. "I just said I understood."

Hapker ignored his hostility. "All we can do right now is wait."

He rested his hand on the boy's shoulder to assure him. Jori glanced at it with an unreadable expression and Hapker pulled away awkwardly.

The boy's severity returned quickly. "What of me? I'm assuming you have a prison prepared."

"Actually, you will stay with me."

Jori's brow furrowed, hooding his dark eyes. "Are you to be my interrogator?"

Hapker's stomach soured. Even the barbarians of ancient Earth didn't compare to the horrors he'd heard about Tredon interrogators. "No! More like your guardian. I… *We* will certainly ask you questions, but we do not torture people."

"You say you'll do everything you can for my brother. Is this contingent upon my cooperation?"

Hapker raised his eyebrows. *Big words for a boy*. "No, of course not," he replied. "We'd be grateful for your cooperation, though. It would help if you told us what happened between you and the Grapnes, but we won't hold you or your brother's life over your head to get that information."

"You swear it?"

"Yes, I swear it." At least *he* had no intention of doing such a thing. Hopefully, Captain Arden wouldn't either.

The boy bored into him with a studious stare. "Good."

Hapker sighed inwardly. No child should be this hard. He had some rough terrain ahead of him with this one.

7
A Strategic Tour

3790:256:13:57. After a moment of tense silence, the boy broke eye contact. J.D. Hapker stepped out and waited for him to dress. When done, reentered and lifted his brows. The black jumpsuit seemed ordinary enough, but the boy somehow made it look like a uniform. Its plainness added to the solidity of his posture and its color enhanced his solemn air.

Jori was tall for his apparent age and had some features identifiable as Tredon—the dark hair and the high cheekbones. If not for his militaristic demeanor, he'd be indistinguishable in the diversity of the Prontaean Cooperative.

Shera returned with a platter topped with a rectangular slab. Hapker's stomach soured at the sight of the dull brownish-grey substance. It was a gelatin of sorts and resembled the wedges of lard his grandmother used in her cooking.

Shera tentatively set the plate on a tray. "I'm sorry. It's not much to look at, but it was the only way to get everything you requested."

Jori sat without comment and pulled it close.

Hapker tilted his head and crossed his arms as the boy ate in measured bites.

Jori looked up with a frown. "Must you stand there?"

"Excuse me?"

"I want to eat in peace."

Hapker stiffened at the boy's grating tone. "We'd rather not treat you like a prisoner, but you *will* be guarded."

"What do you think I'll do? Stab you all to death with this fork?"

A security officer in the room snorted derisively. Hapker raised his eyebrows. "Would you prefer a cell?"

The boy scowled. The silence hung heavy as he ate. When he finished, he moved the tray aside.

"If you're up to it, I can give you a tour of the ship," Hapker said.

Jori's eyes narrowed. "A tour?"

Hapker smiled. "I don't see why not." Except the captain might have qualms about the boy traipsing around his ship.

"This is a trick, isn't it?"

"No. Not at all. I can't let you visit certain parts, but so long as you follow our rules, there's no harm in a basic tour."

If Captain Arden didn't think they should lock the boy up, then he probably didn't intend to confine him to quarters either. If it turned out he had a problem with it, he'd deal with it later.

Jori rose into a rigid formal posture. He locked eyes and jutted his chin. "Very well, Commander Hapker. Show me your ship."

Hapker let the bossy tone pass and put on a friendly smile. "You can call me J.D., or just Hapker is fine."

"You're in charge of me. I will call you Commander or Commander Hapker. You *are* the commander of this vessel, are you not?"

The way the boy's face remained blank of emotion unnerved him. He cleared his throat. "Yes, but you're not an officer. You—"

"I'm a prisoner."

Hapker tried to speak, but nothing came out. He had no idea what the captain intended to do with this boy. Would he send him back to Tredon or would the Cooperative keep and question him?

He drew in a deep breath and considered. Giving assurances when he had none himself didn't seem wise. He'd be willing to bet the boy knew better anyway. Based on his adult-like mannerisms, he seemed to have a good understanding of his predicament.

He decided on honesty. "We don't have enough information to say that yet. For now, let's make the best of things and see where it takes us."

He turned aside and swept out his hand. They stepped out together and left the medical bay. The boy walked like a soldier, straight and stiff, as they headed down the corridor. He seemed not to notice or care about the handful of security guards who trailed them.

"Where would you like to go first?" Hapker asked.

"Doesn't matter."

"Well, let's see… We can start with the lower-level fabrication and processing areas and work our way up."

The boy said nothing. As Hapker showed him the areas and explained their functions, Jori followed with his eyes and leaned in from time to time. The only time he spoke was to give a short and noncommittal reply.

Silence lingered as they visited the gym and the arboretum. It persisted until they reached the engineering section. Jori commented and asked questions that Hapker never would've expected from a child. Despite the boy's limited view from an open observation room, he expressed an amazing aptitude for the engine's inner workings.

"So, you enjoy the science and physics of starships?" Hapker asked casually after leaving.

"I wouldn't say enjoy. I'm required to learn such things."

Jori's demeanor suggested otherwise, but Hapker didn't push it. "If science isn't something you're interested in, what do you like to do in your spare time?"

The boy kept his eyes forward as they moved on to another area. "I have very little spare time."

"Well, what do you like in general?"

Jori stopped and faced him with a piercing stare. "What business is it of yours?"

Hapker's jaw tightened at the boy's tone, but he kept his own voice light. "You and I will spend a lot of time together. I simply want to get to know you better."

"Know your enemy, you mean," Jori replied. "I can understand that."

Hapker moved to massage his temple but changed his mind and shrugged instead. "Well, I suppose that could be part of it. Sometimes when enemies get to know one another, though, they realize they are not so different and become friends."

The boy made an indecipherable grunt and marched away.

Hapker groaned inwardly and caught up. "What kind of games do you like?"

"I don't play games."

"None? No physical or strategic games?"

"I suppose I like those types of games."

"What about barson-hop or treasure house?"

Jori frowned. "Those are for children."

"Fine. How about schemster?" Schemster was his own favorite strategic game. It might be too complicated for someone only ten years old, but it was the first adult game that popped into his head.

"Yes, I like schemster."

"Really?" he said in a spiked tone. Although he had played schemster with his grandfather since the age of twelve, none of his friends had. "Good. How about I show you the lounge and we play schemster?"

"Very well." Jori's formal tone held no hint of either eagerness or reluctance.

They paused at the entrance. Hapker soaked in the lighthearted chatter that buzzed in every section of the room and looked for a place to sit. Most seats were taken at the bar to the right where people talked or watched the selected broadcast on the viewscreen.

Tables of various sizes sat throughout the room—some short, some tall, some surrounded by stools, high-backed chairs, or padded armchairs. One stunted table had cushions all around, but not even plush pillows induced him to sit cross-legged on the floor. He considered the vacant spots in the back-left corner, then changed his mind. A holographic band played nearby and would hinder the conversation he hoped to have with the boy.

He spotted a table in the other corner and led the way around the service bots carrying trays of drink, food, or dirty dishware. Human servers tended as well, adding a warm touch and a feeling of connection to the communal setting.

Patrons chatted and occasionally laughed, creating a lively buzz he hoped would help the boy feel comfortable. When heads turned his way, the din hushed to whispers. Some people stared while others averted their eyes. Mouths either fell agape or frowned. Apparently, word of the boy's presence had already spread.

The rigidness of Jori's posture intensified, but otherwise he didn't react. It couldn't be easy for him to be surrounded by so many enemies.

Hapker chose a table. Jori took a chair against the wall, a spot he would have chosen for himself if somewhere unfamiliar.

A tap on the table brought up a digital image. He selected the games option, then schemster. Three dimensional pieces appeared on the playing board.

Jori moved first. Hapker made the standard counterstroke. The game advanced swiftly at first.

"So, Jori, I've been meaning to ask you..." Hapker hesitated, not sure how to broach the subject. "Was your father on the ship?"

Jori stiffened and his eyes widened. The look disappeared quickly, though. "No."

Hapker's shoulders relaxed. Thank goodness the boy wasn't orphaned. He couldn't imagine suffering such a loss at so young an age. "I'm glad. It means we can get you back to your family."

"You're sending me home?"

"I can't give you a definitive answer yet, but there's no reason to keep you here."

The boy frowned as he moved a piece. "What sort of compensation are you requesting?"

"Compensation? You mean ransom? We won't be asking for anything."

The boy's eyebrows drew together. "So, you're helping us and sending us home without expecting anything in return?"

"That's right." At least he hoped so.

"Why?"

The question caught him off guard. For him, the answer was obvious. Helping people was a normal aspect of his life. It's what his family had done, and what those around him had always done. "We're not just a transport and science vessel. We also help people in need."

"Even your enemies?"

"Yes. It's part of the mission of the Prontaean Colonial Cooperative. To aid, whether it be medical or mechanical, any persons or vessels traveling within our territory."

Jori grunted.

Hapker took his turn, then leaned forward. "May I ask why your ship was in this area to begin with? You're a little far from home."

The boy wore an unreadable expression and didn't answer.

Hapker lifted his palm. "It's alright. You're not in trouble."

Jori's jaw tightened.

"I won't pressure you into answering, but it would help if we knew. Wouldn't you want to know if our situation was reversed?"

The boy's face hardened. "You don't want to know what things would be like if our situations were swapped, Commander."

Hapker's skin prickled. "Maybe not, but how you are being treated here and now should be a point in my favor, right?"

Jori remained stone-faced. He met Hapker's eyes with the directness of a heracu owl but didn't respond.

"Very well," the boy finally said. "We were on our way back from the Depnaugh outpost when the Grapnes confronted us with a demand for our surrender."

"Surrender for what?"

"They didn't state, they simply demanded. We denied them, of course, and that was when they attacked us. They outgunned us and so we ran." The boy twisted his mouth when he said the last word.

Hapker cupped his chin. "I'm not sure I understand. The Grapnes can be greedy, but they're also cowardly. What profit is it for them to attack a Tredon vessel, even if their ship outmatched yours? Did you have valuable cargo?"

"Nothing of interest. Only foodstuffs, supplies, and equipment."

Hapker tapped his index finger to his jawline. Jori's face remained emotionless, but he spoke directly and without hesitation. Plus, it confirmed what his team had found so far.

There must be more to this, though. "If you're not sure, we understand, but surely you overheard something from your other crew members?"

Jori pressed his lips into a thin line, making it clear he wouldn't answer.

Hapker suppressed a sigh. The boy was hiding something. If it wasn't about prisoners or cargo, what was it? Revenge? That didn't sound like the Grapnes.

He wasn't getting anywhere so changed the topic. "When your captain fled, did he intentionally go into Cooperative territory?"

"We hoped the Grapnes wouldn't follow," Jori said, "and we thought the Hellana system would provide us with cover."

This made sense, at least, but it still didn't solve the mystery. Despite his curiosity, he didn't want to further rankle the enemy child who would soon sleep in his quarters. He had already decided not to have security in his room, but the option grew more appealing by the moment.

Neither spoke as they played schemster. Silence and several moves later, Hapker's general got stuck. His soldiers were blocked and three of his key pieces were in danger of being captured. He stroked his chin as he studied the board, trying desperately to find a way out of this mess.

He wasn't sure how the boy had done it. One moment, his soldiers had Jori's caught in a pincher and the next, his general was on the verge of capture. The formation had long since scattered and the boy would win in five moves.

He found his mouth had fallen open and he clamped it closed. He wasn't a professional player, but his major at the Prontaean Galactic Institute was in strategic planning and analysis. Schemster was a required subject for anyone seeking a degree in this field, and he'd been the second-best player that year. Being beaten by a child both shocked and humbled him.

"That's amazing," he said after Jori won the game. "The last person to beat me was a Schemster Master from Harbon." No one could defeat a Harbon strategist.

The boy's eyes narrowed. "Never underestimate your enemy."

A chill ran down Hapker's spine, but he pretended the boy's bluntness didn't bother him. "Shall we play again?"

Jori agreed and they played another game.

Hapker had let children win before—not that he had let Jori win—but this boy's manner sparked his competitive side. This time, he paid more attention to the moves. He spent longer to analyze before moving a piece. Still, the boy outflanked him here and blocked him there. Hapker moved his red colonel to keep Jori's soldiers from getting past his front line. Two turns later, he lost his colonel. Not without sacrifice, though. Jori had lost a major and three soldiers in the process. Unfortunately, it didn't stop him.

Hapker frowned as he studied the board. His strategy wasn't working. The boy's plan seemed to be to win at all costs, even at the loss of important pieces.

After fourteen more moves, Jori won again. Hapker had either lost his edge or Jori was a master strategist in his own right.

He half-expected the boy to gloat, as some children his age tended to do. To his surprise, he took it in stride.

"You take too long to move." The boy's face lacked any expression. "If this had been a real battle, you would've been dead much sooner."

Hapker's skin prickled ominously.

8
Deceivers

3790:256:11:11. Captain Silas Arden's muscles locked up. He was sure his surprise showed on his face. The Grapne on the screen nodded rigorously. "It's true, Captain."

Arden frowned. Grapnes weren't known for their honesty. "Murder? Before you were merely claiming theft and now you are telling me these Tredons murdered one of your people?"

"Yesss, Captain." Captain Seth's voice hissed and crackled from the inferior transmission. "The Tredons are murderous cut-throats and we simply want justice."

"Who did they murder?" He allowed an inflection of skepticism in his tone. He generally addressed others politely, but Captain Seth shot down another ship for no apparent reason.

"A very important dignitary."

Arden pressed his lips. If the Grapne told the truth, he stretched it. "Yes, but who? And how?"

"I cannot provide you with details." The man grinned as he spoke, and his eyes shifted.

"Can't or won't."

"Can't, Captain. Because I don't know. I am only going by the information given to me by my superiors. You understand."

Arden sighed in frustration. "You stated earlier that you yourself are the victim of this theft at the Depnaugh outpost. How is it the Tredons murdered a dignitary during this theft, but you can't tell me who? You were there, after all."

"A misunderstanding, Captain, I assure you. It wasn't me they stole from. They robbed another ship of ours."

Arden gritted his teeth. "Even if what you say is true, I'm afraid justice is out of reach. The crash killed nearly everyone."

"You said there were survivors," the Grapne said. "They must answer for their crimes."

"The survivors are children, and I will not be handing children over to you."

"But they are the ones who committed the murder."

Arden folded his hands and grasped them so tightly that his knuckles turned white. "Forgive me, Captain Seth, but it seems your story keeps changing to fit the situation."

"It's the truth, I assure you," the Grapne replied with that same ridiculous smile. Arden had read somewhere that Grapnes smiled a lot because they thought it would make people believe their lies more easily. "We simply want the justice that the law requires you to provide."

Arden unclasped his hands and spread them flat on his desk. "I'll tell you what, Captain Seth. You show me concrete evidence that these children personally committed murder, theft, or any other crime, and I will consider turning them over to you."

"Our evidence must be supported by their testimony. We must take them into custody so we can build our case. You understand."

The man is smooth. I'll give him that. "I will not be handing children over to you for interrogation without evidence, and that is final."

"What about my four men they killed?"

"That was self-defense. It is not enough to convince me to hand them over."

"My superiors won't be happy, Captain Arden." The Grapne's grin faded. "Your council will hear of this."

"I'll take my chances. In the meantime, report to the Melna check-in post immediately where they will hold a hearing on your actions and disable your ship's weapons."

"But Captain—"

"Immediately!" He drew in a deep breath to calm himself. "If you do not, I will put out a warrant for your arrest. I have authorities expecting you at the station in half a day-cycle's time, so you had best be on your way." He terminated the conversation and plopped back in his chair with a heavy sigh.

"I think they're lying," Director Jeyana Sengupta said.

"I agree," Arden replied.

Both she and Bracht had witnessed the entire discussion. Commander Hapker would have been here as well, but hopefully he was making some headway with the Tredon child.

Based on what he'd observed of Hapker's personality so far, he had a better chance of getting along with the boy than anyone else. Most other crew members held prejudice against Tredons, and he didn't want something to happen with this child that might incite more trouble.

However, Hapker's agreeable character also worried him. Pholatians were good people and Pholatian Protectors had quite an impressive reputation for defusing situations without violence. They'd never faced anyone like the Tredons, though. As such, they tended to underestimate the ugly sides of humanity.

Commander Hapker might very well overlook the danger this child represented. While he admired those who saw good in others, it could backfire if combined with gullibility.

He had another issue with Hapker's character. After three months, the man was proving to be rather insipid—not at all what he expected from someone who'd stood up to Rear Admiral Zimmer.

Perhaps the Kimpke incident had weakened his nature, made him too passive and afraid to act. If this was the case, he might not be such a good fit as his second-in-command.

At least Hapker wasn't as bad as his previous chief commander. Frida Findlay was so by the book that despite his wife's efforts as Steward of Entertainments, the morale on this ship was lower than he'd ever seen it. She was too tough, and her terrible moods were often taken out on the crew.

If she were here now… A shiver ran down his spine. How his wife had hated that woman. No one angered his merry Symphonia as much as Findlay did.

"Killing someone sounds like something the Tredons would do," Bracht said.

Arden pushed his musings aside. He rested his elbow on the arm of his chair and scratched his beard. "Yes, but it doesn't mean they killed anyone in *this* case."

Bracht's wiry blond mustache turned down with his mouth. "Even though that boy killed four Grapnes?"

Arden's jaw twitched. Bracht was a great defense chief, but he could be unyielding at times. "Tell me, Major," he said patiently. "If they shot your ship down and confronted you, wouldn't you react the same way?"

Bracht scowled but didn't answer.

Arden straightened. "Has security reported any problems?"

The major hunched as though disappointed. "None, Sir, but it doesn't mean there won't be any."

Arden gave the man an admonishing look. "Let's hope not. We don't want an incident escalating to war, do we?"

Bracht looked down. "No, Sir."

Sengupta folded her hands. "If his brother dies, the boy may no longer cooperate."

"If he lives, my security team will have two Tredon warriors on their hands," Bracht added.

Arden sighed. "Both your points concern me, but there are larger matters to contend with. For one, what are the Grapnes really after? Two, what will we do with these children? If they're innocent, getting them home won't be easy."

Bracht growled. "They're not innocent."

Arden frowned at him. Until he knew more, he considered them innocent. In which case, he needed to get them back to Tredon somehow. It wasn't as simple as calling on the Tredons. They'd likely see the fact that he had two of their people as suspicious. The Tredons and the Cooperative were already on uneasy terms. If they blamed him for this tragedy, it could trigger conflict.

A coldness swept over him as memories of the Rabnoshk Battle of Grendork came to mind. Never again did he want to witness such atrocities.

Some wanted the Cooperative to wage war on the Tredons for all their crimes against humanity. Not him. War caused good people to hate and kill, good people to die, and it had destroyed Earth and scattered humans to the stars.

The stated mission of the Prontaean Cooperative was to bring the people back together in peace. This was why he'd enlisted all those years ago. The Rabnoshk hadn't changed his view, and neither would the Tredons.

"What if we take the boys to the Chevert outpost and give them what they need to find their own way home?" Sengupta said.

Arden dipped his head at her ability to grasp the depth of a situation. "I'm not sure that's safe." He massaged his brow where a headache developed. "We can't leave them on their own, especially not with the Grapnes after them."

Sengupta bit her lip. "Their behavior is truly bizarre. What if the Tredons find out we have them?"

"I've considered that. Let's wait for Commander Hapker's report. In the meantime, check with the Depnaugh station to see what the authorities know." He certainly wouldn't get anything from the Grapnes.

"Yes, Sir," Sengupta replied.

"Bracht. Report immediately if your security encounters any trouble."

"Yes, Sir."

"Um, Sir?" Sengupta's thin eyebrows drew down into more pronounced arches. "Do you believe Commander Hapker is… Well, is…" She squirmed in her seat.

"Jeyana," Arden said in a gentle tone, intentionally calling her by her familiar name to put her at ease. "You know I value your opinion." *And Commander Findlay isn't here to admonish you for what she'd call questioning my authority.*

The director visibly relaxed. "Do you believe Hapker is the best one to be the boy's caretaker?"

"I hope he is. Is there something about him, other than what we've discussed previously, that makes you think he's not?"

Her forehead wrinkled. "No. His passiveness is my primary concern."

"Let's give him a chance. At the very least, he can provide authority over the child without being overbearing."

Sengupta flicked her eyes toward Bracht. "I see."

Arden suppressed a smile. Bracht's rough demeanor had its uses, but handling a child was not one of them.

Only time would tell whether Hapker had been the right choice.

9
Haters

3790:256:15:42. Corporal Mik Calloway's legs cramped. The urge to shift his weight intensified, but he couldn't do it with Major Bracht watching. The Rabnoshk warrior's nostrils widened, and his eyes penetrated the security officers arrayed before him. When his glare fell on him, Calloway refrained from swallowing the lump welling in his throat.

Something had upset the major. The heat of his mien practically gave off smoke. Calloway only hoped he hadn't found out what he'd done. Fiddling with the reports wasn't really a deception. He had to do it. Harmel was such a goodie-goodie. *Boot licker. I only did it to get the credit I deserve.*

Second Lieutenant Rik Gresher and his crony Sergeant Ander Vizubi entered the security officers' hall. As usual, Gresher wore that stupid smile of his. It wouldn't have been so bad except the man's mouth spread so wide it could hold two sets of teeth. He looked ridiculous. Everyone seemed to like him, though, so no one made fun.

Nobody mocked Vizubi either. He was the oldest PG-Force officer here, yet still just a sergeant. His history as a thug on Depnaugh discouraged people from giving him a hard time.

Gresher and Vizubi nodded to Bracht and took their place in the ranks. The Rabnoshk warrior responded with a glower but didn't chide their lateness like he should have.

"In case you haven't already heard, we have two Tredons on board," Bracht said. "Regardless of how you feel about Tredons, I expect you to do your duty with the fullest integrity of a Cooperative officer."

The major paused a moment, probably to emphasize how highly he regarded duty. As defense chief, he was all about blind loyalty and the fanatic fulfillment of responsibilities. Calloway wouldn't be surprised if the word *duty* had been tattooed on his backside.

Well, at least he hadn't gotten caught, and his recent promotion remained intact.

"What you may not be aware of is how this situation is being handled and the increased danger it presents." Bracht paused again as he gave each of the officers another sour look.

Calloway resisted the urge to tap his feet. He'd been itching to find out more about the two children who had been rescued from a crash. As a corporal now, he had a right to additional information. What good was his new rank if they continued treating him like a private? He deserved better than the ignorant status of a lowly privy.

Bracht's face darkened. "The captain has welcomed them as guests."

Calloway nearly choked. "What the hell?"

Fortunately, his grumblings were swallowed in the gasps and curses of the other officers. The major had already warned him about complaining. "*It doesn't befit a leader*," the man had said. "*You must rise above such petty things and set an example.*"

Well, fuck that. Speaking out about this was his job. "We should exterminate them!"

"Silence!" Bracht's voice resounded against the walls.

Calloway and the others stiffened in attention. His blood ran hot. Tredons had raided his homeworld, slaughtering every person he'd ever cared about.

A coldness swept over him at the memory of his sister dying in his arms. He gritted his teeth against the rising wave, but it swirled into a tsunami anyway. How in the hell did they expect him to treat the devilish little Tredon spawn as guests? It made no difference if they were children. "*The child of a frog is still a frog*," his uncle used to say. Replacing *frog* with *crocodile* applied better to Tredons.

"The older one is in a coma," the Rabnoshk warrior said. "The other is with Commander Hapker. I want you to keep a close eye on him, and *do not* underestimate him."

"Why aren't they locked up?"

"That is not your concern, Corporal Calloway." Bracht's gaze spread out over the other officers. "Your concern is the safety of this crew. At the same time, I expect you to be on your best behavior. Despite what these children are, you will not provoke them. You'll guard them and look after their safety as well."

"*Their* safety?" another officer called out.

"They're barbarians," Calloway added. "Why should we care about *their* safety?"

Others protested. Words like butchers, brutes, animals, and monsters rang out—and he agreed with them all. Only creatures such as these could do the things done to his sister.

"We have our orders," the Rabnoshk warrior interrupted. "The children are not wanted for any crimes and so they will not be locked up unless they give us a reason."

Calloway's nails dug into his palms. "Are we waiting for them to kill one of us first?"

"Watch your tone, Corporal." The man's dark eyes bored into his own.

Calloway gritted his teeth in seething fury but turned away from the Rabnoshk warrior's hard look.

"You have your orders." Bracht faced the officers with a steely bearing. "They are restricted from secure areas and the recreation room which other children frequent. However, they are permitted to visit other public places on the ship. You'll behave professionally at all times. There will be no name-calling and I will not tolerate anyone using force unless it is clearly necessary. Is that understood?"

Most of the officers mumbled, "Yes, Sir," but Calloway said nothing. When he chose to serve the PG-Force, he hoped he'd be fighting Tredons, not babysitting them.

"Is that understood?" the major bellowed.

"Yes, Sir!" they replied. Calloway mouthed the words, but defiantly made no sound.

When the Rabnoshk warrior dismissed them, Calloway stomped out with a storm cloud brewing in his chest. It grew into a rumbling thunder by the time he arrived at the lounge where he'd guard the younger brat. The loudness of the place drowned out his curses but didn't deter his raging march.

10
Unexpected Emotions

3790:256:16:10. J.D. Hapker suppressed a yawn. Third shift had begun—his bedtime—but he and Jori played another game.

He nearly cornered the boy's key pieces, but consternation seized him as Jori beat him once more. Without taking a moment to gloat, the boy pushed out his chair with a raking scrape and stood. "I will see my brother now."

Hapker opened his mouth to reply, but Jori turned and walked away. He snapped his jaw closed and suppressed a groan as he hastened from the table with solid strides.

A security officer with tawny skin and matching tawny hair grimaced at Jori as he passed—Corporal Mik Calloway, recently promoted from private against Hapker's better judgment. The man never did more than he had to, and his attitude was worse than a monkey with a splinter.

Calloway's face straightened when Hapker gave him a hard look. The officer, along with the other three security members, rigidly followed the boy out.

Hapker caught up to his charge. The boy didn't acknowledge him or the officers, so he ignored him in return. He didn't trust himself to speak now anyway. If he let his frustration coil much tighter, he'd strike out and say something that would aggravate the tension.

Jori's posture reflected confidence as he led the way. An uneasiness slithered through Hapker at how he seemed to know his way around this starship. Was this all an elaborate trap? The cowbird came to mind—how it deposited its egg into the nests of other birds. So, was his being here intentional—a part of some larger plan—or had it truly been an accident?

Hapker mentally shook his head. He shouldn't rush to conclusions. The boy was obviously smart. And maybe he didn't ignore him out of arrogance. Being surrounded by enemies probably made him uncomfortable.

They entered the medical bay and Jori pushed on. He strode purposefully to the set of security officers standing before an enclosed patient area. When he stepped between them, Sergeant Addams stopped him. Jori's face turned red and his jaw twitched.

"Let him in," Hapker said to the copper-haired man before a situation developed.

Addams curled his lips but did as he was told. Hapker wasn't popular with security and arguing in favor of the boy undoubtedly worsened relations. He gave Addams a pointed look and followed Jori inside, taking one corner of the room while the now eight officers lined up outside the entrance.

The older boy lay deathly still with an array of tubes coming out of his nose, mouth, and limbs. His skin was pallid, and except for the artificially induced respiratory action of his chest, he lay as motionless as a sleeping python.

Jori examined the medical diagnostics machine by his brother's bed with a clinical air. Hapker crossed his arms. He could make little sense of the lines and numbers marching across the screen, but the boy's eyes roved over the monitor, pausing here and there as though taking it all in.

"Ahem."

Hapker startled and turned toward the sound.

Doctor Jerom stood in the doorway. His light-brown eyes lit up with a kind smile. "I'm glad to see you're well," he said to Jori.

Jori faced the doctor with a wooden expression. "I am, but my brother is not. Tell me of his situation."

Hapker winced at the boy's demanding tone, but Doctor Jerom seemed not to notice. "He has quite a few broken bones and fractures, including to his skull. There's not much we can do until we're sure the brain has mended. Healing nanites won't work on brain tissue. Even if they did, using nanites with this sort of trauma is dangerous." He continued, explaining the internal damage and other injuries. "I'm sorry. We still don't know if he'll survive."

Despite the grim news, Jori remained unemotional. He reviewed the monitor and asked the doctor several specific medical questions. At first, Doctor Jerom answered in layman's terms, but

Jori spoke so technically that the doctor had to respond the same in return.

"Thank you, Doctor. That will be all," Jori said.

Doctor Jerom opened his mouth to say more, but the boy turned away. The doctor scowled, probably at the apparent dismissal. Hapker shrugged apologetically.

Doctor Jerom left with a shake of his head. Jori gave Hapker a look, as though expecting him to go as well. With still crossed arms, Hapker leaned his shoulder onto a support column instead. He did it partly out of spite for the boy's rudeness, but mostly because his demeanor worried him. His brother might die, and he didn't have the decency to show a single shred of emotion.

Jori turned back to his brother. The placidity of his face persisted and he stood like a songless bird in a stark cage.

An ache developed in Hapker's calves. He suppressed a yawn. If the boy thought he could bore him into leaving, he was mistaken. He'd stand here all night if he had to.

His thoughts drifted. He shook his head and regained his focus. Something had changed.

Jori held his brother's hand. His brow furrowed and a pool of water rimmed his eyes. His chin quivered and his jaw knotted as though trying to hold back an urge to cry.

Hapker's skin tingled with goosebumps as the boy gently rested his other hand on his brother's forehead. Considering how emotionless he had been earlier, this seemed surreal.

Hapker's chest panged. He uncrossed his arms and stepped by the boy's side. "He'll be alright."

The boy tensed but otherwise didn't acknowledge the gesture.

*****

3790:256:16:26. Jori's eyes burned. A surge of sorrow threatened to overwhelm him. He clenched his jaw and breathed deeply, hoping to keep the tears at bay.

He didn't want to let these people see this weakness in him, but being here with his brother, touching him, feeling the emptiness within him, stressed the stark reality of his situation. *Come on, Terk. You must get through this.*

A hollow ache billowed inside him. If only things could go back to the way they were before—when he had stayed with Mother, when he and Terk had studied and practiced together… Laughed together.

Life had been much simpler a year ago, before his adult brother Dokuri had been killed. Father always held them to high standards, but Dokuri bore the brunt of responsibilities. After his death, the next eldest brother failed. That left Terkeshi with the burden of duty and too busy to spend time with him. Jori desperately wanted to hold on and not be left behind.

To lose Terk this way, though, would be worse. Flashes of what his life would be like if he died churned in his head—having to face Father's fury alone, comforting Mother's despair, and bearing Sensei Jeruko's disappointment. Then his father's expectations would fall on him, to be carried like a cold and heavy stone.

He wasn't ready. Not at all. He was nothing like Dokuri—or his father. Nor did he want to be.

"He'll be alright," the commander said as he touched his shoulder. Whatever frustration Jori had sensed from the man earlier had gone, replaced by an inner warmth. He tensed at the unexpected gesture and genuine emotion, and his cheeks burned.

He forced the sensations from the commander out of his head. This was his enemy. The sympathy he showed him now wasn't likely to last—not if they found out the bigger secret.

Although Jori had told the truth about the Grapnes not giving a reason for their demand for surrender, he omitted his suspicions. Bok, the loud-mouthed braggart, had gotten drunk at a station bar and said too much and the Grapnes undoubtedly overheard.

A guard coughed, returning him to the moment. None of this mattered if he never made it back home. He might be free to traipse about this ship—with guards in tow—but he was still a prisoner. Commander Hapker promised to get him home, and he sensed the man had told the truth, but whatever he'd promised, he wasn't the man in charge.

A rising fear overwhelmed his emotional pain. *Curse you, Terk, for leaving me here alone with these people.* The burning in his eyes intensified and liquid slid down his nose.

He bit the inside of his cheek and a metallic taste filled his mouth. *Control. I must control this. Emotion is weakness.*

He clenched his teeth. Heat surged within. *Curse you, Bok! Curse those Grapnes! Curse you too, Father!*

He struggled for air and grasped for hope. Terk must survive this.

When his emotions subsided, he turned his thoughts to his present situation. Since the commander had said nothing about nanites, he assumed the Cooperative hadn't discovered them. Hopefully, they were replicating and assembling into their designated functions. Jori resisted the urge to scratch his palm where most would migrate. Soon, he'd have an internal computer with limited applications—scanners, recorders, and emitters being just a few of its functionalities.

The cyborgs had given many promises regarding the safety and effectiveness of the nanites, and Jori sensed they'd spoken the truth, but their blatant use of biotech unsettled him. External and removeable tech was allowed, but these internal biometric enhancements were illegal in Toradon. Not only that, being the best without having to depend on pseudo-abilities was the pride of his family.

However, he needed every advantage now. It was all up to him. He evaluated his surroundings. The commander carried no weapons, making him easier to overcome. Jori sensed a guard with a diminished level of attention. His phaser was stun only and likely protected by biometric authentication, but he also had a knife sheathed at his hip. Taking it would be easy. He'd stab the guard that felt the most vigilant first. The commander would be next since he'd likely be the quickest to react. Then he'd take out the guard reeking of arrogance and hate. Calloway, someone had called him.

His stomach roiled like the swirling storms of Arashi. He should despise these people. His anger was real, but not enough to make him act. He'd killed before. He'd ended those Grapnes. These chima should die too. It's what Father had trained him for.

I can take them. Then what? Even if the device had survived the crash and he was able to get it, he couldn't do that and save his brother too. No. He had to wait for Terk to recover and his nanites to be ready—then deal with these enemies.

Wake up, big brother. I need you.

11
Investigation

3790:257:00:12. The entrance slid open and J.D. Hapker stepped into the empty conveyor. "Docking bay four." The door closed and he stretched his mouth wide. A tingling sensation spread over him. He held his breath at the height of the yawn, trying to hold on to the revitalizing feeling, but the heaviness of fatigue rolled quickly back in.

Locking his bedroom door hadn't eased the anxiety of having the Tredon boy sleeping in his quarters. Not that he was afraid. Uneasy, maybe. Wary. Perhaps even a little concerned, but mostly uncertain—especially after reading the report from the captain about the Grapnes' accusation. Captain Arden had expressed doubt regarding the truthfulness of it, but the notion that the boy could be a murderer unsettled him.

He massaged his forehead, hoping to invigorate wakefulness. He'd woken at his usual time, expecting Jori to be awake. However, the boy still dozed and looked so peaceful that he'd left him there. Even though he'd appeared to recover quickly from his grief last night, Hapker suspected he held back more. Perhaps this brief separation would give him some much needed privacy, and next time Hapker saw him, he'd be more relaxed. The frigid expressions and the autopilot behavior wouldn't help either of them.

The conveyor opened at the front end of the docking bay generally reserved for visiting ships and shuttles. Now it harbored the skeletal remains of the Tredons' Serpent. Seeing it here in the well-lit expanse did nothing to diminish its forbidding hulk. The charred ruin loomed in the background as scientists and engineers dissected the pieces. The once-bright floor was darkened with footprints of dirt and soot. A sour odor like that left by a dead campfire tweaked his nostrils. Though the bodies had been removed, the Serpent's corpse still reeked of death.

Hapker suppressed his disquiet and pulled back his shoulders. He headed to a team of officers and nearly turned away when he saw Canthidius. As a leading science officer, it made sense for the man to be here, but it didn't mean Hapker wanted to deal with him right now. The difficulty of trying to keep the peace with a warrior child who distrusted him was enough.

Well, at least this adult version was harmless. "What have you found so far, Doctor?" he asked Canthidius.

The man straightened and stood respectfully but a gleam of distaste filled his odd-colored eyes. "We recovered some recordings from the cockpit, Commander. They don't tell us much, but there is something peculiar."

"Peculiar how?"

"Well, it seems the older boy was the pilot. In other words, he executed that skimming maneuver I heard about."

Hapker's eyes widened, but he had no chance to verbalize his surprise.

"Pure stupidity, if you ask me," Canthidius continued, "but still extremely difficult. If he had been more than a half degree off… And that's not all. It seems he was also the one in charge."

"In charge of the crew?"

Canthidius wore an indulgent smile that seemed to hold back a cheeky reply. "Of course, Sir," he said in a sickly-sweet tone instead. "Here. See for yourself."

The doctor led him to a viewscreen and played a fuzzy video with disjointed sound.

Hapker leaned in. The static and missing pixels distorted the faces, but he distinguished the boys by their statures.

Sure enough, the eldest boy operated the flight controls. Although the translator couldn't interpret the muddled voices, the tone of the man talking to him seemed deferential.

Hapker scratched his chin. "Can you enhance the audio?"

"If I could have, I would have," Canthidius replied. "Sir," he added with another fake smile.

As if smiling makes you less of a snob. Hapker's jaw tightened but outwardly he pretended the man's attitude didn't get under his skin. "Have you found any indication of what the Grapnes were after?"

Canthidius turned back to the screen. "I managed to pull some incoming vid communications. The sound is just as bad, but Doctor Rosta can read lips. The Grapne captain demanded surrender but never indicated why."

So Jori told the truth about that.

"I also found an outgoing communication, sound only," Canthidius said.

The doctor tapped the play icon on the screen. "*We've acquired some supplies as well as the device you wanted, Father. We are returning home now and should arrive in half a period.*"

Hapker stroked his chin. Without a visual, he could only assume the voice belonged to the older boy. The tone was formal, as though he spoke to a superior officer, but he called the man father. Perhaps his father was a Tredon captain or major. It explained why a boy was in charge. "That's rather vague," he said. "Any other outgoing messages?"

"Just basic docking and departing requests to the Depnaugh station."

"Have you found any unique tech or any other records that tell us anything about this device?"

"Nothing else worth reading or listening to. No unique tech either, but that is to be expected since Tredons are at least smart enough to realize they're too stupid to figure out how to use it."

"Don't be so sure, Doctor," Hapker replied. "The Tredon boy seems pretty darned intelligent to me."

Canthidius huffed. "I hardly consider military intelligence to be an actual form of intelligence."

Hapker bristled. No doubt Canthidius intended the remark to be about him as well as the boy. "Remember that when we travel to Tredon territory to return the children. The intelligence of our military personnel might be all that keeps us safe."

The doctor paled. Hapker suppressed a smile. "Have you found anything else of importance here?"

Canthidius shivered, then cleared his throat. "Nothing significant, but perhaps something curious. This ship's maintenance records indicate it only had two operable crash pods."

"How is that curious?" Crash pods were only installed on vessels designed for landing on planets. Since it was much easier and cheaper for transport vessels to dock at space stations, many of these ships disregarded the upkeep of their crash pods.

"Watch." Canthidius played another video.

Although this recording was worse, it showed enough to give Hapker goosebumps. The warriors yanked both boys away from the cockpit viewer and put them into the crash pods.

His own instinct would be to protect children, but these were Tredons—by all accounts loudmouthed, aggressive, bloodthirsty warriors. What prompted them to commit such a selfless act?

His comm beeped in his ear. "Yes, Sir," he replied to the captain.

"Commander, we have a situation on the planet. Get suited up immediately. Lieutenant Gresher will fill you in at the transport station."

Hapker's heart leapt to his throat. "On my way." He nodded a thanks to the doctor, then rushed from the bay.

The conveyor seemed slower than usual, allowing ample time for his imagination to take flight. What if the Tredons found out about the crashed ship and sent a recovery crew and found their science team instead? He pictured the Tredons unleashing their revenge and using them as human shields when Hapker and the PG-Force arrived.

He wiped his brow and shook his head. *This is what I get for wishing for excitement.*

12
Sly Snakes

3790:257:00:52. J.D. Hapker jogged to the transport pad with his combat helmet under his arm. The nanite infusion of his armor allowed him to move easily despite the thicker material. It had more mass compared to the enviro-suit but didn't weigh him down. His own imagination did that.

He rounded the corner to find two squads of PG-Force officers prepping their weapons, readying their gear, or personalizing the settings on their augmented helmets. Hyped chatter filled the room until heads veered his way. He caught a few snide remarks, but no one spoke to him directly.

Lieutenant Gresher met him with a disarming grin. "You're just in time, Commander. We will be ready in four."

"Give me the sitrep," Hapker said as he turned to the weapons locker.

The lieutenant snapped on his tactical belt and packed it with ammo and utilities. "A shuttle from the Cougar has landed in stealth-mode not too far from our science team."

Hapker's muscles loosened. *Just Grapnes. No Tredons.* He opted for a regular phaser rather than the more powerful RR-5 rifle. "From the Cougar? *Virtuous Dealings* left them behind?"

"Apparently, Sir. Our people noticed them, but not in time. The Grapnes activated a transport-blocker."

"Crap." Hapker shook his head and exchanged the phaser for the rifle. "So they have our people as hostages."

"Yes, Sir. Five."

Hapker groaned inwardly. Whatever these Grapnes were after, they were desperate to get it. "What do they want?"

"We don't know yet. The captain says they're not responding."

"What's your plan?"

"Officer Chandly will beam us just outside the range of their transport-blocker. We'll set up an encirclement and show them what we're capable of. It might prompt them to surrender our people."

"If not, I'll negotiate." Hapker considered the regular phaser again so he wouldn't look intimidating, but the situation was already too volatile. "Sounds simple enough. Will heavy artillery be beamed down with us?"

"Yes, Sir. Chandly is coordinating it so we all arrive at the same time."

"I'll follow your lead," Hapker said with a nod as he donned his helmet.

An officer made a face, no doubt wondering why he allowed Gresher to take charge when he hadn't let Lieutenant Sharkey do it in the initial encounter. He pondered on that himself as he followed Gresher's team onto the transport platform.

The first incident wasn't pre-planned, and he hoped there'd be a chance to neutralize trouble before it started.

No. If he couldn't be honest with himself, who could he be honest with? The truth was he wanted to prove himself to the captain. It would've been smarter to allow Sharkey to take command. She had long since earned the respect of the officers, making her the best one to lead if the situation had worsened.

He phased onto the dismal planet and fell in beside Gresher as the team dashed over to a materializing railgun. Unlike the last time, he didn't run far. An easy sprint brought him in position behind the machine where he watched the other weapons appear. Like a one-minded hive, the officers snapped into their designated roles with precision and focus.

"Two turrets in my line of sight," Sergeant Ander Vizubi called out.

Hapker glanced at the older man, taking in his solemn demeanor. Vizubi opted for the compact helmet, allowing Hapker to see his big nose and his dark, grey-flecked hair. The sergeant might be the oldest PG-Force officer here, but he was hardly the least fit. According to the most recent health evaluation, age had not diminished his eyesight or his reflexes.

"Five turrets reported," Gresher called out. "Fireteam alpha, target the shuttle's aft and starboard. Fireteam beta, port. Gamma, dorsal. Delta, forward."

"Line of sight into port hatch," an officer announced through the comm. "No sign of our people."

Before Gresher could give an order, energy blasts erupted from the turrets. Hapker fired at them in return, then ducked behind his shielded railgun.

"Their shield is holding, Sir," Vizubi called out. "We should use the railguns."

"Our people are inside that ship, Sergeant," Gresher replied. "Keep firing until the shield gives."

Hapker adjusted his rifle to rapid pulse and aimed again. The energy blasts fell onto the shield and dissipated. His power cell depleted to a quarter strength before he stopped. "This isn't working," he said to Gresher. "Do we have a frequency finder?"

"Yeah, but they're masking it somehow."

"If we can get close enough…"

"Cease fire!" Gresher glanced at his power cell. "Scheisse," he cursed. "What kind of shield do they have on that damned thing?"

"It must be a Lazarus shield." A shield within a shield where the depletion of one initiated the other as it regenerated.

"How did they get this tech?" Gresher seemed to say to himself. "God, I hate those things. We'll use half our arsenal before it goes out."

Hapker agreed. "They have our people for a reason. They must want something." He powered down his rifle and handed it to the lieutenant. "I need to find out what it is."

Gresher frowned. "You're going over there? We'll cover you, but I can't guarantee it will help."

"I've got to try. Give me a frequency finder. I'll transmit the information as soon as I can. Do nothing until it's obvious they're not willing to communicate."

"Understood." Gresher detached the small device from the side of his helmet and handed it to him.

Hapker put it on, waited a few seconds for his visor to recognize and accept it. When the icon appeared on his visor, he eye-clicked it. With the frequency finder activated, he inched out from behind the railgun with his hands up. His stomach soured at the thought of Bracht commenting on how he'd surrendered twice now. This set a bad precedent, but it was the best option.

"Cover him," Gresher said through the comm.

Hapker eyed the turrets as he steadily approached. The frequency finder remained at zero and he willed it to move.

"That'sss far enough," a voice hissed from the shuttle.

Hapker's muscles went taut as a Grapne appeared from the open hatch. At first, the man appeared to have only one eye. Hapker activated the zoom feature in his vizor and noted a beige patch covering his other eye. As the portly man lumbered down the gangway, Hapker recalled a story about a mythological cyclops.

A much skinnier man hunched behind him. The figures approached, the leader with a mischievous glint.

Hapker faced the cycloptic man and spoke through the mic. "Where are our people?"

"On our ship. My captain says he will release them when we have the Tredon children."

"What do you want with them?"

"Justice," the Grapne hissed.

"Justice for what?"

"Not your concern. Hand them over and we'll send out your people."

Hapker clenched his jaw. Why wouldn't they tell him anything? What were those children to them?

He stepped forward hesitantly. The frequency finder remained at zero. "We don't negotiate with terrorists."

The Grapne straightened and frowned. "We are not terrorists. We are the victims."

Hapker took another tentative step. "Victims don't kidnap innocent people."

"We must have the children. Give them to us and all will be well."

Hapker moved closer. The frequency finder zipped through some numbers but returned to zero. *One more step.* "Tell me why you want them so badly."

"Tell them," the cowering Grapne said in what would have been a whisper if Hapker's helmet hadn't picked it up.

The one-eyed man smacked him on the shoulder. “If we told them, they’d keep the little devils for themselves, now hush.” He turned back to Hapker as though nothing had happened.

This mystery roiled through Hapker’s gut. These Grapnes wouldn’t tell him anything, though, so long as they had the upper hand. He stepped again and numbers rolled up on the frequency finder.

The one-eyed Grapne raised his palm. “Don’t take another step, or your people are dead!”

Hapker held his hands out in mock innocence as he eye-clicked the information to Lieutenant Gresher. Before the Grapne could say anything else, phaser fire erupted from the squads.

“Defusers activated,” Gresher announced in the comm as he and the other officers flooded forth.

Hapker let his tension fall away. The defusers would keep the Grapnes from shooting their people with phasers. Hopefully, they didn’t have firearms.

The cowering Grapne screamed in a high pitch and covered his head while the one-eyed man flinched at the sound of his turrets being taken out. Then his eye bulged and he threw his hands up. “I surrender! I surrender! It wasn’t my idea. Our captain told us to do it. Please don’t shoot me. I give up.”

“Situation secure,” Gresher announced.

Hapker confronted the Grapnes. “You’re not getting the children so you might as well tell me why they’re so important.”

The Grapne’s dismay changed into a simpering smile that showed his yellowed teeth. “You must arrest us. We have violated your trespassing laws.”

Hapker’s skin prickled. “Why do you want the children?”

“We surrender. Arrest us. We understand if you must impound our shuttle.”

Hapker’s expression tightened. “We will arrest your captain. The rest of you may go, but you must do it now.”

The Grapne’s one eye widened. “No. We can’t go. Our ship is gone. Our shuttle can’t travel far.”

“Crap,” Hapker whispered. Per Cooperative policy, only the higher-ranking Grapnes could be arrested. The PCC wouldn’t allow him to leave the others stranded, and bringing them onto the *Odyssey* was a bad idea. People claimed Grapnes were unintelligent yet devious. Whatever they were after, they would undoubtedly create more trouble to get it.

"Lieutenant Gresher," he said through a private channel. "Do we have enough security to monitor the Tredon boys as well as the Grapnes *and* keep our passengers safe?"

"We can't watch too many people at once unless they all stay in one place, which I doubt they'll do."

Hapker planted his hands on his hips and huffed.

"We have the important places already guarded, though," Gresher added. "And if they're after the children, they have our protection."

Hapker chewed his lip. Gresher made good points. Despite having more misgivings about the Grapnes than the Tredon children, he didn't have enough justification to treat them differently.

"Fine," he said to the Grapne. Get your people out here. After we inspect them and your shuttle, you may park it on our ship."

The one-eyed Grapne bowed. "Thank you. Thank you. Your hospitality is most appreciated."

Hapker held back an eye roll and met up with the lieutenant. "Gresher, they're all yours."

As the man took over with the Grapnes, Hapker gazed over the dull land. A craggy outcrop loomed only a kilometer away. Some slopes appeared flat enough to hike and its cracks and crevices offered good handholds for rock climbing.

He sighed. If only he could go exploring rather than babysit.

*****

3790:257:02:56. J.D. Hapker pinched the bridge of his nose and imagined canoeing the sparkling ruby stream found in the Adosela region on his homeworld. The waterway led to a lake where the clear waters let him view the red-rocked bottom with such clarity that it seemed nothing separated him from its depths.

The first time he'd looked down the deepest part known as the Devil's Eye, fear seized him. He felt like he teetered on the edge of a great crimson abyss. One slight tip of his boat and he'd plummet to the bottom. It shook him so badly he barely kept hold of the paddles as he rowed back to shore.

He'd returned a few years later, and several more times after that. The feared memory changed into calm and awe and was one of many remembrances that inspired his desire to see other worlds.

What was I thinking? Hapker peered through the one-way mirror at the leader of the shuttle on the other side. It had been over an hour since they'd brought the man here and began interrogation. Not even Bracht had induced him to say what he was after. The major never laid a hand on him but Hapker's ears still hurt from the Grapne's wailing of innocence and blaming the Overseer.

He grimaced as the Grapne picked his nose and inspected the blob on his finger. "Any suggestions on how we proceed?"

"Keep him detained," Bracht replied. "Perhaps a few days of sitting in a cell with only his snot to play with will loosen his tongue."

Hapker crossed his arms. "It's possible he's telling the truth. His Overseer isn't likely to share details."

The major harrumphed, whether in agreement or doubt, he wasn't sure.

"We've run out of options," Hapker continued.

"Within the limits of the law." Bracht's mouth turned down with disappointment.

Hapker wagged his head. "Did they really think taking our people would work?"

"Perhaps *this* was their plan all along," Lieutenant Gresher said.

"You mean us bringing them here?" Hapker asked rhetorically. "Perhaps as a backup plan if the hostage exchange didn't work."

Bracht growled. "Whatever those devious little snakes are planning, they won't get away with it."

Gresher ran his hand through his hair. "I wonder what those Tredons did to make these people so tenacious."

Bracht's throat rumbled louder.

Hapker stroked his chin. If Jori was intelligent enough to beat him at schemster, what else was he capable of? However, the boy's words about never underestimating the enemy seemed to apply more to the Grapnes. "Maybe the Tredons didn't do anything. The Grapnes don't usually do things like this unless it profits them somehow."

Bracht bared his teeth. “They’re fools.”

“You said the boys’ father wasn’t on the ship, right?” Gresher asked. “What sort of parent sends his children to a place like Depnaugh?”

Hapker frowned. Not even a PG-Force officer would venture onto that space station without an armed squad. Granted, a team of warriors accompanied the boys, but why risk them to begin with?

The Grapne stood and meandered about the room. He craned his neck this way and that, taking in the bland walls and ceiling. He stopped before the mirror, showed his teeth, and picked something black from between an incisor and canine.

Hapker sighed. “I suppose we should report to the captain.”

“If it’s alright with you, Sirs,” Gresher said, “I’ll review our security situation and make any necessary changes.”

Bracht grunted. Hapker dipped his head and checked the MM tablet on his wrist. “You go on ahead, Major. I’ll check in with the boy.”

Bracht nodded and mumbled to himself. “If only torture was allowed. I’d tie that little snake into knots until he learned how to sing.”

Hapker winced, unsure if the warrior spoke in longing or jest.

13
Mystery Deepens

3790:257:03:24. J.D. Hapker rubbed his brow. The captain couldn't be happy about him bringing both Tredons and Grapnes on board. Plus, he was no closer to determining what this was about. Part of him wanted to blame Canthidius for not finding anything, and the Grapnes for being secretive. Captain Arden would see it for the pettiness that it was, though. Besides, he had also failed to elicit any information from the boy.

Some commander he was. He might as well be a petty officer for all the value he'd contributed to this ship so far. The chances of the captain accepting his commission dwindled by the day.

He filled his lungs and stood straight as he entered the conference room. Captain Silas Arden gave him a slight nod and tilted his head at an empty chair at the table where Director Sengupta and Major Bracht already waited.

Bracht's frame took up twice the space as Sengupta's. Her bushy black hair seemed to outweigh her otherwise diminutive figure, but not in an unattractive way. Bracht's hair was as bushy, albeit wilder and of the opposite color, but it somehow made his build seem shorter and squatter.

"Report," the captain said. His voice was terse and his eyes hard.

Hapker tensed at the captain's austerity, but otherwise kept his nervousness from showing. "I've just sent you a detailed report of yesterday's events, but here are the highlights."

After describing his experience with Jori, he summarized the information on the crashed ship and related his encounter with the Grapnes on the Blue Blight. Afterward, Bracht gave his statement on their interrogation findings.

The captain's mouth turned down. "So, no one knows what the Grapnes want? Not even the boy?"

Hapker stiffened, expecting the captain to chastise him for not getting more information. “I wouldn’t say he doesn’t know, Sir. He said the Grapnes didn’t tell them what they wanted. This seems to be true, but he’s as tight-lipped as they are.”

The captain tapped his bottom lip with his index finger. “The message about some sort of device is concerning. Perhaps the Grapnes want it and they think the children will get it for them. Ask him more about this. Be persistent but gentle.”

Hapker agreed.

“If he still refuses to say anything, I may get Garner involved,” the captain added. “We must get to the bottom of this as soon as possible.”

Garner. Hapker’s insides tumbled. The man’s ability to extract thoughts didn’t work on Grapnes—it triggered them into screaming fits—but it worked on children well enough. There was a small risk it could cause unintended harm, though. “Unless lives are at stake, isn’t using someone like him against the rules?”

“Yes, but there’s a lot of grey area in that regulation.”

“You can’t be serious.” Hapker’s heart skipped a beat. If the captain used Garner against Jori, it meant he was no better than the PG-Force who were too quick to use bold methods. “It’s dangerous and he’s just a boy. Give me a few days. Although he’s being stubborn now, I think I can build his trust.”

The captain’s brows rose. “A few days is a long time. You understand he’s been accused of murder.”

Hapker opened his mouth to speak but the captain put up his hand and continued. “Even though I doubt this accusation, the fact remains that he is capable of killing. We have a crew to protect.”

Hapker shifted in his seat. “I only want to give the boy a chance before we call in Garner. You said we’re not at war with the Tredons and that we don’t wish to be. If Garner harms him, it could trigger a situation.”

Captain Arden nodded. “Has the child given you any trouble?”

“No, Sir. Other than a few biting remarks, he hasn’t misbehaved. A few days will give us a better idea of what we’re dealing with.”

“If there is no change in his behavior… I think that’s fair, Captain,” Sengupta said.

Hapker bowed his head in thanks for her agreement.

The captain tapped his lip again and the focus of his eyes seemed to retreat inward. Hapker resisted the urge to fidget as silence settled in. He took a huge risk in siding with this boy, and not only with his career. If he was wrong and Jori ended up hurting or killing anyone… He dismissed the thought to keep a certain memory from blooming.

The captain drew in a deep breath. "What about the fact that he beat you in schemster?"

Sengupta's brows arched up. "He actually beat you?"

Hapker nodded. Though few on the ship knew him well, everyone seemed to be aware of his skill at schemster. "Yes, he did. I still haven't figured out how."

"Impressive." The captain frowned and steepled his fingers under his chin.

"Yes, Sir. That's not all, though." Hapker leaned in, rested his elbow on the table and rubbed his jaw. He didn't want to report this next part, but it was only fair to provide all the information before the captain decided about Garner. "Jori seems well-educated. This doesn't fit what I've been told about Tredons. Also, his uniform was rather sophisticated. I wouldn't be surprised if the boys were the sons of some high-ranking warlord or something."

Bracht's nostrils flared and his lip curled.

Sengupta's head bobbed. "I agree with your assessment, Commander. If he has a high rank, his intelligence could be from enhanced genes."

"How's that?" the captain asked. "Didn't the Tredons also stop the genetic and biometric enhancements after the MEGA Injunction?"

These words struck Hapker like a lion on a gazelle. As technology that allowed people to alter themselves became less expensive and more common, society grew increasingly alarmed. The MEGA Injunction prohibited mechanically enhanced or genetically altered persons from attaining certain jobs or positions of power. This was why all forms of tech had to be external and removable, except where medically necessary.

"Tredon lords found a way around the injunction," Sengupta replied.

"There's another way to be enhanced?" Hapker asked.

"Not in the way you're expecting," Sengupta continued. "Tredon warlords generally procreate with women who carry enhanced genes from before the universal agreement was established, thereby perpetuating the enhancements through the generations."

"Leave it to the Tredons to cheat." The ends of Bracht's mustache jabbed downward.

"Select breeding is not against the law," Captain Arden said. "However, it's something we should consider with regard to security. We don't know what genetic abilities he's inherited." He looked at Hapker. "You really think you can get him to open up?"

Hapker shook off his unease. How powerful could this boy be after so many generations? "It seems contradictory, Sir. I, too, have conflicting concerns, but it's just a feeling I have."

Sengupta tilted her head. "What is? What feeling?"

"That perhaps there's more good in him than bad."

Bracht harrumphed.

Hapker's jaw tightened. "Even if I'm wrong, Sir, someone has to be the boy's advocate. All children need an adult to represent them."

"Not *all* children," Bracht said.

Hapker ignored him. "Besides, I'm sure our security can handle him." His tone had an unintended sour edge to it.

Bracht's nostrils flared. "Of course we can, Sir," Bracht replied to the captain.

The captain glanced at them but didn't comment on the exchange. "So, do you agree we should hold off on Garner, Major?"

Bracht's lips twisted as though he'd eaten something bitter. Apparently, Garner had the same effect on him. "I don't trust that boy, Sir, but I trust my team."

Captain Arden frowned. "I will consider this further."

Hapker suppressed the uneasiness in his gut. "I understand, Sir."

"In the meantime," the captain said, "let's see if we can determine which warlord these children belong to. Director, you reported the DNA database and facial recognition gave you nothing on the children. Check their crew members too."

"Yes, Sir."

"How much longer before you hear from your friends at Depnaugh?"

Sengupta's eyes tilted apologetically. "Just one friend, I'm afraid. Maintaining contacts at that station has been a challenge. If my friend is still alive, she may take a day or several days to reply."

"Keep me posted." Captain Arden turned to Hapker. "Our doctors found an anomaly in the children's medical scans. They've had a lot of bone reconstructions."

"I have several myself," Bracht said dismissively. "As a warrior, getting hurt during training is common."

The captain shook his head. "No. There are so many, it's beyond concerning. I would say it's alarming, in fact, especially when you consider the Tredons' greater bone density."

"You think they've been abused?" Sengupta asked, echoing Hapker's guess.

"Even if they were, what can *we* do about it?" Hapker added.

"Yes, Director," the captain said to Sengupta. "Doctor Jerom was hard pressed to find bones that hadn't ever been broken. Those that were, happened at different times, which rules out the possibility of them being involved in a single cataclysmic event."

Nausea rolled in Hapker's gut.

"There is not much we can do about it," Captain Arden said to Hapker, "but perhaps you can use this to get him talking."

Hapker dipped his head. "Yes, Sir."

The captain flattened his hands on the table in a way that generally signaled the meeting was over. "Also ask him who to contact so we can send him home."

"Yes, Sir." Hapker stroked his chin as he formulated some possible ways to approach the boy. Somehow, his ideas were either too unrealistic or they ended with more bad feelings. Maybe his father was right. He should've stayed on Pholatia.

14
Holo-Man

3790:257:04:37. J.D. Hapker's fatigue had drifted away. He'd been ordered to spend most of his shift hours with the Tredon boy, so no dull bridge duty and no tedious scheduling or report writing.

Thanks to the captain, he felt as light as a cool mountain breeze as he jaunted to the medical bay where he expected to find Jori. However severe Captain Arden's demeanor had seemed to be, the man was nothing like Rear Admiral Zimmer. The earlier meeting would have gone differently if Zimmer had been in charge. He would have scolded Hapker and ordered him to use more force with the Tredon boy.

Never mind that Jori came from an enemy race and could be as prickly as a porcupine. He'd rather wrestle with that spiny rodent than allow people like Zimmer to stain his conscience again.

"Where's Jori?" he asked a security officer guarding Jori's brother.

"He went to the gymnasium, Sir."

Hapker thanked the officer and left. A game of wall ball was exactly what he needed. Perhaps he could get Jori to join.

After returning to his quarters for a change of clothes, he hummed a happy tune from his homeworld. He'd been worried for nothing. The captain hadn't challenged any of his decisions and agreed with him on most points. If these odd assignments were a test, he'd passed.

He let his song taper off as he entered the gymnasium. Weight machines dominated one part, cardio machines another. Several ball courts lay along the perimeter. An officer from the science lab taught gymnastics in the central open area. Lieutenant Gresher instructed a martial arts class in a space at the back.

Hapker rounded the gym's track to a crowd gathered at the far edge. He weaved through the circle of people and found the boy using a haptic-holo-station.

Jori swung a staff and cracked the side of a pseudo-solidified holographic warrior. Astonished sounds swept through the onlookers.

The holo-man disappeared and a shorter one appeared. The boy reacted quickly, sweeping the holo-man off his feet. He then jabbed the end of his staff into its sternum. The holographic image of the man vanished and a taller one materialized.

Hapker gaped as holo-warriors of various sizes fell to their virtual deaths. Jori moved with the power and smoothness of swift-flowing rapids. He met his opponents' attacks with astounding precision, like a black mamba—fast and dangerous.

The boy made this tough fighting program seem as easy as breathing. Even without a phaser or the strength of a man, he had the potential to be deadly. Hapker's own martial skills paled in comparison. Perhaps he had misplaced his faith.

"He's frightfully good."

Hapker glanced at the woman who'd spoken. Wisps of hair stuck out from Sharkey's bun, making it resemble a mangled nest. Her face flushed from whatever exercise she'd been doing.

"Frightful is right," he replied. "If he was full grown, he'd probably be an even match for Gresher and Bracht."

Sharkey sighed. "Maybe letting him be out and about wasn't such a good idea."

"Everyone deserves a chance," he said, trying not to sound defensive.

"I hope you're right," she replied. "He's barely a decade old, and yet I heard he's already more than a match for you at schemster. Is it true?"

He groaned inwardly. "It is. Believe it or not, I didn't let him win. Either I've lost my edge or he's just *that* good."

Sharkey's brow furrowed. "I vote for the former. I hate to say it, but the Kimpke incident changed you. You're not as confident as you used to be."

Hapker harrumphed. "Being castigated by an admiral will do that to you."

"You did the right thing."

"Did I?" His actions meant nothing since all those innocent people still died.

"Well, I think you did." She touched his arm. Her eyes tilted in sympathy.

He shrugged. "Then you're the only one."

Jori jabbed the next holo-man in the throat, making it blink out of existence. The boy froze in an offensive stance, waiting for more. Sweat dripped from his brow and chin and his chest heaved. His face was red but otherwise calm, as though he'd stepped on an anthill and thought nothing of the multitudes that suffered and died beneath his feet.

Goosebumps prickled Hapker's skin.

"You think you're something, don't you?" someone said.

What the heck? Hapker moved through the crowd to get a better view.

The newly promoted Mik Calloway stood with his arms folded and his lips curled in a sneer. "You're just an ugly little space-thug."

Jori straightened. His face turned darker as he bared his teeth. Hapker imagined his own face coloring. He clenched his jaw as a swelling heat surged throughout his body.

"Corporal Calloway!" He pushed through the group of onlookers and planted himself between the officer and the boy. "What are you doing?"

Calloway paled. "Nothing, S—"

"Nothing? Just because you are off duty doesn't mean you get to shoot your mouth off."

"But he's a murderous—"

"He's a guest on this ship! Were you not ordered to be civil?"

Rather than appear chastised, the man scowled. At least he wasn't stupid enough to make more excuses.

"Don't let me hear another harsh word come out of you again." Hapker glared until Calloway averted his eyes.

I knew I should've denied this man's promotion. Only a few months on the ship and he already had a bad taste of Calloway's caustic character. "Rest assured, this behavior will not go unmarked. I will speak to you about this later." After he cooled down and in private. Reprimanding an officer in public was not something he approved of. It was something Zimmer would do, but not him.

He waited a few moments longer before turning to Jori. He half-expected to see the same angry expression on the boy as before but no trace of it remained. Jori stood in an at-ease stance as emotionless as ever. Hapker's goosebumps returned.

15
The Spike

3790:257:12:07. Silas Arden sipped his now cold coffee and grimaced.

"Captain. We have a small ship with a trajectory on a direct intercept," Triss Stever, the bridge chief, announced on the comm.

"On my way." Arden blinked. His eyes were dry from reading his officers' reports, and he rubbed them briskly. His legs were rubbery as he left his office and entered the bridge. The backs of his thighs tingled, a sign that he'd been sitting for too long.

After giving a wordless greeting to his crew members, he stood by his chair rather than sat and pressed the comm button on its arm. "Commander Hapker. Are you available?"

"Yes, Sir," Hapker replied, his voice made deeper through the link. The comms could be adjusted to be more precise, but he'd found it unsettling to have it sound like the person was right here.

"Should I open a channel to the ship, Captain?" Officer Brenson asked.

"Let's wait for them to contact us."

"Yes, Sir."

Arden reviewed the information on the viewscreen. Their current distance provided few details, other than the vessel was small and still a few minutes away.

Hapker arrived. "Captain," the man greeted with a light half-crooked smile that Arden had come to accept as an almost constant expression.

"We have a ship that looks like it wants to meet us." Arden inclined his head at the screen. "No other information yet."

The Commander stood straight and tall as he peered over the screen. The slight shift of his feet and the way his eyes darted at the data indicated his eager interest.

Ah, to be young again. Arden's own pulse elevated a bit, but mostly out of curiosity rather than excitement. At fifty-two, he'd seen and done it all and it took a lot to get his blood running.

"Sir, it's a Bantam," a bridge officer said.

Not one of ours, then. Bantams were small independently owned cargo vessels with a little firepower. They were a popular choice for those who worked along dangerous borders—and for pirates.

"Shields up." Arden doubted a pirate ship would seek them out. Most likely, it was an ordinary vessel needing repairs or some such, but better to be safe than sorry.

"No communications yet?" Hapker asked Brenson.

"Not yet, Sir," Brenson replied.

More information about the Bantam popped up in a section of the viewscreen. The registration showed it as the C.T.V. *Spike* operated by Captain James Fargoza. The database didn't list any warrants for the man, although he had been cited in the past for minor cargo infractions.

Arden skimmed through the data and halted when something caught his eye. Fargoza was a licensed bounty hunter. Interesting, but not surprising in this part of the territory.

"They're hailing us now, Sir," the comm officer said.

Arden gave him a slight nod. Brenson pressed a button on his console and a man's face popped up in the middle of the front screen.

"Captain Silas Arden of the Prontaean Colonial Cooperative here. How may we assist?"

"Captain James Fargoza of the Bantam *Spike*," the man replied, confirming the registered information. Fargoza appeared to be about Hapker's age. He wore a dark beard and had hair wilder than Bracht's. His nose was wide and flat, and a scar ran across his cheek. "We've been sent for a wanted group of Tredons and we're told you have 'em."

"Told by who?" He couldn't imagine the Grapnes giving these people information.

"Word gets around, Sir," Fargoza replied.

Arden frowned at the man's vagueness. Dealing with these types was almost always like a game of tug-of-war. "What do you want with these Tredons?"

"There's a bounty on 'em, on the two Tredon boys, to be exact."

Arden raised an eyebrow. He glanced at Hapker, who had the same expression. "A bounty? From who? And for what?"

"Authorities at the Depnaugh station, for murder."

Arden's chest tightened. "Send me the report, Captain Fargoza."

"Yes, Sir."

The communication paused and the viewscreen returned to the full information display. The document from Captain Fargoza arrived and Brenson posted it on the screen. "It appears authentic. I'm verifying the code now."

The notice had the Depnaugh seal in the upper right corner. The words *Wanted for Murder* stamped in bold across the top. It gave a ship ID number, and he knew without checking that it belonged to the *StarFire*.

His skin chilled. *So, the Grapnes told the truth about this part*?

Wait. Not entirely. He read the smaller words on the document. The warrant didn't provide any names, not of the victims or the assailants. It broadly identified the Tredons on the *StarFire* along with two children, and nothing more.

Brenson swiveled in his chair. "Sir. The code is out of date."

"The time stamp is only a dozen hours old." Hapker's half-smile turned down and his face paled. "Depnaugh wouldn't issue a warrant with an out-of-date code, would they?"

Arden frowned. They posted the document this day-cycle, nearly a full day after the Grapnes' claim. Perhaps after their failed attempt, they'd contacted the Depnaugh outpost to have a formal warrant written up. Once done, the information became public to bounty hunters like Captain Fargoza.

"What do you think?" he asked Hapker.

"We can't, Sir. We can't turn them over to these people." The commander's brow creased. "This report is obviously fraudulent."

Arden expected his reaction. Hapker had no experience with Tredons. The suspicions about him not being attuned to the danger were proving to be true. Why else argue so strongly on the child's behalf?

Nevertheless, he had no intention of giving the children over to these people. “I agree on both points. I mean, what do you think about the accusation? Did this child murder someone?”

Hapker sighed and rubbed his jaw. “We’ve seen that he’s capable of killing, Sir, but I don’t know. He’s shown how skillful he is… But I doubt he committed such a crime. And if he did, perhaps he had just cause, such as self-defense. Or maybe the adults of his crew put him up to it.”

Arden nodded. His response wasn’t as strong as he would have liked, but it made sense. Though the definition of what a Tredon would consider as a *just* cause might differ greatly from his own.

The commander let out his breath, but the lines on his forehead remained.

“Reopen the comm,” Arden said to Brenson.

Fargoza’s face popped up on the screen again. “Captain. We’re ready to take ‘em off your hands.”

“Not yet,” Arden replied. “The document doesn’t have enough information and its code is no longer valid. Since the children are already in our custody, you must file a claim with the Prontaean authorities.”

“Begging your pardon, Sir,” Fargoza said with a hint of impatience, “but that will take several days.”

“I’m afraid it’s the law.”

“I understand that, Sir, but you understand we’re only trying to make a living. We’ve come all the way out here. Fuel is expensive, and I must pay my crew.”

Arden suppressed a dubious frown. They couldn’t have traveled too far since the bounty had just been set. “I’m sorry, Captain. The Depnaugh authorities will need to provide evidence before we will acknowledge the warrant. Even then, I’m not inclined to hand over children.”

“They’re Tredons, Sir. I’m sure Depnaugh thought that was explanation enough.”

“What do you know of the circumstances?” Hapker asked.

Good question.

Fargoza didn’t answer right away and his eyes narrowed. “Nothing, but you know what Tredons are like.”

Arden's jaw tightened. They were hiding something, too. *Why am I not surprised*? "We're not turning anyone over without more details on their crimes." He managed to keep his tone light.

Fargoza's lips curled. The expression disappeared quickly, as if he held back his temper. His mouth spread into a smile instead. "If I may make one more argument, Captain Arden."

Arden gave his consent although there probably wasn't anything the man could say that would convince him.

"I'm sure you have better things to do than babysit these two murderous little creatures. Yes?"

Rather than reply, Arden stared at the man with mock patience. Yes, Tredons were brutal, and it would save him a lot of hassle if these children weren't here, but he didn't like what Fargoza implied.

"Your directive prevents you from doing what should be done," Fargoza continued. "Let me take care of them for you and no one else has to know the rest."

Arden's stomach twisted. He had no doubt now what was in store for the children if he turned them over. A harsh rebuke came to mind, but he pressed lips together to keep from saying it. "Sorry, Captain," he said politely. "Not without the proper documents."

Captain Fargoza snarled. "It's your funeral." He ended the communication.

The back of Arden's neck prickled. Hapker sagged with the apparent belief that the child didn't commit murder. Was he blinded by his lack of experience with people like the Tredons, or did he see something that no one else saw? Arden hoped for the latter.

If this boy caused any serious harm, he'd need to take action. If the child turned out to be the son of some warlord, that action could lead to war. He'd negotiated his way out of war with another warrior race before and it hadn't been easy. One wrong step and all his hard work with the Rabnoshk would have erupted in cataclysmic flames.

Acid roiled in his stomach at the thought of history repeating itself. "Let's see if we can find out what's going on," he said to Hapker. "Bring the young man to my office."

"Sir." Hapker hesitated. "I don't think Jori will respond well to pressure."

"Understood, Commander. It's time I met the child, though."

"Yes, Sir."

It seemed Hapker wanted to say more but didn't. Arden wished he would. Though the man had the backbone to debate with Bracht, it'd be nice to see such firmness in other areas.

He put the thoughts aside for now. Something was amiss and he needed to get to the bottom of it.

One problem at a time.

16
Clash of Interests

3790:257:12:46. J.D. Hapker attempted the merry tune again as he headed to his quarters, but it seemed out of place this time. His humming withered away, replaced by the murmuring sounds of other crew members going about their day.

Whatever confidence he'd had earlier was gone. The captain's evident disappointment rekindled his doubt. His claim that Jori wasn't as bad as everyone assumed had been contradicted at every turn. Captain Arden probably considered him foolish for taking the boy's side. *He thinks I haven't done my job so he's doing it himself.*

Maybe he was a fool. His dad had thought so too.

He greeted the officers guarding outside his quarters, then went inside. Jori sat at the small dining table eating a hunk of the grey gelatin substance. Hapker's dread must have shown on his face because Jori's placid expression changed into a scowl. "What's the matter with you?" the boy asked tartly.

Here we go. "Something's come up and the captain wants to meet you."

Jori's bearing turned wooden. He shoved the food aside and stood rigidly. Hapker expected the boy to ask a bunch of questions, but he marched out the door without a word. Once again, Hapker found himself taking long strides to catch up.

The boy's pace seemed almost impatient, creating an edginess in the air.

As they reached the conveyor, Hapker halted him with a hand on his shoulder. Jori frowned. Hapker motioned to the following guards. "Give us a moment."

They moved back without relaxing their vigilance.

Hapker returned to Jori. "The captain may also ask you some questions, but don't worry. The captain assigned me as your guardian, which means I'm on your side."

Jori's eyes darkened. "Does the captain want to help me too?"

He paused. Captain Arden had done all the right things, but he had no way of knowing how the man felt. Was he simply following rules, or did he truly agree that handing Jori over to those space vultures was a bad idea?

"I think so," he replied.

"You *think* so?"

Hapker sighed. "I'm fairly certain. Everything he's done and everything he's said indicates he wishes to help you too."

He expected the boy to make a derisive remark, but silence lingered in the conveyor and the rest of the way.

They entered the office together. The captain stood with his hand out and a smile that crinkled his eyes. "Welcome, young man. I am Captain Silas Arden."

The boy glanced at the hand, hesitated a moment, but took it. "Jori."

"Please, have a seat, Jori," the captain said with a gesture.

"I'll stand." Jori assumed a formal stance.

Hapker clenched his jaw at the boy's rudeness.

"Very well." The captain sat at his desk and folded his hands with an unflappable air.

His demeanor matched the tranquility of his office, making Hapker yearn for home. Although the desk contained the same composite material found overlaying the structural framework of the rest of the ship, it resembled wood to such an extent that knocking on it was the only way to tell the difference. The room held a few wooden carvings, all of animals, and pictures of scenery adorned the walls.

This place looked very much like his mother's living room except it had no photographs of people around, not even of the captain's wife, and the décor was sparse and meticulously placed.

"I want to personally welcome you aboard our ship," the captain said in unexpected stately politeness. The man was known for his diplomatic skills, but Hapker expected more sternness with this Tredon boy.

Jori raised an eyebrow but didn't reply.

"I promise you're safe here, and you have my word that we're doing everything we can to help your brother." Captain Arden sounded genuine. Hapker hoped he was.

Jori's eyes narrowed. "Even though he is your enemy?"

"Yes. We treat everyone with equal care here." The captain's gaze didn't waver. "I'm sincerely sorry about the rest of your crew. The crash was severe. You and your brother are lucky to be alive."

"Your presence is part of the reason we are still alive, Captain," Jori stated matter-of-factly. He didn't sound grateful, but at least he didn't sound hostile either.

"Now can we get to the point?" the boy added. "The commander said you wanted more information."

Hapker resisted the urge to groan. *So much for not being hostile.*

The captain didn't flinch. His own expression stayed as flat as the boy's. The two could've had a contest to see who was the most difficult to read.

Captain Arden unclasped his hands and turned the small screen on his desk around so Jori could view it. "We've encountered some very disturbing information and would like to hear your side of it."

If there had been a contest, Jori would have lost. His face darkened as he examined the document. "It's a lie. We haven't murdered anyone."

"Can you tell me what *did* happen?" The captain said in a neutral tone. "Why would they say you did this?"

"I assure you, Captain, that neither myself nor my brother committed any crimes on or near that outpost." The boy's eyes blazed.

"They must be after you for some reason."

"Prejudice." Jori practically spit the word.

"Perhaps you acted in self-defense?" Captain Arden said.

Jori growled. Hapker placed his hand on his shoulder. "It's alright. You can tell us."

The boy jerked away. "There's nothing to tell."

"This is serious, young man," the captain replied firmly.

Jori's jaw tightened.

"Jori." Hapker kept his voice calm even though his insides felt like a pond full of fish on a feeding frenzy. "This is for security reasons and our own peace of mind. Murder is a grievous crime, and we have a right to know if their claims are valid."

The boy's face turned crimson. "I *told* you, we've committed no crime. Not on Depnaugh and not with the Cooperative."

"I want to believe you…" Captain Arden said. Jori's reddened further.

"I *do* believe you," Hapker added. However antagonistic Jori acted now, his reaction didn't fit someone who was guilty. He seemed truly appalled by the accusation.

The captain glanced at Hapker with his lips pressed in a thin line. Hapker's stomach did a flip, but his eyes held firm.

Captain Arden turned back to Jori with a neutral expression. "But there's something going on here, and it has me concerned. I can't help you if I don't know what it is."

"If you knew, you wouldn't help us," Jori said in a flat tone.

Hapker's surety fell. There was more to this. Perhaps not murder, but something.

The captain leaned back with a thoughtful expression. After a few moments, he straightened. "I promise you, even if you or your brother committed a crime as heinous—"

"We didn't commit a crime!"

"Jori," Hapker said sternly. He understood the boy's hostility, but this attitude wouldn't help either of them.

Captain Arden raised his palm. "*If* you did, *if*, it wouldn't change what we're doing to help your brother. Nor will we harm you."

"We did *not* kill anyone." The boy spoke with a frosty tone through gritted teeth. "We did not hurt anybody, and we did not commit any crimes."

"What about the device we've heard about? Could they have been after you for this?"

"No."

The look on Captain Arden's face didn't change. He kept his eyes locked on the boy, perhaps in contemplation or maybe waiting to see if Jori would say more but the boy faced him with a burning glower.

Captain Arden broke the silence by noisily drawing in air. "Two people have come to me with serious accusations. Until I find out what this is about, you will remain here."

"You're keeping us prisoners!" Jori jerked forward. Hapker held him back.

The captain frowned but maintained his composure. "You seem to be forgetting your circumstances and you're not considering mine."

"*Your* circumstances?"

"*My* circumstances. Most of my crew says you're dangerous and I should lock you up. Your hostility is telling me that perhaps they're right."

Jori growled. "We didn't do anything!"

"Alright!" Hapker drew him back and stepped between the two, angling mostly toward Jori. "It's obvious we have some differences here, but we each want the same thing."

He turned to the captain whose left eyebrow rose. Hapker's stomach rumbled like a stampede, but he pushed on. "Sir, it's reasonable to say that we'd all like this to end peacefully. You and I want our crew to be safe. Jori here also wants to be safe, and for his brother to be taken care of. Neither of those expectations are unreasonable."

Though the captain's face was devoid of emotion, the placidity of it made Hapker's mouth go dry. He squared his shoulders and did his best to mask his unease. "Obviously, we should continue our investigation. Meanwhile, please give me some time." He didn't need to say time for what.

He held his breath as Captain Arden drummed his fingers. The man glanced back and forth between them, then folded his hands on the table. "Jori. I want to help you and your brother, and I prefer not to hold you against your will, but understand, I have a job to do and I *will* do it." His eyebrow lifted again.

Jori's mouth twitched, but his face remained blank.

"With that being said," the captain continued, "we shall go on as before. Unless something convinces me otherwise, this includes our efforts to get you home. Can you tell us how to contact your parents?"

"There is a ship we're supposed to rendezvous with at the border at three-four-zero-point-zero-four-five from the Chevert outpost," the boy said. His tone seemed less angry but still assertive.

"Is this where your family is?" the captain asked.

"No, but they'll get us home."

"I'd prefer to take you directly to your parents."

"Trust me, Captain. You don't want to meet my father."

A chill shivered down Hapker's back. If he wasn't mistaken, the captain released a slight tremor as well.

"Fair enough," Captain Arden replied. "We will review the situation and keep you updated. Commander?"

Hapker's heart leapt. He expected a reprimand or a hard look, but neither came. It took him a moment, but he understood what the captain hinted at—get more details. He bobbed his head. "Yes, Sir."

When Jori left the office, the captain fixed him with an unreadable look. He'd overstepped his bounds by intervening and braced himself for the reprimand.

"I certainly have a better understanding of what you mean." No hint of displeasure touched the captain's tone.

"Regarding?" Hapker eased into the chair in front of the desk.

"His apparent level of maturity. His attitude. I find his manners rather unsettling for one his age."

Hapker smiled lightly. Perhaps Captain Arden had thought he wasn't doing his job, or maybe he just wanted to see for himself. Either way, the man now understood what he had to contend with. His jaw hurt from grinding his teeth so often, and he probably sighed in frustration more in these past thirty-six hours than he had his entire life.

"Now that we've spoken to him, what do you think about this development?" the captain asked.

Hapker spoke without hesitation. "I'm sure he didn't murder anyone. He seemed honestly appalled."

"Agreed, though there's a chance he's lying."

"He hasn't lied so far. If he doesn't want me to know something, he simply refuses to speak."

"Yes. I see what you mean." The captain's brow drew down. "I believe he's keeping secrets, but I can't be sure if they're related to the warrant."

"It could be about prejudice, as he said. There's a lot of that going around. I just finished up a reprimand on Corporal Calloway for trying to instigate trouble with the boy."

The captain made a slight shake of his head.

"After hearing some callous remarks from our own people," Hapker continued, "it wouldn't be a stretch for others like Captain Fargoza to take their hatred further. Children are easy marks for revenge seekers."

The captain sighed. "Disturbing, but true." He rubbed his temple. "There's also this device mentioned in the recording and still nothing from the team investigating his ship."

"What about our Grapne passengers?"

"Nope. I doubt these underlings know much anyway."

Hapker agreed. "Overseers like to hold all the cards."

"I never got to speak with the Overseer. Captain Seth insisted he wasn't available."

"He put more stress on the supposed murder."

"Yes. With only his brief mention of a theft, I have no way of knowing if it's related to this device."

"Hmm," Hapker said. "A device could be anything. Perhaps their father wanted a hydration unit."

"I sent a message to the Depnaugh outpost. I'm hoping for more clarification." The captain's forehead wrinkled. "If there truly was a murder and it involved those boys, you realize we must call on the PG-Force."

Hapker suppressed a grimace. "I'm sure it won't come to that."

"I hope you're right."

"In the meantime, Sir, I'll keep trying to get Jori to open up."

The captain nodded.

Hapker hesitated. "May I ask you something, Sir?"

"Of course," the captain replied.

"You told him they would remain here unless we got more information, but you also said you'd send them home. What if we never find out what this is all about? Will you keep them here indefinitely?"

The captain folded his hands and leaned forward with a direct stare. "My intention is to help them return home. My comment was intended to convey how much it disturbs me that he's keeping a secret. Whatever it is, it's serious enough to cause the Grapnes to shoot down his ship and for bounty hunters to come for him. This does not sit well with me, Commander. Not at all."

Hapker swallowed. "Yes, Sir. I apologize for intervening."

"Don't apologize, Commander. Never apologize for trying to do what's right."

"Yes, Sir." The tightness in his chest eased but not by much. One moment the captain seemed to judge him, then he did an about-face and acted more agreeably. It kept Hapker wondering what laid over the next hill. Perhaps he should return home before his career failed again.

No. I must let this play out.

17
Cyborgs and Cats

3790:257:13:32. After the commander left, Silas Arden leaned back and sighed. He wanted to believe the child. Despite not knowing the commander well, he wanted to have faith in him too. However, he also had a responsibility to the safety of his crew.

He folded his arms and stared at the viewscreen without really seeing it. Murder was a serious accusation, one that shouldn't be ignored. Captain Fargoza had been right about it taking several days to file the warrant through the Cooperative. What if they validated it and he had already taken the children back home? Then again, what if someone had fabricated the charge for the sake of revenge?

He rose and ordered coffee from the food fabricor. The rich brown liquid poured from a nozzle into his favorite cup. Steam rose. He took in a whiff and his mouth watered.

After returning to his chair, he accessed Bracht's security report. Deceit seemed most likely with the Grapnes. Captain Seth never checked in with Melna, and the Grapnes brought onboard had already been problematic. Officers had caught them snooping about several times. If only Cooperative law allowed him to hold them all accountable rather than just the one in charge.

He pinched his bottom lip. The only one capable of giving answers right now was the child with a countenance as hard and unyielding as any Tredon warrior he'd ever met. Was it the face of a murderer, though? His gut said no, but Jori definitely kept something back.

Hapker might get the information. The man had finally shown some backbone by interrupting. He liked seeing fire in his new commander but found his unwavering support of the child unsettling. If only he'd be as bold when it came to protecting his crew.

On the other hand, the entire conversation played out well. Although it probably appeared Arden had lost his cool, he'd dealt with enough warriors to know that being firm established his authority and kept him from being viewed as weak.

Perhaps Hapker wasn't aware of this. When he stepped in, though, he might have made a positive difference. The way the child's temper seemed to fade indicated the commander had a chance of gaining his trust. How long should he wait, though? So much could go wrong.

Arden sighed again. He sat up and checked for new messages. There were none. Waiting to hear more about the warrant took more time than he cared to give.

He ran his hand down his face. Should he use Garner?

Liam Garner was a good man, but people were uncomfortable with his talent. They feared that even though he wasn't supposed to use his skills without permission that he'd do it anyway and none would be the wiser.

Their fear was justified. Many like Garner had been convicted of such a crime. The invasion was a violation of one's privacy and rights. And there was a small possibility his ability could cause brain trauma. The Prontaean Cooperative used people like him nevertheless—for situations where lives were at stake.

He opened the communication link and tapped Garner's name. A photo of an elderly man with an oblong face and pale leathery skin popped up on the screen, but the "Contact" button below stared back at him.

Arden was within his rights to give Garner permission to use his skill, but he had to be careful. Was he using him merely to satisfy his own curiosity, to solve this mystery? Or was there a genuine threat to security?

Was the child truly a danger? Or was it Arden's own preconceived notions?

He rested his chin in one hand and tapped the table with the other. A buzz at his door broke him of his thoughts. "Come in."

Director Jeyana Sengupta rushed in. "My contact called."

Arden straightened. "What did she say?"

"Nothing yet. I thought you might want to be in on this."

Arden left his desk to stand in front of the viewscreen. Sengupta touched her MM and the screen on the wall powered on.

A white-haired young woman with bronze skin appeared on the comm feed.

"Thank you for waiting, Ivory." Sengupta broadened her smile. "And thank you for allowing my captain to join our chat."

Ivory returned the greeting with a waving dance of her fingers. "Captain Arden! I've heard so much about you," she said with a high-pitch. "Are you really in your fifties? Because you are one handsome man. Mmm-mm."

Arden cleared his throat and shifted his stance as he admired the woman's smooth neckline and rounded bosom. "Thank you, yes. I'm fifty-two. I appreciate you sharing information with us."

Her smile turned into a mock pout. "I'm afraid I don't have much on the Tredons who visited our station recently. All I know is they purchased something from Shekaka, the black-market dealer, and they traveled with a pair of youths—a boy and a teen."

Arden realized her lush white painted lips had stopped moving and kickstarted his brain to register what she had just said. "Did you get information on what they purchased?"

"Not at all, Sweetheart. I'll keep an ear out, though. I have other intel… Something about their emperor."

"Oh?" Arden forced down his rising internal heat. Ivory wasn't his type, especially since his wife Symphonia was the best woman in the world, but Ivory's garish makeup, flawless skin, and tight-fitting clothes incited a chemical reaction that sent his blood racing.

"Someone's told me he's in league with cyborgs." Ivory's expression turned grave. "And not just any cyborgs, not ordinary thugs with a few enhancements. They're almost robots and their tech is like nothing anyone has ever seen."

Arden's chest tightened. Could this be the secret the child kept hidden?

"What kind of tech?" Sengupta asked.

Ivory tapped a long white fingernail on her cheek. "I'm not sure, but my source said he overheard someone saying they have tech that not even the MEGA hunters can detect. It becomes part of the body or something."

MEGA, mechanically enhanced genetically altered persons. Arden shivered. The people themselves didn't bother him. It was the fact that they voluntarily had their eyeballs scooped out or their arms cut off so they could get machine parts. Equally unnerving were the fanatical MEGA Inspection Officers, also called MEGA hunters, who registered those violating the MEGA Injunction, then blacklisted them from certain occupations.

He shook the feeling off. "May I ask how you came by this information?"

"I know a cargo hauler who makes three or four deliveries to the emperor a year. The man's a scoundrel, so I don't take everything he says as the gospel truth, but he seemed pretty shaken up about this. He said them 'borgs were alive but not alive at the same time—like machines with humanistic faces plastered with fake smiles."

An icy sensation ran down Arden's spine. "Did he say how many he saw?"

"Three. Two with cybernetic eyes and one with computer ports in the back of his metal skull." Her body quivered and she made a revulsive noise. "Just those ones, but another ship docked at the same time as his. He went to check it out but got stopped by the metal-headed cyborg. It creeped him out, he said, and he hightailed it the hell out of there as fast as he could."

The hot blood this woman had stirred chilled in Arden's veins. "I will pass this information along to the Prontaean Council. Thank you, Ivory."

She dipped her head.

"Yes, thank you," Sengupta added. "You have no idea how much I appreciate your intel and value our friendship. I'll send you a little gift through the U-Bank."

"You're a peach, Jeyana. We'll catch up again sometime. And nice to meet you, Captain Arden. If you ever come to the station, stop by for a visit—no charge." Ivory winked.

Arden's entire body flushed.

The communication ended. Sengupta wore a sly smile. "She's beautiful in an interesting way, isn't she?"

Arden's words caught in his throat.

Sengupta returned to her business-like bearing. "It makes her popular and she hears a lot. She's never given me wrong intel."

Arden sat behind his desk with a sigh. "We have two puzzles to solve now. I only hope these children have nothing to do with the emperor's cyborgs."

"This could be big." Sengupta's mouth turned down. "I will tell my other contacts to be watchful."

Arden organized his thoughts. "Have you had any luck identifying the other crew members of the *StarFire*?"

"None at all, which isn't surprising. Tredons live dangerous lives so it doesn't take long for one we've identified to get killed and replaced by another."

Arden hid his disappointment and held up a finger. "I have a couple other ideas. Give me a moment." He minimized the communication link for Garner and opened the one to the medical bay.

"Medic Shera here for Doctor Gregson," the yellow-eyed woman announced.

"Shera, are you familiar with the medical file on our two Tredon children?"

"Yes, Captain."

Arden assumed as much so didn't bother asking her if Doctor Gregson was available. "Did you find any sign that they might have biometric implants?"

"No, Sir, and we checked as part of our security protocol."

"Is there any chance they have implants and we just weren't able to detect them?"

"There's always a chance for that, Sir, though we have very sophisticated detection methods. Not as many as the MEGA Inspection Officers, but enough to mitigate the risk factor."

Arden's shoulders fell. "Thank you, Shera."

She dipped her head. "You're welcome, Captain. Let me know if we can be of further assistance."

Arden nodded and ended the communication. He leaned back in his chair and focused on Sengupta. "Another dead end. My options for sorting this out are one, use Liam Garner or two, send my people to Depnaugh to see if they can unravel things from there."

Sengupta's brows rose. "Neither of those are good. Garner might inadvertently harm the boy and that station is a dangerous place."

Arden agreed. "If these children are hurt under our care, we could spark conflict with an enemy who might have enhanced warriors. If we send our people to Depnaugh, we put them in a risky situation."

"That boy might not have much information and you'd risk him for nothing," Sengupta said. "What about Sergeant Ander Vizubi? He can handle himself and he has a knack for digging up the facts."

"I was considering him. He also knows how to navigate that place and he may still have connections there."

"I believe his brother lives on that station. Honestly, since that station is less than a half a day away, I'm surprised he didn't request leave to visit him."

"His history there is complicated," Arden replied without divulging the sergeant's personal affairs. "Do you think it would help if you accompanied him?"

Sengupta stiffened as though the notion frightened her. He'd never known her to shy from danger, but Depnaugh had a bad reputation and she had no combat skills. "I would probably be more of a hindrance than a help and I don't know anyone else other than Ivory."

"You're right. Vizubi it is then." A heaviness rolled over Arden's chest. Vizubi wouldn't like going, but he was the best choice.

"If something else comes up or the boy becomes a greater problem, you still have the option of using Garner," she said.

Arden sighed. The temptation of using the man remained, but he set it aside.

After she left, he ordered the team on the planet to wrap up. They would leave in two days. Although solving the mystery of the Tredons was his top priority, he also wanted them off his ship. The boy said a Tredon vessel would be near Chevert, and heading there minimized further encounters with bounty hunters.

He prayed for smooth sailing from here on out but didn't hold out much hope. Anything involving Tredons promised trouble.

*****

3790:257:14:27. Sergeant Ander Vizubi sat cross-legged on a cushion on the floor. He stared at the flameless candle set on the altar before him and mumbled his prayers. "Forgive me for the wrongs I've done to others, for the times I stressed out my parents, getting in fights, cheating on my high school history final, breaking Davin's arm, busting Mark's nose…" He sighed. "For hurting all those people when I took the wrong path, and mostly for abandoning my brother."

Thinking of his younger brother always choked him up. He let himself feel the emotion as it twisted and tumbled in his gut. "Help me be a better person and guide me on the rest of my journey."

His comm beeped, snapping him back to the here and now. He kissed the cross hanging on the silver chain around his neck and tapped the tiny device behind his ear. "Vizubi here."

"Sergeant Vizubi, this is Captain Arden. I have an important task for you."

"Yes, Sir." Vizubi imagined the Tredon boy making trouble and stood, bracing himself to jump into action.

"I need you to go to Depnaugh."

A pang stabbed in Vizubi's chest. "Sir?"

"Someone at that space station knows more about the Tredons we have here, but no one is talking. I'm hoping you can contact some old associates to find out who they are and what they're up to."

"Um. Sir? I haven't seen them in a long time. I'm not sure if they'll volunteer anything, even if I paid them."

"I need you to do what you can, Sergeant. You have a talent for finding the truth."

Vizubi slowly inhaled. Ideas on who to contact or shake down for information swirled in his head, then stopped when his brother came to mind. Hesteben also served Guillermo, but unlike Vizubi, he'd fallen deep into that dark and dismal world. Hesteben was still there, presumably still alive. They hadn't spoken in months.

The captain was right, though. He had a talent for solving mysteries. When he'd worked for Guillermo, he wasn't just an enforcer, he was a problem solver.

"If this is something you can do by calling them," the captain continued, "this would be ideal."

"I'm afraid not, Sir." He ran his hand through his hair, noting in the nearby mirror how grey it had gotten since he last visited that station. "Most likely, my contacts won't have much information. They might tell me who does, though, and they wouldn't put me through to them on a video call. I should speak to them in person. I'll need a team to accompany me."

"We can't spare many."

Vizubi nodded to himself. Although the only Tredon threat on the ship was just a boy, he'd seen the fire in his eyes and watched him surpass his own martial skill on the holo-machine. "I'll need at least three, preferably four people."

"Done," Captain Arden said. "I've received information that the Tredons purchased something from Shekaka while they were there. There's also a rumor that the emperor might be colluding with MEGAs. I'm not sure if these two things are connected, but it's important that we find out as much as we can."

"I'll do my best, Sir. When do you want me to leave?"

"As soon as possible. We'll be leaving this planet shortly. Take a Swift and we'll rendezvous at the Chevert outpost."

"I'd rather take a Bastion, Sir. A Swift is too nice of a ship for Depnaugh. A Bastion is more common and is better equipped to defend itself."

"It's your call, Sergeant. Be safe out there and contact me as soon as you arrive."

"Yes, Sir."

"Arden, out."

The comm clicked off. Vizubi reached for his small table-sized console and ended up touching a brownish blob of goop splotched on top. "Aye-ya!"

He quickly found something to wipe his fingers on and turned around with hands on hips. "Damn it, Makala," he said to the cat on his bed.

Makala hoisted a leg up in the air and licked it. His ears twitched, but he continued his ministrations as though no one had spoken.

"Seriously, cat. You'd think you'd show a little gratitude for all I do for you, you ungrateful urchin."

Makala glanced at him, then resumed licking. Vizubi grabbed a special towel just for this type of incident and cleaned up the mess. "I coulda just left you in that dump heap to scrounge for garbage, ya know. You wouldn't be such a damn picky eater then, would ya?"

Makala switched to cleaning his other leg as Vizubi tossed the hairball in the garbage chute. He returned to the console and got everything ready. Once he had alerted his team and hashed out all the details, he made one more call.

"Lieutenant Sharkey," he said. "I have a favor to ask."

"Sure, anything," she replied in a chirpy voice.

"Captain Arden is sending me to Depnaugh, and I need someone to take care of Makala."

"Of course! I'd love to."

His face broke into a smile. He suspected she would. She loved that damn cat almost as much as he did. "His new favorite food is recipe two-one-nine and if he tires of that, try a sardine flavor."

"You got it."

He gave a few more instructions, then disconnected. After packing his gear, he scratched Makala behind the ears. "Don't make any trouble while I'm gone, ya little runt."

Makala arched his head, taking in the rubbing with a satisfying purr.

Vizubi stopped and shook his finger. "And leave that cleaning bot alone or the next time I've gotta go, I'll put you in the closet."

Makala eyed his finger with stiff intensity. His tail flicked. Vizubi enticed him with a finger dance until he gave in and attacked.

Vizubi grunted a laugh. "Damn cat."

18
Gossip

3790:257:18:45. An attendant approached Mik Calloway and his friends. The volume in the lounge seemed louder when everyone at his table fell silent. Shrana set each of their drinks down with a friendly smile. They thanked her in return while he said nothing. After all, she was only doing the same thing the bots could do. Granted, she was better looking but the bessie didn't like him, so why waste his effort?

Shrana left and Private Sindy continued their conversation. "Aw, come on, Calloway. You're only saying that 'cause you got caught." Her voice sliced through his eardrums. She was pretty enough, though her backside was a little bigger than he preferred. Plus, the sound of her shrill tone turned him completely off. "You're lucky you got off so easy."

He took a swig of his Wyndhill ale and grimaced at the initial bitterness. The crisp fruity flavor that followed redeemed it. "Y'all can't tell me you didn't want to say the same thing to that little monster."

Private Frebt huffed from nostrils so wide that Calloway could probably stick his big toes up in them. "Yeah, but we weren't stupid enough to say it out loud." The man slopped his non-alcoholic drink around as he spoke. Something about his body chemistry or some such sent him running to sick bay if he had more than a half glass of a proper drink. Poor pig-nosed dud.

"And with the commander there, no less," Corporal Bret added. His full name was much longer and more difficult to pronounce so everyone simply called him Bret. As if to live up to the superiority of his fancy name, he was the only one drinking wine. The prim and proper know-it-all thought he was better than everybody here, but Calloway needed a drink on his day off and didn't care who he drank with.

“Come on,” he said. “I didn’t notice him there. Neither did any of you. Kinda messed up how he came to the little brat’s rescue and all, isn’t it?”

“Yeah.” Frebt huffed out of his nostrils again.

Finally, someone’s on my side. “I mean, what’s up with this guy anyway?”

“It seems odd that the captain would commission someone who was nearly discharged and jailed,” Bret said.

“I think he’s cute,” Sindy added.

Calloway rolled his eyes. “You only like his rank, which he’s lucky to have.”

“I hear he got high marks at the institute. Top of his class.” Frebt hid his admiration by taking another drink.

“Seriously?” Maybe Frebt wasn’t on his side after all. “His major is security, but can you imagine a Pholatian Protector having any skills in combat? They’re the galactic pussies of soldiery.”

Bret choked on his wine. Sindy cackled, not noticing all the heads that had turned at her outburst. Frebt loudly sucked in air through his wide toe-slotted nose.

“Don’t let the commander hear you say that one,” Sindy said, her voice surprisingly low.

He harrumphed. “All I’m saying is he doesn’t belong here, and neither does that little Tredon monster.”

“Yeah, even the Rabni seems to go along with it,” Frebt said.

“Another oddity,” Bret added. “I thought Rabnoshk warriors despised Tredons.”

Calloway usually hated Bret’s formal haughty tone, but not this time.

“Hey chaps,” a boyish voice interrupted.

Calloway leaned away from big-eared Private Vigan as he neared the table. The short and creepy-looking man moved closer. “Guess what?”

Calloway curled his lip. “What?” Either the nosy munchkin overheard them talking—not good—or he had used his diminutive height to sneak close-by and impose himself on them with another stupid story about his yappy little dog.

Vigan cupped the side of his mouth and lowered his voice. “Those Tredons we brought on board… They’re wanted for murder.”

Calloway scoffed. "Of course they are. Aren't they all?"

"No. I mean there's a warrant and everything."

Calloway's annoyance at the little man's interruption slipped away, replaced by interest. Frebt and Sindy goaded Vigan for more details. The man smiled as he spoke, as though enjoying the attention. He told them all about the ship they'd encountered and about how the warrant was for the Tredon boys.

"No friggin way!" Sindy said.

"I can't believe they're still allowing the brat to walk around freely," Calloway added.

Bret, the ever pragmatic uppity suckpot, made a face. "If this is true, then why didn't the captain turn them over?"

Vigan shrugged. "I didn't pick up on that part."

Calloway slammed down his glass. A slop of ale splashed his hand. "This is going too far. We must do something."

"What can we do?" Frebt asked.

He let out an exasperated breath. "I don't know yet, but we can't go along with this."

"Perhaps there is more to this than we're aware of," Bret said.

He twisted his mouth and scowled at the man. *Uppity prig*. "I know all I need to know about those fucking animals. They constantly raid my planet. Every single family member of mine has been murdered or taken as a slave by those brutes. You don't even want to hear what they did to my sister."

His gut churned as though he'd eaten a slab of rancid meat. His little sister had been so sweet and innocent until the Tredons got a hold of her. She was barely alive after the hours of mauling those monsters inflicted on her. Her eyes still held fear when she died in his arms.

He slammed his fist on the table and the glasses clacked as they bounced. If he *had* eaten rancid meat, his stomach was running it through the grinder now.

Bret looked away, saying nothing. No one else spoke either. The awkward silence lingered, and his drink turned sour. *Just another fucking day ruined by that murderous little space-thug*. He had to do something. He wasn't sure what yet, but he'd figure it out soon enough.

19
Hitting a Wall

3790:258:01:26. J.D. Hapker breathed in a heavy rhythm. A pleasant burning warmed his calves and thighs. Sweat trickled down his back.

The weightlifting area returned to view as he jogged around the track. *Eleven.* One more lap to go.

The same individuals he'd passed earlier were still there. He shook his head at the sight of Bracht lifting a substantial weight on the bench press. If the machine ever malfunctioned, it would take dozens of people to lift the gigantic barbell off him.

He pushed on past the open matted area where Jori did tumbling exercises. By the time he'd taken three strides, Jori had finished a round-off and a series of flips. At a mere age of ten, the boy was good enough to compete in the Prontaean Games. He was fast, agile, and had a great sense of balance.

A crowd had gathered, much like they had done yesterday. After his confrontation with Calloway, though, he doubted anyone would give the boy any trouble. It helped to have Sharkey in charge today. He could always count on her to do every aspect of her job well.

He pumped his arms and increased his pace for the final lap. His leg muscles screamed but he pushed harder, taking ever deeper breaths. *A few more yards. Breathe. Breathe. Almost there.* His heartbeat throbbed in his ears.

Done! He sped by the weight machines then stopped short at the sight of a tall skinny man with a creepy smile and a patch over one eye. Hapker followed his gaze and found Jori glaring right back.

Crap. He moved his legs again as Jori stormed toward the Grapne. The boy's face contorted into a snarl and his pace quickened.

Hapker jumped in front of him. The boy halted. His fists balled as he sidestepped around him.

"No you don't." Hapker snatched the boy's shoulder.

Jori whipped his arm around, removing Hapker's grip. He turned and glared up at him with a murderous scowl. "What the hell is he doing here? He murdered my crew!"

Hapker hardened his expression. "The captain of the Cougar killed your people. This man is a maintenance worker. He had no part in shooting down your ship."

Jori growled. "You dare to accuse me of murder, yet you let him walk about freely? I thought you were on my side."

"You are both walking about freely because neither of you committed murder," Hapker said calmly as Sharkey ushered the one-eyed Grapne out the gym. "We wouldn't hold you accountable for another person's actions any more than we would him."

Jori held a glare so heated that it practically smoldered. "He's not innocent. He came here looking for me, and if I see him again, I'll kill him."

Hapker ignored the chill down his spine. He matched Jori's black look and crossed his arms. "If you want to return home, you won't hurt *anyone* on this ship."

Jori growled. Hapker remained firm until Jori unclenched his fists and his face returned to its usual shade.

"Your workout earlier was amazing," Hapker said, changing the subject.

Jori dipped his head in reply. Whether in agreement or to say thanks, Hapker wasn't sure.

Probably the former. "You ready to go?"

Jori frowned. "No. I've only been here an hour. I will stay a few more."

"A *few* more? Is it normal for you to exercise for so long?"

"Yes."

Hapker didn't let the boy's clipped tone deter him. "How much time does that leave you for schooling?"

Jori's brow still hung over his dark eyes but his mood seemed to taper. "Plenty, which reminds me. I need reading material."

"Of course. What would you like?"

"I'm currently studying Pershornian warfare, fourth generation, and Alkon's theories on quantum mechanics."

"Whoa. That's an impressive reading list."

The boy must have the inherited genetic enhancements Sengupta had mentioned. Some people were naturally more intelligent. Some even had a natural mutation in their genes that gave them greater energy by carrying more oxygen in their blood. For this boy to have super-endurance as well as above-average intelligence and likely a stronger bone density indicated a possibility of nature being manipulated. *What else is this boy capable of?*

Hapker made a mental note to include this information in his next report. "I can get you an MDS. You are welcome to read anything you find there." He wasn't sure how Captain Arden felt about the boy using their electronics, but an MDS should be alright. It only gave access to a publicly available library and couldn't connect to any other network.

"That's acceptable."

The boy's gaze spread over the gymnasium as though looking for something else to do. Hapker considered leaving him with the security officers to work on scheduling. As much as he hated that task, the idea seemed pleasant. However, he had another duty to attend to. Jori's confrontational attitude had abated, so perhaps this was his chance.

"How about a game of wall ball?" He pointed to where two people played in a room off to the side.

"What's that?"

He led Jori over. "Two or more people take turns hitting a ball against the back wall." This was his favorite exercise. It might be a little intense for most children, but this boy could probably handle it.

Jori's eyes followed the ball, but his face remained otherwise placid. "Very well."

*****

3790:258:03:01. J.D. Hapker marveled. The boy never seemed to tire. They played for far longer than he intended. Although his legs had turned to rubber, he enjoyed himself.

Jori presented quite a challenge. He lost most games, but this only inspired him to try harder. His brow furrowed over a bright red face much like he'd worn when Calloway tried to pick a fight. This expression, though, seemed more determined than angry.

Hapker hit the ball. It bounced over to the other side of the court. The boy dived for it and crashed to the floor, his elbow hitting first with a loud smack.

Hapker cringed and rushed over to make sure he was alright. Jori sat up and cradled his arm with a fleeting wince.

"How is it?"

Jori stood. "It's not bad."

"Come on. Let me see." He led him out of the room where they sat on the bench. The boy's elbow held a dark mark but no indications of a serious injury.

Jori flexed and twisted his arm. "I can keep playing."

"We should go to the medical bay to make sure it's not broken."

"It's only bruised."

"It wouldn't hurt to check. At the very least, we can get you something for the pain."

Jori frowned. "I don't need anything for the pain. I would know if it had fractured or broken, so seeing a medic is pointless."

Hapker sighed at the boy's stubbornness. "Alright." He wiped his forehead and exhaled again, this time in hesitation. This was the perfect opportunity, though. "Speaking of broken bones, Doctor Jerom noticed both you and your brother have had quite a few."

"Yes." Jori shrugged.

Hapker waited a few moments but Jori offered nothing more. "It's unusual for someone your age, of any age actually, to have this many bone reconstructions. How did they all happen?"

"Various things."

Hapker gritted his teeth at the boy's brevity. "Like what?"

"In exercises, contests…"

"So, all accidents?"

"Mostly."

An icy dread drizzled down Hapker's back. "Mostly? As in some were intentional?"

"That is correct."

The iciness spread. "From your father?"

"From my father, others, and from my Jintal training."

"Jintal!" Hapker's gut moved like it performed all the tumbling exercises Jori had done earlier. Jintal was a harsh practice used to build up pain tolerance. "Aren't you a little young for that?"

"Yes, but my father persuaded a Jintal master to teach us anyway."

"You know this is wrong, don't you? What your father does to you is abuse, torture even, and it's morally wrong."

"My father is not known for his morality, Commander," Jori stated matter-of-factly.

Hapker's mouth fell open. Jori seemed so unemotional about the entire issue that he wasn't sure how to respond.

"Aren't you worried," he finally said. "Worried that your father will get you killed?"

"I don't think about it. I wouldn't be the first to die by my father's hand, and there isn't much I can do about it."

The urge to vomit welled up. "If you could get away from it, go somewhere else, somewhere safe, would you go?"

"No."

"Why not?"

"Because of my mother."

"You don't want to leave her behind." Hapker gave Jori's shoulder a gentle squeeze.

"Correct. And because I have responsibilities."

Hapker shook his head. "You are too young for so much responsibility."

"Fulfilling my responsibilities keeps me alive, Commander."

That's why he doesn't show any emotion. He's trying to numb his feelings. He patted Jori's back. "You can call me J.D., you know. We don't need to be so formal with one another."

Jori said nothing so Hapker added, "I'm sorry. No one's life should be so harsh."

"Don't feel sorry for me, Commander. My life is not so dark and dismal as this conversation has led you to believe."

"Tell me the good parts, then."

"My brother. My mother."

"They certainly sound good." The knot that had formed in Hapker's stomach loosened. "If you spend most of your day exercising and studying, though, where do you find the time to do anything fun?"

Jori's brows knitted. "Exercising and studying are fun."

Hapker smiled. "I can understand that. I know you said you don't play games, but surely there are things you do simply for the sake of enjoyment."

"My brother and I did some fun things at the Depnaugh outpost."

"Yeah? Like what?"

"We used a holo-suite to visit exotic planet-scapes. And we saw a lot of interesting stuff, including a pair of laverjack beasts being transported by the Hurvans."

"Hmm. I wouldn't mind seeing them up close." Hapker asked more about the planet-scapes and found that Jori enjoyed nature activities like hiking and rock climbing, things he loved to do as well. The boy still kept any emotion from showing, but his eyes betrayed him. They lit up when he talked about a survivalist excursion he recently went on with his brother.

The conversation turned animals. He didn't just express enthusiasm for the ferocious creatures like laverjacks. He seemed intrigued by all animals and even asked about the dogs and other pets he'd seen during their tour of the ship's arboretum.

Their discussion continued for a while longer. Eventually, it led to Jori's interest in the sciences, and the perfect opportunity came for Hapker to bring another issue up. "The logs of your ship mentioned a device. Is it some sort of scientific device?"

He realized the moment he said it that the question was out of place.

Jori's eyes darkened and his jaw clenched. "I see. You're only being nice so you can trick me."

"What? No." He waved his hand in dismissal. "That's not it at all."

"Liar."

Hapker shivered at his murderous expression. "I mean yes, I would like information, but me being nice to you… It's genuine."

Jori stood. "We're done talking," he said coldly, and stormed away.

Hapker slumped against the wall and ran his hand down his face. He had been making real headway with the boy. Now they were back to square one.

20
Depnaugh

3790:258:03:37. Ander Vizubi held his arms out as a greasy-headed man patted him down with a practiced precision that was surprising considering how dazed his hollow eyes were.

"Clean." The greasy man said.

You, not so much. Vizubi recognized the foggy expression of someone coming down off a high. He hoped his brother was in better shape, but it'd be smarter to bet on a turtle in a rat race.

The man moved on to Private Mei Fung. When he patted between her thighs, she slapped the top of his head. "Watch it, bucko."

The man ignored her and continued with his pointless search. Despite Private Ishaq Bari's protests, Vizubi had ordered no weapons. "*They'll be taken away anyway*," he had warned.

Vizubi eyed the armed men and women surrounding him and his team. "Does Guillermo really think I'm so dangerous that he pits two to one against us?"

"You have a reputation," a red-haired woman with a cybernetic eye drawled. "Said you were the best enforcer he ever had—until you betrayed him."

Vizubi scowled. "I didn't betray him. I bought my way out fair and square."

"And joined the Cooperative. Now you're a lawman. Can't be trusted."

"I'm not here to arrest anyone. I just want to talk to him… And see my brother."

The woman harrumphed. "He don't wanna talk to the likes of you."

"Liar. My brother and I may not be as close as we once were, but we aren't at odds."

She smirked. "Was talking about Guillermo."

Vizubi frowned. “So what are we being searched for if you’re not taking us to Guillermo?”

“Didn’t say I wasn’t taking you to him. Said he didn’t want to talk to ya.”

A sourness slithered in Vizubi’s gut. Did Guillermo mean to take him prisoner? “If he’s got a problem with me, fine, but let my friends go.”

“No way, Sergeant,” Corporal Rona Quigley said. “We’re not leaving you in the hands of these scoundrels.”

The red-haired woman’s eyes narrowed. “Who you calling a scoundrel? You think just because you’re from the Cooperative that you’re better than me?”

“I think I’m better than you cause you’re so damned ugly.”

The woman lunged in with a swing of her phaser rifle. Quigley blocked it and punched her in the face. With a snap, Vizubi and the others found themselves staring down the points of several weapons.

The red-haired woman touched the drops of blood coming from her nose. “You bitch!”

When she came at Quigley again, Vizubi stepped between. “Alright, alright. Just take us to Guillermo.”

“Oh no. She’s gonna get hers.”

“Try it and I’ll smash your metal eye in,” Vizubi said through his teeth.

She curled her lip and looked him up and down. “You think you’re fast enough, old man?”

“Let’s find out. Make your move and see what happens.”

Vizubi locked his gaze with hers but still noted the increased tension of his team. Bari clenched his fists and his dark eyes hardened with determination. Fung’s mouth tightened and her small frame went taut. Quigley stepped into a combat stance. Her buxom figure matched the red-haired woman’s, though she stood a half-head taller.

This was not a team these people should mess with. Bari was an expert in jujitsu. Fung was petite, but her swift acrobatics gave her the opportunity to reach her opponent’s weak points. And Quigley knew as many dirty street fighting techniques as he did. If Staff Sergeant Oscar Woolley were here rather than guarding their docked ship, he'd be able to disarm one and take half of them out in a single heartbeat.

The red-haired woman's mechanical eye emitted a green glow. Vizubi tensed, expecting a laser strike. A gridwork of green-lined beams ran down his chest instead.

The results of whatever she had scanned him for made her back off. She kept her hard expression, though, and signaled her people. "Let's move these sacks of meat on in. I'm tired of looking at 'em."

She led them through the security gates and into Vizubi's old life. The dingy walls and dirty floors were exactly as he remembered them, yet somehow gloomier. An odor of stale air mixed with a hint of unwashed bodies since few in this line of work cared about hygiene.

The corridor was wide enough to accommodate five people walking side-by-side, but the group squeezed together every time others passed.

Vizubi scanned all the faces. New ones mingled with old, and none were friendly. *How did that happen?* He'd had friends here, but perhaps becoming a PG-Force officer was too distasteful for them.

They passed through another set of security doors and entered an opulent hallway. Rich tapestries hung on the walls between intervals of glowing sconces and old Earth paintings. The tiled floor gleamed with newness. The boss must've replaced the red and black checkered ones with teal and gold, making this entryway much brighter than before.

Vizubi accidentally elbowed Quigley as they squeezed by the cleaning crew. He recognized one, a woman a little older than him, and his heart jumped. Sasha hadn't aged well. Her skin held more wrinkles and dark circles hung under her eyes, but when she looked up at him, her beautiful smile bore the same genuine kindness.

He had offered to save her from this place once, but she refused. This was her family, she'd said, the only one she'd ever known. Guillermo treated her well enough, so he didn't press it. Saying goodbye to her, though, had been almost as difficult as saying it to his brother.

They came upon a golden door and Vizubi's stomach tumbled. He hadn't been looking forward to seeing his old boss again. They had parted on shaky terms and Vizubi imagined the man held some resentment.

The door opened to a lavish room with a grand crystal chandelier dazzling from the ceiling. His chest tightened as memories of the past flooded through him. He'd once dreamed about becoming the bossman's number one enforcer. But at some point, the compounding atrocities motivated him to turn his life around.

"Ander!" a joyful voice said.

The armed guard stepped aside and Vizubi faced a dark-complexioned man with carbon-steel colored hair and an imperial mustache. Guillermo looked the same except a little paunch pushed against the bottom of his embroidered dinner jacket.

Vizubi put on a smile. "Good to see you again, Sir."

Guillermo shook his hand with warm enthusiasm. "Ha, ha! No need to call me sir anymore. We're just old friends now, eh."

"Yes, just old friends." Vizubi pretended good humor, but it hadn't been so long that he'd forgotten how quickly this man's mood could change.

"That is, unless you're coming back to work for me. I haven't found anyone who comes even remotely close to replacing you."

"No, I'm afraid not. I'm not in the business of hurting people anymore."

Guillermo's eyebrow rose. "Yet you work for the Cooperative."

Vizubi took in a deep breath. Not wanting to argue, he went straight to the point. "My captain sent me here to find out some information. I'm hoping you can help me."

Guillermo swept out his arm. "Please, sit my friend."

Vizubi sat in the lush red velvet chair as his old boss placed himself behind his mahogany desk. The armed guards pressed in around Quigley and the others. Quigley made a face, but Bari and Fung kept their expressions neutral.

Guillermo poured two glasses half full of copper liquid. "Tell me, how are they treating you over there? You look great."

That's because I'm not dependent on that starhash shit of yours anymore. Vizubi covered the smartass reply by sipping the bourbon and letting it warm his tongue. "Good stuff, thank you."

The man smiled. "Nothing but the best for my best enforcer."

"They treat me well enough," Vizubi said, answering his question. "There's not as much action, but I'm getting too old for that shit anyway."

Guillermo laughed and raised his glass. "Such is life, my friend."

They clinked glasses and drank again. Guillermo smacked his lips in satisfaction. "So, any woman in your life yet?"

Vizubi rubbed his forehead and hesitated. He never felt comfortable sharing his personal stuff, and certainly not with his team within earshot. "I've never been good at holding on to relationships."

"Not with all those beauties out there. How a man can choose only one is beyond me."

Vizubi shook his head. Too many women wasn't the problem. It was more like keeping one interested in him long enough to stick around. He couldn't count the number of times he'd fallen for someone only to have her break his heart because he wasn't good at talking or sharing his feelings.

"So, what do you need?" Guillermo asked.

Vizubi swirled his drink, taking in the sweet odor it emitted. "A group of Tredons were here a few days ago. They had two children with them."

Guillermo sat back. "Ah, yes. They bruised up Shekaka's men. They wouldn't have pulled that off if he had you as his enforcer."

"I doubt that. I've met one recently and he might give me a run for my money, despite his young age." Vizubi finished his bourbon. "Do you know what these Tredons were after?"

"Not at all, my friend. I know they purchased something from him, and that rascal doesn't tell me anything."

"Did they make any trouble while they were here, say, with some Grapnes?"

Guillermo's mouth puckered. "Ah, don't get me started on those conniving little snakes. They're up to their usual tricks but there hasn't been any mention of them having issues with Tredons."

Vizubi sighed. "Damn it." He massaged his temple. "We got word that this station issued an arrest warrant for those Tredons. Any tidbit of information you have will help."

"Sorry, friend. That's Shekaka's department. All I know is they had a bit of a scuffle with them, but it didn't amount to any killings that I'm aware of. You might ask Diptera, though."

"He's still around?"

Guillermo laughed. "He'll hole up from time to time, but that little maggot knows how to stay alive."

"Where can I find him nowadays?"

"Last I heard, he took up residence somewhere in the water treatment center."

"Figures." Vizubi shook his head. This assignment wouldn't be as easy as he'd hoped.

"Come to think of it," Guillermo continued, "someone saw him talking to some Grapnes the other day. What in the hell do they have to do with any of this?"

"That's part of what I'm here to find out."

Guillermo leaned forward. "Well, good luck to you. What's your station ID? I'll send you the access code to get down there."

Vizubi hid his surprise at the man's agreeableness, and gave him his ID.

"Tell me what you uncover," Guillermo added.

"Sure."

"I mean it, Ander." His old boss' severeness returned. "Information is more valuable than tellurium around here, and I need to know if Shekaka is colluding with the Tredons."

"Of course. I'll find out what I can and pass it on. One more thing, though…"

"You want to see Hesteben, right?" Guillermo asked. "He's at the Pink Lady's lounge, in my private office sleeping off last night's celebrations."

"Same as always, huh?"

The man shrugged. "Some of us are satisfied with this life."

Vizubi masked his disgust. His brother wasn't satisfied. He was just too weak to get out from under the addiction Guillermo had him under.

He wore a smile instead and thanked him.

"If you ever want to come back, Ander, I have a place waiting for you!" Guillermo called as the guards led Vizubi and his team out.

As they advanced through the stronghold, Vizubi reflected on how amiable his old boss had been. Had time tempered his anger or was he being careful because Vizubi was a Cooperative officer now? Depnaugh didn't fall under the Cooperative's jurisdiction, but the leaders here maintained enough of a relationship with them to avoid their unwanted attention.

Guillermo wanted information. He might have also heard about the Tredon Emperor working with sophisticated cyborgs. People out here still opted for enhancements despite the MEGA Injunction, but if soldiers were being enhanced—that was a gamechanger.

"Hey." The red-haired guard planted her palm on his chest to halt him before he passed through the exit. "Maybe I'll see you at the Moon Pit sometime."

Vizubi glanced at her hand, then at her easy smile. "Oh. Uh, yeah." He took in her rough yet somehow still soft complexion and imagined their drink in the bar leading somewhere else. "Yeah," he said more enthusiastically, then shook his head. "Not this visit, though. I've got a job to do and only a short time to do it."

One side of her mouth rolled up and her eye roved over his torso. "Heard that about you. You just as tenacious outside of work?"

Vizubi's ears burned. He fumbled for a reply, but nothing came out.

She stepped aside with a wink, letting him off the hook. "See ya around."

He managed a small smile and dipped his head goodbye. Quigley gave him a knowing smirk as they joined the crowd of travelers, marketers, and thugs.

He and his team fit right in with the rougher folk. Their PG-Force uniforms would have attracted trouble, but this mismatched armor deterred it. The fabricor had done a nice job of making their garb look well-used. The fibers of his own vest were discolored and realistically scorched in places. Fung's armor was also marred and no longer held the smoothness of new material. Bari wore a dented breast and backplate along with other metal coverings of various hues. Quigley opted to wear a smock, but the way her bosom flattened to one smooth hill suggested she wore tight-fitting armor underneath.

For the most part, people veered around them. He occasionally caught the hard glare of a warrior, but holding a disinterested expression usually made them move on.

"You should go see your brother," Quigley said. "We can look for this Diptera guy after."

Vizubi considered it, then discarded the idea. "No. We stick to the mission and we stay together."

"Are you sure, Sir? It's been a while since you've seen him, right?"

Vizubi's stomach knotted. "It has, but it can wait a few more hours."

"Your call, Sir. So where do we find the water treatment center?"

"On a lower level, just one up from the sewage processors."

Quigley's nose wrinkled. "Sewage?"

"I'm afraid so."

"Damn, and me without my ballgown."

Private Bari's eyes lit up. "You have a ballgown?"

Quigley raised her eyebrow and Bari looked away with an innocent expression. Vizubi hid a smile. He still couldn't remember how it happened, but somehow during their early team-building activities their rivalry had turned into casual teasing.

"Sir," Fung said. "I keep seeing the same Grapne. I'm pretty sure he's following us."

"Yeah, I've seen him. If this lead doesn't pan out, we'll talk to him next."

Bari and Quigley casually peered over their shoulders at different times. "The man who can't even stand up straight, right?" Quigley asked.

"That's him," Fung replied.

The Grapne hunched around a corner as they recovered their weapons from a locker. The man continued to follow at a distance until they reached and entered the conveyor.

After entering the code provided by Guillermo, he and his team took an uncomfortable ride down. The initial acceleration of the long trip made him glad he hadn't eaten in a while. The walls rattled until the slowing stop squealed and jarred his knees.

When the doors opened, Quigley pinched her nose while Fung and Bari grimaced. The chemical odor stung Vizubi's sinuses too, but his reaction occurred with a string of memories. How many times had he come down here looking for someone? How often had he taken a high vantage point and laid in wait? He knew this station from top to bottom, and no one evaded him for long.

He led the way, methodically checking under and around every machine, vat, and pipeline. They located everyone from couples making out to kids smoking starhash and vagrants drowsing. Only workers were allowed down here, but people found ways to skirt the rules.

"Who is this Diptera guy, anyway?" Quigley asked.

"He looks like any other drug-addled wanderer around here, but he's sharper than people give him credit for. He has a way of going unnoticed when he snoops around or listens in on conversations."

"Like a spy," Bari said.

"Yes, but he doesn't work for anyone in particular."

Vizubi stopped and sniffed. Something smelled different here. He followed it to a series of vertical pipes and squeezed through. He ducked under another, weaved, then hoisted himself over a pipe with a meter-and-a-half diameter.

"Here!" he called out to his team. The terrible odor struck him full force, making him gag. *Shit. This isn't good.*

Fung slid over the pipe to his side with ease. "What's that smell?"

Bari crossed over and grabbed Quigley's hand to help her. "Smells like something died."

"I think something did," Vizubi replied, indicating the skinny man curled in a fetal position. He rolled Diptera onto his back. Glazed eyes stared at nothing. The man's usually dark flesh had faded to a sickly grey.

"Is that him, the one we're looking for?" Quigley asked as she covered her mouth.

"I'm afraid so." Vizubi tugged at the silver chain around his neck and pulled out his cross. He kissed it and spoke a silent prayer.

"Didn't know you were religious, Sir," Bari said when Vizubi opened his eyes.

"Just respectful," Vizubi replied vaguely. The last thing he wanted was to discuss how faith had helped him turn his life around. He tucked the cross back under his vest, then searched the body for injuries.

Fung knelt beside him. "What do you think killed him?"

Vizubi shook his head. "No wounds. It could be bad drugs or bad food."

"He was poisoned," Bari said.

"How can you tell?"

Bari pointed. "Look at the marks on his neck. It's as though he clawed at himself. This tells me that whatever happened, it happened quickly."

"Good observation." Vizubi picked up the fork by Diptera's side and used it to break open the half-eaten bowl of mush.

"Who do you think did it?" Quigley asked.

Vizubi scanned the small area Diptera called home and sifted through his meager belongings. "I have no idea. Poison isn't a method used by the usual suspects." The Grapnes came to mind, but he didn't say it out loud. Those people were mostly thieves, not murderers. Then again, they shot down a ship, killing several Tredon warriors.

"Maybe he knew something he shouldn't have."

Vizubi sighed and rubbed his temple. "This is a dead end."

Quigley huffed. "Literally."

Vizubi stood. "Let's head out. If we see that Grapne again, nab him."

21
Captain's Table

3790:258:12:22. J.D. Hapker dragged his steps as he and Jori headed to the lounge. The captain had arranged a special dinner as a gesture of goodwill, but Jori's stone silence at the invite and his curt attitude now made Hapker more wary than a prairie dog sentinel. No doubt the boy saw this as another attempt at bribery. *Yep. This will be interesting.*

He eased his clenched teeth. Jori's behavior irked him, but he needed to be more understanding of the opposing perspective. He couldn't give up—not yet. If they had a genuine conversation before, they could do it again.

"I believe the captain has requested Genevian dishes for dinner," he said. "Have you ever had Genevian?"

"It hardly matters, does it?" Jori replied.

Brat. "Probably not," he managed to say lightly, "but I'm only asking out of curiosity. There's no harm in that."

"Ask your questions, then, but do not think you can trick me by being nice to me, and then asking."

"No one is trying to trick you."

Jori grunted.

Hapker sighed. *Patience. Patience. Patience.*

They entered the busy lounge. Funny how many people visited at the same time the captain scheduled a dinner. At least with him present, everyone would be on their best behavior.

He glanced at the boy's unyielding demeanor. *Well, not everyone.*

Captain Arden stood with his wife at the head of a long table. His generally stoic mien seemed relaxed as his eyes crinkled with a smile. "Welcome, Jori."

Jori acknowledged him with only a tiny gesture.

"I'd like to introduce you to everybody," the captain said unperturbed. "This is my wife, Symphonia."

Despite the woman's silver-streaked dark hair, her brown flawless skin made her look young. She smiled in warm sincerity. Everything about her came across as genuine.

The captain indicated the man closest to him. "You remember Doctor Beck Jerom?"

"Yes," Jori replied.

"This is Chandly, our top operations officer." The captain dipped his head toward the young-looking man with a tuft of hair sticking up at the back. "Major Bracht, my defense chief, Director Jeyana Sengupta, our intelligence officer, Officer Sara Fisher from engineering, our bridge chief, Triss Stever, then our security officers, First Lieutenant Hanna Sharkey, Second Lieutenant Rik Gresher, and Sergeant Siven Addams."

Jori greeted each one with a nod, offering no pleasantries. Hapker relaxed somewhat. At least the boy hadn't been rude.

The captain pulled out a chair. "Please, have a seat."

Jori did. Captain Arden sat beside his wife. Hapker placed himself between Jori and the captain. Bracht sat on Symphonia's other side and the widely grinning Gresher took the seat on Jori's right.

"So Jori," Symphonia said. "Have you ever had Genevian food?"

"Yes."

Hapker spoke a silent thanks that the reply wasn't as caustic as the one given earlier.

"I hope you like it." The captain smiled again. "If not, we can order something else for you."

"It's fine."

"My wife has organized an orchestra." The captain pointed to the crew members prepping on the corner stage.

"They'll be playing in the Quavian baroque style," Symphonia added. "Have you heard of it?"

"I do not have much of an ear for music," Jori replied.

"I think you will find it relaxing," Symphonia said.

Jori bowed slightly.

Hapker glanced at the strangeness of the boy next to him. He'd read that the Tredon elites sometimes used bowing as a sign of deference, but didn't they also view women as inferior? Perhaps Symphonia's genuinely pleasant manner affected him. Most likely, this was the calm before the storm.

"So, how do you like our ship so far, Jori?" Gresher wore a broad smile that was almost a permanent feature of the man.

"It is surprisingly well maintained."

"You should see our cells," Addams whispered.

Stever snickered and Chandly grinned, betraying the innocent tone of the comment. Bracht let out a grunt that sounded like approval.

The captain's fork clanged on his plate and his irises turned from sky-blue to indigo. "What was that, Sergeant?"

Addams paled. "Nothing, Sir."

"What's the matter, chima?" Jori's eyes bored most pointedly at Addams and Bracht. "Are you afraid a child will overwhelm your crew?"

Hapker cringed inwardly. *The storm has arrived.*

Bracht's lips curled as he snarled. The combination of his wild yellow mane and sharp teeth made him resemble a lion.

Jori bared his teeth like a wolf pup.

"Major Bjornicibus Bracht!" The captain's eyes flared with each enunciated syllable.

The Rabnoshk warrior purpled. An uncomfortable silence that seemed louder than the music fell over the room. The conversation lagged as everyone stared at their plates while they ate.

Sengupta set down her fork, interrupting the hush. She leaned toward the boy with a small smile. "So, Jori. I understand you are a talented warrior. How long have you been training?"

Jori swallowed his food. "Since I was three."

Sengupta's arched eyebrows rose. "Really? You started quite early. What's the first thing you learned?"

"Balance and stances."

Chandly wiped the side of his mouth with his napkin. "How old were you when you learned to use weapons?"

"I began studying marksmanship with firearms and phaser weapons when I was five. Other weapons came later."

Stever's eyes narrowed. "When did you make your first kill?"

Jori's face darkened. "Human or animal?"

A sour taste filled Hapker's mouth and he gave Stever a firm look. "That question isn't appropriate."

Stever glanced from Hapker to Jori and back before returning to her plate.

"I understand you are also quite intellectual." Sengupta said before any more awkwardness set in. "Is this common in Tredon, I mean Toradon?"

"No," Jori replied tersely.

"So, you're rather special?"

Jori's brows drew down and a fire lit in his eyes. "What the hell do you mean by that?"

Sengupta pulled back and placed her hand over her heart. "I'm curious, is all. Different cultures fascinate me."

"You would not like my culture."

She dipped her head. "Probably not. I hear they don't give women much freedom."

"They enslave them," Stever added in a bitter tone.

Jori's jaw tightened.

Hapker frowned at the bridge chief. "Let's keep the questions and comments civil, shall we?"

"Yes, let's," the captain replied with a scowl.

Sengupta's smile seemed forced. "So, tell me something about your culture I might like."

"Some places aren't so bad," Jori replied.

"No?" She leaned in.

"Lord Tanaka's district isn't so violent. His people have it better than most."

"So, they aren't slaves?" Stever's face appeared innocent enough, but Hapker caught the accusation in her tone.

Jori's nostrils flared. "No."

"What else?" Sengupta said. "Music? Dancing? Do you have any special holidays?"

The heat in Jori's eyes dwindled as he faced the director. "The Feast of Sato in the Nagra Province is quite popular."

Gresher grinned, showing all his teeth. "A feast. How wonderful. What are some foods served during this festival?"

"Mostly anpan."

Sengupta pulled her shoulders back and smiled. "A bread filled with varying jellies, if I'm not mistaken."

Jori nodded. “Usually a bean paste. Sometimes with nuts or tubers or even fruit.”

“It sounds delicious,” Captain Arden said. A few crew members mechanically agreed.

“I know you’re not much interested in music,” Symphonia said, “but do they play music at this Feast of Sato?”

“Yes, but I’m not sure what the style is called.” Jori gestured to the stage crew. “It’s faster than this and the sound is very different.”

“Well, any music is good music, if you ask me.” She winked.

Jori’s darkness seemed to abate. Hapker’s shoulders relaxed.

“Do you have any other brothers or sisters?” Gresher asked.

A weight fell over the boy’s features. “Only the one brother.”

“So, it’s just you, your brother, mother, and father?”

Jori nodded.

Sharkey leaned forward. “What’s your mother like?”

Jori shrugged.

“Does that mean you don’t know or don’t ca—want to tell us?” Fisher’s tone sounded casual, even as she corrected herself, but her eyes held a coldness and her lips curled.

Hapker frowned at her.

“What?” she asked. “I’m only trying to get clarification.”

“Tell us about your father, then,” Captain Arden said cheerfully while also giving Fisher a look of reprove.

Jori’s mouth pressed into a thin line.

“He must be a warrior, like you,” the captain continued, seemingly unaware of Jori’s changed expression.

Hapker cringed.

The captain’s obliviousness persisted. “Perhaps he’s a leader.”

Jori banged his fork onto the table. “It is not your business!”

Hapker tensed and groaned inwardly. Bracht rushed to his feet and the security officers on guard duty hastened forth.

Captain Arden stiffened and his mouth tightened. He regained his composure and motioned for Bracht to sit. “Is this how it will be between us then?” he said to the boy in a cool tone.

Jori’s eyes hardened. “I assure you that if you try to torture the information out of me, you will *still* find out nothing.”

The brewing storm threatened to turn into a hurricane. Hapker’s clenched jaw sent a spike of pain down his neck.

The captain sat back. “Torture? We’re simply trying to get to know you.”

“I suppose you have a right to *interrogate* your prisoners.” Jori replied with a twist of his mouth. “Shall I sit in a dark room while your Rabnoshk warrior goads me?”

“Jori, that's enough.” Hapker slammed his hand on the table, making the eating ware bounce with a metallic ting. “You seem far too mature to be acting like such a child.”

Jori glowered. Hapker returned the expression in kind. The silence crackled. The anger in the boy’s eyes deepened. Hapker held the glare. Jori’s fingers twitched. Hapker’s heart spiked. The sound of shuffling feet whispered through the stillness as the security officers moved behind the boy.

Jori’s jaw tightened and he clenched his fist. “I can tell how every single one of you feel about me. You call it *getting to know me*. You *don’t* want to know me, and I *don’t* want to know you.”

He pushed out his chair and shot to his feet. The security officers poised their hands over their holsters. Jori turned and growled with his fists at his sides.

The officers twitched like panthers ready to pounce but Jori was no scared rabbit. His body held the same edginess as theirs. His knuckles whitened and the twisted features of his face indicated his readiness to handle whatever they had to bring. The hush of the room vibrated as they glowered in return.

Private Agni pulled out his phaser and aimed. Before Hapker or anyone else could do or say anything, Jori jump-kicked the weapon out of his hand.

Hapker sprang between them. “Stop!”

A standoff ensued as he eyed Jori and the officers to make sure no one moved. The boy puffed in and out, but he stayed put.

“We’re just leaving,” Hapker said.

“Lucky you,” Agni mumbled as he glared at Jori.

Jori’s face turned scarlet. “Lucky *you*, chima. None of you matter. You’ll all be dead soon anyway.”

Hapker suppressed a shiver. “That’s enough, Jori.”

Captain Arden stood. “Let them leave.”

The officers eased their hands away from their holsters and hesitantly stepped back. Jori stomped forward in a huff.

Hapker kept pace. An unnerving stillness hovered over them as they headed out. Each heavy step echoed against the walls. Others in the hall stepped aside as they passed. The boy ignored them all as a swirl of fury burned within his eyes.

Hapker's own anger boiled and festered. As soon as they reached his quarters and the doors closed them inside, he faced the boy with hands on hips. "What in the heck were you thinking? Do you have any idea how close you are to being sent to the brig?"

"He pulled out his weapon for no reason. All I wanted to do was get the hell out of there away from your stupid friends!"

"Did you need to be so rude about it?"

Jori crossed his arms. "Me?"

"You!" Hapker jabbed his finger. "The captain was trying hard to be polite and make you feel comfortable. I don't expect you to spill your secrets, but it's not unreasonable for you to be courteous… And perhaps show some gratitude."

"We are not friends."

"We don't have to be friends to get along."

"Is that your rule? I must be courteous and show gratitude or my brother dies?"

Hapker threw up his hands. "How many times must I say that we won't hold your brother's life over your head? All I'd like to see is a little civility. Is that so much to ask?"

"It's not the only thing you've asked for."

"What do you expect? Of course we'd like to know other things, but no one will torture the information out of you, and no one is trying to *trick* you."

"I'm not stupid, Commander. I know you don't want me here. Half your crew would rather see us dead than help us."

"That's not true."

"It *is* true. Your Rabnoshk warrior did nothing but give me murderous looks and your captain can't wait to be rid of me."

"Maybe if you'd quit acting like a childish brat!"

Jori flinched. A shade of fear seemed to fill his eyes.

Well, darn it. Hapker hadn't meant to yell, but his frustration got the best of him. His jaw throbbed from biting down so hard and his head felt ready to explode.

Hapker took a deep breath. A cramp shot up both his arms and he realized his hands were balled in fists.

A sudden chill swept over him. Had he raised his fist while yelling? Jori probably thought he would strike him.

His anger fell away as a coldness settled in. He ran his hand down over his face. “I’m sorry, Jori. I’m upset at you, but I won’t hurt you.”

Jori’s mouth twisted and his eyes darkened again. “I’m not afraid of you.”

He sighed. “Nor should you be.”

The boy’s glare disappeared, and he put on his emotionless mask.

I hope he’s not thinking about killing me in my sleep.

22
Betrayal

3790:258:21:16. Jori rolled over, pulling his covers with him. Hours had passed and he still hadn't fallen asleep. Different faces kept popping into his head. His father's came first with sharp eyes and lips curled in a snarl. As Father raised his hand to strike him, the face turned into Hapker's.

He shoved the image away. Hapker was no warrior, certainly no one to be afraid of. What a ridiculous notion. One couldn't have a father like his and be afraid of a man like him. The commander was far too weak, a puny paring knife next to a katana blade. When Hapker's fists had clenched as he called him a brat, Jori had frozen like some stupid rabbit watching a blackbeast close in.

Jori clutched his pillow as though to squeeze out the fear and let it drop into a pool of hatred. How dare this man threaten him. How dare he treat him like a half-feral dog, teasing him with honeyed bread one moment and then kicking him in the next.

So much for the so-called enlightenment of the Cooperative. Everything Jori had watched or read about these people was no more real than the dragon lore of his ancestors. No wonder Father hated them. The two-faced chima thought so highly of themselves for no reason.

Jori punched his pillow and growled. *Childish brat, indeed!* He threw off his covers and crept to Hapker's bedroom door. It didn't open automatically the way it did when Hapker had entered. *Figures*. Of course he'd lock it. *Coward.*

He quietly opened the side panel and reached in. The dinner scene replayed in his head. They'd started it with their little comments and their prodding questions. He had a right to be upset. Their hatred had burned so hotly, he felt like he stood in front of a furnace.

They weren't the worst. Hapker and Captain Arden had provoked him with their prying. They couldn't find out about Terk.

Terk's condition remained critical. Nothing had changed in the past few days—not a single thing. He might as well be a spent shell-casing.

He could tell the doctors cared. He also sensed the captain and commander weren't lying about helping him, but he was no fool. Things would be different if they knew.

The truth was none of their business. So what if he'd been rude. It was their own fault.

Jori toggled a component and the door slid open with a hiss. He froze and concentrated his senses. Certain Hapker still slept, he tiptoed inside. His thumping heart smothered the sound of the commander's soft breathing.

It would be so easy to kill him now. His nanites were ready.

He poised his palm over Hapker's chest. One command and the nanites would send a jolt into him.

Hapker's breathing remained smooth but Jori's heart pulsed hard enough to make his eardrums hurt. He could kill him. He *should* kill him. This was his enemy.

His hand trembled. He swallowed. *Do it, damn it!*

He opened his mouth to speak, but the command wouldn't come. A sweat broke out, chilling him. His hand shook even more.

Jori clenched his fist and pulled away. *Killing this way is cowardly.*

He backed out of the room. The pounding in his chest turned to a rapid patter. He relocked Hapker's door and crawled into bed. Hapker deserved to die. They all did. Now wasn't the right time, but it would come.

He closed his eyes and tried to sleep, but the image of Hapker with his clenched fists wouldn't leave. How dare he call him a brat.

Jori's cheeks burned. He growled again and turned over onto his stomach, pulling the pillow over his head.

The commander was wrong. *He's a stupid chima.*

His gut soured. Maybe he had been a brat. So what? How else would he keep them from asking so many questions?

What would Sensei Jeruko do? He'd probably refuse to say anything at all, or he might be polite to put them off their guard.

He plopped his head back onto the pillow. Fine then. He'd try to be like the sensei. If they pried again, he'd either give them as little information as possible or not answer at all. Perhaps he'd even be more civil about it. Not too much, though.

Not enough to give Hapker the idea that he'd been right.

*****

3790:258:23:32. The lights emitted a soft glow, mimicking the coming of morning. The shadows of the commander's main chamber lightened into dull shades of color. Jori sluggishly studied the room from the cot that had been set up for him in the corner.

An ugly yellow couch, two brown padded chairs that leaned back with the press of a button, and two low tables sat in the center of the living space. One table held a few animal statues. Three were small, half the size of Jori's palm. The tallest with a length just short of Jori's forearm was a silver-gilded water bird of some kind. It resembled something he'd seen in his mother's chambers. A decorative mug sat on the other table. It, at least, was manlier. It had a huge handle, a thick rim, and appeared to be made from an animal's horn.

The wall across from Jori held several ancient-looking artifacts. His favorite was a length of wood that resembled a baton except it had an intricate scene carved into it. Hapker had said it came from his homeworld. The wood was ironwood, and the carved animals were native.

The man certainly had a fondness for nature. Other than the comfortable padding of the chairs and the pretty bird, his décor had a rustic outdoorsy vibe.

Jori covered his face with the crook of his arm. His head ached from lack of rest and his eyes felt as though someone pressed on them. His thoughts churned like a typhoon. The more he sensed Hapker waking from the smaller bedchamber off to the side, the faster the typhoon spun.

Jori sat up as the commander came out of his room.

"Good morning," Hapker said.

Despite the cooler tone, Jori didn't sense any anger or frustration from the man. He prodded and found disinterest instead.

He swallowed down the lump forming in his throat. He wanted so badly to be angry at Hapker for talking down to him and calling him a childish brat, but his temper had cooled.

"Sleep well?" Hapker asked in a detached tone.

"Well enough." If the commander didn't care whether he had a good rest, then why should he tell him how he tossed and turned? Besides, he might ask why and what reason would he give him? *That I felt bad for my behavior last night? Hell no.*

Hapker ordered his breakfast through the food fabricor and ate without comment. Jori retrieved his and spooned up his bland meal in uneasy silence. Hapker didn't start a conversation, nor did he try to convince him to eat something with more flavor, like he had done in previous days.

The man's mood didn't alter from the cool neutrality, but the churning of Jori's stomach increased to the point that he couldn't finish eating.

Hapker glanced at the half-eaten food but not a hint of concern emanated from him. "You should get dressed now. The captain wishes to speak to you."

Jori mechanically changed clothes. *Maybe I should say something, but what, damn it?* He had nothing to say and it wasn't like they were friends.

They left in silence. Jori's cheeks grew hot. He clenched his teeth as a burning sensation moved through his sinuses and to his eyes. *Don't cry, you stupid fool.*

He bit his tongue and jutted his chin. *To hell with him.*

The air seemed to chill as they wound through the corridors. When the captain's office door opened, a biting draft brushed Jori's face.

Captain Arden greeted him with a pleasant smile, but his emotions were hard and humorless. Jori steadied himself against a rising unease.

"Welcome, Jori." The captain's smile faded. He sat with his elbows on his desk and his hands folded together. "After last night's dinner, I realized we should speak with you more formally and come to an understanding."

Jori suppressed the urge to swallow at the captain's ominous tone. He jolted into alert mode and took stock of his surroundings. A man he had never seen before hovered behind the desk. An eerie smile creased his leathery face, but no emotion emanated from him.

Jori frowned. This was worse than the commander's aloofness. He should at least be able to sense this man's lifeforce, but there was nothing. It was as though he wasn't there.

"This is Officer Liam Garner." Captain Arden said. "He's here to help me today."

Something about this man was wrong. Jori set all his internal turmoil aside and put up a mental shield in the manner his mother had taught. He nodded to the man with a polite grimness and steeled himself for whatever was about to come.

"Now Jori," the captain said. "I've made it clear that you are a guest here and we will not mistreat you, but you must understand I still have a job to do. I not only have a crew to protect, but I have a responsibility to my superiors and to the Cooperative as a whole. This means Commander Hapker and I will question you from time to time."

"I understand, Sir," Jori replied. Guilt crept up and he mentally forced it back down. Garner's eyes bored into him and his concentration almost faltered.

"To be fair," the captain continued, "from now on we will only ask you questions in a more formal setting such as this. This way, you do not need to worry about anyone manipulating you."

Jori nodded in reply, glancing again at Garner. The man's empty smile never wavered. Jori shivered inwardly but kept his concentration on his mental shield.

"Good," Captain Arden said. "Then I must ask you more about your mission. We verified everything you've told us so far, but we also know there's more. We suspect it has something to do with what your crew purchased from the black-market dealer named Shekaka, so tell us what it was."

Jori pressed his lips together. A slight tingling sensation buzzed in his head. *What the hell?* His concentration almost slipped away. *No, not slipping.* He met Garner's deep-set eyes. *He's trying to pull it.* His pulse raced. "What is he doing?" he asked in alarm.

"What is who doing?" Hapker asked.

"Him!" He pointed at Garner. "Get out of my head!"

"He's a reader, Jori. An extraho-animi, to be exact," the captain replied calmly. "He won't hurt you."

"How do you know? Tell him to stop!" Jori's heart galloped. People like this were dangerous. They delved into a person's innermost thoughts and he couldn't risk certain things being exposed. "I want him out!"

The buzzing intensified. Jori threw his arms over his head and backed away. "Stop!" His eyes darted about, searching for something to fight with.

The captain's hand rose. "Garner, stop."

As the buzzing abated, Jori's panic swirled into anger. He scowled and a slew of curses waited on his tongue, but he wasn't about to make the same childish mistake as last night. He held in his temper and kept his tone neutral. "It wouldn't have worked, Captain," he said through gritted teeth. "I know how to defend myself against these mind-rapers."

Captain Arden's mouth turned down. "We received a report about your crew's dealing on Depnaugh. Since you won't elaborate on it, I had no choice but to bring in Officer Garner."

Jori's emotions spun in chaos. A deep settling angst boiled into fury, then spiraled back into fear. To hell with the device. If they ever found it, so what. It was nothing compared to his brother's secret.

His body shook as the adrenaline wore off. "You act like my friend," his voice trembled. "You pretend to care with your promises of helping my brother, but this… This! There can be no trust between us, can there?"

The captain steepled his fingers under his chin. "I want to trust you, Jori," he replied in an annoyingly calm tone, "but how can I do that if you won't tell me anything?"

"I've already told you I'm no murderer. There is nothing else you need to know." He stomped his foot and turned his back to them. So what if it was childish. He'd had enough.

Neither Hapker nor the captain attempted to stop him as he stormed out.

*****

J.D. Hapker sighed.

Captain Arden faced the reader. "Garner?"

The older man tapped his finger to his lips. "I sensed nervousness from him for a moment. He blocked me after that."

The captain's thick eyebrows twitched. "So he *was* able to defend against you."

Hapker stiffened. "He realized what you were doing?"

Garner shrugged. "It's not unheard of. It's mostly people who are closely in touch with their animus who are able."

Hapker glanced at the captain. "Another inherited genetic ability?"

They already knew of Jori's high intelligence and Hapker had reported his greater endurance. Neither of these disturbed him as much as the possibility that Jori might be like Garner, though.

Garner's shoulders rose again. "If he has such a skill, I'd guess he's only a sentio-animi. He never tried to come into my head, and I never sensed him trying to get into yours."

That was a relief. If the boy perceived that he told the truth about helping him and his brother, it would explain why he hadn't acted in the violent way everyone expected of him.

"I will talk to him." *For whatever good it would do*. The boy's attitude wasn't so pleasant before. It surely wouldn't be any better now.

*****

3790:259:00:13. Jori stalked out of the office, away from the captain and his pet reader, and ignored the sound of his guards scurrying to catch up. He'd had it with these people—them and their false backstabbing niceness.

A rising heat swelled within him. How stupid did they think he was? They said he wasn't a prisoner, yet they still treated him like a villain. *Why won't they believe me?*

He marched down the corridor toward the gym, eager to vent on the holo-man program. His thoughts whirled—Calloway's nasty comments, Hapker ignoring him this morning, the sight of his crashed ship and dead men, Hapker calling him a childish brat, Hapker's raised fist, the reader attempting to get inside his head and Hapker watching, Hapker's coldness earlier, his brother lying lifeless… Hapker's genuine warmth on that day when he nearly cried over Terk. He misstepped and dipped low to regain balance. *He was faking. That wasn't real.*

He shook the memory away, but the man's sympathy kept resurfacing. Was he pretending? Emotions couldn't be faked, could they? He clenched his jaw and his fists in determination. *It wasn't real! Even if it was... He betrayed me!*

A deep hurt spiked in his chest and grew like a dying star. Only instead of cooling like the star, it burned hot enough to smother out the fire of his anger. His sinuses tingled. He blinked at the growing wetness in his eyes. *Don't cry. You're being a baby again.*

He turned the corner and found himself in the infirmary. He didn't mean to come to this place, but Terk was here. His brother, the only one who understood him—the only person he had here on this forsaken ship. If only he wasn't dying.

A tear fell down his cheek and he swept it away. "Get out," he snapped to the guards watching his brother.

They couldn't move fast enough. One glowered. Jori flashed his teeth in reply. He would have growled too but was sure it would come out sounding more like a wail.

When the guards closed the privacy curtain, his head fell to his brother's bedside. A sob escaped. He should be furious. He wanted to be, but the stupid tears had to fall instead. *Why the hell am I crying? Why should I care about what the commander did?* Maybe Hapker was right. He was a spoiled brat.

He pressed his lips together, trying to keep anyone from hearing his anguish, but his facial muscles seemed to have a mind of their own. A low moan escaped his mouth. He cradled his head in the crook of his arm and let the racking sobs loose.

A swarm of emotions spiraled around like space debris on the cusp of an event horizon. One by one, they crossed over, falling into the lonely singularity that was him—all alone with no one to protect him, no one to trust, and no one to comfort him.

23
Brothers

3790:259:00:42. Ander Vizubi shouldered his way through the crowd of sweaty bodies. The murkiness of the club contrasted with the merry faces of people drinking or smoking stubs. Colored lights flashed in time with the pounding music from the nearby dancefloor. A rush of nostalgia sent his blood running, but the idea of getting drunk or high and staying up late no longer had the same appeal.

He glanced behind him, making sure his team still followed. Quigley shoved a young, bearded man in the chest as he moved his head in too close to hers. "Your loss, sweetheart," the man called out above the high-pitched synthesizer playing in the background. She rolled her eyes and caught up.

The rabble thinned and the team meandered through a labyrinth of occupied tables, couches, and lounge chairs. A cluster of young men at a table off to the right hollered and laughed as they played a drinking game. A fat, hairy man made out with two women on a nearby couch. Further down, several people lounged in a set of matching sofas and armchairs and passed around a bong.

Vizubi recognized his younger self within every group. With any luck, these kids would grow up one day and realize what a waste this lifestyle was. Exchanging short-lived fun for long-term misery wasn't worth it.

He glimpsed the familiar gold sectional in the corner. Hesteben lounged there smoking a stub as four women lolled about him. *Some people never grow up.*

Before he reached it, two hefty men blocked his path. "Find someplace else," the blond-haired man said. "This spot's taken."

"That's my brother." Vizubi pointed. "Tell him I'm here. He'll want to see me."

The man's lip curled. "You look nothing like him."

Vizubi's hackles rose. Before he could say something smartass, the black-bearded guard leaned in. "You Ander?"

Vizubi peered closer at the grizzled face. "Rocky?"

The man broke out into a grin. "Yeah. Well, what do ya know." He swatted the blond man on the shoulder. "Hey, man. This is Ander. He used to be an enforcer for Guillermo. Was a damned good one, too."

The blond man exchanged his stern expression for a friendlier one. "Yeah? I've heard stories about you."

"Made up ones from my brother, no doubt," Vizubi replied.

"Naw," Rocky said. "Everyone talks about you. You're a legend around here."

A mixture of pride and regret rolled in Vizubi's gut.

"How have you been, man?" Rocky asked.

"Good. I'm here on some business, but I thought I'd look in on my brother."

The man stepped aside. "Go on ahead."

As Vizubi passed, he thumbed the three people behind him. "These are my friends. They won't make any trouble."

The blond man frowned but allowed them to pass while Rocky greeted them, adding a wink at Fung who raised a brow in return.

Vizubi stopped in front of his brother and waited. The women sluggishly glanced at him, but Hesteben was out of it.

Vizubi cleared his throat.

Hesteben's half-lidded eyes blinked. "Oh, hey. You want in on this, man? There's plenty to go around."

"It's me, Steben. Not one of your junkie friends."

Hesteben frowned, then his face lit up. "Andy!" He jolted upright, confusing the woman who had been resting on his shoulder. "I can't believe you're here, man. I thought you said you were never coming back to this place."

"I'm looking for something here. Once I find it, I'm leaving again."

"Awe, that's too bad. Things are good here. Guillermo made me the CTO of his tech department and now I'm living the high life."

Vizubi kept his comment about the hollow title to himself. "You keep living like this, it will kill you. You've lost a lot of weight since I last saw you."

Hesteben dismissed him with a lazy wave. "I feel great, man. If I die, so what. It's not like anyone would miss me."

Vizubi sighed at the gibe. "You know I care about you."

Hesteben rolled his eyes. "Yeah, right. That's why you left."

"Come on. You're a grown man. You didn't need me anymore."

"Yeah, yeah, yeah, whatever."

Vizubi gestured sharply. "Damn it, Steben. I tried to stay here for you but all you want to do is throw your life away with this shit."

"This shit is the only thing that makes life worth living, man."

"Bullshit. I remember what it feels like. Sure, it's great for a few hours. Then you spend the rest of your day wishing it were over."

"Naw, that was you. You smoked it because you wanted to bury your pain, but it came back on the slide down. I got nothing to hide and no regrets, so I enjoy the full ride."

"If you've figured all this out, what the hell are you complaining about me leaving you for?"

"When you took off, you left me to the wolves. Without my big brother, the enforcer, I had to beg Guillermo for protection."

"It looks like he treats you alright."

"Yeah, I'm doing much better now, no thanks to you."

Vizubi rested his hands on his hips and looked up with a sigh. "You could have come with me, you know."

"What, to the Cooperative, our enemy?"

"The Cooperative was never our enemy. They're the enemy of your boss, the same person who uses you, and then hurts you when you make a mistake."

"That's life, man."

"No, it's not. I don't get a beating when I mess up. Hell, they don't even dock my pay. My life is peaceful, and I'm treated with respect."

"Well, good for you. Excuse me for not wanting to leave our home."

Vizubi rubbed his forehead. "Look, I didn't come here to argue. I came—"

"You came to brag about how great your life is."

"I came here to see you."

"Bullshit. You're here for a job."

Vizubi huffed. Before he could reply, Quigley approached and spoke in his ear. "Sergeant. Sorry to bother you, but you-know-who is here."

Vizubi glanced over her shoulder. The Grapne's drab clothes and cringing demeanor contrasted with the rest of the crowd. Timidity didn't belong in a party club. The man was as out of place as a worm in a salad.

"What do you want us to do?" she asked.

"Get around him but keep your distance. I'll talk to him in a moment." He returned to Hesteben, who lit another stub. "Since you're obviously in no mood to talk, I'll go do that job now."

Hesteben waved him away. "You go live your life. I'll stay here and live mine."

Vizubi shook his head. "I should have known this would be a waste of time. You haven't changed."

"Neither have you!" Hesteben called out as Vizubi marched off.

The Grapne ducked behind a patron. Vizubi pretended not to see him as he moved in, but the skinny man slid away anyway. Bari blocked the man's path. He dodged in another direction. As he scampered on, he bumped into a burly man with a brambled beard and a mop of brown hair.

"Watch it!" the man said with a shove.

The Grapne leaned in with a grin and held something in his hand. The man snatched the item and inspected it, making Vizubi's neck prickle. The Grapne spoke. When he pointed at Vizubi, the burly man nodded with a menacing smile.

"Crap." Vizubi raised his palms and stepped back as the man approached. "I don't want trouble. I just want to talk to that—"

The burly man swung. Vizubi pulled away as the breeze of his fist swept by. A second swipe came at him. He blocked.

"Look, I don't want any trouble," he said, deflecting another strike.

"Too bad, bub. Do you know how much that little man offered to pay me?"

Vizubi parried, smacking the man's thick wrist with a thwack. "Do you really believe he will pay you?"

"For the amount he's paid so far, I'm willing to take a chance."

This time, his fist landed. Vizubi grunted from the plunge to his side. Fortunately, the hit wasn't high enough to reach his kidney and adrenaline masked the hurt. He reacted with a strike to the man's chest, missing the solar plexus.

An all-out boxing match ensued. Vizubi received a pop to the jaw and gut, but he bashed his opponent's nose and upper lip and spawned a gush of blood that matted his beard.

Just as the man wavered and Vizubi targeted an opening, something wrapped around his neck. The meatiness of the choking arm indicated this man was bigger than the other. Vizubi dug into the hairy forearm with his chin while also jabbing his fingers behind him, hoping to hit his attacker's eye.

A wet squishiness and a yelp told him he'd succeeded. The chokehold loosened enough for Vizubi to lower his jaw to his neck and keep his airway open.

The burly man popped his knuckles into the center of Vizubi's face. A burning sensation spread from his nose and blackened his vision. He roared away the pain and jerked his head back into the man choking him. The hold broke off. Vizubi twisted and charged the burly man. He slammed into him, forcing his opponent to retreat a few steps. He tossed strikes into every vulnerable spot he could find.

A metallic sound rang behind him. He turned and dodged the knife swipe from the giant hairy man. The swing circled around. Vizubi blocked. He grappled the man's wrist and threw his weight into it, making him drop the weapon.

Vizubi snatched it up in time to make the two men halt. The burly man pulled his own knife and lunged. Vizubi sidestepped and stabbed him into the side of his neck.

The man went limp and fell like a stone as blood gushed. The horror of it smashed into Vizubi's awareness. He discarded the weapon and gaped, then dropped to his knees. His heartrate galloped and his head swiveled as he looked around for a way to stop the bleeding.

A hand grabbed his shoulder. He knocked it away.

"Sir!"

A woman's voice pierced his eardrum. He peered up, but a moment passed before he registered her.

"Sir," Quigley said more calmly. "He's dead."

Vizubi swallowed the bile rising from his throat. He breathed deep, in through his nostrils and out through his mouth, until the sting of his adrenaline fizzled away.

He faced Quigley, noting her busted lip and unruly blond hair.

She flicked a stray strand from her eye. “I’m sorry, Sir. I tried to jump in sooner but that conniving little Grapne sent someone after me too.”

“Are you alright?”

“Better than you, I think.” She gestured at his face.

A wetness and the tangy smell of blood touched his awareness. He winced from the pain shooting through his nose. His physical discomfort, though, was nothing compared to his internal affliction. He knelt beside the dead man again and pulled out his cross. With a whisper, he blessed him and asked for forgiveness.

“He doesn’t deserve your prayers,” Quigley said. “He was about to stab you.”

Vizubi stood and met her eyes. “Everyone needs someone to pray for them.”

She withered and looked away. “Yes, Sir.”

Four uniformed officers surged in around them. “You there! Hands up!”

Vizubi surrendered.

Quigley’s face turned red. “This wasn’t his fault. They attacked him!”

“Show your hands, lady,” the brown-haired officer said.

“Me? I didn’t do anything.”

“Hands up!”

“Quigley,” Vizubi murmured. “Put them up.”

She harrumphed. “This is ridiculous.”

“Hold on there,” another voice cut in. Rocky pushed through. “I can vouch for them. They acted in self-defense.”

“It’s alright,” Vizubi said. “I killed a man. I should answer for it.”

“Not here you don’t,” Rocky replied.

Hesteben approached. “Let them leave.”

As the officers lowered their weapons, Vizubi gaped at his brother. Did he really have this much pull now?

Three officers left as the fourth called for someone to clean up the mess. Vizubi sighed with an upward glance. He messed up, big time. He might get away with this here, but Captain Arden would not be happy.

Quigley tugged at his arm. “Let’s go. Fung and Bari have the Grapne.”

*****

3790:259:01:24. Ander Vizubi towered over the cowering man as Bari held him up by the collar. Technically, restraining him was illegal since he had no jurisdiction here, but he was too pissed to care. Sending thugs after him and forcing him to kill one was too much.

“I’ll ask you one more time. *Why* are you following us?”

“Ssso sssorry, the Grapne hissed. “I was ordered to keep an eye on you.”

“Were you also told to attack us?”

The coward wagged his head. “No. No, please. I only did that so you wouldn’t come after me.”

Vizubi puffed in an attempt to rein in his temper. “Who gave you this order?”

“The Overseer.”

“Why?”

“I-I don’t know.”

Vizubi growled.

“I swear. I swear.” The Grapne’s eyes welled and he clasped his hands in supplication. “He said I must watch you and report to him. I swear, I have no idea why.”

Vizubi planted his knuckles on his hips. “Contact this Overseer. Tell him I want to talk to him.”

“That’s not possible.”

“Now!”

The Grapne whimpered. “Okay. Okay.” He touched the comm behind his ear with a shaky hand. “Sir? U-um, well, the Cooperative officers are here, and they wish to speak to you.”

Vizubi ground his teeth as the Grapne winced and nodded. If only he could hear the other side of the conversation.

“But-but they won’t let me go otherwise,” the Grapne said with a whine. “I think they might hurt me. Please help me, Overseer. I’ll forever be in your debt.”

Vizubi crossed his arms as the man nodded several more times.

The Grapne broke into a smile and his head bounced like a speed bag. “He says he will meet you later, oh-nine-hundred, on the outside of the casino in section G.

“Tell him he had better be there. If he’s not, I will hunt him down. I want answers, damn it.”

After releasing the Grapne, Vizubi gave his team permission to get R&R while he found a dark corner in some pub and ordered a stiff drink.

24
Viewport

3790:259:07:42. Jori stood with his hands behind his back as he peered out the viewport. The width of the mock window spanned an impressive six meters. Since an actual window was impractical on a starship, he admired how cameras projected the scene from outside.

Stars and distant galaxies dotted the velvet black sky. The Milky Way laid a sporadic gauze over the points of light. He wished his own ship provided a view like this. The vastness of space awed him. This time, it also deepened the hollowness within his core.

The blue planet's star stood out with a soft white glow. As the *Odyssey* left it behind, it shrank with each passing hour. Although operating the arc drive distorted how close the stars looked, the presence of the Shuku nebula indicated the ship probably headed to the Chevert outpost.

Good. He must get away from this terrible place. Staying with the commander had become unbearable. Every time he sensed the man's flat emotions, his gut twinged. He should've used his nanites to end him. For some stupid reason, though, he couldn't bring himself to do it.

His sinuses burned and threatened to make him cry. He clenched his fists and dug his nails into his palms. Why the hell was he so upset?

A group of officers entered this smaller lounge, intruding upon his brooding. He marched out, ignoring their whispering and dirty looks.

With his guards in tow, he entered the hall that would lead him to the gymnasium. His mind churned from one unpleasant thought to another until a whiff of distinctive lifeforces grabbed his attention. He bit down hard and balled his fists. *Grapnes*.

He quickened his pace, hoping to get ahead of the guards and take revenge on these sly snakes for killing his crew. Something metallic at the edge of the corridor caught his eye. His heart lurched and he threw his arms over his face. A bursting pop struck his eardrums as blazing brightness gleamed through his eyelids. The guards cried out.

Jori blinked the spots from his eyes in time to make out four Grapnes coming at him. Heat flared in his chest. He bellowed out his fury. His attackers halted and their jaws dropped. *That's right dumbasses. I blocked your flash bomb in time.*

Jori stormed in, then spun with an arm-swipe into one man's gut. The Grapne doubled over. Jori rotated low and swept his leg out, taking out two more attackers. He lunged for the fourth, causing him to scream and jump back.

The first Grapne recovered and rushed at him with a hypospray. He chopped at the man's wrist, prompting him to drop it. With a dive, Jori grabbed the instrument, then somersaulted out of the way and to his feet.

The man screeched with frustration and came at him again. Jori ducked under his arm and jabbed the hypospray into his thigh. The Grapne fell with a thud.

"Stop!" a guard called out.

A phaser blast whipped by Jori, striking a Grapne. The two remaining attackers squealed and ran off. Half Jori's guards gave chase.

The rest aimed their weapons at him. "Drop the knife!" the curly dark-haired guard named Sergeant Naran said.

"It's a hypospray, you idiot." Jori tossed the useless thing aside.

Naran holstered his weapon and pulled out cuffs. Jori backed up and analyzed his options.

The other guard kept his aim. "Don't move!"

Naran twirled the handcuffs. "You better do as he says. You're already in a lot of trouble."

"I didn't do anything!"

"Sure you didn't."

Jori roared and swooped in low. Naran's eyes widened. He sidestepped but not enough. Jori clipped him on the left hip. As they tumbled, he snatched the man's phaser. The other guard fired his weapon, and everything went black.

*****

3790:259:08:03. Silas Arden drummed his fingers on his desk. "So the facts are as follows. The Grapnes set off a flash bomb that temporarily disabled the officers. They then came at the child with hyposprays, one containing a knock-out drug and the other a micro-reader." A crafty move on their part. If they injected him and no one discovered it, they could have left the *Odyssey*, then used their transport to lock onto the reader and beam him over. "Then the child charged Sergeant Naran and stole his phaser."

"Naran said he thought Jori had a knife and that he discarded it when ordered," Commander Hapker added.

Major Bracht scowled. "Then attacked them."

Hapker returned the expression. "Both officers claimed he didn't act against them until they approached him with the restraints. He was being attacked on two fronts."

Bracht's lip twitched, almost into a snarl. "My officers did not attack him."

"He perceived it as an attack." The commander huffed. "He threw down the hypospray, not a knife by the way, so the officers had no reason to restrain him."

"They saw him fight the Grapnes. They didn't realize at the time that he acted in self-defense."

"Who else would have set the flash bomb?" Hapker exaggerated a shrug. "Jori couldn't have done it."

Arden took in their words but wished both men would speak without sounding quarrelsome. Their behavior reminded him too much of his previous commander.

"I agree they made a mistake," the major said, "but that is no reason for the boy to take their weapon."

"You admitted he acted in self-defense," Hapker replied with a sharp pitch.

Bracht growled. "He disarmed an officer! If their phasers hadn't had bio-sensors to keep unauthorized people from using them, he could shot them."

The commander shook his head. "With a stun weapon. Besides, he probably only intended to disarm them. Considering his intellect and warrior status, he had to know the weapons wouldn't work for him."

"We can't make that assumption. He's too dangerous!"

"Enough!" Arden threw up his hand before tempers worsened. "We're venturing into speculation here. Misunderstandings likely occurred on both sides. Although I agree with you, Major, that the boy has the potential to be dangerous, last evening's dinner has shown me that our people are too quick to take action against him."

"Because he's dangerous," Bracht replied in a less heated tone.

Hapker grumbled.

Arden sighed. Perhaps he should hand the children over to a PG-Force ship. As much as he wanted to preserve peace, recent events showed this to be too problematic.

No. Not yet. They were just children. "Is your team unable to manage him?" he asked the major.

Bracht's jaw hardened. "We can handle him, Sir."

Arden leaned back and laid his palms on the table. "Good. We will keep things as they are. Speak to your people about not being so quick to pull out their weapons. The only way I will be comfortable locking this child up is if he is the one provoking the attack."

Hapker exhaled while Bracht pressed his lips into a grim line. Arden raised an eyebrow at both men. The commander still seemed to favor the child over his own people and the major couldn't see the situation from a warrior's perspective. If someone came at him when he had done nothing wrong and after he gave a sign of surrendering, he would react the same way.

"Sir, what about the Grapnes?" Hapker asked.

Arden rubbed his temple. How much easier would this be if they'd never come aboard? Bracht had induced more information out of them. They said the Overseer promised a handsome reward if they captured the children. However, they insisted they didn't know why the Overseer wanted them. "The four who attacked the child will stay in the brig. Major, have a stern talk with the remaining five. If they come anywhere near these children, we will arrest them too."

“Sir,” Bracht snapped. “We’re locking up the Grapnes, but not the Tredon?”

“The children are constantly under our watch. Since we don’t have enough resources to monitor the Grapnes all day as well, we will give them a warning and follow up if they don’t heed it.”

“Yes, Sir.”

Arden placed the flat of his hands on the desk again. “That will be all, gentlemen.”

After they left, he massaged his forehead. He was getting too damned old for this kind of stress.

25
The Overseer

3790:259:08:36. Ander Vizubi stood before the door and rubbed the back of his head, hoping to get rid of the headache. He regretted drinking so much last night. He didn't care for the stuff, nor did he like how it made him feel. So why did he do it?

He'd told himself it would help him rest since his sleep schedule was off. The truth was he feared he'd have a nightmare about the man he killed. *Please, God. Forgive my sin and give me the strength to stay off this path of self-destruction.*

He inhaled slowly and pressed the buzzer.

"Yeah. Who is it?"

"It's me," Vizubi replied.

"Come on in."

The door swished open, revealing a luxurious apartment. *Damn. He really has done well for himself.*

"I'll be with you in a sec," Hesteben called from a back room.

Vizubi sniffed the air, surprised at its freshness. Where was the sweet odor of starhash? He studied the plush burgundy couch and the feathery white rug and didn't find a single stain. The place was dust free and no trash lay about. What had happened to his messy, disorganized brother?

Hesteben emerged wearing a silk blue shirt. "Hey, Andy! It's good to see you again. What are you doing here?"

Vizubi scowled. "I just saw you about eight hours ago. Don't you remember?"

His brother's brow creased. "Oh, yeah… You got in a fight with some rogues."

Vizubi shook his head as Steben practically danced to the kitchen area. In one rapid movement after another, he opened the fridge, pulled out food, set it on the counter, and prepared his meal with the precision of a robot. Watching him made his skull hurt more.

Hesteben was at his best when he was high, but it didn't last long. Vizubi eyed him for any signs the drug was wearing off but found none.

Good timing. He let himself relax. "Thanks to you, I didn't get in any trouble with the authorities."

Hesteben flicked his hand. "No worries. You took care of me all those years. It's the least I could do."

Damn. He's like night and day. "You're not still angry with me?"

"Angry with you for what?"

"Never mind," Vizubi muttered. His brother understood seven forms of computer language but didn't remember much when he came down from starhash.

"So what's up?" Hesteben picked up his sandwich laden with lab-grown meat and fabricated cheese and shoved nearly half of it in his mouth at once.

Another side effect of that damned drug. Everything on the short ride up and nothing on the long ride down.

Vizubi kept his criticism to himself. "I came here for a mission and thought I'd check in on you. It looks like you're doing pretty good."

"Good?" Hesteben broke into an open smile, causing breadcrumbs to drop from his mouth. "I'm doing great, man!"

"But how long does the high last nowadays before you fall? An hour? Two?"

Hesteben laughed. "It's not the quantity, it's the quality."

Vizubi sighed. "It seems this way now, but there's so much more to life. I can show you. Come with me to the *Odyssey*."

His brother frowned and smiled at the same time. "Leave here? Not a chance. I got everything I want right here, man."

"Remember those days when you'd spend hours designing some new program or another? Remember what it felt like when they executed perfectly?"

"Of course I remember. I still do those things."

Vizubi silently conceded. Why else would Guillermo provide him with this luxury if he wasn't doing things for him in return? "What about your dream to create the perfect android?"

"Just the silly dreams of a silly kid, man."

"It's not silly. As intelligent as you are, you can do it without someone like Guillermo peering over your shoulder."

Hesteben darkened. "Can't you ever just visit for the sake of visiting? I don't want to change, alright? I like my life, so quit trying to fix it, damn it."

"I'm only looking out for you." A pang swelled in Vizubi's chest. His brother was on a short walk down a long corridor. Although his current happiness sparkled in his eyes and spread across his face, in another thirty minutes or so, he'd look like a miserable drifter and stay that way until the next day.

Hesteben brightened. "I don't need your help anymore, man. I got this."

"Well," Vizubi said, "if you change your mind, I'm just a call away."

"Yeah, man, sure." His brother grinned.

"Alright. Well, I've got to go. My mission is nearly over."

Hesteben reformed the same frown-smile. "Leaving so soon? We didn't even get to hang out."

"I know, but it's hard for me to come here. Maybe when my leave comes up in a few months, we can meet somewhere."

The two said their goodbyes with an embrace and empty promises. Vizubi left with a hollowness in his gut. Looking back, he regretted all the terrible choices he'd made. Hesteben's addiction was his fault. He'd gotten him into this life. Too bad he couldn't get him out.

Quigley met him in the corridor. "How'd it go?"

"It went," Vizubi replied.

"That bad, huh?"

"Not too much, but I didn't convince him."

"I hope this isn't overstepping, Sir, but you can't save someone who doesn't want to be saved."

Vizubi agreed, but it didn't stop him from wanting to rescue his brother anyway.

*****

3790:259:09:00. Ander Vizubi contained his anxiety as he waited by the casino. Bells, whistles, and dings assaulted his ears.

Smoke from stubs and who knew what else wafted by, stinging his sinuses and sharpening his headache.

"Here they come, Sir," Quigley said through the comm.

Vizubi straightened and peered down the corridor. A tall lanky Grapne with a fake smile plastered on his face headed over with a poised gait. He touched his fingertips together and bowed a greeting to those he passed. Unlike the man from yesterday, this one walked with his head held high and wore the clothes of an aristocrat—purple robes embroidered with gold around the collar and cuffs.

Vizubi grimaced. Overseers considered themselves royalty despite not ruling any territories. Their planet had become inhospitable some generations ago because of the outrageous pollution their factories spewed. Nowadays, the only thing they ruled was their ships.

"Sssergeant Vizubi, I presume?" the Overseer hissed with a stupid grin and a snaky tone.

Vizubi clasped his hands behind his back. "That's me. I'm surprised you came."

"Well, you made it crystal clear on what would happen if I didn't." The Overseer held up his finger. "I'm not giving you anything for free, though. I've put a lot of expense into this venture, so if you want to know what I know, you will pay me."

Vizubi ground his teeth. He tapped the MM on his wrist and pulled up the figure in his mission's expense account. "This is all I have."

The Overseer lifted his nose. "That's barely enough to cover the cost of my man's wages." He glared down at the Grapne spy cowering beside him.

"Do you want it or not?"

The Overseer tapped his finger to the side of his mouth and looked up.

Vizubi crossed his arms. "Listen here. I have other ways to find out. Take it or leave it."

The Overseer's stupid smile widened. "Very well. I suppose you should know who you have on your ship."

A chill ran down Vizubi's spine all the way to his toes. He swept the goosebumps away and prepped the account for transfer.

After receiving the man's bank information, Vizubi sent the money. "There. Now tell me."

The Overseer checked his tablet and his eyes lit up. "Very good." He crooked his finger, urging Vizubi to come close.

"Just tell me, damn it."

"We can't have spy tech picking up on our conversation now, can we?"

Vizubi huffed but leaned in. When the Overseer whispered two words, a coldness like the void of space engulfed him. He pulled back with his jaw hanging. "Impossible."

"It's true." The Overseer's stupid smile seemed real for the first time.

"Why would they come here?"

The Overseer exaggerated a shrug. "They purchased something from a dealer here, but I don't have information on that."

"So you putting out a warrant has nothing to do with them killing anyone?"

"The Tredons confronted a couple of Capsian pirates, but I'm not sure if they killed them."

Vizubi flushed as sweat broke out over his torso. After verifying the Overseer had no other information, he hustled to the nearest communication station.

"What is it, Sir?" Quigley asked as she jogged to keep up.

"You'll find out in a minute." He had to hurry. Those children were a propellant waiting to ignite.

26
Secret Revealed

3790:259:09:25. J.D. Hapker stopped short as a tall bot with six arms zipped by. It emitted a high-pitched beeping, which could have been to communicate with other bots or to alert him to watch out. The machines should avoid getting in people's way but docking bay four was too crowded.

The robots had helped the crew disassemble the *StarFire* into thousands of smaller pieces. Several bots like the one he almost ran into hauled the parts to specific spaces, based on their identification. Various other units of different sizes and shapes analyzed each component using spectrum analyses, x-rays, and many others that Hapker didn't remember.

A rectangular bot on wheels placed an object through its opening, then closed the hatch. A blue light flashed for about three seconds. A taller and narrower robot retrieved the item, then rolled off. Close by, a cylindrical machine with a rounded top illuminated a larger piece of the *StarFire* with red laser lines from its electronic eye.

At the center of this madness stood his least favorite person. Doctor Canthidius shook his finger at a young scientist with a black braid that hung nearly to the floor. His grey face carried a pink tint.

His words reached Hapker's ears as he approached. "How could you be so careless? Only an idiot—"

"Hey!" Hapker's blood pressure spiked. "There's no reason for name calling."

Canthidius straightened with flinty eyes. "This is not your concern, Commander."

Hapker ground his teeth. "Verbally abusing the crew is every bit of my concern."

"She moved the—"

"I don't care what she did. You don't insult her to reprimand her. After you're done here today, you will re-read section fourteen-dash-a on reprimanding employees, then write me a report on it. I want it first thing tomorrow."

Canthidius' lip curled. "Yes, Sir."

Hapker faced the young woman. "Will you give us a moment, please?"

She dipped her head and retreated with a swift gait.

He returned to Doctor Canthidius. "I will put this incident in your file."

The man jutted his chin. "You don't know the situation, Sir."

"I'm not arguing with you about this. If you disagree with my disciplinary report, you can make a rebuttal. Captain Arden will review it and decide what to do from there."

At the captain's name, Canthidius' grey skin paled.

He opened his mouth to speak and Hapker raised his hand. "Let's move on. Give me an update on what's happening here."

The doctor's nose tilted up. "We have scanned and catalogued half the ship's contents so far, and it has proven futile. There is nothing of interest here."

Hapker suppressed a biting remark. "Is that what you're putting in your formal report?" he said instead.

Canthidius' snooty expression faltered. "No, Sir. I'm merely giving you an update."

Sure you are. "Then give me a *proper* update."

The doctor rattled on with far more detail than necessary. Hapker listened with mock patience. His jaw ached from clamping it so hard, but he had to keep himself from violating section fourteen-dash-a.

A distinctive beep sounded in his comm. *Thank goodness*. He forestalled Canthidius with a gesture and answered. "Yes, Captain."

"I need you in my office right away. Sergeant Vizubi has solved our mystery."

Hapker's heart jolted. He ordered the doctor to carry on and hurried to the command level.

*****

3790:259:09:54. J.D. Hapker resisted the urge to tap his foot as he waited with Captain Arden for the others. The man's expression was unreadable but a sheen of sweat beaded his forehead. *What've you been hiding, Jori?*

Bracht arrived first and Sengupta came soon after.

When she took her seat, the captain tapped his deskview screen and turned it toward them. "Tell them what you told me, Sergeant."

Vizubi dipped his head. "Major, Commander, Director. You won't believe this."

Hapker's neck prickled.

"The children we have onboard are Emperor Mizuki's sons," the grey-haired officer continued.

Sengupta sucked in a breath. The major's throat rumbled with menace.

Hapker's heart did a double-flip. He jerked forward. "Are you sure? I thought the last of his sons were dead."

His study of the Tredon's recent history stated one of the emperor's sons had died while battling a rebellious lord. *Wasn't another prince killed by the Emperor himself?* Every limb prickled as though zapped by the tentacles of a giant jellyfish. The conversation he'd had with Jori about why he had so many broken bones ran through his head. "*I wouldn't be the first to die by my father's hand.*"

"I didn't know he could still have children," the major said.

Sengupta leaned in. "I believe the rumors about him not being able to sire any more offspring, even artificially, are true. However, it's believed that the incident corrupting his genetic coding happened about ten years ago—after these boys were born."

Hapker rubbed his chin. "If these are his sons, why haven't we heard of them before?"

"Perhaps he protected them until they came of age."

Hapker's brow tightened. Could the boys really be the sons of the Dragon Emperor himself? "Assuming Jori continues to withhold information, how can we verify this?"

"Let me try something." Sengupta tapped the MM on her wrist. "This will take a few moments."

Hapker shifted in his seat. "While we're waiting, I have another question. Why would the emperor send his children all the way out here?"

"I'm not sure, Sir," Sergeant Vizubi replied. "A contact of mine confirmed they purchased something from Shekaka, but he doesn't know what it was."

Captain Arden's dark brows turned down. "Have you heard anything that connects them with MEGAs?"

Hapker's mouth went dry. If anyone knew about the emperor's dealings with cyborgs, it would be Jori, but he wasn't likely to tell them.

"Nothing like that at all, Sir," Vizubi said. "Do you want us to stick around here and keep investigating?"

The captain stroked his chin.

"Sir," Bracht said. "We have the best sources of information right here."

Hapker stiffened. "Regardless of who they are, they're still children. We must consider that before we try any more interrogation methods on them." He cringed inwardly at Garner's attempt to pull thoughts from the boy's mind.

Captain Arden nodded. "I agree, and the fact that they're the emperor's sons makes this an even more sensitive issue."

Sengupta bounced her head up and down, making her bushy hair bound with it. "The Dragon Emperor will surely war with us if something happens to these two."

The captain sighed. "Return to the ship," he said to Vizubi. "I'll pass this up the chain and let them decide what to do."

"Yes, Sir. There's a couple of things I need to wrap up, if that's alright."

"That's fine. Coordinate your flight schedule so we can meet at Chevert at around the same time."

"Will do."

"Is that all you have, Sergeant?"

"I'm afraid so, Sir."

Captain Arden ended the conversation.

"May I?" the director asked, pointing with a trembling hand at the large viewscreen on the opposite wall.

The captain indicated for her to proceed.

Hapker and Bracht turned to watch.

Sengupta tapped her MM and a man with jet black hair and hard eyes popped up on the screen.

"The Tredon Emperor." Bracht's rough voice held a hint of disdain.

The director rapped her tablet again and close-ups of the boys appeared beside the emperor's portrait.

Hapker whistled. *Dear god.* Jori's brother could have been the emperor when he was young. Jori didn't look as much like the man but he strongly resembled his brother.

"I did a quick facial map analysis. The results show a likely relation."

"I can't deny that the resemblance is uncanny," the captain replied.

Bracht growled. "I told you he was trouble."

The loudness of the Rabnoshk warrior's voice broke Hapker's stare at the screen. "His behavior has been ill-mannered at times, but he hasn't made the kind of trouble I would expect from the son of our enemy."

The major's fists whitened. "Sir! We must lock him up."

Captain Arden folded his hands. His eyes flickered across the images. "If they are the Dragon Princes, then we have an even more delicate situation than we first thought."

"They're vicious criminals!" the major barked.

The captain's composure remained calm. "Their father is a criminal. I have no evidence that these boys are."

Bracht snorted. "Their heritage is evidence enough."

Hapker's initial shock wore off. Pieces came together. "This is probably what Jori's been hiding." It made sense. The boy's secrecy. His defensiveness. "He's been trying to protect his brother." It was like someone had thrown him into ice-cold water. Only instead of opening his eyes to a raging river, a swell of understanding washed over him.

The captain nodded. "It would explain what the Grapnes were after."

"And the bounty hunters." Hapker added.

"I imagine the price for the heads of the last two Mizuki Princes would be substantial," Sengupta said.

Hapker frowned. "Or someone could use them to get revenge on the most hated man in the galaxy."

Captain Arden tapped his chin. “If you think about it, this is a great opportunity.”

“Opportunity for what?” Hapker’s tone was sharper than intended. His imagination took flight as all sorts of gruesome *opportunities* came to mind.

Bracht smiled, showing his pointed canines. “If the emperor can’t have any more children, as Sengupta says, then we have the power to end the Mizuki reign once and for all.”

Hapker’s heart clenched. “Kill them?”

The captain raised his palm. “No one will be harmed.”

“Keep them.” Bracht’s eyes hardened. “Force the emperor to abdicate.”

“You mean take them hostage and hold them for ransom?” Hapker asked.

Bracht bared his pointed teeth. “Yes, and urge them to tell us what they know of the emperor’s plans and military might.”

Hapker tightened his fists. “You can’t. They’re not pawns in some game. They’re children.”

The major squared his shoulders. “Children of a man who’s committed genocide.”

“No,” the captain said sharply. “The opportunity I’m referring to is the opportunity to sow peace.”

Hapker relaxed at the seriousness of the captain’s expression.

“Making friends with the boys won’t make us any allies,” Bracht scoffed.

Captain Arden shook his head. “Perhaps not now, but if these are the heirs, then maybe someday.”

Bracht’s mouth twisted as though he were a lion who’d just eaten a skunk.

“Commander.” The captain leaned in. “Why don’t you talk to Jori? Send him my apologies for using Garner and see if we can help assure him he’s still safe.”

The major’s face grew darker. “We’re supplicating ourselves to them!”

“Do you mean to tell me, Major,” the captain said in a hard tone, “that you truly advocate locking these children away and subjecting them to torture? The same as was done to your brother by his enemies?”

Hapker’s eyebrows shot up. This wasn’t in Bracht’s file.

The Rabnoshk warrior looked down and shifted his stance. "It's not the same thing," he mumbled.

"Isn't it?"

Bracht didn't raise his head. Whatever had happened to his brother, it seemed to have left a powerful impression.

"This violence and hate must stop somewhere," the captain said. "We can either try to make peace with our enemies or we continue to commit the same atrocities. I think you know very well where I stand on the matter. It's why you're here, isn't it? Why you chose to serve on this ship?"

The captain spoke to Bracht, but Hapker couldn't help but feel like he was talking to him as well. He hadn't accepted the position on the *Odyssey* just because it was the only decent offer he'd received. He accepted it because of Captain Arden's reputation as a peacemaker.

From what he'd read about the man, he'd earned a commendation for brokering the peace between the Cooperative and the Rabnoshk people. Was the major a part of that too?

The captain glared but Bracht continued to stare at his feet. "Yes, Sir."

The captain's eyes softened. "I'm not saying we should let our guard down. Not in the least. I'm merely stating we must give the child a chance—the same chance you and I once gave to each other."

Hapker wanted to cheer. Not because Bracht was being rebuked for his hateful behavior. If anything, he saw the man in a whole new light. It was because of how genuine the captain's words had sounded.

"Commander?" The captain said.

"Yes, Sir?" *Oh, wait. He's waiting for my reply.* "I mean, yes, Sir. I'll talk to him." He doubted it would do much good at this point, but he wanted to try.

27
A Flood of Truth

3790:259:11:18. The curtain to the small room opened, making the sound of a sword sliding over a whetstone. Jori didn't bother looking up as the commander sat beside him.

Hapker's warm hand rested on his shoulder. "No change?"

A pang welled from deep within Jori's core. He kept his head down to hide his tears. *You're not my friend. You betrayed me.*

The man patted him. "There's still a chance he'll make it."

An urge to tell Hapker to leave him alone sprang up. He swallowed down the saliva building in his mouth instead. When the man's compassion poked through his own turmoil, he pushed it away.

They sat a long time without speaking. Despite his best attempt to deflect it, the commander's concern swept over him like a fresh blast of air into a hot engine room. His tears dried, though his cheeks remained flushed. The more he calmed, the more Hapker's emotions crawled their way into his head. Something about them niggled at him so he probed.

Dread. Dread tainted the man's sympathy. Jori's insides whirled. He met Hapker's eyes. "What's going on?"

Hapker's brows shot up and a spike of unease emanated from him. "What do you mean?"

"Something's wrong. The captain wants to interrogate me, doesn't he?"

"No. No one will hurt you."

"Then what is it?" His voice came out hard, but his gut wriggled with worry.

Hapker sighed. "I need to discuss something with you. Later of course. After you've spent some time with your brother."

"I can come back to see him again."

"Are you sure?"

"Yes." *Might as well get this over with.*

Hapker stood. "Let's go to my place where we can talk in private." He gave a significant glance toward the curtain where guards waited on the other side.

Jori swallowed against the lump in his throat. They walked in silence, but at least their earlier tension had gone. The commander felt apprehensive, but he had an odd mixture of sanguinity with it. Was he going to say sorry? Did he expect him to apologize? *Does he hate me?*

Hapker had tired of him. That must be it. He wanted to pass him over to someone else or lock him up.

Jori's chest tightened as they entered the quarters. They each sat on a padded brown chair. The commander leaned in with his elbows on his knees. Jori almost tasted his unease and it compounded his own.

Hapker looked away as though in thought. After a long moment, he took a deep breath and spoke. "What happened with Garner, we didn't want to do it, but it was necessary."

Jori frowned. A tart reply came to his lips, but he kept it to himself.

"We understand now. You were afraid of what we would find out and that we'd hurt you or your brother because of it."

Jori's throat caught and his pulse quickened.

"Well, I promise you it changes nothing," Hapker said in a warm tone. "We'll continue to do everything we can to help your brother, and we'll still get you home."

Jori dared not speak. His heart throbbed painfully while blood drained from his head, leaving a cold and numbing sensation running over his jaw and down his neck.

The commander hesitated. "We know you and your brother are Emperor Mizuki's sons."

Jori couldn't breathe, as though someone pressed on his lungs. He pulled back and assessed his chances for escape.

"It's alright. We won't hurt you." Hapker touched his hand.

Jori flinched. He tried to read the man, but his own emotions spiraled out of control. "Why?" His voice came out in a croak.

"Because no matter what our opinions are of your father, you've done nothing wrong."

Jori grunted. "You don't believe that."

"I do."

Jori struggled to see through the whirling sensations. Somewhere in the mix was a sense of sincerity. It wasn't his own so it must be Hapker's.

"Jori." The commander clasped his hand and gave a slight squeeze. "Our people may be enemies, but you and I don't have to be."

Does he mean it? Or is he manipulating me? Jori snatched his hand away and bound to his feet. "I'm headed to the gym."

"Huh? Now?"

"Now." His emotions threatened to overflow.

"I'll go with you."

"No. Leave me alone." He stiffened in resolve, trying to force the torrent down.

Emotion is weakness. Emotion is weakness. He repeated the mantra over and over, but the flood rose too fast.

A sense of resignation emanated from Hapker. It contained a hint of disappointment as well. The sensations nearly sent Jori over the edge. *I don't get it. I'm his enemy.*

He raced out. The guards yelled for him to stop.

"Let him leave," the commander called as a guard came close enough to tackle him. "Just follow."

Jori ran on in a blur. Before he knew it, he had activated the holo program in the gym.

His emotions struck like a solar flare and, at the same moment, he took out the first holo-man with an uppercut to the chin. The fire within him rolled out in a raging yell. Tears streamed down his face, but he moved so fast and furiously against the haptic image that he doubted anyone noticed.

28
The Truth Hurts

3790:259:11:37. J.D. Hapker stepped out, intending to follow the boy. Jori had known something was wrong. Was he a reader? If so, he must realize he'd told the truth.

He went back inside and plopped into his chair with a heavy sigh. Anything he said now would undoubtedly be met with resistance.

"*You just need some time*," his dad had told him in their most recent conversation. This was good advice for letting someone process hard feelings. When he had made this comment, though, he meant it as an admonition.

The memory prompted him to his console where he tapped the file of recorded communications. He opened the one from last month and his mother's face with her usual warm smile popped up on the screen. "J.D., what a surprise," she had said.

"Hello, Mom. How are you doing?" his recorded voice replied.

"I'm doing very well, thank you. The weather is perfect. It's spring here, you know. Do you remember those tiger lilies I told you about?"

Hapker had nodded, so the recording didn't pick up his response.

"They bloomed so beautifully. I cut one for Merele to put in…"

Hapker skimmed through the part where Mother had gone on about her friends and her garden. She beamed the entire time, keeping her tone upbeat. She tended to go on about ordinary things as though they were the most interesting subjects in the universe, but at least the topics were positive.

Hapker hit play again.

"We saw Shannah the other day." Mom had spoken in a way that implied seeing her was the highlight of her life.

Hapker had groaned, but not loud enough for the recorder to pick up. “That’s great, Mom.” It made no sense for her to bring up his ex-fiancé except as a reminder that he should come back home and marry her, like they had originally planned for him. She was perfect, they said, but he found her dull.

“She baked this wonderful quiche,” his mother had rambled on. “It was delicious, better than the one I tried to make last Christmas. Remember that? How it was burnt on top and mushy on the inside?”

“I remember,” he had said, though he doubted she heard him.

“Hers was not an ordinary quiche either.”

Hapker skimmed ahead again.

“Here comes your father,” she said in the video. “He just came in from the garden. Oh, and he’s brought in some dates. I should make some jam. Goodbye, son. I love you.”

“I love you too, Mom.”

She stepped away, leaving behind the image of their living room wall. He smiled as he listened to her gush over the dates as his dad contributed ideas on what to do with them. Though Hapker didn’t want the life they lived, he missed their affectionate bickering.

His father’s face appeared on the screen. “How are things going, son?”

“Great, Dad,” Hapker had said. “It’s different from the PG-Force, but in a good way.”

“Yeah, well, if it doesn’t work out you can always come home.”

Hapker cringed at the idea.

“Your position with the Protectors is waiting for you,” Dad continued. “They really miss you.”

“I don’t miss them.” Hapker didn’t say this in the actual conversation, but saying it now satisfied him.

“Lieutenant Aronson has been asking after you,” his dad said.

“Tell him hello for me.” Hapker detected the terseness in his recorded voice, but it didn’t seem his father did.

His mom rejoined the chat. They mentioned more friends and reminded him of all the good times he used to have. Hapker skimmed through it. The discussion tensed when his dad brought up news reports about the Cooperative. Somehow, he put a negative spin on everything they did. He spoke as though they were an evil organization bent on corrupting sons and daughters everywhere.

Hapker resumed the recording near the end.

"We hope to see you soon, son," his dad had said. "You don't belong there."

"Please, not this again."

"Well, it's time," he replied in a lecturing tone. "You almost got discharged, for goodness' sake. And for what? For making the right decision?"

"It's not like that."

"It's proof of that the Cooperative still has a long way to go before reaching our level of understanding."

"Dad, we discussed this already," Hapker had said with exasperation. "I want to give this other option a turn."

"Alright, alright," Dad replied with a disappointed expression. "You just need some time. Then you'll see how much happier it is at home."

They spoke their goodbyes with an attitude of unresolved discontent. The video ended. Heaviness returned, just like on the day of that conversation. What if his dad was right? As the days progressed, it became more apparent that he didn't belong with the Cooperative.

This low mood needed a lift. He shut down his console and left. A cheerful buzz met him in the lounge, but his frame of mind didn't allow him to embrace it. After finding an isolated stool at the edge of the bar, he tapped the screen on the counter and placed an order for a stiff drink.

A bot arrived with a glass of amber liquid. He took a sip, letting it bite the tip of his tongue and warm his throat, and tried not to think about Jori.

Tried and failed. The boy's abrupt behavior after he'd made a sincere overture of friendship stung worse than the alcohol. He'd given his trust and it meant nothing.

Doubt crept in. Perhaps Captain Arden had assigned the wrong man for this job. He shouldn't even be here. What the heck had been going through his head when he decided to leave home? His position as a Pholatian Protector held promise. A couple more decades and he would have reached the same exalted rank as his father.

That was the problem, though, wasn't it? He'd be living the life his dad wanted instead of the one he wanted.

His father was a good man, great even. Hapker didn't want his life, though. He wanted to escape its predictability and do something better.

Only he wasn't doing better. According to his dad, he'd made one poor decision after another. First, breaking it off with Shannah. Next, relinquishing his duty as a Pholatian Protector. The Kimpke incident, however, had brought out the worst of his dad's temper. Hapker wasn't worthy of the family name, the man had said.

He wasn't entirely wrong. If Hapker couldn't make this job on the *Odyssey* work, it would be the last felled tree that would crush his dad's heart.

As he lifted his glass to take another drink, someone dropped into the seat next to him.

"I hardly ever see you here." Sharkey's thin lips curved into a small smile, making her sharp cheekbones stand out.

Even though she shattered his respite, he didn't mind. Sharkey was the only person on this ship he knew well, and she was easy to talk to.

"I needed a drink," he said.

"The Tredon boy's giving you trouble, huh?"

He sighed. Jori's presence was certainly troublesome, but in looking back, his behavior made perfect sense.

"Not so much," he replied. "It's…" *It's what? The son of the notorious Dragon Emperor has a way of shining a light on my complete inadequacy as a Prontaean officer?* He couldn't tell Sharkey about Jori yet. Not in this setting. He ran his hand down his face and rested his chin on his fist.

Since Sharkey didn't order through the counter device, the bar bot interrupted with a distinct click. She asked it for her usual lunch, and it wheeled off to comply.

She folded her hands and her expression turned thoughtful. "It can't be easy for him here."

"No, it can't. Whenever he comes close to opening up, something happens, and I have to start all over again."

"That's understandable."

"Understandable but frustrating."

"Put yourself in his place," she replied. "He just needs a little time to realize you're trying to help him."

"It's more than that." The fear on Jori's face when Hapker had angered popped into his head. He closed his eyes and replayed the scene in his mind, too ashamed to speak of it out loud even to his friend. The situation following that was nearly as bad. "The captain called in Garner."

Sharkey shivered as though spiders crawled up her back. "No wonder he's upset. What happened?"

"It didn't work. Jori realized what he was doing and resisted."

"Is he alright?"

"Yeah. He's not hurt." Hapker sipped his drink and the sharp taste of the alcohol hit him like a lightning bolt. *Jori's angry because I told him I was on his side.*

The liquor struck like a fiery meteor as it plunged down his throat. It was bad enough the boy had expected Hapker to strike him, but then he'd delivered Jori to Garner the mind-thief.

Thinking of the man and his ability to dig around in people's minds always unsettled him, but this time guilt corkscrewed with it. No wonder Jori kept pushing him away.

If he had sided with the boy, though, he would have gone against the captain. How should he have handled it without alienating them both?

He set down his glass. "This isn't the prevailing opinion of the crew, but he's not the monster everyone makes him out to be."

"I agree with you, but I can understand how they feel."

"He's only a boy."

"A boy who's probably seen more death than any of us combined." She leaned back and shook her head. "Do you wonder what sort of impression that's made on him?"

The corkscrew sensation wrenched Hapker's gut. He imagined Jori standing beside his father as the man tortured someone. His heart ached as he recalled the conversation with him about why he had all those broken bones. The boy had no choice but to live up to his father's expectations.

Hapker drank again, keeping the liquid in his mouth long enough for the bite to numb his tongue.

"You know," she said, "you're perfect for this assignment. Not only are you open-minded, but you're also the only person who has any remote possibility of being a good influence on him."

His cheeks warmed. "Yeah?"

"Yeah."

"I wish the captain and the rest of the crew believed it too."

She shrugged. "They don't know you well enough yet."

Her tone indicated she avoided something. "What? You know their opinions of me, don't you?"

She averted her eyes. "It's like I said. They don't know you."

"What are they saying?"

Sharkey touched his arm again. "It's nothing. You shouldn't worry about it."

He pressed his lips. "Tell me. I can take it."

Her shoulders fell. "They think you're naïve." She straightened and spoke in a rush. "But it's not true, and you standing up for the kid is the right thing. They're letting their prejudices affect their judgment."

The confidence built up by Sharkey's earlier words came crumbling down. "You said before that I've lost my edge. I believe you're right."

Her mouth turned down in pity. "No. I said you're not as confident as you used to be."

"Same thing."

"C'mon, Hapker," she said in a lighter tone. "You did what was right then and you're doing what is right now. Some people won't like it."

He shook his head. "I'm not so sure it was right. My decision with Kimpke backfired. A lot of innocent people still died. Taking Jori's side could backfire as well." He imagined his dad's disappointment and a pang filled his chest.

"You made an impossible choice…"

"And the choice was the one that made me the least accountable," he said.

"It was an *impossible* choice. Nobody could have known what he would do. Besides…" She turned, fully facing him. "Wouldn't you rather have given Kimpke the chance than wonder whether it could have ended differently?"

He frowned. "I already wonder."

She let out an exasperated breath. "What about with Jori? Wouldn't you rather give him a chance than mistreat him for things he *might* do later?"

"That's just it," he said. "What he *might* do isn't something remote. It's highly probable. He is dangerously capable. Perhaps the crew is right. I *am* naïve."

"Forget about them. Be who you are and don't worry about what others think. You've been around him the most, so no one is more qualified than you to judge him. If your decision to help him backfires, then at least you gave him a chance. It's probably more than anyone else will ever give him."

"That might be true about the crew, but not the captain. I *must* keep this position. I can't go home a washout."

"Captain Arden is more reasonable than you think. He's a good man and I'm sure he both understands and respects how you're handling this."

He rested his jaw in his palm, hoping she was right. The captain had agreed with him more than once. Hapker was so close to getting Jori to open up, too. If he could only help him see what life was like without cruelty, maybe he could show the boy how to make better choices.

He should try, at least. Despite his misgivings, he wasn't ready to give up.

*****

3790:259:15:03. J.D. Hapker had just finished changing into his nightclothes when Jori returned. A glance at the boy's blank face disheartened him. "How are you doing?" he asked anyway.

"Well." The boy's eyes didn't even flicker.

"Can we talk?"

Jori clasped his hands behind his back and took an attentive at-ease stance.

Hapker suppressed a despondent sigh and sat facing him. "I realized something earlier. I should have stood up for you when the captain allowed Garner to pull your thoughts."

Jori's brow furrowed. "You believe you should have gone against your captain?"

It wouldn't be the first time going against a superior. "I told you I was on your side, and I failed you in that. I'm sincerely sorry. You shouldn't have to face all this alone."

Jori's throat bobbed and his eyes glistened. He remained silent as he studied Hapker as though searching for something. "You really do still want to help us," the boy finally said.

"Yes."

"I wish to speak to Captain Arden." His tone was hard, but not demanding. "You say this, despite who we are, but I must hear it from him."

Hapker straightened. "You *are* a sentio-animi, aren't you?"

Jori's eyes darkened. "I can't do what that man can do. He's an extraho. He plunders peoples' thoughts like a pirate."

"I didn't mean to make it sound like an accusation."

"I can only sense emotions that people give off." Jori's tone softened. "It's barely any different from reading body language."

Hapker nodded. The Cooperative considered the skill of a sentio-animi to be nominal. They only regulated those of extraho-animi and higher because of the damage they could do.

Even so, the idea that Jori could read his emotions made his insides squirm. "Can all Tredons do this?"

"No. Only my brother and I… And our mother."

"Not your father?"

"No."

Hapker sighed inwardly. "I bet this ability comes in handy."

"It is why I didn't *shoot* you when you and your men confronted me on that blue planet," Jori replied humorlessly. "It's why I trust you when you say you will help save my brother and why I must speak to the captain directly."

Hapker flushed at the word *trust*. Perhaps he'd been a positive influence after all. "Fair enough. I'll arrange it for tomorrow. Don't worry too much in the meantime. I'm certain the captain intends to help you."

Jori dipped his head. It was a good thing Hapker was more confident about where Captain Arden stood now. Otherwise, the boy probably wouldn't have believed him.

29
Brimstone

3790:260:01:15. Silas Arden sipped his coffee. Black, bitter yet smooth, and just the stimulation he needed for the weighty decisions he had to make. The presence of the Mizuki Princes held implications far beyond the security of this ship. If the emperor found out they had them…

He rubbed his brow. He must handle this situation delicately lest it get out of hand. The Cooperative and Tredons hated each other. If something happened to the Dragon Princes, then nothing would stop an all-out war.

The coffee turned sour on his tongue. He wanted to give the child the benefit of the doubt, regardless of his heritage. After all, peace began with trust. If Bracht's people became allies after decades of being enemies, then so could the Tredons.

The conference room doors slid open. Commander Hapker entered with the Dragon Prince at his side. Major Bracht and Director Sengupta followed.

"I must protest, Captain," Bracht flicked his hand vehemently. "This boy is extremely dangerous and must be locked up."

If one didn't know the Rabnoshk warrior as well as Arden did, they'd think he made a demand. The man could certainly be brusque, but he'd trust him with his life.

Bracht's notion tempted him, but it still didn't resonate. Barring the child's attitude, his behavior had not been overly concerning.

Hapker's firmness with him had been quite unexpected. More surprising was how the child backed down. Was it because he realized he didn't have a chance? Or was it because the commander had gained his respect?

"He might kill the commander in his sleep," the major continued.

Jori's face darkened. "I do not kill people in their sleep."

Bracht snarled. The child didn't flinch or cower, and his predatory stare matched his.

"Major," Hapker said in a low tone.

The staring contest broke. Jori turned away and faced Arden with a cool composure. He stood alert like a soldier—body erect, legs shoulder-width apart, and hands clasped behind his back.

"Welcome, young man." Arden smiled, but the child remained unmoved. Only the bold confidence of his dark eyes reflected any emotion. "I'm sure Commander Hapker extended my apologies, but I appreciate this opportunity to give them to you in person."

Jori nodded.

"I sincerely wish I hadn't needed to use the reader on you. As I said, though, I have the safety of my crew to consider. Although it pleases me a great deal that I have been able to help you and your brother, your presence here poses a number of concerns."

"Will you continue to help us?"

Arden rested his elbows on the table and interlocked his fingers. "I assure you that nothing has changed regarding you or your brother's well-being. Now that I have a better understanding of why those people were after you, I see no reason to keep you here."

"And you will let us return home?"

Arden nodded.

"Even though we are your enemies?" His eyes flickered into disbelief.

"Yes. We treat everyone with equal consideration here."

"Despite what you say, I can't help but feel my brother's life may be contingent upon my cooperation."

"As next in line, I'd think you wouldn't care," Bracht said.

Arden glanced at him pointedly, but the man didn't seem to notice.

"Do not speak of what you do not know," Jori warned the Rabnoshk through gritted teeth.

A growl rumbled from Major Bracht's chest. The child's poise remained cool, but his eyes burned.

"That's enough, Bracht, or I'll have you wait outside." Arden admired the man's tenacity… Most of the time. It's what made him an excellent security officer. However, he needed to handle this with diplomacy.

He turned back to Jori. “No contingencies. My intentions remain the same.”

“It would not be so for you if the situation were reversed.”

Jori’s soberness sent a tingle down Arden’s spine. “Nevertheless, it is not our way to let anyone needing medical care die, nor to keep children as prisoners.”

“He's no ordinary child,” Bracht muttered.

Jori kept his scrutiny on Arden. “What if my father had been on the ship? Would you have saved him too?”

Sengupta sucked in a breath. Bracht grimaced while Hapker’s throat bobbed. His own hands twitched. *Thank goodness this wasn’t the case.* His answer remained the same, though. “Of course. We would do our best to help, even if it were your father's life on the line.”

“Why?” The child said in a flat tone as his eyes reflected puzzlement.

“The Prontaean Cooperative does indeed consider your father a criminal, but we would still attempt to save him so he could stand trial for his crimes.”

Jori’s mouth twitched. “I find your justice system bewildering, Captain. You know he's guilty. My father knows he's guilty. Why waste time with a trial? It would be simpler to let him die… Assuming you had that opportunity.”

Bracht grunted in agreement.

“We believe every person has a right to a fair trial, a right to defend their actions, and a right to receive impartial judgment,” Arden said.

The child shook his head as though in disbelief. “What keeps you from putting my brother and me on trial?”

“So far as I am aware, you’ve done nothing illegal.”

“Not in your territory, but aren’t you worried about us doing so later?”

“What you do is your own choice. Your family history doesn’t have to presage your future.”

The placidness of Jori’s face broke with a wrinkling of his brow. “We are enemies, Captain.”

Arden brought his folded hands up and rested his chin on the point of his index fingers. "But we don't need to be."

*****

3790:260:01:49. Jori blinked. Hapker had said the same thing. *Did* they have to be? Father thought so, and he sensed the enmity from several other Cooperative officers. Just because the commander and this captain attempted to be friendly didn't mean they were friends.

This is another trick. He's trying to trick me.

His cheeks grew hot and he clenched his fists.

The captain folded his hands. "Now that you know our intentions, I'd like to clarify a few things. Your reluctance to tell us who you are is completely understandable. Since you didn't lie to me and only withheld the information, I assume you've been telling the truth on the other questions we've asked."

"I'm no liar."

"I believe you, but I must make sure. Were those people after you because you are Emperor Mizuki's sons, or is there more to this?"

He scowled. Just because the captain had discovered his identity didn't mean he had to spill all his guts. It made sense to tell the truth in this case, though. "I suspect they were after us strictly because of who we are. It should have been kept secret, but one of my men let it slip." Bok was a braggart, even when sober. Add a little drink while visiting a pub, and he became a loudmouth.

"I see," the captain said. "Why would your father send you both out there? Wasn't he worried about the danger?"

Jori made a face. *Father worried about danger?* "How will we gain experience if all we do is play simulated games? This should have been an easy mission."

"What was your mission?"

He clenched his fists. The captain was pushing it. "Just a simple purchase of supplies. No thievery. No killing." *Simple, and yet we still failed.* His cheeks burned again, but this time in shame.

"Supplies such as a certain device we heard mentioned on a communication with your father?"

Jori blinked. So, they hadn't found it. Either it had been destroyed in the crash or it remained hidden. Whatever the case, it didn't mean he'd tell them anything. "That's none of your business. I've already made it clear we've done nothing illegal." He bit the inside of his cheek at how close he came to lying. Although they purchased it fairly, the legal sense was fuzzy since the Cooperative had laws against purchasing stolen items.

Captain Arden's mouth worked as though he considered his reply. "Could this device have something to do with your father's interaction with MEGAs?"

Jori hid his surprise with a scowl. How did this man learn about the cyborgs Father had dealt with? He probed the captain's emotions. "You're fishing. You don't know anything about my father's activities."

"I know he spoke to an engineered man who supposedly has a way to hide biometrics from us."

Jori's heart skipped a beat, but he kept his cool despite the sudden heaviness of his nanite infused hand. "It's not illegal to talk to cyborgs."

The captain's emotions dripped with dread. "It depends on why he's talking to them."

Jori scoffed. "Your laws don't apply to my father."

"But…" Director Sengupta hesitated. "Doesn't Toradon have laws against genetic and biometric enhancements as well?"

Jori enjoyed the level of fear coming from everyone here, but if he let them assume the worst, they might scan him for biometrics and find the nanites. "Yes. Although my father is in charge, we must maintain our legitimacy through natural means or answer to numerous lords."

Captain Arden shifted in his chair. "Of course, you can circumvent the lords with undetectable tech."

Jori flinched inwardly while also admiring the man's shrewdness. "If there is such a thing, someone somewhere will eventually find a way to detect it. My father would be foolish to risk it." The captain wasn't the only clever one. Jori congratulated himself for speaking the truth without revealing anything.

"So nothing came of this talk your father had with a MEGA?"

"I will tell you no more," Jori replied firmly.

The captain emitted hesitation as he studied him. No doubt he wanted to press the matter, but Jori stood steadfast.

"Fair enough." Captain Arden sighed. "Now, how can we contact your father?"

Jori tensed. What would Father think if he found out he was here being treated as a guest on a Cooperative ship? *He'd suspect I'm a traitor. That's what.* "Speaking to my father isn't a good idea."

"Don't you want to tell him you're alright?"

Jori huffed. "He would never believe I'm safe here, even if I told him so myself."

"He'd realize we took good care of you." The captain's confident tone held a hint of uncertainty.

"Not if my brother dies."

The captain radiated alarm. Sengupta and Hapker did as well. Bracht stewed, but not as hotly.

"I see your point. So, tell me more of this ship waiting for you near Chevert outpost. It's not your father's ship?"

"No. It's General Sakon of the *Brimstone*."

The captain's uneasiness increased. Jori suppressed a smile. People feared General Sakon almost as much as Father.

"General Sakon," Hapker said. "I've heard of him."

Jori shrugged. "He's the one who taught me to play schemster… Among other things."

The trepidation emanating from Hapker did not give him nearly the same level of satisfaction as it did coming from the captain. He was beginning to like the commander a little too much. *Curse him.*

"Are you sure you can trust him?" Captain Arden asked. "I'm not well versed on Tredon politics, but there must be some leaders who'd love to see an end to the Mizuki reign."

"The general is loyal. He'd be a fool to make an enemy of my father." Not to mention that Sakon couldn't do half the savagery he enjoyed so much if he didn't have Father's permission.

"Very well," the captain replied. "I will contact him soon."

"I must speak to him myself."

"Of course."

"He will want the remains of our ship," Jori said. He still needed the hidden device, after all.

The captain emitted a hint of suspicion. "I'm afraid that won't be possible."

Jori's mouth dried. "Why not?" he replied harshly.

"You were in Cooperative terr—"

"Doing nothing illegal!"

Both the captain's face and emotions hardened. "It's the law."

Jori glowered. He wanted to argue the point further but didn't bother wasting his breath.

"I hope that's not too much of a problem," the captain said.

Jori struggled to keep his frustration in check so as not to give the man a reason to suspect anything. "No," he replied a little too sharply.

A smugness emanated from the captain, but he kept his face neutral. "That's good. I'm glad we don't need to make an issue of it. Thank you, Prince Mizuki."

"It is *Second* Prince Mizuki. My brother's *not* dead."

Sengupta stepped forward. "So, there are only two of you, then? Two princes, I mean."

A flash of heat surged through him. He wasn't supposed to reveal that. *Curse these Cooperative people.* He gave her a dirty look.

The captain seemed to pretend he hadn't heard her. "My apologies. Thank you, Second Prince Mizuki," he said. "Though may I suggest we keep your identity between us? For your safety, of course."

"Very well."

The captain smiled. "I appreciate what a wonderful guest you've been so far. I hope we can continue our cordial relationship."

Wonderful guest? Cordial? This man was full of sickeningly sweet politeness.

The captain seemed to wait for a response but Jori wouldn't lie and make empty promises. When Terk woke up—*if* he woke up—they still had to atone for their losses to Father, especially if the captain kept the remains of their ship… And therefore, the hidden device.

30
Captain and Commander

3790:260:02:27. Silas Arden waited for the door to close as the young prince left. “Well, that was an interesting conversation.”

Commander Hapker sat. Both he and Director Sengupta dipped their heads in agreement. Bracht kept glancing at the door as though he wanted to follow the boy out and keep an eye on him personally.

Arden smiled inwardly as he recalled how the man had struggled with his new position because he tried to do everything himself. Perhaps this time he shouldn’t delegate, though.

The child had seemed rather upset about the fate of his damaged ship and he held things back. Arden rubbed his forehead. Should he be more concerned about the mysterious device or the emperor’s connection to the MEGA? Both weighed down on him, but the latter laid beyond his ability to investigate.

“Commander,” he said. “Follow up with Doctor Canthidius and Chief Simmonds regarding that ship.”

Hapker nodded.

“How soon will you contact the Tredons?” Sengupta asked.

Arden hesitated. He didn’t relish the idea of setting up a meeting with the notorious General Sakon. “I want to get this murder charge sorted out first. Depnaugh still hasn’t commented on it.”

Hapker folded his hands in front of him. “Now that we’re fairly sure he’s innocent—”

“He’s not innocent!” Bracht barked.

Arden looked pointedly at the Rabnoshk warrior. “Regarding this matter, I’m certain he is.”

“General Sakon isn’t,” the major replied. “He’s as bad as the emperor himself.”

Arden nodded. Worse in some ways since Sakon was more directly involved in kidnapping people to take as slaves. "I plan to wait until the very last moment to contact the *Brimstone*."

Hapker dipped his head. "So he doesn't have time to lay a trap."

"We should notify the PG-Force as soon as possible," Bracht said.

Arden agreed. It hadn't been his initial intent to get them involved, especially since galactic relations were still in his jurisdiction, but the stakes had grown.

Sengupta's brow drew down. "Have you notified the admiral?"

"I reported that we have Tredon children here, but I can't tell him who they are until we reach the next communication hub. Admiral Zimmer will get the update in about ten days."

Hapker stiffened. His history with the admiral had not been a pleasant one. While Arden wasn't particularly fond of Zimmer himself, the man was an able leader.

"Your talk with Jori went well?" Arden asked him.

The commander's rigidness abated. "Not great, but not as bad as expected."

"Has your opinion of him changed?"

"I understand him better. Now that his secret is out, I'm confident it will improve our relations."

Hapker's reply sounded hopeful, but was it too good to be true? Arden still suspected the man was too trusting of the child.

"Don't be fooled, Commander," Bracht said. Then he turned to Arden. "Sir, I must alert security about this increased risk."

Hapker's face tightened. "Sir, it's bad enough most of the crew has heard these boys are Tredons. If they hear they are also the Mizuki Princes, it could generate more trouble."

Arden agreed. The behaviors of some crew members had been more negative than he'd expected. Perhaps Commander Findlay's antagonizing attitude had rubbed off on them. "I meant it when I told the child his identity should be between us. I understand the crew has strong feelings about having Tredons on board, and I don't want them intensified to the point where they do something irrational."

Bracht squared his shoulders. "I trust my lieutenants and sergeants, Sir. They must know who they are dealing with."

Arden brought his folded hands up to his chin and touched his index fingers to his lips. Telling more people risked the information getting out, but he had a good crew. He should have faith in them. It was important to their safety that they understand the increased risks—as well as the increased sensitivity—of the situation. "You may inform the lieutenants and sergeants only. Make it clear they are to keep this secret."

"Yes, Sir," Bracht replied.

"I know feelings against the Tredons run deep, but I will not have you or anyone else instigating conflict. As security, your job is primarily to protect our crew, but it's also to protect the child from those who wish to take their grudges out on him. Is that clear?"

"Yes, Sir," the major said in a more subdued tone.

*****

3790:260:02:48. J.D. Hapker considered the characters of the lieutenants and sergeants. He trusted Sharkey and he had a good impression of Gresher. Some sergeants were a different matter, though.

"That is all." The captain laid the flat of his hands down.

Sengupta stood. The major moved to the door.

"Captain, a private moment?" Hapker said.

The captain tilted his head again, prompting Bracht and the director to leave. "Yes, Commander?"

Hapker considered his words with care. It had become apparent that Captain Arden and the Rabnoshk warrior were close and he didn't want to offend. "I'm wondering about Major Bracht, Sir. It's obvious he doesn't like the boy and I'm worried his prejudice may rub off on the others."

"I've known him for many years," the captain replied casually. "He is outspoken in this room, but I assure you he is not one to instigate trouble."

"It seemed he tried to instigate trouble here," he said, careful to keep his tone from sounding accusatory.

"I understand your concern, Commander. I've spent a lot of time around warriors like Bracht and of other races. This behavior is their way of establishing their boundaries. You'd be surprised at how well two men who hate each other can get along once they're done posturing."

"Hmm." It made some sense.

"I also believe he is a good deterrent for anything the prince might be considering," the captain said. "I've given this child our trust, but Bracht has established that we won't allow him to take advantage of it."

Hapker sat back in his chair. "I never thought of it that way." He quickly replayed the scene in his head and saw the major differently this time around. The Rabnoshk warrior was harsh, but only at first. Same with the boy. Toward the end of this encounter, both appeared mollified.

"There's something I'd like to ask *you* about, Commander," the captain said.

"What is it, Sir?"

"What is your opinion of Rear Admiral Zimmer?"

He tensed at the name but hoped the captain hadn't noticed. "Uh… Well." The room seemed to shrink.

"It's alright. I realize your previous assignment left you with some unpleasant feelings, but putting that event aside, what is your honest assessment of the man? This is strictly between you and me."

"He's an arrogant blowhard," Hapker replied bluntly. Captain Arden raised an eyebrow. *I should be more tactful.* Every time someone mentioned the name Zimmer, though, he imagined them shaking a hornet's nest. "This was my first impression, so I'm not just basing my feelings on how he nearly ended my career."

"Your own actions nearly ended your career, Commander."

Hapker's anxiety spiked. Not once since the captain appointed him a few months ago had he brought up that incident. "I realize this, Sir, and I'm not trying to shift blame," he replied more calmly than he felt. "I meant to say his method of command compelled me to the actions that nearly led to my dismissal from the PG-Force."

"What do you mean by his method of command?"

"He refuses to listen to the advice of his officers, even when presented with compelling evidence. While many admire him for his intelligence and years of experience, I believe his ego and prejudices limit him. He never admits when he's wrong and when things don't turn out the way he expects them, he somehow makes others look and feel responsible." His heart raced but speaking out about Zimmer lifted his mood.

The captain looked thoughtful. "And you came to this opinion before you got into trouble?"

"Yes, Sir. I could cite you several examples if you'd like."

Captain Arden flicked his hand. "No, that's quite alright. I'm familiar with how the admiral operates. Do you know why I requested you as my commanding officer?"

Hapker leaned forward. "I've been wondering, Sir."

"As subordinates, we should do as we are told, even if we disagree. Your previous actions imply that you will disobey the chain of command whenever you do not want to do something."

He opened his mouth to protest but the captain held up a hand.

"I don't, however, believe this one incident sets a precedent. You no doubt felt strongly about what was happening and you faced a moral dilemma."

"Yes, Sir." *Maybe someone finally understands.*

"Although following the chain of command is important, we shouldn't always do so blindly. I actually find what you did to be noble. You were backed into a corner and had to choose between doing something against your conscience or disobeying and risking a court martial."

"I don't make a habit of disobeying orders, Captain," Hapker said, "but it would have plagued me for the rest of my life if I had done what he ordered."

"That's what I hoped for when I took you on. Out here, we are often confronted with moral dilemmas. There will be times when we must do things we don't agree with. At the same time, it is our responsibility to speak up when we are directed to do something we consider immoral. I am currently faced with such a dilemma."

"Regarding Jori."

"Regarding both him and his brother. While I admire the fact that you're acting as his advocate, the safety of our crew—and our people—must always come first."

Hapker swallowed down the lump rising in his throat. "I understand, Sir."

"I hope so. There's something else as well. What do you think the admiral will do when he finds out we have the Mizuki Princes on our ship?"

The room chilled. "He'll order us to bring the princes in for questioning."

"Exactly what I was thinking." The captain frowned. "I worry about the consequences if we do such a thing."

The pit of Hapker's stomach twinged. "If Emperor Mizuki found out, he'd have a valid argument for getting several other dignitaries to side with him against us. We'd have war."

"How do you feel about a war with the Tredons?"

"Despite how disagreeable they are, warring with them would be a terrible mistake."

"Are you telling me this because you think it's what I want to hear, or is this your true opinion? You are a strategist, after all, and strategy is a war tactic."

"Yes, but I didn't choose to be a strategist so I could fight in a war."

"Tell me more." The captain's attentiveness reflected a genuine interest.

Hapker relaxed. "I assume you know I was a Pholatian Protector for a while."

"You received a medal during that time, if I remember correctly."

Hapker smiled. "Well, my father was one too. As was my grandfather and great grandfather."

The captain's eyebrows rose. "A family of Protectors. That's quite a legacy. How do they feel about you being a strategist for the Cooperative?"

Hapker sighed. Protectors differed from the militaries of other cultures. They were entirely true to their name—always on the defense, never on the offense—and they never sacrificed innocent lives.

In the eyes of his father, the Cooperative fell far short of these ideals. "Opinions vary." His cheeks burned. "On the one hand, my family worries I will get caught up in a war. On the other, they understand fighting is sometimes necessary to protect people."

"But you don't think war is necessary now?"

"No. Not at all, Sir. My father taught me that strategy isn't just about fighting. It's about safeguarding ourselves and others while incurring as few casualties as possible. If we go to war with the Tredons, many will die, and not only the fighters. The Tredons will probably use our value of human lives against us. They will strike at military bases as well as homesteads. So, the best strategy in this case is to *avoid* warring with them."

Captain Arden nodded. "I'm glad we're on the same page in all this. So what if the admiral orders us to bring the children to him?"

The notion sent a cold sensation into the marrow of his bones. "Must we tell him?"

"We do. Although I'm given a lot of leeway to make my own decisions without involving our superiors, I must inform him about this."

Hapker swallowed a lump in his throat. "What about your promise to Jori?"

The captain sighed. "I'm hoping for the best, Commander. I'm hoping the admiral will share my opinion."

The hardness in Hapker's throat constricted. His face flushed with heat and his skin prickled as air from the vent whispered over the sweat on his neck. "Sir. We promised the boy."

The captain looked him dead in the eyes. "Our first promise is to the Cooperative. If the admiral orders me to send the boys to him and I agree, what will you do?"

Hapker turned away. He sat back, elbow on the chair arm, and stroked his chin. If he disobeyed again, his career would be over. Worse, he'd return home and try to make it up to his father by living as his clone. If he obeyed, though, he'd betray Jori's trust and for no reason other than to satisfy Zimmer's political desire.

His father had warned him about this. The Cooperative was still wrought with political differences that complicated their ability to decide the best course of actions needed to obtain a greater good. Pholatia had its share of politics, but at least the greater good had already been achieved.

This was why being a Pholatian Protector wasn't enough. He yearned for more. Being a part of the Cooperative gave him the opportunity he'd sought while also satisfying his desire to explore the universe.

Perhaps he wasn't cut out for this life. The choices were too difficult. He wanted to fulfill his promise to Jori, but at the same time, he had developed an admiration for Captain Arden. The man was nothing like Rear Admiral Zimmer. He wasn't only logical, he was wise. He didn't just listen to his crew, he listened with respect and consideration.

Hapker met the captain's eyes. Serve him or return home? The choice wasn't easy, but he'd already decided when he left Pholatia. His only option now was to see this through. "I trust you, Sir. If you truly believe letting the admiral take the boys into custody is the right thing, I'm more inclined to go along with your decision than his."

The captain stared into his eyes as though weighing the truth of his words. "We haven't known one another for long, so I greatly appreciate your support. However, if the admiral gives such orders and I follow them, it won't be because I believe it is right. It will be because of my loyalty to the Cooperative."

Hapker shook his head. "My loyalty is inspired by individuals. Although I'm loyal to the ideals of the Prontaean Cooperative, not everyone is."

"That's a matter of perspective. There's seldom a one hundred percent agreement on the right thing to do. If we are given the order, we must trust it. After all, they might have information we don't."

Hapker resisted the urge to wipe the sweat from his brow. "Yes, Sir, but please don't make me take part. If the admiral won't allow Jori to go home, let me be off duty. It will be hard enough for me to live with such a decision. I don't want to see the boy's face when I betray him." Nausea rolled in his gut.

The captain sucked in a breath. "Better to betray the Tredons than the Cooperative. No one ever said serving would always be easy. If you can't serve the way you're supposed to, perhaps you should go back to being a Pholatian Protector."

Hapker's skin burned as though something had stung him. Was this what the captain wanted or was it simply the kindly advice it seemed to be? The captain's face betrayed nothing, but his tone suggested the latter.

"You're right." He sighed despairingly and sat back in his chair. "This is what I signed up for."

Although the captain's expression didn't change, he seemed pleased with the response. "And none of us can know how it will all turn out."

"*I'll just have to wait on Brinar's Bluff until then,*" his mother's favorite phrase chimed in his head.

"Have faith in the system," the captain added.

Hapker's stomach soured at that. He couldn't bring himself to have faith in Zimmer, but he peered deep into the captain's eyes and saw hope.

*****

3790:260:07:23. Armed guards entered the bar, radiating purpose. Ander Vizubi suppressed a groan as they marched over.

"You were right, Sir," Quigley whispered. "There's only four, though. We can take them."

Vizubi took a swig of his beer, then plunked the bottle onto the table a little too loudly. "My orders stand."

"You sure? They don't look happy."

One guard approached with a direct stare that reflected a no-nonsense attitude. His physique matched Vizubi's but his weapons and armor gave him an advantage.

"I'm sure." Vizubi stood to meet the man while his team remained seated. Though his instinct told him to fight, he kept his posture open and relaxed. "Hey. How's it going, friend?"

"Guillermo wants to talk to you," the guard replied in a decidedly unfriendly tone.

Vizubi shrugged. "Sure. No problem. You mind if a friend of mine comes along?"

Bari rose.

The guards tensed. "Just you," the lead said.

Shit. Guillermo must be pissed. Vizubi signaled for Bari to sit and wore a smile for the guard. "Okay. I'm all yours."

After Woolley's request to depart from the station had been denied, they'd suspected this moment to come. There wasn't a damned thing they could do about it except give in and hope to talk Guillermo down.

He suppressed the rising angst as the guards escorted him. Not telling Guillermo what he'd discovered had been a risk. Considering the Grapnes' efforts to get the children, he wouldn't put it past his old boss to try something too.

They reached Guillermo's office. Vizubi inhaled deeply as the lead guard pressed the comm and announced him. The golden door swished open.

"Ah, you've returned, my friend!" Guillermo said with arms spread about as wide as his fake smile.

"Yeah, I got what I came for, but you won't like what I found out."

Guillermo leaned back into his chair with a stern glint. "Hence the reason you didn't share your intel before submitting your request to leave."

The subtle accusation sent a twinge through Vizubi's gut, but he didn't react.

He'd been considering how to pass along the information while omitting the key piece. There was no dancing around the truth, though. He might as well spit it out and hope for the best. "The Tredon children that were here earlier are the emperor's sons."

Guillermo's eyes popped as he lurched from his chair. "His heirs! You mean I had the most wanted creatures in the galaxy right under my very nose? Mierda! I could have arrested them." Guillermo sat back down and tapped his chin. "Then traded them for ransom or sold them to the highest bidder."

"I believe that's what the Grapnes intended to do," Vizubi said. "But that wouldn't have been wise. The last thing you want is to earn the wrath of the Dragon Emperor."

Guillermo laughed. "My friend, surely you know me better. I would have made it seem Shekaka was behind it."

Vizubi shook his head. Guillermo had been trying to undermine his rival for years, but this wasn't the way. "The emperor would attack this station regardless of which of you abducted his sons."

"Hmm. Perhaps you're right. There's information that I could've gleaned from them, though, and information is money, my friend." Guillermo's eyes lit up. "Your captain has them in his custody, does he not?"

Vizubi's insides tumbled. This was the part he'd worried about. "Yes, but he won't trade me and my team for them."

Guillermo cocked his head. "No?"

"No." Vizubi held an unyielding stare. "Not only will you make an enemy of the Tredons, you'll also invite trouble from the

Cooperative. They're already encroaching on this station's independence."

Guillermo leaned back and stroked his chin. Vizubi forced himself to remain still in the unsettling silence. If only he had another card to play. If this didn't work, he and his team would be screwed.

The silence stretched. Sweat formed on Vizubi's brow and upper lip as his old boss held the reins to his fate.

Guillermo puffed. "You're right, of course."

The tightness in Vizubi's shoulders eased. "I'm sorry about the lost opportunity, but it's probably for the best."

"Yes, yes, my friend." Guillermo flicked his hand. "Did you find out anything else?"

"Nothing."

"No word on Shekaka's doings? Nothing about what the emperor is up to?"

"Not a thing. You have my word."

Guillermo's eyes narrowed.

"I keep my word," Vizubi stressed. "Some things about me have changed, but that's not one of them."

Guillermo rose with a tight smile. "Very well. You are free to go." He raised his palm before Vizubi turned away. "Next time you visit my station, though, you had better not procrastinate on coming to see me. Friends or not, I will not tolerate disrespect."

"Understood. It won't happen again." Vizubi resisted the urge to swallow. He'd come up with a reasonable excuse for why he hadn't reported earlier. However, giving it now would sound like the bullshit it was.

"Good. I'll release the hold on your ship."

Vizubi dipped his head. "Thank you." Guillermo would likely delay their departure a little longer just to make a point, but he hoped the man wouldn't change his mind.

Vizubi headed for the exit, keeping his pace normal despite the urge to get the hell out of this place.

31
A Seed is Planted

3790:261:00:24. Mik Calloway stifled a yawn. Eight hours of menial safety inspections took a toll. The job was simple, boring as hell, but one that any greener could do. His new status should have meant this kind of monkey-work was beneath him. *Blast that suckpot of a commander.*

He licked his lips and imagined a hard drink running down his throat. It must wait, though. He hadn't worked out in a couple of days and a bout of boxing would do him some good.

He stepped into the conveyor. "Deck five, quarters." His mouth soured when he said it.

Thanks to the commander, he still shared a bunk with three privies. When he received his promotion, he should have moved out and into his own quarters, but the reprimand pushed the date back by thirty days.

The conveyor let him off at a congested hallway. It reminded him of his dorm room at the PG Institute. A pair of women giggled as they passed him. Another gave him a dirty look, which he promptly returned. One night and she assumed he belonged to her.

A group of privates chatted further down. One man leaned casually against the wall with a stupid grin on his face as he talked to Celenia. He was wasting his time. No way she would give herself to that joker.

Two guys sat on a bench studying something on a tablet. Calloway expected it to be work-related but glimpsed cartoon characters. *Spiffle, the Kooky Alien.* What idiots. Everyone knew there was no such thing as aliens in the cosmic sense. Humans had explored much of the galaxy and there had never been a single sign of extraterrestrial intelligence. Animals, yes, but nothing even close to beings like him. He was superior.

He reached his room and the door slid open automatically.

"Are you friggin kidding me? The boy can't be—" His roommate, Agni, clamped his mouth shut. Sergeant Naran pressed his lips together and gave Agni a warning look.

"What? What's going on?" Calloway asked.

Agni shrugged. "Nothing."

Calloway huffed. "It's about that Tredon brat, isn't it?"

"It's not your concern," Naran said in an authoritative tone, like he had any pull over him when off-duty.

Calloway pointed at his roommate. "But it's his?" Agni and the sergeant were best buds, as though being from the same planet and the same continent made them brothers or some stupid shit.

Naran glowered. "Mind your own business."

"Tchah. Whatever. I couldn't care less about what you duds are talking about."

He opened the lower cabinet of his desk. The sonometer he used for keeping track of his vitals and stats while working out was near the top, but he pretended to rummage about until he located the recorder.

This device had helped him a great deal over the years. He'd gotten one of his roommates at the institute kicked out when he learned of and reported the man's selling of unsanctioned foodstuffs. He didn't say how he found out, of course. Then there was the time he recorded a woman's confessions of what she liked in a mate and used this knowledge to charm her.

Mostly, the recorder kept him apprised of all the juicy gossip.

Once he triggered the bug, he grabbed the sonometer and gathered his workout gear.

"See ya," he said as he headed out the door. *Chumps.*

*****

3790:261:02:58. Mik Calloway flinched. "He's what?"

The pounding of his heart increased each time he replayed the recording—and so did the heat flaring in his chest.

"No fucking way." Calloway threw the recorder into his desk drawer, sending an echoing crack around the room. If his bunkmates had been here, they'd have acted like his outburst was an intrusion—as if their very existence wasn't already an intrusion. "I can't believe this rubbish."

He left his quarters without bothering to put his other stuff away and fumed. Why was this being kept secret? Everyone should be told. He had to be careful, though. He couldn't afford another reprimand.

People moved out of his way as he stormed down the corridors and into the lounge. A sharp grinding pain surged from his jaw down to his balled fists. He plunked onto a stool at the far end of the bar and fumed.

"Vodka, neat," he barked at the attendant. He could have ordered from the counter device. Like most others, though, he preferred an actual person when they were available. The man moved slower than the machine, but not by much.

As soon as the attendant set down his drink, he downed a mouthful and grimaced as the pleasant burn washed down his throat. The heel of his foot drummed the floor without rhythm. *All this time.* He couldn't believe it. That boy was the son of the same monstrous taipan responsible for his family's death.

Tasha's dead eyes rolled back into his thoughts. He slammed his glass on the counter. "Another!"

The attendant served a second drink. Calloway stared onto its liquid surface at his reflection. In it, he imagined his face caked with blood. Some was his, but most belonged to her.

Her dead, beautiful eyes dominated his attention now. The memory of that nightmarish day flashed in his brain. Her torn, blood-soaked clothes barely covered her thin little body. Her arms jutted out at crooked angles. Tooth and claw marks raked her bronze skin.

Those fucking animals! He slapped his glass down again. A splash of his vodka spilled out.

The attendant frowned and turned back to whoever he was talking to. The two people were close enough for Calloway to discern their voices, but not close enough for him to understand what they said. He ignored them and gulped down the rest of his drink.

He waved to the attendant to get another but stopped when he saw the man's conversation partner.

Young Sergeant Siven Addams, the too-good-looking, boot-licking monkey with his pretty copper hair. Other than the attendant, Addams sat alone. He probably waited for his girlfriend,

Felissa—a woman he'd do himself in a heartbeat if she'd ever bothered.

Lucky suckpot. The sergeant didn't deserve that woman, or his position for that matter. His excellent marksmanship didn't justify his rank.

His rank. Then he already knows! Calloway signaled the attendant for another drink.

He had to act quickly before Addams' girlfriend showed up, along with a herd of his other snooty friends. As soon as he received his vodka, he moved to the seat next to the man. "Perfect time for a hard drink, huh?"

"I'm drinking a virlini," Addams replied blandly.

Non-alcoholic then. *How does a wuss like this get a woman like Felissa?* "Really? I'd think you'd want something harder after having to deal with the spoiled little prince all day."

Addams' copper brows rose. He set down his glass and glanced around. "How in the heck did you hear about that?" he hissed.

"I overheard Sergeant Naran tell Agni." Calloway smiled inwardly. One of two things would happen here. Addams would make a report against Naran for telling a privy or he would figure that since the secret was already out, he could tell a certain someone else. Either way, Calloway wouldn't be implicated.

"Damn. No one's supposed to know." Addams' dismay turned into anger.

"Everyone should learn about this, especially your friend… What's his name? The medic?" Calloway tapped his finger to his chin in mock thought. "Oh, yeah… Laren."

Addams remained silent. The man didn't much care for him, but that was fine. He hated him too. Still, they had this one thing in common. He bet the sergeant didn't enjoy protecting the little dragon spawn either.

"Wasn't he working as a medic at a small outpost when the emperor attacked it?" Calloway continued. "His wife and child were killed, right?"

Calloway and Laren had connected once. They'd both lost people they cared about to the Tredons. They had a bit of a falling out, though. Something about Calloway screwing his girl. Whatever. It wasn't his fault she preferred him over the stupid medic with a weirdo-haircut.

It wouldn't work to tell Laren about the princes himself, but Addams was perfect for the job. The two were best buds, like cell mates who watched each other's backs and kept each other company at night.

"Can you imagine what it must be like for him?" he said, rubbing it in. "Having to try and save the life of the older brat while the little one walks free, all without a care in the world for all the people his father has murdered?"

"They're just children," Addams replied stiffly.

"Yeah, but they will grow up someday. Hell, the young one's already shown how dangerous he can be. Hammer said he saw that child kill four Grapnes. You were part of the team that went down to the Blue Blight, right?" He knew the answer so didn't bother letting Addams reply. "The little monster is already a killer and he's only ten cycles old. I can't imagine what we will have on our hands if his big brother wakes."

Addams still didn't comment, but he seemed to consider it. The seed had been planted, and so Calloway left it alone for now. Perhaps later, he'd make other comments to help the seed grow.

32
Intercept

3790:261:03:41. Ander Vizubi placed his hands on his hips and gazed over the crowds that filled the vastness of the docking port. He closed his eyes and inhaled the stale scent of the place he used to call home. A heaviness fell over him at the same time. A few fond memories but numerous regrets.

He turned away and entered the skywalk, leaving the echoes of the past behind. His pace quickened as he neared the tranquility of the present.

"Andy, wait!"

Vizubi jerked to a halt and whirled around. A skinny man waved as he sprinted to the gateway.

Vizubi crossed his arms "What the hell are you doing here?"

Hesteben reached him and bent over to catch his breath. "I want to go with you."

Vizubi's throat caught. "Go with me?"

His brother straightened. A broad smile etched his face. "Yeah, man. Go with you."

Vizubi evaluated him with a squint. The light in Hesteben's eyes indicated he was high. His expression reflected his eagerness. The large duffle bag he carried meant he'd had time to pack and consider his decision.

Vizubi bit the inside of his lip. "What made you change your mind?"

"Well, I realized you're right. I can't keep living like this under Guillermo's constant scrutiny. I need to be my own, man."

"If you go with me, you must give up the drugs."

Hesteben flicked his wrist in a dismissive gesture. "You said the Cooperative will help me overcome my addiction."

"In part, yes, but it also takes a lot of willpower. Your decision seems too rash for me to believe you want this."

"Pfft." Hesteben frowned. "First you want to rescue me from this place, and now you want to discourage me from leaving?"

Vizubi rubbed his brow. "I don't want to discourage you. I just need to make sure this is what you really want."

"Yeah, man. Of course it is." Hesteben's eager grin returned.

Vizubi stroked his jaw. He'd been wishing for this, but it came about too easily and unexpectedly. Was this his brother's idea or did Guillermo put him up to it?

Either way, he couldn't say no. Whatever trouble his brother brought, he'd deal with it when it came. "Alright. Let's go."

After an introduction to the crew and getting Hesteben set up in the sleeping area, he ordered his pilot, Staff Sergeant Woolley, to head out. As his brother fell into the slump of coming off his high, Woolley disembarked from the station. The process was as uneventful and dull as the slow crawl through the station's buffer zone.

Vizubi stared at the navigational controls without really seeing them. As copilot, he had nothing to do until they could activate the arc drive, and that was still ten minutes away—enough time to chew over his brother's sudden change of heart.

The console flashed red. Vizubi jerked forward and examined the readings. His hackles rose. "There's a large ship in the vicinity. It seems to be on an intercept course. I'm prepping weapons."

"Ya think it's intentional?" Woolley asked.

Vizubi initiated active sensors. "I'm not sure, but I'd rather be safe than sorry."

He sat on the edge of his seat and leaned over the console, waiting for results. When the other ship's information came in, he cursed. "Oh, shit. We're in big trouble. Change course."

"Yes, Sir." Woolley dipped his head, causing his light curly hair to jounce. "What is it?"

Vizubi broke into a sweat as he alerted the crew and activated shields. "It's the *Virtuous Dealings*."

"What?" Woolley barked. "I thought they were supposed to turn themselves in at the Melna check-in post."

"They were." *Damn the Overseer*. He must have planned this.

"Fuck."

Vizubi's stomach heaved as his pilot turned and increased speed. The sensors indicated the Cougar stayed on them and approached fast. He stabbed the comm. "Captain of *Virtuous Dealings*. The Cooperative won't hand over those children. It didn't work on the Blue Blight. It won't work now. All you'll do is piss off the PG-Force."

His shoulders tightened he waited for a reply. Seconds passed, then minutes. "They're not answering."

"And they're still closing in," Woolley said.

"Is there something you can do?"

"Other than activate shields and use our weapons? Nope. There's nowhere to hide and that ship is faster than ours. We don't even have time to return to the station."

Vizubi pulled out his cross and kissed it before opening another channel. "Depnaugh, this is Ander Vizubi of the Bastion-class, *Fortification*. I'm being pursued by an Angolan Cougar-class ship named *Virtuous Dealings*. This ship is wanted by the Cooperative. If you help us, I'll make sure you're compensated."

"They won't get here in time." Woolley's upper lip beaded with sweat.

Vizubi swallowed. "Maybe not, but I sent it as a general broadcast. Other ships will hear it and it might convince the Grapnes to back off."

He glanced at the display. Long range sensors showed the Cougar approaching firing distance but no other vessels nearby.

"Sir?" Woolley's forehead crinkled. "How did they know where to intercept us?"

"The Overseer probably bought the information and passed it on to the Cougar."

"It can't be that easy, Sir. There's a lot of space around the station. They shouldn't have known which direction we headed, yet their course indicated otherwise."

Vizubi's stomach knotted. "Maybe they paid other ships to look out for us."

"I suppose."

Vizubi didn't like the uncertainty in his pilot's tone, but how else could they have done it? "Two minutes to firing range."

"I can increase speed into the red zone," Woolley replied.

"Will that give us enough of a lead?"

The pilot's throat bobbed. "I doubt it, Sir. That ship caught up to a Serpent vessel. It'll undoubtedly catch up to a Bastion."

"Then let's stay alive." Vizubi swallowed the dryness from his mouth. He might as well succumb to the inevitable. Besides, he still had a team of warriors and a fighting chance.

The minutes passed. The anticipated blast still caused him to flinch. He returned fire in rapid succession.

It didn't do any good. The enemy's shields were stronger.

The *Fortification*'s energy cannons alternated between discharging and regenerating. Only so much energy could be replenished at a time, and soon the weapons died. *Damn.* Shields were down to eleven percent. Vizubi glanced at the projectile weapon storage. Could he spare one or should he let the enemy think he was out? It depended on whether the Grapnes meant to kill them or take them captive. He guessed the latter and silently prayed he was right.

Another energy strike landed. Shield strength dropped to three percent. He gripped his armrests as his heart raced.

Woolley turned to him with wide eyes. "We're done for, Sir."

The ship rocked. Vizubi braced himself for the end.

The tremor subsided. *That wasn't so bad.* Vizubi checked the stats. Shields were down, but the hull had no damage. Some of that blast should have gone through.

He blew out. He'd been right. They wanted them alive, so they had fired at less than half power. He jabbed the internal comm. "Everyone suit up! Prepare to be boarded. The Grapnes are coming."

Woolley unbuckled and jumped to his feet. Vizubi did the same. They dressed in two minutes, then spent a minute or so prepping their phaser rifles.

The pilot lowered himself back into his seat and checked the stats. "They've sent a message," he said. "Text only."

Vizubi noted the enemy's shields were down and debated whether to use the projectiles. With the right aim, he could damage their ship enough to cripple them, but projectile weapons were slower. The enemy would detect them long before they arrived and take the opportunity to eliminate them or evade.

"They're telling us to surrender," Woolley continued. "Come quietly into our starboard docking bay."

Vizubi rubbed his jaw. Battling from here was pointless. They were outmatched. If they docked, though, they'd still have a fighting chance. Grapnes generally had little combat skills. With the prowess of his people, they might have an advantage. One problem—Hesteben wouldn't be in any shape to fight.

He activated his comm. "Bari, make sure my brother is suited up. Don't give him any weapons."

"Yes, Sir. What's the plan after that?"

Vizubi responded by opening the primary channel. "The *Fortification* can't take on the Grapne ship, so we're taking the fight to them. They've instructed us to dock in their bay and we're complying. However, we won't just give up. Stock up on as many weapons as you can carry and prepare to shoot our way to their bridge."

*****

3790:261:05:12. Ander Vizubi hoisted his RR-5 rifle. Quigley positioned on the opposite edge of the exit. Bari and Fung crouched at their feet while Hesteben leaned against the back wall without a care in the world.

The gangway lowered, opening the hatch on the port side. Vizubi tensed. He kept his breathing even and his mind hyper focused.

Pitch blackness spread out before them. He eye-clicked the floodlight atop his helmet. The team followed suit and illuminated nothing more than shadows. No weapon bots, no drones, and no Grapnes.

"Where are they?" Quigley said.

"Lights out, try thermal view." Vizubi clicked over. His visor darkened, making him blind.

"Nothing," his crew replied one by one.

"Night vision," Vizubi ordered. "Steben, stay here. I'll call you when it's clear."

"Yeah, man."

He took point, checking down the left side of his ship with Bari while Quigley and Fung headed to the right. Nothing jumped from the shadows. No unusual objects lurked in the corners. The dock was empty. Glancing at the stats on his visor, it seemed not even air hid in this bay.

He met Quigley behind their vessel. Without a word, they parted and followed the walls around. When he reached an entrance to the body of the Cougar, he stopped and waited for her.

"I didn't find anything," she said.

"Not a damned thing," Bari added.

"Alright," Vizubi replied, "let's get the hell out of here. Hesteben, come on."

His brother ambled out. Vizubi eye-clicked through a series of files and found schematics for an Angolan Cougar. "After we get through, we go right. Ready?"

"Ready," four voices responded.

He punched the panel beside the door. Nothing happened. He hit it again. "Shit. I think they locked it. Fung, do you know how to unlock this?"

"I'll give it a try, Sir."

She popped open the casing and fiddled with the insides. At one point, she fired into it with a low-level burst. Nothing worked. Fifteen minutes passed. Hesteben fell asleep.

Fung sagged. "Sir, I'm out of options. I just can't get this without damaging the door and locking us out here permanently."

"Did we bring a thermite torch?" Vizubi asked, though he knew the answer.

"I'll get it, Sir," Bari replied.

He returned with a foot-long cylinder, six centimeters across, and an armload of cartridges. "Sir, these doors are thick. They're designed to withstand an impact of a docking ship coming in too fast. I don't think I have enough thermite to burn out a hole."

"Can we cut a hand-sized one here?" Vizubi pointed on the door beside the panel. "If we can reach a hand through, we'll open this from the other side."

"Possibly, but it will take a while, and we've only got one chance. The thermite won't last."

Vizubi sighed. "Meaning if they seal off other areas inside, we're screwed."

"Can we go outside and cut an easier hole elsewhere?" Quigley asked.

Vizubi shook his head. "The entire hull is just as thick. The only places to get in are places we don't want to go."

"Sorry, Sir," Quigley said. "I didn't think to bring equipment to infiltrate a starship."

"That's alright, Corporal. Neither did I."

"Why are they doing this?" Woolley asked.

"All they need to do is hold us until they can make arrangements for the trade," Vizubi replied.

"If the Cooperative won't trade, all they need to do is open that hatch and let us out into space," Bari added.

"Devious little snakes, aren't they?" Fung said.

Vizubi looked up and huffed. He caught sight of a black semispherical object in the corner and an idea sparked. "They're watching us."

"And probably laughing their asses off," Bari muttered.

Vizubi ignored him as his thoughts churned. They were out of options. They could remain here and wait it out, or somehow get the Grapnes to bring them further into the ship. "If we stay out here, we have enough air and food on the *Fortification* to last several days. However, if the Cooperative won't negotiate—"

"Which we know they won't," Quigley said.

"—they will easily be able to get rid of us by opening the exit, letting us out, and blasting us into oblivion. We have to get inside."

"What good would that do?" Bari asked.

"If we get inside," Vizubi continued, "they will lock us away, but maybe we can figure out how to escape. We also have a chance of convincing them this idea of theirs won't work and that releasing us is the best way to keep the PG-Force from hunting them down."

"There's no guarantee they'll feed us," Bari said.

"They wouldn't gain anything by starving us to death," Vizubi replied.

"Until they learned the Cooperative won't trade," Quigley added.

Vizubi moved to massage the headache from his forehead and bumped his helmet instead. "Anyone have any ideas?"

No one responded.

"I have one, but you won't like it," Vizubi said. "Everyone put all your weapons back, then meet back over here."

"Sir?"

Vizubi pointed to the corner. “If they’re watching us, they’ll see we’re unarmed. Perhaps they’ll let us in.”

“Then we can take them out in hand-to-hand combat.” Woolley’s voice carried his enthusiasm.

“Only if there aren’t too many,” Vizubi said.

Everyone complied while Hesteben continued to snooze. When they were ready, Vizubi lifted his brother to his feet and jostled him. “Wake up, Steben, and raise your hands.”

“Wha—?” Hesteben swayed. “What are we doing, man?”

“Surrendering.”

“Oh. Alright.”

“Raise your hands,” Vizubi said again.

His brother gained his balance and put up his hands along with the team. They stood like that for nearly five minutes before the door light flashed red.

The tension in Vizubi’s neck relaxed. “We should be in shortly. No one make a move unless I give my say-so. If the odds are too great, we’ll go peacefully.”

The double doors slid apart, revealing a smaller room. They stepped inside where another red light blinked, creating a crimson glow. After they were shut in, pressure equalized and air filled the area. When the light turned green, Vizubi removed his helmet and hung it on his belt clip. “Get ready.”

The next entrance glided upward. Vizubi tensed, expecting to meet a handful of Grapnes with weapons aimed. He found a dozen armed bots instead and froze.

“Shit.” No way they could get past those.

“Looks like they’ve got us in a noose, Sir,” Quigley said.

“Those devious little bastards,” Bari added.

Vizubi sagged. *Damn it.* He should have expected this.

33
Sacrifice and Slaves

3790:262:08:13. J.D. Hapker waited as Jori's eyes darted over the schemster board. He undoubtedly noticed the trap and was trying to figure a way out.

Hapker smiled inwardly. Not only would he finally win a game, Jori seemed more at ease. The past two days had been peaceful. They played schemster and wall ball every day. Their competitions were fierce but friendly. They even had polite conversations, though the boy remained distant.

Jori took a key piece from Hapker. He held a stony expression, as usual, but his eyes radiated a confident satisfaction.

Hapker pulled back. "Huh?" He rubbed his jaw and examined the playing field. He couldn't ignore the boy's colonel. Taking it would force him to break his trap but leaving it would mean certain death for his general. "You've lost all your colonels," he said as he removed the game piece.

Jori shrugged. "I don't need them to win."

His spine tingled at the boy's dispassionate tone. "I hope you aren't as ruthless in a real battle."

"Why wouldn't I be? If they can't do their jobs well enough, there are plenty of other men ready to take their place."

The comment shouldn't have surprised him, but his jaw dropped, nonetheless. "You would sacrifice your own people?"

"That's the biggest difference between you and me, Commander. If I want something, I will fight for it no matter what the cost. While you, on the other hand, are so worried about what will be lost that nothing is ever gained."

Hapker frowned. Admiral Zimmer had made a similar remark. "I'd rather gain nothing than sacrifice others," he said with more confidence than he felt.

Jori swept his arm across the holo-board. "If these were real men, they gave their lives when they chose to become warriors."

"What about the slaves?"

Jori tilted his head.

"What if this were a space battle?" Hapker continued. "Your ships carry slaves, don't they? Slaves for trading, slaves to do the menial labor the warriors are too good for, slaves for…" E*ntertainment.* He suppressed a shiver. General Sakon of the *Brimstone* was best known for raiding the planets along the Cooperative borders. Those he didn't butcher or leave for dead were taken and never heard from again—no doubt working in Tredon mines… Or worse.

"We wouldn't be able to function without them," the boy said carefully, as though sensing a trap.

"All the more reason not to sacrifice them."

Jori's eyes narrowed. "We live in different worlds, Commander. You have no idea what the stakes are."

"You're right. I don't understand your lifestyle, but where I come from, people don't sacrifice others for their own selfish interests."

Jori made a non-committing grunt.

Hapker tapped his chin. "When you have a chance, perhaps you should look up Xien Zhang's *Treatise on Humankind* on your MDS."

"Sounds like something my father would disapprove of."

"Maybe that's a reason to read it."

Jori shook his head. "I doubt it would do any good."

"Then what's the harm?"

Jori didn't answer but he had a gleam of interest in his eyes. Hapker applauded the boy's enthusiasm for reading. Security intelligence monitored his MDS and reported a diverse selection—more than just Pershornian warfare and Alkon's theories.

*****

3790:262:08:59. J.D. Hapker leaned back with a whistle. Despite his earlier confidence, he lost to the boy once again.

He tapped off the tabletop and the holographic image of the schemster game disappeared. “You’re amazing at this. You said General Sakon taught you to play?”

“My mother taught me first. Then I apprenticed with General Sakon for a few months.”

“Really?” Learning from a general didn’t surprise him, but the part about his mother sparked his interest. What he had read on Tredon culture never mentioned empresses, let alone ones who contributed to the education of their children.

“So, is your mother a warrior too?” he asked. If she taught Jori schemster, then perhaps she wasn’t as repressed as other women of Tredon.

Jori harrumphed. “Far from it,” he said in a dismissive, but not derisive, tone.

“Does she live with you on your ship?”

“Yes.”

Hapker didn’t let his brevity deter him. “So, she’s the empress, then?”

“Not exactly. No one has used that title in over a century.”

“No?” No wonder he hadn’t read about any.

The boy’s expression flickered with annoyance, but he still answered. “She’s my father’s concubine.”

“Oh, I see. She’s a slave, then.”

Jori darkened. Their earlier talk of sacrifice and slaves was probably why the boy didn’t want to discuss her, but at least he had his mother with him. The galaxy would be a much better place if everyone had a mom.

“What’s she like?” Hapker asked.

The boy’s lips pressed to a thin line.

“Don’t worry. I’m not trying to pry any secrets from you. I’m curious, is all.”

Jori’s face softened. “She’s kind.”

Hapker determined not to let Jori’s unwillingness to share bother him. He told him about his own mother and how she always seemed to know how to cheer him up. Despite the boy’s silence, the intensity of his focus indicated this subject interested him.

“I still love my mother,” Hapker added, “so it’s not childish or unmanly if you love your mom.”

“That’s a matter of opinion,” the boy said flatly.

He suppressed a sigh. “True enough, I suppose, but I’m not ashamed to admit it.”

“She sounds nice,” Jori replied in a surprisingly warm tone.

“Best mother in the galaxy.” Hapker smiled.

“So, your father didn’t consider her an influence of weakness?”

“No. Not at all. Moms are sometimes overprotective and are more about getting in touch with their feelings than dads are, but it’s a complementary balance. I don’t suppose you see much husband-wife relationships in the Tredon Empire?”

“It’s more common among the lower classes, but I doubt it’s the same as it is here.”

“That’s a shame. You know, women are just as intelligent and capab—”

Jori lifted his palm. “I’m not in the mood for another lesson on ethics, Commander. I can’t refute your logic other than to say, what is known and what is practiced are two different things.”

Hapker’s eyebrows lifted. From what he understood, Tredons viewed women as inferior. If their treatment was true, Jori didn’t seem to agree but went along with it anyway.

Hapker considered his reply. Since it wouldn’t do any good to press the issue, he changed the subject. “You don’t need to call me by my rank. We’ve gotten to know one another well enough to be on a first name basis. Call me J.D.”

Jori nodded but didn’t speak.

“Well.” Hapker rose. “What do you say we forget the mental exercises for the day and get some physical exercise?”

Jori stood. “Wall ball?”

Hapker grinned. “Wall ball.”

34
The Pack

3790:262:11:12. Jori swung at the ball and missed. The commander raised his fists in the air. "Yes!"

His exultation blew like a gust of wind into Jori's senses. It almost made him smile, but he dared not let the man see such a thing. *Emotion is weakness*.

Hapker panted as sweat poured down his red face. Wetness blotched the front of his shirt and armpits.

Jori's heart pounded and his breaths were deep, but neither strained. Hapker appeared tired but his own body was just getting warmed up.

Despite having lost another game of wall ball, it had been exhilarating. Hapker's height and reach gave him an advantage, but Jori liked the odds being against him. An easy challenge wasn't worth it.

It helped to sense Hapker's enjoyment. When his emotions mixed with his own, he forgot his worries for his brother. The swell of hostility from his surrounding enemies didn't affect him as much either.

The commander was different from anyone he had ever met. The man's kindness should have been a weakness, but Jori found his nature difficult to exploit.

He should hate this man and Hapker should hate him. Unlike the four guards standing outside the court, though, the commander held no hint of negative emotions. It puzzled him, but also put him at ease.

The man wore a huge grin, one that emphasized the crookedness of his mouth. Jori pressed his lips together to keep from smiling at his cheerful and annoyingly infectious humor. "You seem to take a lot of pride in being able to beat a mere boy, Commander."

Hapker laughed and clapped him on the back. "It's J.D., remember?"

Jori's grin pinched into his cheeks.

They exited the court and sat on a bench. As Jori basked in the commander's mood, something else crawled through his senses. The hairs on his arms and neck prickled like a hundred thousand tiny needles stabbing him at once. He focused on the guards where the swell of hateful emotions originated.

"Something's changed, hasn't it?" he asked Hapker.

"What do you mean?"

"The guards. They know, don't they?" Jori sensed the man's guilt, which answered his question. "I thought the captain said it was between us."

"Well, yes," Hapker replied. His feeling of dread nearly overwhelmed the ugly emotions of the guards. "But after discussing it more, he decided to inform the lieutenants and sergeants. Don't worry, though. They're to keep it to themselves."

Jori's body tensed and he clenched his fists as he analyzed them. They each exhibited about the same amount of hatred, yet their insignia indicated no lieutenants and only one sergeant. Since his senses told him Hapker didn't lie, perhaps their shared animosity was a coincidence.

"Are you alright?" Hapker asked.

"Yes," Jori replied despite the level of hard emotions pressing around him.

"You sure?"

Meeting the commander's eyes triggered his ability to focus on him and to push the guards' animosity aside.

"Yes, I'm sure," he replied, surprised that he really was alright. He should've been angry at the betrayal, but he couldn't ignite any ill feelings against this man.

Hapker stood. "Well, I'm done here for the day. Are you staying?"

Jori glanced at the guards and a pang of fear stabbed him. He gritted his teeth and forced it aside. *They don't scare me.* "A little while longer."

Hapker seemed unaware of Jori's apprehension. "I will see if Lieutenant Sharkey can come by. I bet she'd enjoy a game of wall ball."

Jori shrugged. Although something about the woman suggested she could hold her own against a man, the idea of exercising with her unsettled him. Then again, she didn't seem to have the same hostility toward him as the others.

"See you later for dinner," Hapker said.

Jori watched the man retreat and followed him with his senses. Each step away took the cheerful emotions with him like a slowly dimming light.

When Hapker had gone, the weight of the surrounding animosity struck him once more as his guards glared at him like ill-tempered blackbeasts.

He clenched his jaw, determined not to let them intimidate him, and headed to an empty mat to warm-up for his martial exercises. They trailed him but kept their distance.

"—cking monster."

Their overheard words stung, but Jori forced himself to concentrate on his moves. Front-snap kick. Jab. Jab. Upper cut.

"—grow up to be a psychop—"

Focus. Ignore them. Block. Dodge. Roundhouse kick.

"—see how he'd like it if we cut—"

Jori's emotions swayed between anger and shame. He'd seen enough horrors committed by his people to understand why the guards felt this way. *They think they're any better? They're nothing but a bunch of cowards.*

Block. Strike. Block. "Kee-ya!" Take-down.

The guards snickered. Heat spread over Jori's face. *Chimas!*

Control. Sensei Jeruko's advice echoed in his head. He relaxed his clenched fists and unclenched his jaw. After closing his eyes and focusing inward, he willed his tightened muscles to relax.

Calmness returned. Without giving them the satisfaction of knowing their words bothered him, he ignored them and strode to another part of the gym.

A small group gathered around the holo program. They burst into laughter. Jori found an open spot. The scene before him sent a heated spark through his body. *Calloway.* That chima fought a holo-man that looked like a Toradon senshi.

Jori's bottom lip trembled. *Don't you dare cry.* His throat ached from trying to hold back the swell of emotion.

Calloway noticed him and a grin spread across the man's face, along with a surge of gloating satisfaction.

Jori's internal heat intensified, burning away the hurt and shame. He clenched his jaw and stood as motionless as a blackbeast waiting to pounce.

"What?" Calloway said. "You got nothin' to say?"

Jori's heartbeat roared in his ears, muffling Calloway's voice. It took him a moment to register what the man had said.

Control. He forced himself to speak. "Yes." He managed to keep his tone even. "I suggest you try a mock-fight with a Munchani. This way if you win, it'll be more realistic."

Calloway's face darkened. Jori jutted his chin, satisfied the man had heard this slang term applied to a race of dwarf-like pacifists.

He broke eye contact and glanced at the control console. "What do you have this set at anyway? Level five?" He harrumphed. "Figures."

He'd beaten level five when he was eight years old. Granted, the holo-man had been programmed to match his relative strength and height, but the skill still applied.

A surge of fury emanated from the pompous chima. Darkened emotions closed in from all around as the guards and onlookers stepped closer.

Jori's heartbeat deepened and a cold sweat fell over him. Being surrounded and outnumbered by people full of hate hardened him. He balled his fists, ready for an attack. They held back, though. Perhaps they waited for him to make the first move, but he was no fool.

He wasn't a coward either. He glared at the men and women before him. Outwardly, he wore the raging mask Sensei Jeruko had taught him. Inwardly, he resisted the instinct to run away.

They didn't scare him. He'd faced far, far worse.

"Someone needs to teach you a lesson, boy," Calloway said.

"Really?" Jori huffed derisively. "You think you're capable of teaching me?"

Calloway stepped forward. "I know I am."

Jori stood his ground and bore his eyes into the man. "Go ahead. Give it a try."

He braced himself. If Calloway made a move, he'd slam his heel into the man's knee. Then he'd send his fist in an upward thrust to the chin as the man bent to keep his balance.

It wouldn't end there. The guards and the other onlookers inched closer. Jori kept his eyes on Calloway but surveyed a broader view for potential weaknesses and openings from the others. *I could take them all if I wasn't so small!*

"I promise, the only way you'll succeed is if all of you join in at once," he said. "Even then, *no one* will walk away." His voice hitched, but he maintained the menace.

Calloway harrumphed. "Why don't you show us what you've got?"

"Because I am not a fool."

Calloway crossed his arms. "That's right. You know better than to start trouble."

Jori narrowed his eyes. "I don't start trouble. I *finish* it." His blood raced like a raging river. His stance remained rigid but ready to strike at a moment's notice.

Someone else snorted derisively. "Your people start trouble all the time."

Jori jerked his head and glared at the man who spoke. "I'm not the one starting it this time, though, am I?"

Once Calloway fell, Jori would roll away and come up beside this brute, then swipe his long legs out from under him. The man would drop like a stone and he'd elbow him in the throat. He'd jump to his feet and swing his arm into the gut of the next person who came for him.

Calloway took another step. Jori snapped his attention back to him. His body bristled in anticipation. A vibration hummed through him. He clenched his jaw to keep from quivering.

An uneasiness cut through the turbulent storm of malice surrounding him.

"Shark-face," someone whispered.

A sense of guilt spiked through the crowd and a low murmur spread.

"Lieutenant Sharkey," another person said.

A surge of anxiety emanated from Calloway. "Saved by a woman." He twisted his mouth as he stepped back.

Jori's heart fluttered. "Yes, you were."

The crowd disbursed. Calloway's hatred seethed, but he left with the others.

Jori relaxed. His skin tingled as the adrenaline slowly wore off. It was over… For now.

*****

3790:262:17:10. Jori gave up on trying to sleep. His thoughts spun like a pulsar. One moment his temper flared as he replayed the scene with Calloway. The next it turned off as he analyzed his conversations with the commander. Round and around it went.

He sat up and probed with his senses to determine which guards were on duty. Not that he feared Calloway, but he needed some time to think without his negative vibes interfering. After seven going on eight day-cycles, Jori easily recognized the unique lifeforces of those who kept watch over him. Two of the four outside the quarters now carried animosity against him but they never expressed it. Another man had a bland character. The fourth person held a lighter essence—Lieutenant Sharkey, or Shark-face as some called her.

He didn't know her well, but her presence reassured him. She reminded him of a female blackbeast. Not in an outwardly ugly way. When this creature cared for young, it fostered a deep contentment. If danger came, her spirit exploded into a hellfire. Not that he'd seen Sharkey angry, but she seemed oddly protective of him. That, and Hapker trusted her.

He dressed quietly and left the chambers as Hapker slept. Sharkey gave him a small smile, but no one spoke as they followed him.

The ride on the conveyor and his stroll to the center of the ship promised the quietude he needed. When he entered the arboretum, the guards remained close enough to keep an eye on him but far enough to give him a solitude. A fair number of people strolled about or sat among the bushes and flowers, yet they kept their distance too.

He found a secluded bench under a small tree. Some sort of carmine fruit hung, gleaming with ripeness. He stared into the branches in awe of the red-capped bird chirping above. He didn't get to visit the wilds on the planets of his home territory often, but when he did, their array of life captivated him. To have a forest, albeit a tamer one, on a spaceship amazed him.

He sat back and admired the view as well as the calm sensations surrounding him. Despite people like Calloway, an overall tranquility permeated this ship. On his own ship, he had to shut out most of what he sensed or go crazy. The anger of those who dominated often clashed against the feelings of helplessness and bitterness of the others. Women who serviced his father and other men emitted resignation or fear. The slaves who did the hard and dirty manual labor required to maintain the ship's functions radiated dejection.

Part of the reason Jori had begged Terk to allow him to come along on this mission was to reconnect with him. The other part was to get away from the madness.

His ship wasn't all bad, though. The camaraderie of the warriors bolstered his own. Competition among them could be fierce but it mostly remained friendly. The slaves enjoyed their occasional periods of reprieve. The women also found their moments of happiness, his mother especially. Father had never treated her well, but he seldom paid attention to her nowadays.

An ache swelled in his chest as he thought of her. As the youngest, his father had allowed him to stay with her longer than his brothers had. Even though Father forbade him from visiting her anymore, he often snuck into the harem anyway.

If she were here now, she'd help him sort through this tangle of feelings. He hated the Cooperative when he thought of Calloway, but not when it came to Hapker.

The absurdity of Calloway's threatened attack made his lips curve into a smile. He almost laughed out loud. The man wouldn't last a minute against an adult senshi. Hell, when Terk woke, he'd easily turn him into a pile of meat.

Though Jori's smallness prevented him from taking on most adults, he could handle Calloway by himself. If not for the others nearby, he probably would have. Come to think of it, that foul man probably wouldn't have antagonized him if all those people weren't there to protect him when Jori thrashed him.

The more he considered the ridiculousness of Calloway's behavior, the more his mind settled. The heaviness of fatigue set in and relaxed him. He lay with his hands behind his head. The nattering of the songbird became a lullaby and the combined peacefulness of the others on the ship became a blanket. His consciousness fell into darkness while holding on to a comforting warmth that he hadn't felt in a long time.

35
Suffering and Death

3790:263:08:27. Ander Vizubi twiddled his thumbs with boredom. He could only do so much meditating and stretching before his mind imploded.

At least their cell had a food and water dispenser because they hadn't seen their captors for two days. Fortunately—or unfortunately—Hesteben had his drugs in his pocket. His highs had been annoying, but he would be a bigger pain in the ass when he ran out.

Vizubi eyed the mismatched artillery bots on the other side of the clear security door. Some were short rapid-fire machines, while others stood tall on two or three legs. All appeared to be outdated, but they still had deadly potential. Breaking out would be easier than getting past them.

Bari sat against a wall with one knee pulled up. Quigley lay on a cot, her arms folded behind her head as she stared at the ceiling. Fung and Woolley chatted quietly while Hesteben slept soundly.

The swish of a door jerked Vizubi into alertness. He rose to his feet as the Grapne Overseer entered the cell block with a wide grin.

"We meet again, Sssergeant," the skinny man hissed.

Vizubi bit his tongue. It wouldn't do any good to antagonize his captor. "This won't work. The Cooperative has a strict policy about negotiating with criminals."

"The Dragon Emperor is the real criminal. I'm only seeking to make the galaxy a better place."

"And make a profit," Bari muttered.

Vizubi gave the private a look that told him to remain quiet. "They're just kids," he said to the Overseer. "It's not right to keep them in captivity for something their father has done."

The Grapne darkened and his face twisted into a snarl. "Something? You mean everything. Do you have any idea how many of my people have been enslaved by that man? How many of our children he has murdered?"

"He's a monster. I get it, but who's to say his offspring will follow in his footsteps?"

The Overseer snickered. "Do you want to bet on it? I'll take you up on that wager."

Vizubi clenched his fists at the futility of arguing with the man. "What will you do with us when the Cooperative won't negotiate?"

"They'll negotiate. They always seem to fold when it comes to helping their own."

"Not without trying other tactics first, ones that will likely get your people hurt in the pro—"

"Hey, man," Hesteben said to the Overseer with a friendly smile. "How about letting me outa here?"

The Grapne shook his head. "No one is leaving this cell."

Hesteben frowned. "Hey, we had a deal, man."

Vizubi's heart constricted. "Deal? What the hell are you talking about?"

His brother waved his hands. "Wasn't my idea. Guillermo's the one who worked something out with these guys. I'm just along for the ride, man."

A smoldering heat rose to Vizubi's face. "You betrayed me? Your own brother? For starhash!" He crossed his arms to keep from strangling him. An overwhelming ache bloomed at the same time. *How could he do this to me?*

The Overseer's grin widened. "He's also got a transmitter in his bag. It's how my ship found you."

Vizubi's fury comingled with his deep hurt and created a whirlpool that threatened to drown him. "You won't get away with this."

The Overseer bowed. "I already have."

As the Grapne left, Hesteben rushed to the cell door. "Hey, man! We had a deal! I need my stuff. You've gotta let me out of here!"

Vizubi clenched his teeth. "You did this to yourself, Hesteben. I pray your withdrawals won't kill you, but I also hope you writhe in pain."

He unjustly wished harm upon his own brother, but he was too furious to care. *Damn it.* All of this was his own fault. He should have known Guillermo would do this. Hell, he should've known Hesteben would sell him out for starhash.

He plopped onto the edge of his cot and dropped his head in his hands. No matter how hard he tried to stop it, all the terrible ways this could end kept swirling through his brain.

*****

3790:263:10:15. J.D. Hapker doubled over and panted. His chest heaved. "You're getting better at this." He was in great shape, but an entire hour of full-on cardio was a little more than he was used to. He'd never sweated so much in his life. Nor tried so hard to win.

"I've learned to anticipate your movement patterns," Jori replied.

Hapker shook his head. *Who analyzes movement patterns?* Professional players, maybe. "Well, you've certainly got me figured out," he said instead. "I haven't won a game all day."

Jori bounced on his toes. "Want to try again?"

He looked so eager, Hapker had to grin. "One more, but I warn you. If I drop from exhaustion, you'll need to carry me out."

The boy quirked his mouth. *Was that almost a smile?*

The game began anew. Although they played with the same intensity, Jori's demeanor seemed lighter. He appeared to enjoy this just for the fun of it rather than as a fight against him. Still, Jori scored again and again. Hapker's legs move like gelatinous ooze while the boy ripped around like a cheetah chasing an impala.

Hapker swung and the ball clipped the end of his racket, sending it askew and with barely enough of a bounce to reach the wall. He took advantage of the reprieve and bent over again to catch his breath. "You know," he said between gasps, "it wouldn't hurt for you to give an old man a break."

"You want me to let you win?"

The dumbfounded look on the boy's face made Hapker laugh. "I do have my pride." He shook his head. "At least I used to."

Jori smiled this time.

Hapker inhaled, then blew out and stood. "Alright. I changed my mind. Give me all you got."

Despite his bravado, his performance did not improve. He missed his next shot. As Jori trotted down the court to retrieve the ball, he picked up his bottle and gulped down water. He considered ending the game, but Jori served. Hapker hit the ball just in time.

Rather than return the ball, Jori caught it. “I must see my brother.”

“Now?”

“Now.” Jori’s face twisted in anguish. He dropped everything and ran out.

Oh no. Hapker abandoned his own gear and followed the boy, hoping he didn’t sense something regarding his brother.

A rush of adrenaline burned away Hapker’s fatigue. They reached the medical bay together. His heart clenched at the sight of the elder prince’s room. Doctor Jerom yelled out instructions. Medics rushed about in a frenzy. Mechanical beeps sounded in alarm.

He grasped Jori’s shoulder to keep him from rushing in and to provide reassurance.

“What's happening?” Jori asked a medic as she hurried by, but she seemed too harried to hear.

“It’ll be alright,” Hapker said. “They will do everything they can.”

Jori didn’t reply. He stood rigidly but Hapker felt his body tremble.

The medics bustled about. Hapker swallowed down a rising sense of dread. The risk of war was only one reason he didn’t want this young man to die. Jori was the other. Hadn’t he seen enough death and suffered enough pain in his short life? “He’ll be alright,” he said again.

Jori looked up at him. His forehead wrinkled and his eyes glistened like liquid wells of despair.

Hapker’s throat tightened. He gently squeezed the boy’s shoulder. “Doctor Jerom is the best. I’ve never met a doctor more skilled and more dedicated.”

The panic of the medical team heightened. Their yelling intensified. Hapker only discerned a few words, but he understood what was happening.

“—defib—” “—start compressions—” “—epinephrine.”

A med bot rolled up. A medic rushed in with a hypospray. Six medics and the doctor surrounded the young man's bed in a crowd of blue and white. Although masks covered most of their faces, the intensity of their eyes expressed the seriousness of the situation.

Jori's head swiveled as though searching for a way to help. "No," he said in a low, heart-wrenching tone. Tears rolled down his cheeks and his chin quivered.

Hapker embraced him around the shoulders. To his surprise, the boy slumped against him, then turned and buried his face against his chest. He didn't make a sound, but his body shook as though sobbing. Hapker enveloped him and squeezed.

Jori let out a muffled wail that drowned in the din of the medical team. Hapker held tighter and the boy surprisingly returned the gesture by wrapping his arms around his waist. Consoling words wouldn't be enough, so he provided solace in silence while the boy melted against him.

The medics calmed. "He's stabilizing," one said.

Jori let go and turned to check.

Hapker noted the pulse on the heart monitor. "He's alright."

Tears still fell from Jori's red eyes. Hapker hugged him close again. It struck him that the boy didn't resist. If the circumstances hadn't been so dire, he might be elated over this breakthrough between them.

They remained in an embrace as they watched the medics calm and disperse. Someone closed the privacy curtain. Jori let go and stepped forward, breaking Hapker's hold.

Doctor Jerom blocked the way, though probably unintentionally. His brows wrinkled inward. "We don't know what happened yet. He inexplicably convulsed and his heart went into defib."

"Will he be alright?" Hapker asked on Jori's behalf.

"He's stable. That's all I can tell you for now," Doctor Jerom said solemnly. "I'm sorry."

"Can I see him?" Jori's voice croaked.

"Let us examine this first." The doctor gestured to an area off to the side. "You're welcome to wait here and I'll let you know when you can go in."

Hapker moved out of the walkway. Jori did too, but at a reluctant pace. The boy returned to his stiff and formal composure. His eyes dried and he wore his standard placid expression.

Hapker gripped his shoulder with reassurance. Jori didn't react but neither did he dissuade the show of compassion. Something had changed between them, something deeper he couldn't quite define.

They waited a half hour with the medics coming and going before Doctor Jerom returned and gave Jori permission to enter. The boy spent the rest of the day by his unconscious brother's side.

36
Perantium

3790:264:00:41. The corridor lay empty, so J.D. Hapker arched his back to loosen the stiffness created by sleeping in the chair all night. Jori dared not leave his brother and Hapker didn't want to let him carry this burden alone.

He still had his duties to attend to, though. He stretched one more time to rejuvenate his muscles before entering the conference room.

Captain Arden glanced up from his deskview. He made a sweeping hand gesture. "Please, have a seat, Commander."

Hapker gave the chair a sour glance but sat and waited for the others to arrive for this morning's meeting.

The captain turned off his screen. "Doctor Jerom reported the situation with the elder prince. How's the younger one taking it?"

Hapker let out a heavy sigh. "He's distraught."

"That's understandable. Any anger?"

"No, Sir. He must realize we're dedicated to doing everything we can."

The captain's eyebrows rose. "Good to hear."

"In fact, I believe the incident's brought us closer."

The man's brows lifted further. "Really?"

"Yes, Sir." Hapker smiled. "I'm actually getting to like him. I think he feels the same for me."

"That's wonderful news, Commander. It's unfortunate it came about in this way, though."

Hapker's smile fell away. The same thing had occurred to him. No doubt Jori had felt lonely in that moment when his brother almost died. "Yes, but I'm sure we would have gotten there eventually."

"He trusts you," the captain replied. "He has good reason to. You've done a fine job, Commander."

Hapker's heart swelled.

"But it's not over yet," Captain Arden added.

His heart shrank. "No, Sir. There's still a chance his brother won't make it."

The captain dipped his head. His forehead creased. "A real possibility, I'm afraid. There are more concerns, which I will get to shortly."

Hapker leaned back and blew out a breath. *What else is going wrong?*

The conference room door slid open. Bracht stomped in with his usual manner. The lion-maned warrior nodded a greeting, then sat.

Sharkey came in next. Her posture was rigid, and her expression strained.

"Lieutenant Sharkey, I wasn't expecting you," the captain said.

"She has important information, Captain," Bracht replied.

Hapker perked up like a mongoose on lookout duty. He studied Sharkey's features to try and get a hint of what she had to report, but all he discerned was its seriousness.

The captain nodded and motioned for her to sit. She'd been a part of their conferences before, but this time her striking blue eyes darted about as though nervous.

Director Sengupta arrived last. She, too, had an edgy look about her.

Hapker worked his jaw, trying to wet the dryness of his mouth.

"Lieutenant Sharkey, why don't you begin," the captain said.

Sharkey cleared her throat. "Sir, there's a lot of resentment among the security officers going around. I believe the information about Jori being the emperor's son has gotten out and spread in a bad way."

The captain frowned. "In what way is that, Lieutenant?"

Sharkey stared down at her hands. "I suspect some of our security people tried to pick a fight with the prince the other day."

Hapker stiffened. "When?"

"At the gym, after you left." She averted her gaze from his, as though she felt guilty for telling on him. Not that he'd done anything wrong by leaving. "I don't know the details, but apparently, someone thought it was funny to program the holo-man to look like a Tredon. Words were exchanged and I believe things came to near violence. Based on what I was told, it broke up just before I arrived."

Heat swelled in Hapker's chest. "How could you let this happen?" he asked the major.

Bracht's jaw tightened. "*I* didn't."

Hapker bristled. "Didn't you? We all know how much you hate him, and your team took your attitude as encouragement."

The major's dark eyes lit up like fire. "I know my duty, Commander," he said in a rumbled tone. "The only attitude I've expressed outside these walls is the danger the boy presents."

"And your hate," Hapker replied heatedly.

"The Tredons are murd—"

Hapker slapped his hand on his thigh. "Jori has done nothing."

Bracht's face turned red, but he didn't reply.

Sharkey and Sengupta averted their gaze while the captain's eyes flicked between them. If the man had an unfavorable opinion about his outburst, he kept it to himself.

Hapker swallowed down the hard lump in his throat that didn't have anything to do with the captain. Bracht wasn't entirely at fault. He should've stayed with Jori that day.

"Jori hasn't mentioned this," he said in a calmer tone.

"Why wasn't this reported?" The captain directed his glower at Sharkey.

Her mouth turned down apologetically. "I only heard it second-hand an hour ago, Sir. When I asked the officers who were on duty, they told me nothing worthwhile happened."

"One brought up the holo-program while the others denied it, which makes me think there's something to this," Bracht added.

"I hate to say it, Sir," Sharkey said, "but having security wear body-cams might not be a bad idea."

The captain shook his head. "Studies have shown that officers wearing such devices don't deter negative behaviors by either party, especially in tense situations. Besides, they only present one side of a situation."

"We also don't want our people to second-guess themselves," Bracht added.

"Nor do we want to create an atmosphere of distrust." Hapker's mouth twisted at the memory of Zimmer using security cameras to rebuke the officers rather than as training tools.

“I will question everyone again, Sir,” Bracht said.

“Find out what you can, Major,” Captain Arden replied. He turned to Sharkey. “You say the information about the boy has spread?”

“I’m sure the entire security team knows, Sir. Probably beyond them as well.”

“Then perhaps I should address the crew. This behavior is unacceptable.” The captain’s eyes hardened as he gave them a firm look.

Hapker’s gut churned. “I’ll stay with the boy at all times from now on, Sir.”

“You or Lieutenant Sharkey,” the captain replied. “Can we trust Lieutenant Gresher to do his duty and keep his personal feelings aside?”

“I should’ve been able to trust all of them to do so.” Bracht’s tone came out angry, but Hapker suspected it held a hint of shame too.

“I’m sure we can rely on Lieutenant Gresher, Sir,” Sharkey said.

The captain dipped his head. “Very well. Work out an arrangement.”

“Yes, Sir,” Hapker and Sharkey replied at the same time.

“Bracht,” the captain added. “I can’t emphasize enough how important it is that our people are not the antagonizers.”

“I will make every effort to stress it to them, Sir,” the Rabnoshk warrior said.

Yes. Please do. Hapker suppressed a sigh. Poor Jori. Because of his father, nearly everyone here hated him. *Well, he has me. I don’t care who he is or what his father’s done.*

“Now for the next item of discussion.” Captain Arden gestured to the viewscreen. “If you will turn your attention to the screen. A friend of Director Sengupta’s shared this footage from a cargo ship. It’s a view from the outside.”

Hapker leaned in as the video of the calm starscape erupted with chatter from the vessel’s crew.

“Captain! A Tredon warship just appeared on our scopes. It sees us!”

“Shit! Get us the hell out of here.”

“There’s no way we can outrun it, Sir.”

"Try anyway!" the captain roared. "How close are we to the Galunta system?"

"Not close enough."

"Are there any asteroids or anything nearby—to put something between us?"

"Checking, Sir. So far there's nothing."

"Keep looking," the captain replied. "Maderu, do everything you can to evade those bastards."

When the camera view lurched to focus on the gigantic warship, a biting tingle ran down Hapker's spine. The ship's black hull barely reflected the light from the nearest star, making it resemble a hulking shadow. Its turrets lit up like menacing eyes. He imagined a hundred bats waking from a dark cave.

The video image shook. "We're taking fire!" a crew member yelled.

"No shit," the captain said. "Return fire!"

"Our weapons won't do anything against that monster."

"Do it anyway. Use every damned weapon in our arsenal if you must."

The shaking view continued in rapid succession.

"Shields at sixty-two percent and dwindling fast."

"Evade, damn it!"

"I'm trying, Sir!"

"Fifty-four percent." The image shuddered twice more. "Thirty-nine!"

"We won't last much longer. What do we do, Captain?"

"Christ! I don't know. Anyone have any ideas?"

No one answered. Red dots of firepower heralded more rattling of the camera. An explosion resounded, followed by the yelp of a crew member.

"Shields at ten percent, Sir! They've got us."

The captain released a spew of curses. "Get your damned weapons, now! Those fuckers might disable our ship, but they won't take us alive."

Muffled sounds of the crew scuttling about put Hapker on the edge of his seat. The firing stopped and a small blue maw like an opening eye glowed from the shadow as the Tredon ship opened its hangar.

"Shields down, Sir. They're coming!"

"Fight as if your life depends on it!" the captain bellowed. "Because it does."

Another crew member whimpered.

"Suck it up, Maderu. There are worse ways to die."

The viewscreen clicked off. Hapker nearly fell out of his chair as his own reality came back into focus.

"Sengupta," the captain said, "do you want to tell us the rest?"

Her eyes dropped to her lap where her hands fidgeted. "Another vessel found the ship two days later. Inside were nineteen dead bodies. The ship's roster indicated a crew of forty-six so we can only assume the others were taken captive."

Hapker gulped.

The captain's forehead wrinkled. "Their records showed the vessel that attacked them was the *Brimstone*."

A frigidness overtook Hapker's entire body, making him shiver. "The ship Jori wants us to take him to."

"That's not happening," the captain replied in a harsh tone. "The *Brimstone* can send someone to Chevert to pick them up. I will also make sure we have PG-Force ships nearby before we stop there."

Hapker dipped his head.

Captain Arden regarded him and the other crew members with tired eyes. "Now for the other piece of news." He pressed the comm button on his desk. "Doctor Canthidius and Chief Simmonds, I'm ready for you to come in."

The saliva in Hapker's mouth soured as Canthidius entered. His distaste had little to do with the man himself. His presence here meant he had more to report regarding Jori's ship—something Jori might have hidden or lied about.

Hapker's suspicions heightened when Engineering Chief Sam Simmonds arrived a few moments later with a solemn expression. Simmonds was generally a cheerful man. His genial personality would have blended right in on Hapker's homeworld.

The man's sense of style could be jarring, though. Simmonds sported a mustache and long sideburns that grew down to a point that ended at the start of his bald chin. When he wasn't in uniform, he wore colorful clothing that would have shamed the birds of the parrot family. Combine these traits with the way his large nose turned red at the tip whenever he got agitated, and he reminded

Hapker of the jocose performers in the traveling bazaars back home.

Canthidius glanced at Simmonds with an ugly twist of his mouth. *So I'm not the only one the fish-man has a problem with.*

Hapker had heard about recent friction between the science officers and the engineers assigned to investigate the Tredon ship. Apparently, Canthidius and Simmonds had both bypassed him and taken their arguments directly to Captain Arden. Supposedly, the captain was not at all happy about it. Whether his displeasure was because they skipped the chain of command or that they couldn't handle their differences on their own, Hapker wasn't sure.

He suspected Canthidius was the primary instigator. Getting involved in the rumors that flowed throughout a ship wasn't something he did. A few whispers reached his ears, nevertheless. They said Canthidius and the previous commander were close allies who tended to be at the center of much dissent.

Whatever the truth, the captain welcomed both officers with equal professionalism.

The captain addressed the chief science officer. "Doctor Canthidius, tell us what you've found."

Canthidius cleared his throat. "We've discovered a chunk of perantium on the *StarFire*."

Hapker cocked his head. "Perantium?"

Canthidius smiled in a way that Hapker assumed he intended to be patronizing. Before the man could show off his intelligence while belittling Hapker's ignorance, Simmonds answered. "It's a rare and non-replicable crystal capable of enhancing waves to an enormous magnitude." Simmonds' eyes widened, but the expression reflected wonder rather than alarm. "It's so rare that we consulted Director Sengupta regarding its origins."

"It's part of a wave-emitter prototype. Someone stole it from Thendi some months ago," Sengupta said.

Oh no. Hapker leaned back in his chair. "So Jori lied."

Sengupta glanced at Hapker with eyes tilted in sympathy. "The thieves were Zervians. It's possible the Tredons purchased the device in the underground market."

"Shekaka." Hapker exhaled, somewhat relieved that Jori still hadn't outright lied.

Captain Arden's brow wrinkled. "Could this perantium have been obtained by the Tredons in another way?"

"The closest source is nearly a year's travel from here. We believe this particular piece is from Wendar, an uninhabited planet in the Xenar system," Canthidius said.

"The Thendi are a lot closer and they have a much bigger piece they purchased legally," Simmonds added. "They are building a larger wave-emitter based on this prototype. This crystal will help them send waves into their planet's crust. They hope to ease the destructiveness of the plate movements."

Canthidius flicked his hand as though to downplay Simmonds' information, but Hapker suspected a connection. "So, what could the Tredons do with the smaller device?"

"The enhancement of certain waves can cause a lot of destruction," Simmonds replied.

"The size of this prototype probably won't do any more damage than a torpedo," Canthidius said in a dismissive tone.

Simmonds' demeanor tightened. If the science officer irritated him, though, it didn't come through in his voice. "But if they create a larger wave-emitter like the one on Thendi and get their hands on a bigger chunk of perantium, they could use it to destroy an *entire* planet."

The hairs on the back of Hapker's neck rose.

The captain's frown deepened. "You found this hiding on their ship."

Simmonds nodded. "Yes. In pieces. By themselves, the parts looked innocuous, like nothing more than simple wave-emitter components. When we discovered the perantium, though, we fit the pieces together, so to speak."

"Shouldn't the parts themselves have raised suspicion?" Sharkey's eyes tilted as though she was nervous about interrupting the conversation.

Canthidius pressed his lips at her unintentional accusation. Hapker tightened his too, but only to suppress a smile. Canthidius' mistake of not recognizing the parts as important before was understandable considering the destruction wrought throughout the ship, but the arrogant fish-man probably didn't like the oversight pointed out.

"Wave emitters are generally rather weak." Simmonds appeared to take no offense at Sharkey's words and even seemed eager to answer. "Granted, this particular device had modifications we'd never seen before, but it never occurred to us it could be anything so dangerous."

"It's not dangerous," Canthidius' fish-face had a pinkish tint to it, and he shifted in his seat. "The Tredons don't have enough information to build a larger device based on this tiny prototype."

Hapker recalled the charred remains of the vessel. "How did it not get destroyed in the crash?"

"Perantium is a very hardy substance," Simmonds replied. "Only certain intense waves can break it. It's what makes it such a powerful conduit for Thendi's purposes."

"Commander?" The captain gave him a meaningful look.

Hapker rubbed his hand across his aching forehead. "I'll ask him about it, but I think Director Sengupta may be right. If they had stolen it, the report from Depnaugh would have mentioned it."

"Not if it had been stolen to begin with," Bracht said.

Hapker frowned. The Rabnoshk could be right too.

The captain stroked his beard. "Unless we find they were a part of the original theft, I see no reason to hold them. We can't allow them to have it back. However, we should still return them home as promised."

Hapker's shoulders fell in both relief and in disappointment. They wouldn't keep the boys against their will, but they were more culpable than he'd hoped.

37
The Attempt

3790:264:07:52. J.D. Hapker left Bracht's meeting with the security officers feeling that he'd just been strung through a singularity. The Rabnoshk warrior's lecture had come down like an avalanche. Everyone seemed to have a beaten look about them as they hastily returned to their duties.

He, himself, had only been there as an observer, but the quake of the major's voice tremored down to the core of his bones. The shame, disappointment, and anger the warrior had expressed left even him with a hard knot in his stomach.

The experience impressed him. His respect for the man grew by the day. However boorishly Bracht had behaved toward the boy, he was proving to be much more compelling, not at all the one-dimensional brute he'd first assumed.

"Hey, Jori," he said as he entered the elder prince's room in the medical bay. "Is he any better?"

Jori shook his head. A deep sadness filled his eyes.

Hapker pulled up a chair and sat beside him. "We found the perantium."

Jori shrugged without a change in his expression. "So?"

Hapker blinked. "What were you going to do with it?"

"Give it to Father."

"Do you know what this device is capable of?"

"Of course," Jori replied as though they were talking about dirt.

"This doesn't bother you?"

"It's no more dangerous than your weapons."

"Yeah, but…" Undoubtedly the emperor had already been aware the prototype could help him create a much larger and more perilous device, but he best not hand out any ideas. "If you don't think it's dangerous, why dismantle and hide it?"

"My brother's idea."

Hapker shook his head in disbelief. "Jori, you lied to us."

Jori scowled. "No, I didn't. I told you we didn't steal it and that's the truth."

Hapker sagged against the chair's back. Sengupta's speculation had been right. "When we get you home, we can't let you take it with you. Shekaka stole the item and we must return it to the original owners."

"Return it, then."

Hapker frowned at the nonchalant attitude. When Jori's doleful expression returned, he understood. Whatever importance the device might have had before, it paled compared to his brother.

He brought up the other issue. "What happened in the gym the other day after I left?"

"Nothing worth mentioning."

"Are you sure? I got the impression some people harassed you."

"It wasn't anything I couldn't handle."

"Why didn't you say something?"

The boy's brow furrowed. "Why would I?"

"If they tried to start trouble, then their behavior was *way* out of line."

"Why? After everything my father's done, they have a good reason to hate me."

Hapker considered his first unfair impression of Major Bracht. "We should judge people as individuals. You shouldn't be blamed for his actions."

"Maybe that's true for ordinary people, but I'm a prince. My entire reputation is built upon my father's."

"You're still your own person. You might need your father's authority, but you don't have to be like him."

Jori lowered his eyes. "In some ways I do."

Some ways, as in being the best fighter and the best strategist by practicing and studying every waking moment? "Perhaps, but it doesn't give anyone the right to antagonize you."

"It *was* cowardly."

"Yes, it most definitely was. Tell me if it happens again, alright? *I don't* think they have a good reason to hate you at all."

Jori raised an eyebrow.

"I mean it," Hapker said with a smile. "You know I do."

The boy scowled. "Yes, but I don't understand why. I've been nothing but a brat since I arrived."

True enough, but... "It's alright. You're under a lot of stress."

"That is no excuse," Jori replied. "I can control my emotions."

"So I've noticed. Rather unusual for one your age."

"Sensei Jeruko taught us the importance of maintaining control."

"Sensei Jeruko, huh?" *So not his father.* "What else does he teach?"

"Most of our fighting techniques, except strategy and aerial combat." The boy's voice trailed off as though he wanted to add more to the list but feared being too forthcoming.

"Hmm. He must be a good teacher. I've seen your skills in the gymnasium. Pretty impressive."

"I still have a long way to go."

"I bet when you grow into your strength, you'll be quite adept."

"I must be more than adept. My brother and I have to be the best. Otherwise we will not be fit to lead."

"Sounds like a lot of pressure," Hapker replied. Jori's world differed from his own. Climbing trees, playing ball, and swimming were probably frowned upon where he came from, unless they had combat applications.

Jori's mouth turned down. "Despite what many think, being a prince doesn't mean living a life of privilege. It means I have a lot to live up to."

"That's rather insightful. I've met a few nobles and dignitaries who think otherwise." Dignitaries who complained because the bed wasn't soft enough or their room didn't have a vase of fresh flowers.

"Then they're fools."

"Yeah, they were." *And less mature, that's for sure.*

Hapker studied the peaceful face of the other prince. How much were these two alike? Would this boy have Jori's same level of maturity? Would he be as cooperative? Or would they have an angry warrior on their hands when he awoke?

"Does this pressure to be the best pit you and your brother against one another?" he asked, remembering what Sengupta had said about other Mizuki princes in history.

"It won't." Jori's tone held confidence. "Sure, we compete, but we also try to complement our abilities. We each have our strengths and weaknesses."

Hapker stroked his chin. "He sounds like a good brother."

"He is." Jori's face fell.

Hapker squeezed his shoulder. Jori didn't react, not like the day before when he'd cried in his arms.

They remained quiet for a while. After the flood of information Jori had shared, he didn't want to pressure him for more.

After some time, Jori turned to him.

"I am confused about something, Commander," the boy said.

"J.D. Remember?" Hapker replied.

"Jaydee?" Jori said, pulling the two sounds together.

"J.D." Hapker emphasized each letter.

"What does it stand for?"

"My birth name is Jairo Damark. My family and friends have always called me J.D."

Jori's mouth curved up. "J.D., then."

Hapker grinned.

Jori glanced away with shyness. A softness filled his expression. "The captain doesn't seem like a warrior, but everyone here does what he says. How does that work?"

Hapker cleared his throat, taking the moment to revel in his joy before turning his thoughts to the question.

When he had been Jori's age, he considered authority as a given. After he'd taken a class on leadership at the PG Institute, he learned the complexity behind it. Jori probably only knew one aspect. "There's a lot more to leadership than forcing people to do what you want."

"Like what?"

"Like trust. A good leader doesn't just give orders. He takes an interest in those who serve him. He respects them and cares for their well-being. In return, his followers don't just obey. They give him their loyalty because they trust he will look out for them."

Jori stared blankly as though considering his words. "Are you loyal to Captain Arden?"

Hapker looked up and stretched his mouth to one side. "Yes, I am."

"Why the hesitation?"

Hapker smiled. *The boy doesn't miss a thing*. "He hasn't been my commanding officer for long. The more I get to know him, though, the more I respect him."

"You've had commanding officers you didn't respect before?"

"Oh, most definitely." *Zimmer*. A hardness formed in Hapker's gut.

"You obeyed them anyway, yes?"

"Most of the time, but…"

"But?"

Hapker hesitated.

Jori leaned in.

Hapker stroked his chin. *Where to begin?* "They ingrain the importance of obeying orders from the very first day we enter the institute. That's what I do, even when I don't like the orders. However," he paused again. He hadn't fully discussed the Kimpke incident with anyone other than the review board and, on a more personal level, with Sharkey.

"However," he continued, "I couldn't bring myself to do it this one time. I was the tactical officer of a PG-Force ship under the command of a rear admiral. We came upon a civilian cruise liner where intel had told us a dangerous criminal named Jokko Kimpke was on board. The admiral had been pursuing this man relentlessly for months. We asked the captain of the vessel to turn him over, but he wouldn't. Some civilian ships have an aversion to military personnel interfering with their affairs, but I suspected Kimpke had influenced—no, I mean threatened him. The admiral was furious and decided the captain's lack of cooperation meant he intentionally harbored the criminal. Nothing we said would change his mind. So when he ordered me to open fire on the ship, I refused. Kimpke escaped." *And killed the captain as well as many more people on that ship*. The boy didn't need to know this part, though.

Jori, who had always seemed so careful about masking his emotions, appeared riveted now with his eyes wide and his mouth hanging open. "What did they do to you as punishment? You can only guess what my father would have done if someone had disobeyed him."

"Oh, I can imagine." A shiver ran down Hapker's spine. "My punishment was harsh, but nothing like that. They put me in the brig. The admiral charged me with willful insubordination. I was nearly convicted of the crime, but the court determined that the orders were unlawful—unlawful because of the civilians who would have been killed—and acquitted me."

"So, the court ranks above an admiral?" he asked, his tone a pitch higher.

"Only with judging crimes. This system is a way of applying checks and balances so the authorities don't overstep."

"We have nothing like that." The boy shook his head.

"This means when you and your brother come to be in charge, you must be mindful of the fact that just because you can do whatever you want, doesn't mean you should."

Jori nodded. Hapker slouched as comfortably as was possible in his chair and enjoyed the peacefulness. Other than the state of Jori's brother, everything was perfect—his relationship with Jori, the captain, and even his budding respect for Bracht. He only hoped it would last.

*****

3790:265:00:05. J.D. Hapker jerked awake. A twinge burned in his neck from sleeping in the chair again.

"What is that?" Jori demanded the medic standing on the other side of Terkeshi's bed with a hypospray.

"It's hippoceretine to help him recover," the man with the funny round haircut replied.

Jori stared at him as though reading him.

"It's the same injection we've been giving your brother every two hours," the medic added.

The intensity of the boy's expression put Hapker on edge. "What's wrong?"

"Let me see it" Jori circled to the other side of the bed to where the man stood.

The medic withdrew and held the hypospray out of reach. "No."

Hapker's neck prickled at the darkness in the man's eyes.

Jori held out his hand. "Give it to me."

The medic shrank back against the medical monitor. His face twisted. "No!"

Hapker indicated Jori. “Let him see it…” *What’s his name again? Lelan? Loren? Logan?*

The medic huffed dismissively. “It's nothing, Sir. It's just hippoceretine.”

“He's lying,” Jori said to Hapker while keeping a hawkish gaze on the man.

“Why would I lie?” the medic replied.

Why would either of you lie? Hapker hesitated. Something had Jori worked up. Since a sentio felt the emotions of others, they could use this ability to determine whether someone told the truth.

Hapker scrutinized the man. *Laren. That’s his name.* Laren clutched the hypospray against his chest. His eyes, normally hooded and narrow, were wide now. Perspiration dotted his upper lip.

“Let him see it,” Hapker said more forcefully.

“You really want me to hand over this drug to a child?” Laren asked with mock incredulity.

“I gave you a direct order, Laren. Give it to him.”

“Sir, it's just hippoceretine.”

Laren's reluctance convinced him something was wrong. Before he could react, Jori used his brother's bedside to hoist himself up and snag the hypospray out of the medic’s hand.

Laren attempted to grab it back, but Jori dodged him and backed away.

Hapker rushed in and pressed the man back. “I gave you a direct order.”

Laren paled.

“Let me go!” Jori shouted.

Hapker found Sergeant Addams grabbing a hold of both Jori’s arms and attempting to pin them back. The boy jerked his body low, forcing Addams to let go. As Addams reached for him again, Jori rammed his elbow into his solar plexus. The man doubled over with a gasp. Jori twisted away with the unused hypospray still in his fist and backed into Hapker, putting them between Laren and the guards.

Another officer moved to lunge at him, but Hapker swept out his palm. “Leave him be.”

“Sir!” The red-faced officer pointed. “Look what he did to Addams.”

Addams knelt, holding his chest and hitching his breath. The thought of the pain he was suffering brought a phantom ache to Hapker's own chest, but Addams would be fine soon enough.

"Why the heck did you grab him anyway?" Hapker asked.

"Sir?" The man pointed first at Jori, then at Laren. "He attacked him."

"No, he didn't. He merely took something from him. It's not the boy you should worry about. Take Laren into custody."

The officer's mouth dropped open. "Wha—"

Laren pushed past Hapker and snatched for the hypospray but Jori ducked out of reach. The medic lost his balance. Hapker grabbed him by the back of his shirt before he fell. "Arrest him now!"

The officer complied. Laren resisted. Two other officers arrived and restrained him.

"Don't you know who he is?" Laren shouted. "He's a monster. They both are!"

The medic jerked away from the officers' grips and charged at Jori. The boy stepped into a defensive stance and faced him with a grim stare. An officer yanked Laren back before he got too close.

"Your father killed my family!" the medic screamed. "Gonoro. Do you remember Gonoro? My wife and daughter are dead because of you!"

Laren continued shouting as the officers hauled him away.

Hapker turned to Jori. The boy maintained the same stance, but his fists hung at his sides and his face whitened.

"Are you alright?" Hapker asked.

Jori darkened. "Your people just tried to kill my brother," he said venomously between clenched teeth. "You told me you were helping him!"

Hapker chilled as blood drained from his head. He had no doubt what Laren had been up to. "Oh, Jori. I'm so sorry. This wasn't supposed to happen."

The boy's lips curled. "You expect me to believe that? My brother almost died because of you!"

Hapker swallowed down the lump in his throat. "I'm really sorry."

"Keep your damned sympathy!" Jori slammed the hypospray on the counter.

Hapker sighed and ran his hand down his face. *One step forward. Two gigantic leaps back.* It didn't help that the boy had a right to be angry.

What was Laren thinking?

Ah, yes. His family. What a mess this all was.

38
Criminal Revealed

3790:265:00:24. J.D. Hapker's shoulders fell. "I'm really sorry about what just happened."

Jori snarled. "If I hadn't been here, that man might have killed my brother."

"I didn't expect anyone to take things so far," he replied.

Jori's eyes burned with hate. "How can I trust you now? How can I trust anyone? Who will try killing my brother next? Will it be you?"

Hapker ground his teeth "That's not fair. You know I don't condone this. I messed up, though. I underestimated my crew." He sighed and rubbed his brow, then ran his hand down to his chin. "My dad was right," he spoke to himself. "Hate runs deep outside of Pholatia."

Jori looked away. "Why don't you hate me?"

"What? Why would I hate you?"

The sound of Addams trying to catch his breath on the other side of the curtain diverted his attention. "Hold on," he said and stepped over.

Addams perched shirtless on the exam table in the room next door while a medic did a body scan.

Hapker noted the cherry redness below his breastbone. "How are you doing, Sergeant?"

Addams made a wry face. "It's nothing, Commander."

"He will be fine, Sir," the medic added. "A hit to the epigastric region is painful but not life-threatening."

"Did you alert the captain?" Hapker asked the sergeant.

"Yes, Sir. He's on his way here now."

Doctor Jerom entered. Hapker stayed as the medic explained Addams' symptoms and the pain reliever he planned on giving.

The doctor nodded his approval, but Addams refused the treatment.

"Doctor," Hapker said before the man left. "I need you to analyze this." He handed over the hypospray. "I was told it contained hippoceretine, but I believe it might be something harmful."

Doctor Jerom's brows lifted. "Why? Who in the universe would do that?"

Hapker heaved a sigh. "Laren stated the Tredons killed his wife and child."

Doctor Jerom's light brown eyes seemed to lose their color. "Oh dear. I had no idea. There was no mention in his file."

He must've kept it a secret. He shook his head and returned to Jori and his brother. Jori's normally stiff posture slumped. Instead of having the usual blank look, he held a haunted expression.

"This wasn't your fault," Hapker said, suspecting Jori overheard him speaking to the doctor.

"Yes it was," Jori replied. "I was there."

Hapker cocked his head. "You were where? You were at Gonoro?"

Jori hesitated. He glanced at his brother, then averted his gaze to the floor. He fidgeted with his hands before finally meeting Hapker's eyes. "I killed them. I killed that man's family." The boy's throat bobbed.

Hapker tensed. "What? How?"

"It happened three years ago." Jori's voice was low. "My father attacked the small outpost. My brother and I watched. At some point, he let us take over the tactical station. He never allowed us to fight in a real battle before, so we eagerly agreed. We…"

Hapker's shock turned into dread. He knelt to the boy's level. "You're not to blame."

"I am." Tears streamed down Jori's reddening cheeks. "We had fun doing it, too. We even competed to see who could make the biggest explosion."

Hapker swallowed down the hard lump in his throat. "Oh, Jori. You didn't know what you were doing."

Jori shook his head as if to disagree. "Yes we did, but we didn't consider the aftereffect. After our soldiers secured the outpost, our father brought us there. There were so many people, a girl—" Jori suppressed a sob.

Hapker moved to comfort him, but Jori raised his hand to hold him back. "I felt the ones who were still alive," the boy continued, "but they didn't get to live for long."

Saliva welled up in Hapker's mouth along with the urge to vomit. *That monster!* What kind of sick mind would teach his children to murder innocent people and show them the gored bodies? "Your father did this, not you."

"I'm a criminal." Earnestness and guilt filled his eyes. "You should take me into custody and let me answer for my crime."

Hapker wagged his head. "You're not a criminal. You're mature for your age, but your youth still limits your understanding."

No seven-year-old could have fully comprehended what destroying that outpost meant. Even Admiral Zimmer with all his experience had seemed blind to the real consequences of firing on what appeared to be nothing more than a hunk of metal.

"I understood when we visited the station," Jori said.

Hapker laid his hand on the boy's arm. "You now understand the effect of your actions and you won't want to do it again, right?"

"No. I won't, but my father will want me to. I won't have a choice." The boy's brow furrowed into a pained expression.

"Someday you will. Then you can make better choices." Hapker pulled him into a hug. The boy didn't resist.

A warmth fused through Hapker's body, followed by a wave of heat as he contemplated Jori's experience. The emperor had manipulated this innocent boy. Jori later understood he'd done something terribly wrong and regretted it. Would he carry what he learned from the experience to adulthood or would he harden himself against it and follow in his father's footprints?

Hapker eased away from the boy when Doctor Jerome slid back the curtain and motioned for him. He gave Jori a comforting pat on the shoulder, then followed the man out to where Captain Arden waited.

The captain's mouth turned down and his brow pinched in the center. "How's the child taking this?"

"He was angry, but he's calmed down now."

The captain's eyes reflected relief. "What happened?"

He explained Laren's reluctance to hand over the hypospray and the events that followed.

"So, he sensed Laren was up to something?" the captain asked.

"Yes." Hapker turned to the doctor. "Have you figured out what he was up to?"

"I'm not sure what's in the hypospray yet," Doctor Jerom said, "but whatever it is, it certainly isn't hippoceretine."

Hapker's gut tumbled. "So Laren *was* trying to harm the boy." He didn't want to believe a member of the Cooperative crew would do such a thing. Now, he had no choice.

Doctor Jerom nodded. "If you don't mind, Captain, I'd like to run a few more tests."

"Of course, Doctor," the captain replied. "Commander, I should apologize to the child."

"Yes, Sir."

He led the captain to the room where the next shift of guards kept watch. When he opened the curtain, Jori stood and moved into his usual formal posture with his hands clasped behind him and his shoulders pulled back. He wore the blank mask. However, it didn't deter from the red rims around his eyes.

The captain matched his pose, though it wasn't as stiff. "Jori, I'm so very sorry about what happened. I assure you I will do everything I can to make sure this doesn't happen again."

"You're aware it isn't gullibility that makes me believe you, Captain," Jori said in a rigid tone.

"Yes. The commander told me about your sentio-animi ability," Captain Arden replied.

"Good." Jori's eyebrow cocked over his dark blazing eyes. "Because if I sensed you were lying, this conversation would go *very* differently."

Hapker's mouth fell open. Since things had been improving between them, he'd forgotten how blunt he could be.

The captain didn't seem ruffled by the tone. "I understand. I hope you can sense my sincerity when I say I want your brother to recover."

"Then why haven't I been able to speak to General Sakon yet? I thought you intended to take us to our people."

"That is still my intent," Arden said, "but General Sakon has a dangerous reputation and I will not risk my crew to get you home.

You already told me he is near the Chevert outpost, so I will allow you to contact him just before we arrive. He can then pick you up from the station."

"Someone nearly murdered my brother and now you deny me the right to speak to my people. Are we prisoners or are we guests?"

"I must consider the safety of my crew."

"But not my brother's safety, apparently."

The captain's jaw twitched but he maintained an agreeable mien. "I will do everything I can to ensure something like this doesn't happen again."

Jori didn't respond. Nor did his deadpan air betray his thoughts. An awkward silence hung until Captain Arden excused himself and left.

Hapker crossed his arms and gave the boy what he hoped was reprove. "Did you have to be so rude? This wasn't his fault."

"He's the captain," Jori said. "That makes him responsible."

"And he is taking responsibility."

Jori's mouth curved down and the anger dwindled from his eyes. "Listen, J.D. You and I have come to a better understanding of one another, but I must keep my guard up. I can't afford to expose my weaknesses like this."

Hapker's heart leapt at the use of his casual name and all annoyance about Jori's behavior left him. "Do you mean your emotions? Being upset about your brother is not a weakness."

Jori pulled back his shoulders and his face reverted to his typical placid mask. "Such sentiment is weakness. Emotion is weakness."

"Is this what your father tells you?"

"Yes. Sensei Jeruko too."

"They probably meant you should control your emotions, not eliminate them. Hiding them could be important in some situations. Having emotions is not a weakness, though, unless you lose control of them or let them control you."

"You know how I feel about my brother. If you wanted to, you could use my sentiment against me."

"Sadly, there are people in this world who would do such a thing, but this doesn't make you weak. Having compassion for others is a good thing. If you don't care, then you're just a bully."

“I'm supposed to be a bully. It’s what being a Mizuki is all about,” Jori said with sarcasm in his tone.

“If this is what your father tells you, I think he's wrong. There are better ways to lead.”

“Maybe,” Jori replied. “If you weren't the man you are or I was on another ship, perhaps my emotions would have made me vulnerable.”

“That’s quite possible but consider this. Your sentiment for your brother saved his life. I bet he would do the same for you. Together, you are stronger because of your emotions.”

Jori’s expression turned thoughtful, but he didn’t respond.

39
Withdrawal

3790:265:05:43. Ander Vizubi seized his brother from behind, enveloping him in a tight hold.

Hesteben twisted and bucked. “No! It’s going to get me!”

“There’s—” Vizubi grunted. “—no Chupacabra!”

“Help! It’s coming for me!” Hesteben tossed his head back, butting onto his top lip.

“Damn it! There’s no such thing.”

“No! Get away. Get away!” His brother kicked out, striking the edge of the bed.

“Get his legs!”

Bari grasped his foot and struggled to keep it from swinging out. Woolley grabbed the other, and together they eased a little of Vizubi’s burden.

Hesteben squirmed, but only his hips and head moved. “Ah! It’s biting me!”

Vizubi gritted his teeth and advanced to the cot. “It’s not a Chupacabra!”

Quigley ripped up a sheet as he tried to figure out how he would maneuver Hesteben on the bed without letting go. He dropped onto it and turned his torso, trying to get his brother’s writhing body situated.

“Tie his feet!” Woolley pressed his weight on Hesteben’s left leg.

Quigley rushed in at the same time Bari lost his hold of the right. She caught the foot in her gut but held on. The private regained control and she strived to bind the delusional man’s ankles together.

Vizubi’s muscles ached as his brother jerked from one side to the other and screamed. Adrenaline and determination were all that kept him from letting go. Sweat dripped from his brow by the time she secured Hesteben's feet to the bed.

Now for the hard part. Vizubi lowered his brother down further while maintaining a tight squeeze. Woolley settled his weight on Hesteben's chest while Bari did the same to his legs. Quigley maneuvered between them with the stripped sheet.

"No! It's eating me. Help!"

Vizubi's body burned with exertion as Quigley bound his brother's arms to his sides. Hesteben rocked and rolled, but he held on. A twinge exploded from his side, indicating he'd pulled a muscle.

Quigley's hair stuck to her forehead as she bent in to shove the end of the strip down between the cot and the wall. She grunted and huffed, then crawled under the bed to pull the cloth through. She puffed as she rose. After a brief pause, she wound the strip around Hesteben's torso and tied him down.

It wasn't enough.

Fung held out another cover. "Here, use the whole thing."

Quigley angled in the middle of them again. Her breast pressed into Vizubi's face. He turned as much as possible but couldn't avoid her softness. More than once he'd admired her curvy figure, but now wasn't the time to get distracted. He focused on keeping his brother still as she worked the cover into the gap by the wall.

They both heaved a sigh of relief as she straightened. The job wasn't done, though. He struggled to keep Hesteben down while she hunched under the bed again. A few grunts later, she pulled the blanket through, giving herself ends long enough to knot together.

Vizubi let go. He flopped onto his own cot, leaned back, and banged his head against the wall. His arms spasmed from the exertion. His throat ached with the pain and anger he tried to keep at bay. Hot liquid in his eyes blurred his vision. How could he have been so stupid?

He glanced at his team members and a pang of regret hardened in his gut. Because of him, they had to suffer. Bari nursed a sore jaw. Quigley lay with one arm over her forehead and the other over her stomach. He hoped she didn't hurt from where his brother had kicked her. Woolley sat with a scowl. He'd been the most upset by Hesteben's betrayal and was no doubt still vexed. Only Fung seemed unaffected. She had helped in the beginning by maneuvering Hesteben to a place where Vizubi could get behind him, but she didn't have the strength to assist further.

By the time Vizubi stopped sweating, Hesteben had calmed. His yells turned into soft cries. "I need a fix," he whimpered. "Please."

"After all the shit you've put us through, we're not doing anything for you," Vizubi replied.

"Please, Andy. I love you, man," his brother wailed from his cot.

His chest constricted. "You did this to yourself, Steben. Now you're suffering the consequences."

"I need a fix. Please. It hurts. It hurts." Hesteben blubbered, turning his words into nonsense.

A volcano erupted in within Vizubi and he bolted upright. "What the hell do you expect me to do, damn it? Look where I am! I'm in a shit-hole cell because of you."

"Please, please," Hesteben whined. "I can't take it anymore. Help me."

Vizubi fell back against the wall with a growl. Quigley's eyes and mouth tilted. He appreciated her sympathy, but it wasn't enough to help him quell his raging emotions.

The others avoided looking at him. He hated that they pretended nothing was wrong. How could they not be angry with him? This was his fault. He was the one who brought his brother along.

He had apologized to them a dozen times already. Despite their forgiveness, he recognized their disappointment in him. Some leader he was.

"Andy, you've got to help me." Hesteben's voice came out more coherent than before. Perhaps the worst was over. "Please. Tell the Grapnes to bring my bag. I have more stuff in there."

"Of course you do," Vizubi muttered.

"Come on, Andy. I can't take much more of this."

"You should have thought about that before you agreed to betray me."

"I had no choice, man."

Vizubi slammed his palm on his thigh, making a smack that echoed from the cell walls. "Yes, you did! You always have a choice."

"They won't hurt you, man. Guillermo promised."

"Yeah? He also promised that you'd be out there instead of in here. That's what you get for trusting—"

Hesteben convulsed. Vizubi's heart leapt to his throat. He sprang to his brother's bedside and pressed his hand onto his chest to keep him from hurting himself as he thrashed against the bindings.

"Damn it, Steben! I shouldn't have let you come." Vizubi glanced around. "What do I do? Do any of you know?"

His team shook their heads. He fumbled with the restraints, trying to tighten them without harming his brother. He'd seen people go through withdrawals before, but not like this. Had anyone ever died? None that he recalled. Seizures were bad, though, and he had no idea how to stop them. *Please, God. Help him. I'm sorry I wanted him to suffer.*

The convulsions continued. Each jerk of Hesteben's body made Vizubi's heart skip a beat. "I'm sorry, little brother. I'm so sorry," he whispered.

The seizure ended. Hesteben didn't move. Vizubi held his breath and checked his brother's pulse. The faint and rapid rhythm shocked him into breathing again. He considered waking him but decided to let him sleep.

He patted his brother and stood. One hand rested on his hip while the other rubbed his jaw. Sweat beaded on his brow as he paced. Someone going through withdrawals usually needed a medic nearby to help them. His own journey had involved well over a week of doctors constantly monitoring him. He didn't stop all at once, either. They had weaned him off. Hesteben didn't have that luxury. Not while locked in here.

He approached the front of the cell. "Hey!" He pounded on the plasti-glass door. "Hey! My brother needs medical attention!"

"Sir, they'll probably think this is a trick," Quigley said.

Vizubi resumed his pacing. She was right. He examined the artillery bots. They undoubtedly had optical sensors, but were the Grapnes watching through them? If so, they had to know Hesteben's symptoms were real.

He knelt before a shorter bot. "Please. You've got to help my brother. He has a terrible drug addiction, and the withdrawals are killing him. If you have any doctors that can help, please send them. I promise we won't try anything. Please."

Some bots had lights on their domes or panels, but those only indicated they were prepared to shoot. He had no way of knowing whether these machines transmitted anything. Surely the Overseer had someone keeping an eye on them.

After several minutes with no response, he turned his back on the robots and cursed.

"He's okay now," Quigley said as she pulled the blanket up to Hesteben's chin. "His heartrate has slowed, and his breathing is normal."

Vizubi fell into his cot with a creak of the bedsprings. He hung his head in his hands and grasped at his spinning thoughts. They refused to settle, so he whispered prayers instead.

"Sergeant!"

Vizubi snapped upright. Bari pointed outside the cell to where the Overseer stood with a grin.

Vizubi jumped to his feet and rushed to the gate. "Did you hear me calling? My brother's in trouble. He's been dependent on drugs for years. He needs a doctor."

"We don't have doctors for thisss kind of thing," the Grapne hissed.

Vizubi's stomach clenched. "Then get his bag from our ship. His drugs are in there."

"I will do what you ask, but you must do something for me."

"Anything. Just help him."

"When we reach your ship at the Chevert outpost—"

"What makes you think our ship is there?" Quigley asked.

"They have our ship, remember?" Woolley whispered. "They probably looked at the nav."

The Overseer nodded. "—you will speak to your captain and convince him to trade you for the children."

Vizubi's deflated. "It won't work."

"You must make it work."

"You're asking me to relinquish the lives of children."

"Those brats are the last of the Mizuki reign. Ending them, ends the Tredon Empire."

Vizubi's gut lurched. "I won't help you kill children. Not even for my brother."

"What about for your crew?"

Vizubi balled his fists. It was his fault they were in this mess. "You expect me to trade lives?"

"The lives of your crew over potential genocidal murderers? Yes. Besides. I don't mean to kill them. My intention is to exchange them for my people—and perhaps for a little monetary compensation."

Even if the man told the truth, the fate of those children would certainly end in death—and he'd have a hand in it. What else could he do, though? Playing along now might help him later. Besides, what were the lives of the Dragon Heirs compared to his crew?

He glanced at them. Bari was a good man. His quippy comments and optimistic nature had a way of lightening moods. Fung was quiet and composed unless someone crossed her. He admired her boldness. Quigley's unquestionable loyalty had helped him through many tough times. He didn't know Woolley as well yet but hadn't noted any fatal flaws.

Bari dipped his head. Fung didn't react, but she didn't speak against it either. Quigley's expression softened, telling him she'd go with whatever he decided. Woolley wagged his head back and forth.

"Sergeant, please share your objections," Vizubi said. He tried to sound encouraging but his voice came out haggard.

Woolley pointed at Hesteben. "He betrayed all of us, not just you. We're here because of him."

Quigley's brows furrowed. "If he doesn't get help, he'll die."

Woolley threw up his hands. "That's not my fault. We can't give in to the enemy."

"The Grapnes already have us," Fung said. "The only thing Sarge is agreeing to do is talk to Captain Arden directly."

"And the captain is smart enough to know we're speaking out of desperation," Quigley added.

Woolley shook his head. "It still feels like giving in. If we do that, what else will he want? It never ends with these people."

A heavy weight seemed to fall over Vizubi's shoulders. "Look, I'm the last one who should decide this. Sergeant Woolley, you're my second. You make the call."

Woolley's eyes darted to each of the teammates. "If I say no, you all will hold it against me, won't you?"

"Leaders must make tough calls sometimes." Part of Vizubi's burden lessened. It wasn't fair to push this onto his new staff sergeant, but he didn't trust himself to be rational. "I respect your argument and swear not to hold anything against you."

"Same," replied Quigley.

"We're all in this together," Bari added, "but consider the option that buys us more time."

Fung nodded.

"My patience is wearing thin," the Overseer said. "Decide to help me and all of you will live. Refuse and all of you die."

Vizubi shivered at the man's cold smile.

Woolley stormed up to the man. They would have been nose-to-nose if not for the thick sheet of plasti-glass. "What guarantee can you give?"

The Grapne sneered. "We are not Tredons. We don't keep slaves, torture people, or commit murder."

"But you kidnap them."

"For the greater good. Help us get the dragon spawn and you go free. Everybody wins."

Woolley sighed. "Alright, snake." He pointed at the Overseer. "We'll do what you want, but only because we dislike the Tredons more. You had better hold up your end of the bargain, though."

Vizubi swallowed and faced the Grapne. "You have your answer, now help my brother."

"Good choice." The Overseer showed his teeth in an oily smile. "I will have someone bring your brother's bag, and when we get closer to the *Odyssey*, I'll send for you."

Vizubi held down the rising nausea. He hated himself for doing this. If only he could change the past. Not just at the station with Hesteben—all the way back to the first time they did starhash together.

He flopped down on his cot and closed his eyes. Wishing was as futile as his chance at redemption.

40
Guilt and Allies

3790:265:09:09. Jori face sagged. The lifelessness of Terk's hand countered its comforting warmth. *Come on, Terk. You can pull through this.* Jori clenched his jaw to keep the rising tide of tears at bay. The burning in his sinuses threatened to overwhelm him. He breathed steadily like Sensei Jeruko had taught him, and the sensation receded.

He squeezed his brother's limp hand, hoping against hope he'd return the gesture. It couldn't happen, though. Not in this state.

He detected only a vague feeling of his brother's lifeforce. Terk had lost weight from lying here so long. His sickly grey skin accentuated his thinning form. He might have awoken by now if not for that koshinuke medic. The lump in Jori's throat hardened. *Please wake up. I need you.*

Even as Hapker—J.D.—napped in an awkward position, his goodness gave Jori comfort. He was the only trustworthy person in this cage of blackbeasts. Everyone else could go to hell for all he cared.

His sadness ebbed, only to be gorged by a flow of anger. The hatred emanating from his guards gripped his attention and spurred his temper. Their emotions inflated his own until his vision darkened with a bloody haze. If Terk died, he'd make these people pay—somehow.

Why wait? He turned Terk's hand over to the palm. Most of his defensive nanites should gather here. If they were operational, Jori had no way to know since only his brother could activate their functions. Had the healing nanites used by the Cooperative destroyed them?

It didn't matter at this moment. Jori had already tested a few of his own nanite functions. Just when he believed he wouldn't need to use them, this shit happened. He flexed his fingers open and closed while considering his options. A zap to someone's chest with his palm would be so easy.

He glanced at J.D. and his gut churned. No. Not him. Anyone else but him.

This weapon was only good for one kill or three stuns anyway. He should hold on to it in case he needed it later.

Another idea sparked—something he could start right away. Since the captain didn't allow him to speak to General Sakon, his nanites offered a way to get around it. His lips curled upward.

Why in the hell have I been so compliant all this time? He'd been behaving himself. He hadn't caused any trouble, yet Terk remained in a coma, all because of the Cooperative.

That cowardly medic did this when his brother had lain helpless. *How could anyone murder someone so defenseless?*

The fire within him sputtered out. *Gonoro*. He killed those defenseless people. He was a monster, just like his father.

The image of a girl his age with lifeless eyes popped into his head and his gut twisted into a painful knot.

He wasn't sure what he'd expected when his gravitational boots first allowed him to step into that station. Dead warriors perhaps, but not the elderly man with his sliced neck and mangled body. Not the old lady with the bottom half of her torso missing. Not the woman clutching the infant, both who appeared to have been hurled against a wall by an explosion. And not the little girl with dead eyes who still haunted his dreams.

Nausea rolled. His mouth watered. He bit down and took in air through his nostrils to keep from heaving. He squeezed his eyes shut, hoping the image of the girl who might have been the medic's daughter would go away.

It didn't.

We didn't mean to. Terk doesn't deserve to die. The wave of burning tears threatened again. He clenched his fists and inhaled.

The sensation faded as heat rolled back in. What he had done to the Gonoro station was a mistake. He'd only obeyed his father's command, and he didn't understand the consequences until later. J.D. had said so himself. That medic, on the other hand, acted intentionally. He wasn't the only one here who wanted to harm him and his brother, though.

The privacy curtain slid open. J.D. jerked awake as Doctor Jerom stepped in. The doctor smiled but the gesture didn't touch his bloodshot eyes. His posture slumped and a brief sensation of remorse mixed in with his fatigue.

"I have some *good* news," he said, his emotions spiking with optimism.

Jori straightened. "Will he be alright?"

Doctor Jerom waved his hand. "Now, now. I'm not sure yet. I'm sorry."

A heaviness fell over Jori's shoulders. "What's the good news, then?"

"Well, the drug our medic gave your brother has no lasting effects. It's out of his system now."

"What was it?" J.D. asked.

"A form of ciculata. It's a poisonous plant. How Laren acquired it, I don't know. It's not something we have available on the ship. He administered it in small doses so our monitors wouldn't pick it up. You caught this in time. If he had continued, the poison would've caused severe and irreversible consequences and eventually death."

A prickling sensation ran up Jori's arms and down his back. That man almost succeeded. "So, its effects have been reversed, but he could still die?"

Doctor Jerom sagged. "Yes. Your brother has suffered a severe trauma from the crash. I'd like to say he's improving. Many of his external and internal wounds have mended, but brain injuries aren't so easily repaired."

Jori swallowed hard and clenched his fists. His eyes watered. Brain damage would be worse than death.

J.D. rested a hand on Jori's shoulder. "He'll pull through. If he's half as strong as you, he'll make it out fine."

The commander's words gave him hope. The tears threatened again. *I'm not strong. I'm weak.*

"He's right," Doctor Jerom said. "I agree, your brother's pretty tough. His immune system is the best I've ever seen."

Jori nodded. Even without medical nanites, both he and his brother had an extraordinary healing ability.

He sensed the doctor's honesty as well as his compassion, and it confused him. The hate from that medic, from Calloway, and from various people on the ship scorched through his senses. Somehow, the concern from Doctor Jerom and J.D. subdued them. These two were not so bad. Captain Arden was also sincere.

Fine. So not everyone here deserved payback if Terk died. He still had to contact General Sakon, though. They had to get out of here before someone else attempted to kill his brother.

He leaned back in his chair and planned.

Tonight, while Hapker sleeps.

*****

3790:265:16:06. Mik Calloway stretched and readied himself for another long shift of looking after that brat. He eyed the door to the commander's quarters and his gut soured. As much as he hated watching over both monsters when the boy slept in the sick bay, at least more went on over there to keep him alert.

He glanced at his security partner and suppressed a groan. It was going to be a long night.

Jacques Harmel, or Jack Hammer, as everyone called him, was a joke. He was nothing like the huge industrial machines used in demolitions. His slight frame would snap in two if an adult Tredon attacked him. How in the hell had he ever made the cut as a security officer to begin with?

The man fidgeted more than usual. As much as Calloway disliked him, he needed to keep from falling into boredom.

"You look stressed," he said.

Harmel the hammer sighed. "Yeah. I just got roped by Major Bracht."

Oh, hell. Calloway suppressed the urge to swallow. If the major had privately questioned Hammer… *Did he tell on me?* "So, what did you say?"

"Nothing. I can't afford a write up."

Calloway's shoulders fell. That no one wanted to get in trouble for antagonizing the Tredon Prince had saved him. If that wuss of a commander found out he'd been calling the brat names again, he wouldn't just postpone his promotion. He'd revoke it.

So unfair. The little monster deserves it.

Although everyone probably felt the same, he worried someone would rat him out. If anyone snitched, it'd be Hammer. With a personality as weak as his stature, it shocked him that Bracht hadn't already caused him to spill his guts all over his shiny black combat boots.

"Same here," Calloway replied. "I wonder how he heard about it to begin with."

"I bet the Tredon boy told them."

"Naw. If he had, he would've pointed us all out to the commander." *His new best friend, apparently.*

No, it wasn't the little warmonger. Maybe an onlooker had whispered something to their bedmate and it somehow got back to Shark-face. Fortunately, the rumor didn't include the names of those involved.

Calloway shifted his stance. His calves ached from standing so long. At least they'd taken him off the menial work. Not that the current task held any more excitement.

"How about that lecture he gave?" Calloway asked, referring to the rant from the Rabnoshk warrior about the importance of keeping the peace. As if the Tredons had any interest in peace.

Hammer shook his head. "Yeah, that was a ringer."

A ringer? Calloway frowned. By the context, he guessed Hammer didn't mean laughable. Major Bracht would make them shit their pants before he ever made them laugh.

So unfair. The Rabnoshk hypocrite hated Tredons as much as everyone else, but he was such a boot licker with the captain.

Captain Silas Arden, a man of peace. What a joke. If not for him, they wouldn't be putting up with the barbaric Rabnoshk warrior to begin with—or the little Tredon monsters.

He dared not say this to Hammer, though. Nor to anyone else, for that matter. Most of his fellow officers were oddly loyal to Bracht and the captain. Loyal to a bully and his wuss of a captain. This new commander was turning out to be a wuss as well. *How in the hell did I come to serve on a ship like this to begin with?* Captain Richforth would've tossed the spoiled little prince in a cell without so much as a bone to chew on.

"I don't get it. We should lock those two up, not pander to them," Calloway said.

"I agree," Hammer replied. "Even if they are kids."

Calloway jerked in surprise. The rubber hammer agreed with him? Maybe he wasn't such a pushover after all. "Murderous little cutthroats, you mean. You saw that child murder four Grapnes in less than ten seconds."

Hammer huffed. "Yeah."

Since this man never disagreed with anyone, Calloway couldn't be sure his sentiment was real. It was worth pursuing, though. Laren had failed, but he might be able to incite others to try.

"Too bad that medic didn't succeed," he said.

"I know, right?" Hammer's tone seemed genuine.

Good. "We should do something."

Hammer's eyes popped. "No way! I can't get in trouble."

"Naw. I don't mean something as drastic as what the medic did." The details of Laren's attempt eluded him. A dozen different stories circulated already, but not one was a first-hand account. The only two verified facts were that Addams received a good jab in the chest and Laren was in the brig. *Where the fucking princes should be.*

As far as he was concerned, Laren deserved a medal. Well, he would've if he'd actually succeeded.

"Remember in the gym?" Calloway said. "We should try it again. Provoke the little monster. Get him to act out so we can kick his backside and lock him up. Then there'd be no way the captain would let him and his brother go home. They'd languish in a prison instead." *I wonder if I'd get a medal for taking care of that little taipan.* Not from Captain Arden, but maybe from a higher-up.

"Hmm." Hammer's mouth twisted. "We must be careful, though. Gresher and Sharkey are keeping a close eye on us." His eyes flicked over to where the lieutenant stood.

"You mean Cheshire-cat and Shark-face? Yeah. We've gotta watch out for them."

Eagerness burned within him. This idea could work. Only one problem. His shift took place when the wussy commander and his little pet monster slept. An opportunity was bound to come, though. He just needed be patient. Then his sister would be at least partially avenged.

41
Sneak Attack

3790:266:13:26. Jori reclined on the couch, pretending to read his MDS. His insides fluttered and he juddered his foot with impatience.

Why can't they just shut up already? The snide comments from two of his guards didn't bother him as much as the way they kept looking his way to see if he was listening. They weren't making this easy. If he didn't carry out his plan soon, his stomach would tie itself in a knot.

The front of the couch where Jori lay faced a viewscreen displaying an ocean and sunset. Birds and the rhythmic whoosh of waves sounded from a speaker as irregular soft gusts of salty air swept from the upper vents.

Jori had chosen this small lounge for a reason. In another frame of mind, he might've enjoyed the oceanic motifs and calming atmosphere. This time, though, he selected it for its proximity to his target. Plus, the back of the sofa faced his irritating guards, providing him with easy cover.

Other than the rude remarks, the guards left him alone. All he needed to do was sneak over to the lower wall vent. He ran his palms down his thigh for the tenth time. If only those chimas would stop trying to needle him and get engrossed in their own conversations instead.

Hacking into J.D.'s console had been too easy. He'd worried the biometric authentication system would detect the malware his nanites had embedded on the surface of his skin and in his eyes. However, his nanites got him in without a hitch. Sending a message proved to be more difficult. The Cooperative used a sophisticated security AI that monitored transmissions and flagged those that seemed out of the ordinary. Messaging General Sakon directly was impossible. He must contact him through someone on the Chevert space station instead.

To dispatch it from J.D.'s console would've triggered the AI. The commander didn't send many communications, and when he did, they weren't to the fringes of Cooperative territory.

Only one person on this ship had a good chance of sending a message without alerting the AI. An inspection of Director Sengupta's communication files indicated she'd sent several over the past thirty days. The AI marked two for review, but only as a normal part of its quality control mandate.

A distinct sensation prodded his senses and made him freeze. Timid emotions coupled with the feeling of being hunted triggered a heat within his core.

A damned Grapne. He sat up with a huff and tight fists. As he swung his legs off the couch and sprang to his feet, the Grapne passed by. The man halted. His eyes bulged, and a smile spread across his face. Jori growled.

"Hey!" Lieutenant Sharkey's voice sounded from further down the hall. She jogged up and threw her palm up in front of the Grapne. "Move on, friend."

When the skinny man didn't leave, she grasped his elbow and led him back the way he'd come.

Jori stopped short of going after them. Since the attention of all the guards now focused on the Grapne, he pulled the tool from his pocket and darted over to the vent. His heart raced as he used the device taken from the utility box in J.D.'s room to undo the fasteners.

"We should let the Grapne hang around and see what happens," Calloway whispered loud enough for Jori to overhear.

Jori gritted his teeth has he worked. Calloway didn't usually start his shift this early. As much as he hated the man, at least if he got caught, they'd blame Calloway.

"We do our duty," Addams replied, though his emotions didn't reflect any offense at the idea. "Especially not with her here."

Jori removed the last fastener and eased open the vent cover. At fifty centimeters square, it provided enough room for him to crawl through. He slipped inside and pulled the cover back in place. As he inched away, the patter of his heart tapped in his chest. The tiny sounds of his movement echoed in the small space.

Little by little, he slid his way to an intersection. Thanks to the recon he'd done earlier using the nanite sensors in his palm, he had a map of the vents. His sensing ability had already told him where the director's quarters were, but the vent wouldn't lead there.

Jori turned himself around at the intersection. He used his elbows instead of his sweaty hands to crawl down the next tunnel toward the exit. As he reached the end, the tool slipped from his hand, clanking with a sound that pierced his eardrums. He held his breath as the soft tread of feet passed by the opening.

The laughter of two women broke out, then faded away as they moved on. Jori exhaled. He remained motionless when his senses picked up another person nearby. Several heartbeats later and the hall cleared. He hastened with the magnetic side of the tool and loosened six fasteners before anyone else passed.

Jori's nose itched as he worked. The sensation broke his concentration and he struggled with the last fastener. *Come on, damn it.*

The fastener snapped off. He halted and spread out his sensing ability. The nearest people were his guards, and they were too far around the corner to hear. He slipped out with ease. After replacing the cover, he bounded to his feet and hurried to the director's quarters. Using the nanites in his palm, he tricked the biometric reader into opening her door.

The squawk of a bird made his heart jump. He'd sensed the animal during his earlier recon, but the unexpected noise jarred his focus. He forced himself to concentrate. *So far, so good.*

With Sengupta on bridge duty, he shouldn't have any trouble here. He sat before the console and activated it. As he waited for his nanites to bypass security, the yellow bird paced on the perch in its cage. Its sharp pitched peeps grated his eardrums. Its nervousness fed into Jori's own and sent his thoughts racing.

Contacting General Sakon meant alerting him to the *Odyssey*'s potential flight plan. He'd likely attack this vessel, taking down its shields. Then he'd send a team to infiltrate the ship and rescue Jori and Terk. Jori wanted to get out of here, but Sakon's men were brutes. They'd probably kill anyone they came across, including J.D.

Jori's insides squirmed like a pit of snakes. Maybe he shouldn't contact the general yet. Captain Arden had said he'd take them to Chevert. Perhaps he could just tell Sakon to meet them there.

Jori sat up straight as the director's console lit up. He worked the dryness from his mouth as he clicked open the communications section.

His fingers hovered over the keypad. The address to the Chevert contact lay right there in his memory, but his hands wouldn't move. His eyes darted over the screen. All he needed to do was type.

Even if he told the general to pick them up from Chevert, he'd probably still attempt to waylay the *Odyssey*. *J.D. could die, but so could Calloway and those stupid Grapnes.* What about Lieutenant Sharkey? Although he didn't know her well, she always smiled, and her lifeforce reminded him of a sunlit body of blue sparkling water. He could use his nanites to stun them. That would keep Sakon's men from harming them.

His fingers finally moved. When the jumpiness in his gut intensified, he pressed his lips together and hardened his resolve. The medic, Calloway, and those damned Grapnes all deserved to die.

*****

3790:266:14:17. Jori inched back through the duct. As he neared the lounge, he sensed more Grapnes. Five lifeforces to be exact. Those *koshinuke!*

Their voices rang out, more piercing than the frantic bird in the director's quarters. "Where is he? He should be here! Find him, quick, before we get caught."

Jori's muscles tensed. He rolled out from the vent and swept the feet out from under the first person he came across. Another Grapne shrieked. He tossed the tool at him, striking him in the center of the forehead. The man fell back with a cry. One with a patch over an eye dived for him. Jori leapt out of the way. Two more pounced. He twisted and turned, kicking and hitting as he did so.

"Get him!" the one-eyed man squawked.

The shortest Grapne lunged. Jori spun away, but not far enough to avoid him. The man caught his arm and they tumbled to the ground. The one-eyed Grapne came at him with his yellowed teeth bared and a hypospray in his hand. Jori kicked the shorter man off him and jumped to his feet.

One-eye swiped at him. He leapt back into the viewscreen with a thump. The man charged again. He ducked away and rushed at another Grapne, ramming his head into his gut. The one-eyed man reached his backside, but the hypospray didn't make contact long enough to do anything.

Jori hopped over the couch and caught sight of his guards on the floor near the exit. He rolled over to one and snatched his phaser. Before he could get it to work for him, though, two Grapnes tackled him. His heart jumped to his throat as their weight pressed on him. *Chusho!*

The one-eyed Grapne showed all his teeth in triumph as he leaned over him with the hypospray. "I've got you now."

Jori jerked his body, trying to get out from under his captors. The other two Grapnes piled on, knocking the wind out of him. He tried to push them off or wriggle out, but to no avail. He lay helpless as the one-eyed Grapne leaned over and pressed the hypospray to his neck. The man's cackle dissipated into blackness.

42
Bombs Away

3790:266:14:35. J.D. Hapker sprinted down the hall. His lungs ached from the exertion. He barely recovered in the conveyor before daring through the opening doors and racing anew. The emergency call had said Jori's four guards were down. Hapker's heart had lurched at the thought of the boy hurting Sharkey, but then they stated five Grapnes held him hostage.

Jori had to be alright. He could defend himself, but against five?

I should have been there. His gut twinged. He'd failed him again.

He turned the corner and found several officers with their weapons aimed into the lounge. His eyes locked onto Sharkey's sprawled body and he broke out into a cold sweat. *Please, just let her be unconscious.*

He darted up to the armed group. In the center of the room stood the one-eyed Grapne grinning as he held up a small black device. Four other Grapnes did the same. The tallest carried an unmoving child-sized bundle over his shoulder.

Hapker stepped forward. "Jori?"

"Ah-ah. Thisss thing in my hand is a detonator, the cyclops hissed. "Don't think of shooting me either. It has a dead man's switch."

"We each have one." This other Grapne bobbed his head. "You can't shoot any of us."

"That's right." The one-eyed Grapne laughed. "Five detonators, five bombs."

Hapker swallowed.

Major Bracht's neck muscles knotted as he aimed his phaser. "You won't get away with this."

The one-eyed Grapne tittered. "Oh, yes we will. We have the upper hand. Let us go and we won't blow up your ship."

"You're lying," Hapker said. "You don't have any bombs. This is a trick."

Bracht snarled. "We know you how you people operate. Lies and deceit."

Cyclops elbowed a Grapne with a missing tooth. "Snyder, go ahead."

The man cringed. "But they'll shoot me."

"We have more weapons, idiot, now do it!"

The man released the dead man's switch. The one-eyed Grapne cackled. "No lies this time, Rabni."

Bracht opened his mouth as though to speak. An emergency alert sounded in Hapker's ear and likely the major's too. "Explosion on deck five, info center! Medical and security needed now! Fire bots responding!"

Hapker fought off a wave of dizziness as the blood drained from his head. They hadn't been lying. He took in the pale faces of the security officers.

"Shit," one said.

"What do we do now?" asked another.

Bracht's face twisted from white to red. "If anyone is hurt, I will tear you limb from limb."

Cyclops tsked. "Why all this trouble? We're trying to help you. The galaxy doesn't need these two monsters."

Hapker shook his head to clear it. "What do you want?"

"We're leaving, and we're taking this boy with us. Meet us in the docking bay with the other boy, and we will go. No more bombs."

"Not a chance," Hapker said.

"We don't negotiate with terrorists," the major added gruffly.

The Grapne replied, but Hapker didn't hear through the other alarm sounding through his comm.

"Fire out, smoke cleared," the reporting officer announced. "No injuries. Info console seven is damaged. We're still looking into what happened."

Bracht pressed his comm. "Ship-wide alert. Bomb threat initiated. Follow protocol five point eight. All hands to emergency stations. Civilians to the safety depots." He tapped again and informed Captain Arden of the situation.

"That was just a small one for demonstration," the one-eyed Grapne said. "There are more but you won't find them all. Let us leave and you have no need to worry."

Bracht growled. "Commander, what are my orders?"

Hapker dipped his head to the Grapne. "Alright. You may go."

The major shot him a black look. "You're surrendering again?"

Hapker bristled. "For now."

Bracht rumbled.

Cyclops frowned. "You better not try anything. We still have four more bombs."

Hapker wet his lips. He had to try something, but what?

The officers moved aside, keeping their weapons aimed, and the Grapnes inched by with wary eyes.

Hapker stepped back and gave the Rabnoshk warrior a significant look. The officers followed the five men and boy out while he and the major lagged.

Bracht glared at their backs with lips raised. He turned to Hapker with an expression nearly as dark. "I trust you're familiar with protocol five point eight. Are you also familiar with protocol nine point seven?"

Hapker nodded. The first initiated the bomb squad, comprising officers and a slew of bomb detecting robots. The second referred to hostage negotiations. "Letting them head to the docking bay will buy us time. If we're lucky, we can find and defuse them all before they leave."

Bracht's frown eased. "Yes, Sir. Good idea."

Part of the tightness in Hapker's shoulders let up. "They're headed to the conveyor. We should lock out the exits closest to their ship and make them walk. Send more officers down there, maybe an assortment of maintenance bots too. It'll hinder them a while longer."

"Yes, Sir."

*****

3790:266:15:01. J.D. Hapker zoomed to the conveyor exit Bracht had designated. A crowd of officers carrying or dragging materials blocked the way.

"Get out of my way!" the one-eyed Grapne screeched. "Now, or I'll set off another bomb!"

The Grapne pushed his way through. An officer dropped his load, sending engine parts clattering to the floor. The commotion drowned out Cyclops' ranting as he treaded through the mess, stubbing his toe in the process. He sneered at Hapker and Bracht. "Delaying us won't work! Tirad, let go of your detonator."

"No!" Hapker lunged forward.

"Stop!" the one-eyed Grapne shoved his palm at Hapker's chest. "Do not test me!"

The alarm sounded in Hapker's ear. His stomach dropped. *Not again.*

"Explosion in the aft lounge in section eight!"

Hapker's dread must have shown on his face because the one-eyed Grapne smiled. "You think I'm tricking you. This is your fault!"

Hapker raised his hands. "Alright. Calm down. Let's discuss this."

"No talking. You know why we're here, yet you hinder us. We are doing humanity a favor!"

"He's just a boy," Hapker said. "He hasn't done anything to you."

"Yet! Now get out of my way or I swear I will blow your ship to smithereens."

"Let's at least talk about it. We can work something out."

"No talk!"

Hapker hesitated as more information came in through his comm. "Three to sick bay. Minor injuries only." A new message clicked in. "Two bombs found. Deactivating them now."

Hapker sighed. That left one more. He stepped aside, letting Cyclops storm by. The other four Grapnes scuttled behind him, two still holding up their dead man's switch detonators, which would soon be useless.

Hapker leaned in, inspecting the boy thrown over the tall Grapne's shoulder. They'd bound his hands and feet. Drool dripped from his open mouth as his body swayed over the man's back.

"Bring me that other boy!" The one-eyed Grapne jabbed his free hand at Bracht. "You have five minutes!"

Hapker subtly shook his head, but it was unnecessary. The storm on the major's face indicated he had no intention of letting these Grapnes get away with threatening his ship.

The one-eyed Grapne huffed. "I want to hear you make the order!" His shrill stabbed Hapker's eardrums.

Bracht pressed his comm. "Medical, prep the boy for transfer and bring him to auxiliary docking bay seven." He paused. "Yes, Doctor. I understand." He let go of the comm. "The doctor says it will take fifteen minutes, at least."

"Fifteen minutes!" Cyclops stomped his foot. "I said I want him here in five!"

Bracht glowered. "If you want him dead, we can get him here sooner. Otherwise wait."

The one-eyed Grapne's mouth twisted. "You lie."

"Test me, if you dare, but I promise you're not half a stubborn as I am."

Hapker raised his brows in appreciation.

"He's awake!" The Grapne carrying the boy held tighter.

Jori's arms and legs twitched and a moan escaped his lips.

"Jori!" Hapker said. "Are you alright?"

The boy groaned. "You cowards," he mumbled. "Let me go."

An idea sparked in Hapker's head. "Jori, listen to me. The Grapnes say they've set bombs and will blow up our ship if we don't allow them to take you and your brother. Don't worry, we won't let that happen."

Jori growled. His body squirmed.

"Stop, or I'll set off another bomb!"

"You're not taking me," Jori replied. With a jerk of his shoulders, the tall Grapne screamed and let go. Jori fell with a thud.

Hapker knelt before him. "Jori, wait. I need to know if they're telling the truth. They say they have five bombs. Can you confirm that?"

Jori glowered but made a slight move of his head. Hapker held his breath, hoping he understood.

“Pick him up!” the one-eyed Grapne said.

“Don’t touch me, you cowards.” Jori kicked out. “You don’t have a bomb big enough to blow up this ship.”

Cyclops stomped his foot. “Do too! And if you don’t behave, I’ll prove it by blasting this ship into pieces.”

“He’s lying.” Jori spoke to Hapker but his dark eyes remained on the one-eyed Grapne.

“I’m not! I have bombs!”

“Five?” Hapker whispered.

“Five?” Jori copied.

“Yes, of course I have five. One for each of us. The detonator I have in my hand is the biggest.”

Jori barked a laugh. “I knew it! You’re lying!”

Hapker dipped his head at the major, hoping the man could read that he believed Jori. Bracht’s lips pulled back and he shook his head.

“I’m not lying!” the one-eyed Grapne bellowed.

“Another lie!” Jori replied.

“Are you sure?” Hapker asked quietly.

“I’m sure. I can practically smell the stench of deception on him,” Jori said in a low tone, barely moving his lips.

Cyclops jumped up and down. “I’m not lying! Tan, Clyde, let go of the detonators. Let go now!”

The eyes of the two Grapnes bulged and they shared a look. “Are you sure, boss?”

“I’m sure, you fools. Do it!”

They released the detonators. The one-eyed Grapne showed all his teeth. “See what you’ve done? Your crew is doomed.”

Hapker’s skin prickled as he waited for another communication.

“Well?” Cyclops said. “What are you waiting for? Pick up that brat and let’s go!”

Hapker jumped to his feet. “Enough!”

“Sir!” Bracht bellowed. “There’s one more!”

The Grapne moved back. “That’s right! One more. Don’t you come near me or you’ll all die when I let this go.”

“He’s lying,” Jori replied. “He’s impotent.”

“No! It’s true.”

Hapker stepped forward. “I don’t believe you.”

"Sir!" Bracht's tone carried his horror. "What if the boy is wrong?"

"He's not wrong." Hapker snatched the detonator from the man's hand.

The scene froze. No one dared even to breathe as they all waited for something to happen.

"See." Jori broke the silence. "I told you he was lying."

The one-eyed Grapne's face turned purple. "You brat!"

He leapt for the boy with a snarl, but Hapker grabbed his arm. Cyclops yelped as he pinned his hands behind him. Bracht took over and cuffed him, giving Hapker a look of reprove in the process. Security moved in and restrained the others.

Hapker crouched and placed his hand on Jori's shoulder. "Are you alright?"

The boy glowered. "How did I get here? We're almost to their ship."

"No. I never would have let them take you. If you hadn't woken up, I don't know what I would have done to stop them—but I would've done something."

Jori looked away with a frown. "Then why do you feel ashamed?"

Hapker examined his feelings as he removed Jori's bonds. "I'm not ashamed. I'm just sad that I had to let Captain Arden down."

"How?"

"He will see this as me putting your safety over the safety of our crew."

Jori's brow furrowed. "But he knows I can tell when someone is lying."

Hapker nodded. *He will still see my action as foolish and too risky.*

"Will you be in trouble?" Jori asked.

"Don't worry about it." Hapker clapped Jori on the shoulder. "I was right to trust you and now you're safe."

"Thank you," Jori said.

Hapker warmed. No matter what happened from here, he'd done the right thing.

43
The Dragon Wakes

3790:266:22:48. Jori awoke with a gasp and found himself surrounded by a swirl of darkness. His body stiffened as he strained to listen. Nothing but the sound of his pounding heart.

Earlier, he'd had a nightmare about being helplessly bound again, but it didn't feel as though one had woken him this time. He blinked at the shadows. Light filtered in. The blackness turned to greys. Shapes became more defined. The silence from J.D.'s quarters put him at ease.

What woke me up? His mind churned, trying to recall. No fleeting images teased his memory. Nor the lingering sensations of a dream. The feeling that he was missing something important overwhelmed him, though.

He focused his sensing ability. His mind's eye pictured a sun shining through the broad leaves of a hardimen tree, bringing him a warmth and strength he associated with J.D. The subdued peacefulness drifting from him meant the man slept soundly.

Jori rubbed his eyes. Whatever had woken him up didn't have any effect on the commander.

He fanned out his senses. The four guards standing outside radiated boredom. One also had a stench of sorts, making him think of the smelly cage of a blackbeast. *Calloway.* His nose wrinkled and he tightened his fists. Perhaps he was the reason he woke up.

No. The foulness of Calloway's lifeforce lurked in Jori's awareness but kept its distance.

He stretched out his senses a little further. A few other Cooperative officers passed now and then, but none felt threatening. He lay with a sigh, too tired to contemplate it further.

The heaviness of sleep eased over him. Then a sensation like a brush of wind tickled him. He bolted upright and froze, concentrating on the delicate impression.

"Terk!" His brother's lifeforce blazed. *He's awake!*

The covers flew off in one wild swoop. He leapt out of bed and zoomed to the door. It slid open too slowly for his pace, forcing him to twist his body sideways through the opening.

The slick floor of the corridor met his bare feet and he faltered. He recovered his balance and sprang forward.

Calloway grabbed him by the elbow, jerking him to a halt. The man glanced back at the commander's now closing door. "Where in the hell do you think you're going?"

A low growl escaped Jori's throat. "To see my brother." He jerked his arm, but Calloway held tight.

A swelling heat ignited in his cheeks. He gritted his teeth and yanked at an angle out of the hold, just like Sensei Jeruko had taught.

Calloway glowered. "No you don't. You're staying right here."

Jori balled his fists and stepped into a defensive fighting stance with the weight of his legs equally balanced. "I dare you to try and stop me."

As much as he wanted to hurry to his brother, a part of him had been looking forward to confronting this man. He was perfectly poised to make a quick kick into the side of his knee. Calloway would double over, allowing him to send a sidekick across his jaw. When the other guards came after him, he'd leap over him and use him as a shield so they all couldn't rush him at once.

The plan would work—if he had more strength. Instead of five weak Grapnes, he faced four sturdy guards. The urge to fight them fled as he imagined being helpless and bound by Calloway.

The foul man planted a hand on his hip. "Oh, please. Give me a reason. I'd love to throw your royal little tail in the brig."

Jori jutted his chin. "Not only do you lack the skill, you insignificant chima, you also lack the authority."

"You don't know anything, you little shit." Calloway's face twisted. "I'm in charge here now and if you try to leave, I'll kick your backside. Then I'll tell the commander I had no choice because *you* attacked me."

Jori's fingernails dug into his palms. J.D. wouldn't believe this cowardly liar, but everyone else might.

He glanced about and used his heightened senses to reevaluate the situation.

An alternative came to mind, prompting a shrewd smile. "There's one problem with your plan."

"What's that? You think—"

Jori darted around the man, twisting and ducking at the same time with his leg out so it swept the back of Calloway's knees and sent him tumbling.

"You're too slow and stupid!" Jori barked a laugh and raced down the hall.

"Blast it!" Calloway's voice carried despite the growing distance.

Jori's bare feet pattered rapidly, but his short strides allowed his guards to close in fast. He turned the corner and found more people in this corridor. He weaved around them with ease and sprinted to the conveyor.

Someone behind him yelped. "Watch out!" Calloway responded.

Jori laughed to himself as his guards ran into people and lost their gain. These Cooperative weaklings should take their martial and agility practices more seriously.

"Stop him!" Calloway's voice resonated with rage.

The conveyor opened. Jori brushed past the woman about to go in.

"Don't let him leave!" Calloway's ugly face appeared through the crack a half-second too late.

"Infirmary," Jori said to the computer, hoping the officers wouldn't implement security controls in time.

The conveyor jerked into motion but didn't move fast enough. Winded from the exertion, he worked to get his breathing under control. He tried to calm his racing heart, but his anticipation kept him from concentrating. Terk was awake but did he have brain damage?

The door opened to the hall across from the infirmary. Although his blood rushed through his veins with a prickling electricity, he forced an outward composure. He maintained a steady walk as he entered. His heart thumped as he neared Terk's area where Lieutenant Sharkey and three other guards kept watch.

Calloway exited a conveyor down the hall and charged him. "Stop, you!"

Jori met him with his hands clasped behind his back. He almost smiled. Calloway's light hair twisted every which way, and his face resembled the ripened red fruit he'd seen in the arboretum.

"It's about time," Jori said. "If you had come a moment later, I would've had to tell Lieutenant Sharkey you must not have been paying attention and didn't see me leave."

Calloway flashed his teeth.

"Shark-face," another guard whispered.

The foul man glanced over Jori's shoulder and paled.

Jori gave him his best smile and turned around.

"Saved by a woman," Calloway grumbled.

Jori's mouth soured. Running hadn't been his bravest idea, but it was the smartest. If Calloway pulled that shit again, though, Terk would be there.

His heart swelled as he entered his brother's room and absorbed his enlivened lifeforce.

44
Grappling with a Dragon

3790:266:23:39. J.D. Hapker stepped into the prince's room and stopped short. Something was different. Jori slept by his brother's side. Nothing unusual there. However, his brother had his arm draped over his shoulder.

Is he conscious? He checked the monitor. The numbers meant nothing to him. The ups and downs of the various monitoring systems could have been recording subspace signals for all he knew.

He glanced down at the boys and his heart jumped. Terkeshi stared right at him.

"You're awake," he said with unintended loudness.

Terkeshi made a slight nod. "You must be Commander Hapker," he croaked.

Hapker forced himself to smile. "Welcome, Prince Mizuki." He'd meant to call him by his casual name but thought better of it.

"First Prince Mizuki," the Dragon Heir corrected.

A shiver sizzled down Hapker's spine. Terkeshi spoke with the same bluntness as Jori, but with a deeper and more ominous tone. "Yes, of course. My apologies, First Prince Mizuki."

Terkeshi dipped his head, hopefully indicating the slight was forgiven.

"How are you feeling?" Hapker resisted the urge to shift his feet. *Don't be stupid. Prince or no, he's still a person.* He wasn't the first dignitary he'd ever spoken to, nor the highest ranking. *But maybe the deadliest.*

"Tired, but glad to be alive," the young man replied. "I understand I have you to thank for it."

Hapker tensed at the seemingly bitter tone, but he put on a smile anyway. "You really have Captain Arden to thank."

"Yes. I suppose so, but it's you Jori has spoken so well of."

There was no mistaking the bitterness this time. Hapker resisted the urge to swallow. “I feel the same for him. I hope you and I can be friends as well.”

Terkeshi raised an eyebrow.

Another shiver ran through him, all the way down to the tips of his toes. “If not friends, at least not enemies,” Hapker added.

“We shall see. For now, leave us be,” the young man said. “My brother is asleep, and I am tired.”

Hapker flushed at the dismissal but dipped his head and left.

Here we go again.

*****

3790:267:00:51. Jori awoke from the jaggedness of Terk’s emotions. His lids felt heavy, but more in a state of relaxation than sleep.

“I don’t get it. What do you see in him?” Terk said in a tone that belied his fatigue. “The commander is weak. It’s obvious he wants to play nice. Friends? What an idiot.”

Terk’s harsh words against J.D. stung like the bite of a giant hae fly. “It’s not so foolish to want to be on our good side,” Jori replied. “The Cooperative knows how strong we are.”

Terk made a noncommittal grunt. “It’ll only make it easier for us to redeem our failure.” He spoke in their secret language so the guards with their translators couldn’t understand.

Jori sat up, wide awake now. “What do you mean?”

Terk frowned. “I mean we kill our enemies and get out of here. Maybe we can steal some of their tech while we’re at it. We might even get help from General Sakon and destroy this ship.”

Jori sucked in a breath. “We can’t!”

Terk scowled. “Why the hell not?”

J.D. The commander trusted him enough to risk his crew and save him from the Grapnes—and probably got in trouble for it, too. He hadn’t told his brother about this yet, but his life being saved should be enough. “They’re not all bad—”

Terk pressed his lips. “Don’t be stupid. Father will stomp my head in and toss me out into space when he finds out I lost all his men, his ship, and the cargo. I’ve failed completely and there’s only one way to make up for it.”

Jori folded his arms. “I’m not being stupid. These people saved our lives. We’d be dead or under torture right now if it weren’t for them.”

“Yeah, yeah, yeah. You explained this to me already.” Terk flicked his wrist and the way it flopped about showed how weak he’d become. “Just because they helped us doesn't mean we owe them anything.”

“Don’t we?” Jori gestured sharply. “I, for one, am glad they saved you. Why shouldn’t I be grateful?”

“The fact that they rescued us makes them stupid.”

“They are far from stupid,” Jori snapped. “I've been watching them. I know we don't *have* to owe them, but there are certain people here who shouldn’t be hurt. If we must harm anyone, I'd rather do it to people who deserve it. Besides, Captain Arden has promised to take us to the Chevert space station and General Sakon knows to meet us there.” *Assuming he wouldn’t decide to ambush the Odyssey instead.* He ignored the twist in his gut and wore a stern expression.

“They are *all* our enemies.” Terk’s eyes darkened.

“Why? Because our father says so? Everyone is Father's enemy.”

Terk’s jaw muscles twitched. “If we don't come back with something, Father will beat us.”

“Father will do that no matter what. Besides, I don't care if we get into trouble.” He did care, but the prospect of punishment was distant. Their father never ran out of things to punish them for anyway.

Terk huffed. “Stubborn brat. You’re being stupid. Now leave me alone so I can regain my strength.”

Jori flushed with hurt. He wanted them to be close again, but Terk still treated him like a pesky flea.

If only he could help him understand. Sure, some guards could be hateful. Their hostility wafted over his senses even now. Not everyone was so bad, though. J.D. certainly wasn’t. The thought of betraying him to appease their father made his stomach writhe like he’d just eaten a bowl of worms. He never should have contacted Sakon.

45
Back to the Beginning

3970:269:01:18. Ander Vizubi's lungs burned. He gave into a cough, but of course, that led to another. His diaphragm jabbed his insides with each one and brought him to his knees.

"They're not coming!" Woolley's eyes watered as he covered his mouth with his cupped hand.

"Get on the floor!" Vizubi yelled hoarsely in between gasps. Smoke drifted upward, creating a haze. He blinked the liquid from his eyes only to have the fumes sting them into producing more tears.

Fung fell to her hands and knees. "I told you this was stupid."

She was the only one who had objected to the plan. Vizubi should have listened. Setting a fire in here, hoping the Grapnes would come so they could tackle them and escape, was not working out.

Vizubi's chest prickled, and he imagined a million tiny lacerations cutting into his lungs. "Put the—" He coughed. "—damned thing out."

"Done, S—" Fung gagged as she broke into a fit of coughs.

Vizubi glanced up. Tendrils of smoke obscured his view of the finger-sized holes near the ceiling. Since their cell door was plasti-glass, those small vents were their only source of fresh air. He kissed the cross hanging around his neck and prayed the smog would dissipate.

Bari blocked his nose and mouth with the crook of his arm. "They'll come. They can't afford to let us die."

"This won't kill us—at least, not right away," Quigley replied with a gravelly texture in her voice.

Vizubi pulled in a halfway decent breath. This had been a terrible idea, but damn it, it was the only viable one they'd come up with. Since the plasti-glass door had a transaction drawer built into it, the Grapnes hadn't needed to open it when they passed over Hesteben's drugs. Pretending Quigley was in pain didn't work either. Nothing they'd done enticed their captors to open the cell.

The air thinned. Vizubi's coughs subsided. Woolley panted, Fung and Bari wiped tears away, and Quigley closed her eyes and moaned. Hesteben had slept through this whole fiasco.

"If that drawer thing there was just a little bigger," Woolley said, "Fung could squeeze through it."

"Ha ha. Funny," Fung replied in a humorless tone.

Bari sat on the floor and thumped the back of his head against the cell door. "I was so sure this would work."

Fung glowered at him. "You should have listened to me."

"Yeah, yeah, yeah. You were right. So the fuck what. I don't see you coming up with any ideas."

Fung growled.

"Give it a rest, you two!" Vizubi called out before their nerves frayed completely. "Yes, so it didn't work, but we wouldn't have known that unless we tried. And we'll keep trying, damn it. We're not giving up."

They fell silent. He dropped onto his bed with a plop. There had to be a way out of this. Surely he and his team of experts could come up with something before the Grapnes reached the *Odyssey*.

*****

3790:269:02:25. J.D. Hapker zoned out. Terkeshi slammed the MDS down, making him jump in his seat.

He's more childish than his little brother. Hapker opened his mouth for a rebuke but thought better of it and pressed his lips together instead. It probably wouldn't do any good anyway.

"I gotta get out of this flea-ridden bed!" Terkeshi threw the covers off and swung his bare feet to the floor.

"The doctor advised you to rest one more day," Jori said in a flat tone.

"I don't care. If I lie here for a minute longer, I will implode with boredom."

Hapker clenched his jaw and braced himself for another tantrum. Terkeshi's outburst yesterday had nearly caused an incident. In a bout of frustration, he had sent his tray crashing into the wall. When security rushed in with their stun guns ready, his face turned fire red. Thankfully, the palimyogenesis treatment had still been in progress and the prince was incapable of reacting with anything other than curses.

Terkeshi swayed. Hapker kept his reproof to himself. The young man didn't have Jori's enthusiastic desire to learn or his level of concentration. While Jori spent as much time studying as he did in the gym, the elder prince only used his MDS to find instructional or entertaining martial vids. No wonder he was bored.

"Let's play a game of schemster." Jori's eyes lit up. Terkeshi twisted his mouth as though he'd eaten an unripe pomelo, but Jori didn't seem to notice. "I bet after a few games, you'll be ready to go to the gym. They have a great holo-program, better than ours. They also have an enclosed court for playing sports. J.D. taught me to play wall ball and it's a lot of fun."

Hapker smiled. Jori's liveliness reminded him of how his own little brother had idolized him.

His comm beeped. "Commander, come to Doctor Jerom's office, please," Captain Arden said.

Hapker excused himself, then met the captain along with Sengupta and Bracht. He noted the room's orderly side with its perfectly placed wall art and desk décor. Then he marveled at the chaotic side of the office with its book congested shelves. Various volumes stacked horizontally or vertically. Tall thin books sat by short fat ones. Even the arrangement of their subjects was mismatched. He made a mental note to ask the doctor later why he had physical books when everything could be digitized.

Doctor Jerom entered and shut his door.

"How is our patient?" Captain Arden asked.

"Very well, physically. There's no sign of brain damage and the palimyogenesis treatment is complete. He will be on his feet soon."

Hapker suppressed a shiver. "How soon? I know our medical teams can do wonders, but he just woke up from a coma a couple of days ago."

Doctor Jerom smiled at the compliment, then turned serious. "Although his muscles have atrophied, the palimyogenesis machine helped rebuild his cells. So rather than spend weeks or even months on rehabilitation, the young man will be back at his full strength in no time."

Everyone's gaze darted away as though they too were uncomfortable with the implications.

"How is he doing non-physically?" the captain asked Hapker.

He sighed. "Attitude-wise he's no worse than Jori was when he first arrived. However, I get a sense that he has more of a temper."

"He's probably better able to act it out, too," Sengupta added.

The captain's brow furrowed. "Do you get the impression he'll act out, Commander?"

He shrugged. "He seems moody, but not hostile. However, he's been giving the security officers ugly looks."

Doctor Jerom shifted his feet. He likely felt out of place now that the topic had changed from a medical standpoint.

"If I may, Sir," Bracht said. "We should keep the children separate so they don't collaborate."

Hapker rubbed the back of his neck. "It sounds like a good idea on the surface, but Jori and I are getting along well. He might be a positive influence on the older one."

The major huffed. "We're playing with a couple of Aurichian warheads here."

Hapker cringed at the exaggeration. The Rabnoshk people had coined the idiom after a weapons-factory accident obliterated a city.

The captain let out a weighted sigh. "What are the repercussions of keeping them separate?"

Captain Arden directed his question at Hapker, but Sengupta answered. "The elder prince might worry about what we are doing to his brother and perceive the forced separation as hostile."

"He won't have the benefit of knowing he can trust us." Hapker added. "He will learn the slow way, like Jori did. Not to mention that they haven't given us a reason to separate them. It seems wrong to be so strict with them when we weren't with the Grapnes."

"And together?" The captain glanced at everyone, including the doctor.

"As the major stated, they could collaborate and cause trouble," Sengupta said.

Captain Arden pinched his lower lip and stared at the floor.

"If we are seriously allowing them to stay together," Bracht replied, "the number of guards should remain the same."

"He's right," Hapker said, surprised he agreed with the man. "Remember, Jori is a level nine in hand-to-hand combat. He's too small to use his skill effectively, but that's not true for his brother."

"That's hardly a point in favor of keeping them together," the captain replied.

"No, Sir, but the major makes a good case and I'm only trying to be objective."

"We should also restrict them from the common areas," Bracht added, as though emboldened by Hapker's concession.

A spark ignited in his chest. *Back to this again*. "We should give Jori's brother the same considerations."

The Rabnoshk warrior frowned. "You said yourself the elder prince has a temper and has been giving my officers challenging looks."

"Looks only," he emphasized with a wide sweeping gesture. "Considering the last reprimand you gave, I expect them to have enough restraint to not be provoked by a few hard stares."

Bracht's nostrils flared. "I guarantee it won't be my team doing any provoking."

Hapker drew in a breath and let it go. "All I'm saying is we shouldn't overreact without them giving us a reason."

Bracht grunted. "Perhaps just restrict them from the workout room, then."

Hapker shook his head. "Why?"

"Because it's where most of the trouble has been."

"By *your* team."

The major huffed. "You don't know whether the boy started it. You weren't there."

"Even if he did, he's a child and these officers are mature adults. They should know better than to escalate things."

Apart from this single-mindedness to lock the boys up, the Rabnoshk warrior had been rational at times. So Hapker reasoned with him instead. "Consider what happens when soldiers get bored. These boys won't be any different."

Bracht grunted again, presumably conceding the point.

Captain Arden dipped his head as though in approval. In the past, the man had shown no reaction to their disputes. Perhaps he did now because Hapker kept his tempter this time.

The captain faced Hapker. "If we keep them together, does it mean you will have both children in your quarters?"

He wiped his hand down his jaw and sighed. "I believe it would be best."

The captain's eyebrows popped up. "Very well. Doctor Jerom? Anything else we should know?"

The doctor shook his head. "No, nothing more."

"Very good," Captain Arden replied. "Do you mind if I use your office a few moments longer?"

"Not at all, Sir."

"Thank you. Now, if you'll excuse me, everyone, I'd like a word with the commander."

When they left, Hapker braced himself. "Sir?"

The captain let out a long exhale. "Does the older prince know someone attempted to kill him?"

Trepidation wound through Hapker's insides. "I doubt it, Sir."

"What do you think will happen when he finds out?"

Hapker's insides shifted. "There'd be trouble. I can talk to Jori, try convincing him not to tell him."

"I'm not sure that will work."

"Maybe I—" *can remind Terkeshi that his actions against Gonoro were what precipitated it.* He couldn't say this out loud, though. He'd never told the captain about Jori's confession. His duty obligated him, but he feared the reaction. Every time he thought he understood the man, he found himself standing on shaky ground. He admired the captain for his understanding and moral integrity, but what if they conflicted with his sense of duty?

"—I can reason with him," he finished.

Captain Arden's face tightened. "You're placing an awful lot of trust in the child. You realize how much this puts our crew at risk."

Hapker rubbed his brow. Though he hadn't been reprimanded for risking the crew's safety by believing Jori about the bombs, he felt his chance of being accepted into this position on a permanent basis drifting further away. "Yes, Sir, but until he does something, we shouldn't overreact."

"What if that something is him killing someone?"

Hapker gulped. "Yes, but what if we treat him like a prisoner? You said yourself that we should take advantage of our opportunity to make peace. These boys are the future of Tredon."

The captain frowned. "I don't like this one bit."

"The circumstances aren't ideal, Sir."

"No, certainly not." Captain Arden sighed. "Very well. We continue as before. I'm trusting you to know when we can no longer safely manage this situation."

In other words, if anything bad happens, it's on me. "Yes, Sir. I will do my best."

*****

3790:269:08:45. Jori held Terkeshi's arm. "At least take it slow."

His brother didn't listen. He stood, stepped, and stumbled. Jori tightened his grip and let the weight fall on him.

Terk pushed him back. "I don't need your help." He puffed in and out as though he were about to try a difficult maneuver, then walked.

Jori noted a slight wobble, but his brother kept his feet without having to hold on to anything. By the time he dressed, all signs of instability had gone.

Terk slid open the curtain. "Let's go." He glared at the guards, then easily strode by.

Jori jutted his chin. Those bastards wouldn't dare mess with him now.

They met J.D. and he followed them out. Terk's upper lip perspired, but his jaw set in apparent determination as they headed down the corridor. His dark eyes glowed with intensity, as though he couldn't decide whether to be angry at himself for feeling so weak or excited about finally getting out of bed and doing something other than browsing an MDS.

They entered the gymnasium and Terk let out a low whistle. Jori beamed as he pointed out the various activities, ending the tour at the section where Lieutenant Gresher sparred with Sergeant Addams.

Terk narrowed his eyes. "So, Commander, what do you say you and I have a little sparring competition?"

Jori flinched.

J.D. emitted uneasiness. "I'm not sure that's such a good idea."

Terk's mouth twisted into a smirk. "Are you scared?"

"No. Just practical."

Terk barked a laugh. "Yeah? How's that?"

"If you beat me, especially despite your condition, I will look bad in front of my crew."

Jori glowered at his brother's broadening smugness.

"If I beat you," J.D. continued, and Terk huffed, "I'm afraid it will sour our relationship. We only have a few days left together. I'd like to make the best of it."

Terk's hostility fizzled out and Jori relaxed.

His brother turned to the guards. "How about any of you?"

Jori hid a smile as some darkened, two frowned, and another's eyes widened.

"No," the commander said. "If you wish to spar, use the holo-program."

Terk faced him with a glare. Jori intervened by pulling at his arm. He gestured at the far wall. "Over here. You've got to see this."

"Fine." Terk strutted by the guards with a wide mocking grin, making them turn darker.

Jori showed him the holo-field. "Do you want to try it?"

Terk's brows rose. "This is much bigger than ours."

"And better. Watch." Jori adjusted the machine to a lower level. Despite Terk's determination, he wouldn't be able to do this for long. Best not set him up for failure and increase his agitation. When his brother would take on more than he could handle and failed, he'd mask his humiliation with outrage.

He didn't mind Terk's hostility with the guards, but the hatred toward J.D. worried him. It bothered him so much that he hadn't told him about the Grapnes, Calloway, or the medic. Even though the commander had nothing to do with those things, his brother would explode and take out his rage on the first Cooperative officer he came across.

Jori wouldn't let that happen. Since Terk was as tall as many of the officers here, he left the height level of the holo-man on its current setting. The haptic image appeared, ready with its hands up and its legs planted in a balanced fighting stance.

His brother jumped into action. Strike. Strike. Block. Kick. His movements started out awkward, but he soon gained a moderate rhythm.

Jori watched with satisfaction. Terk moved slower than usual, but fast enough for this level—enough to inspire sensations of either awe or disquiet from the onlookers.

Terk's exhaustion crept into Jori's senses, but he didn't stop. Before his fatigue caused him to make a mistake and set off his temper, Jori stepped in. "Let me take a turn."

He worked the same level for the same amount of time so as not to show his brother up. When he finished, he barely sweat while Terk's face still sheened a bright red.

"It's hard to believe you were in a coma not too long ago," Jori said, hoping to mitigate his brother's rise of annoyance. "I doubt any of these Cooperative people could recover so quickly."

The tactic worked in one way. Jori sensed Terk's inflated pride, but it bolstered into arrogance.

"So, what about you, Commander?" Terk swept his arm toward the holo-program. "If you won't spar with me, let's see how you do here."

"No, thank you," J.D. replied.

"Why not?"

J.D. sighed. "My own skills are not as good as yours."

Terk cocked a smile. "You admit it?"

"I have no shame in who I am."

Jori soaked in the commander's emotions. He told the truth and spoke with confidence. He wasn't afraid either. Although Terk meant to be intimidating, J.D. only exuded a calm sense of wariness. Cooperative people were strange, but Jori couldn't help but admire the man.

His brother, however, radiated disdain. "You should be ashamed of being a coward."

J.D.'s eyes narrowed. "Taking advantage of those who are not as skilled as you is what's cowardly."

Terk darkened. He squared his shoulders and planted himself in front of the commander. "You wouldn't last a day in the Toradon Empire."

"Stop it, Terkeshi," Jori whispered.

Terk and J.D. glowered at one another. While Jori's stomach rumbled, his brother's antagonism grew and the commander's mixed with anxiousness and irritation. Whatever the man's nervousness, though, he didn't back down. He met Terk's eyes with one brow raised in a dare.

Terk tightened his fists and Jori's heart leapt to his throat. "Stop!" He stepped between them and nudged his brother back.

"Some other time, then," Terk said, acting as though it was his idea. "I've got better things to do anyway." He turned and marched off.

Jori fumed. *Why must he be like that?* Anyone but J.D.

46
Kimpke Again?

3790:270:13:16. J.D. Hapker sat at the far end of the bar, the same spot as the last time he'd been here. His head rested on his hand as he leaned on the counter and absently stirred his drink.

"I haven't seen you like this since the Yendunian dignitaries tried to blackmail you."

Hapker startled. He'd tuned out the hum of the lounge and hadn't heard her approach. "Oh. Hey, Sharkey. Yeah. The Yendunians. I'd take them over the Tredons any time."

"More trouble?"

He looked up and rubbed his chin. "Let's see. The elder prince has been giving the security officers dirty looks since the day he woke. He tried to pick a fight with me yesterday. And today… He provoked Bracht."

She whistled.

"Nothing came of it. The major kept his composure. He'd made a good point the other day, too—I'd be better off playing with a couple of Aurichian warheads."

"That explains why I'm seeing you here again so soon."

He sighed. "It's the only place I feel like I can get away." His shoulders ached from holding so much tension. "I've never had such a need to practice meditation."

She let out a short laugh and tapped the side of his glass. "So, you're taking up the methods of the Zurenian monks?"

He chuckled. They'd met a Zurenian monk at the PG Institute. The man loved to drink. It was common with his order, he'd said. According to him, they drank a liquor made from a certain plant that grew in the mountains where they lived. Since he didn't have access to it at the institute, he quested to find a close substitute.

"I can't count the number of times I saw him in a stupor," Hapker replied of the monk, "or the number of places."

She snickered. "Remember that time in Professor Minski's class?"

"We must've let a dozen of his mice loose in his clothes before he woke."

"I've never heard a grown man scream like that."

They burst into a fit of quiet laughter.

"Remember how he flailed his arms?" Hapker mimicked the movement, not caring if anyone else saw.

"He made up a new dance!"

Hapker shook with laughter at the memory of how the man's robe had almost come loose as he bounced around in circles and flapped about like a mad bird.

"The look on his face…" He copied the expression.

Sharkey pounded the bar with her fist.

He laughed until his sides hurt, then they both fought to catch their breaths.

She wiped her eyes. "Minski was so angry."

"He threatened to turn his pet snake loose so it could find what was left of its food," Hapker added.

"Lucy," she said. "I wouldn't have minded. She was so sweet."

"Sweet? I never would have thought of it as sweet."

"Definitely sweet."

Hapker let out one more small chuckle, then regained his composure. "Thank you for that," he said regarding the memory.

"You looked like you needed it. I haven't seen you laugh since you've come to this ship."

"You mean since Kimpke." All mirth left him as the weight of his worries returned.

"Please don't tell me you're taking up drinking because of him."

"This is non-alcoholic. I only came here to get a break."

She patted his arm. "Jori was challenging too, but you became friends. It'll happen with the other one as well."

He wished he had her confidence. "I don't know. He's very…" *Rude? Confrontational? Moody? All the above?* "Surly."

"And older."

"And stronger." He sank forward, chin on fist. "This is it, Sharkey. I think my career is over."

Her eyes popped. "Don't say that! You're doing great."

He gave her a dubious look.

She raised her hand, forestalling his comment. "Okay, so your confidence is still low. It's coming back, though. Just a few days ago, you whistled in the halls and walked around with a frozen smile on your face."

"That's because of Jori. Now we're dealing with the Dragon Heir and he's threatening to be a real dragon. Jori can be curt with his remarks, but he never tried to goad anyone into a fight."

Terkeshi's attitude didn't bother him as much as the captain's unspoken criticism. He wanted to serve him, but he also wished to do right by the boy. Adding the trial of the elder prince's confrontational behavior, he practically saw the mountain he was about to crash into.

He opened his mouth to confide in her when his comm beeped. "Hapker here."

"Commander," the captain replied. "I'd like to speak to you privately in my office, please."

The man's voice had a hint of urgency to it. Hapker ran his hand down his face. *What now?* "On my way," he said instead.

*****

3790:270:14:07. J.D. Hapker fell heavily in the chair without meaning to.

Captain Arden didn't seem to notice. The man closed his deskview down. His hands wiped the flat surface of his desk in a motion that seemed distracted. Then he folded them and inhaled noisily. "Admiral Zimmer has ordered we bring the children to him."

Hapker froze as if struck by wind from the ice planet, Sardeer. He opened his mouth to protest but the captain had more to say. "There's a PG-Force Destroyer nearby…" Hapker gasped. Captain Arden gestured for him to listen. "…But I've convinced the admiral we escort them ourselves for diplomatic reasons. We will meet him at the Chevert outpost while they search for the *Brimstone* to make sure it doesn't interfere."

"Sir! You can't do this."

The captain lifted his eyebrow at his tone.

"You promised them," he continued, trying to control his rising panic as their previous understanding unraveled. "If you go back on your word, there's no telling what they'll do."

"Then we must make sure we're ready to handle them when they find out."

Just when Hapker thought he was on solid ground, the earth crumbled beneath him. "Sir, you can't! You know it's wrong. They're not criminals. I admit the elder prince is a handful, but what happened to making a good impression on them for the sake of peace?"

The captain raised his palm.

Hapker ignored him. "What happened to trying to avoid a war? If Admiral Zimmer takes them into custody—"

"Enough!"

He snapped his mouth closed, cutting off the dozens of other arguments that spun around in his head. He breathed heavily while gripping the armrests of his chair.

"I know the potential consequences," Captain Arden said in a moderate tone. "As do you, but we have our duty to the Cooperative."

Hapker had wondered earlier whether the captain would choose duty over morality, and it seemed his question was answered.

"It's not something I want to do," the man continued.

"Then don't do it." *How can he be so calm?*

The captain raised his palm again. "We have our orders."

The gravity of the man's tone pressed down upon him. "Did you tell him how much headway we've made with the youngest?"

"I told him as much as he'd allow. You know how he is. He has his mind made up and he stopped listening."

Hapker leaned forward and almost folded his hands together in a prayer of supplication. "Can't we appeal to a higher admiral?"

The captain nodded. "I'm already working on a report, but I wouldn't count on it having any effect anytime soon. If the higher admirals disagree with his order, it will take time to trickle down."

"We don't have time, do we?"

"I'm afraid not."

Hapker sat back with a slouch. The warmth he had once experienced in the captain's office now felt frigid. The carved wooden animals on his desk reminded him of dead things with empty eyes. Scenic pictures on the wall resembled distant places he wished he could be instead of here. One painting of a mountain struck him with its formidability and starkness.

"Commander," the captain said, snapping Hapker's attention back. "We've talked about this before, but some things have changed—especially between you and Jori. Can I still count on you to do your duty?"

Hapker pinched his lip and stared at the painting of a mountain without really seeing it. He was a strategist. He should think of something. This wasn't right.

He couldn't go home with his career in shambles, though. He didn't want to live as a failed copy of his father, and he certainly didn't want the shame from his father hanging over him like a dismal cloud.

Besides, Bracht would stop him if he tried to prevent this. In the end, Jori would still wind up in Zimmer's hands. To defy these orders was pointless.

"I don't like this, Sir," he said in a low thick voice, "but I'll do my duty."

Captain Arden's eyes softened. "Sometimes we must make hard choices. I don't like it either, but I'm glad you'll see it through. I'm not ready to lose another commander."

Hapker hung his head despite the captain's comments. "Did you contact the *Brimstone*?"

"No. I decided to wait until after I spoke to the admiral. Now it seems there is no need."

Hapker nodded. It made sense. If only he'd contacted the Tredons first, though. Then there'd be an additional reason to let the boys go home.

"What about the warrant?" he asked. "If the *Brimstone* got wind of it, they may already know the boys are here."

"There's no longer any record of it."

Hapker frowned. "Do you think they pulled it when they found out we had them?"

"Since they generated it falsely, Depnaugh authorities probably deleted it."

Darn it. He had no way out of this, no argument left. Hapker leaned forward and planted his elbows on his knees. "May I suggest, Sir, that we say nothing to Jori and his brother about this until the last possible moment?"

"Excellent idea."

"Is there anything else, Sir?" Hapker asked tonelessly.

"No. I think that's quite enough. Don't you?"

Hapker's limbs were almost too heavy for him to move, but he managed to stand. "Yes, Sir." *Quite enough.*

He moved toward the door.

"Hold on," the captain said. "I have one more thing to add before you go."

Hapker turned and clutched the chair back to keep the sinking feeling from taking over. "Sir?"

"This conversation is strictly between you, me, Major Bracht, and Director Sengupta. I won't make the same mistake as last time, so no one else will know sooner than the children."

"Yes, Captain," Hapker replied solemnly.

47
Reality Threatens

3790:270:15:22. Jori shifted from his reclined position on the couch. J.D. had told them he would be out for a while, so he read the treatise he mentioned.

"Terk, you should read this."

"Why?" His brother said absently as he watched something on his MDS. His leg hung over the arm of his chair.

"It's very interesting," Jori replied, too excited to keep this discovery to himself. "It shows how our mining facilities and factories would earn so much more if they invested in making them faster and more efficient."

"How does that even make any sense? Spend money to make money?" Terk's eyes never left the screen. He was probably watching one of those rediscovered movies from the twenty-first or twenty-second century where all the action was grossly fantastical but still entertaining.

"Because they're making the mining and manufacturing machines faster and more efficient," he repeated.

"If we do that, then what will all the slaves do?"

Jori suppressed a flippant reply. "They could learn other trades and create more and better products," he said instead. "We get to expand our trading capacity and, in turn, make everyone richer."

"You mean make them richer and us poorer."

"No. We'd earn money off the trade by charging taxes."

Terk glanced away from his screen and frowned. "What the hell are you reading anyway? It sounds like something Father would beat you for."

"That's because he thinks everything undermines him. We're falling behind technology-wise because we limit our people's ability to learn."

Terk scoffed. "Why do we need to learn anything if we can just take what we want?"

Jori scowled at his brother's short-sightedness. "Because while we're still relying on outdated weapons, everyone else will develop more effective ones."

"Not everything we have is outdated." Terk pointed at his palm but was referring to Jori's since his own nanites had not taken effect.

Jori showed his own hand. "Yes, but how much did Father give up to an outsider to get this?"

Terk rolled his eyes. "Stop reading that crap. You talk like that around him, you'll end up like Montaro."

A chilling wave curled in. The memory of what happened to one of their other brothers was too brutal to contemplate—and one that often found its way into his nightmares.

Montaro had been next in line after their eldest brother Dokuri had died. However, he was so incompetent that Father killed him. Both Jori and Terk worried about this for themselves and for each other. They were the only two heirs left. Father couldn't have any more children, but this didn't stop him from trying to pit them against one another.

Terk twisted around to face him. "Seriously. Put that away and help me find a way we can recover from the disaster the Grapnes created."

"You're not still talking about hurting these people, are you?"

"Of course I am. I told you, we *have* to."

Jori set the MDS down and sat up. "No, we don't. We can tell Father they kept us prisoners the entire time."

"I won't go home a complete failure." Terk returned to his MDS as though the matter was settled.

Jori leaned forward and growled to regain Terk's attention. "These people saved our lives!"

His brother turned back to him with his face dark and his eyes darker. "Do you want to end up like Montaro? Do you want *me* to end up like Montaro?"

Jori flinched. "No."

Terk huffed. "Then use your sensing ability to find that stupid prototype."

A bitter taste rose in Jori's mouth. What his brother wanted him to do was simple enough. The captain had several areas of the ship guarded. All he had to do was search for emotions related to those on guard duty—boredom, unfocused thoughts, and perhaps a touch of vigilance—and use his knowledge of the ship's layout to deduce the device's location.

Taking it would mean going against J.D, though. His chest tightened as various scenarios played through his mind. In one situation, Terk fought and killed the commander. In another, they waited until he was off doing something else and battled others instead. Not just those like Calloway, either.

His imagination carried him to where his brother snapped Lieutenant Sharkey's neck. Then he found a weapon and shot down guards, medics, and anyone else he came across. At the end of this imaginary scene, they ran into J.D. anyway. Jori practically heard the commander asking why they were doing this.

The meal Jori had eaten earlier threatened to come back up. *Maybe no one has to die.* He replayed events, this time with no lives lost. The image of the commander asking why returned, and somehow made him teary.

No. He couldn't do it. He wouldn't betray J.D. He considered saying as much, but his brother could just do it himself. He had the same ability, though not as keen. Maybe if he let the matter drop, Terk would forget about it or decide for himself that these people didn't deserve to die. Maybe nothing bad would happen with General Sakon either, and they'd meet him at the space station soon.

Jori's brooding thoughts had not eased by the time J.D. returned. He glanced at the commander, hoping he had recovered from his mood with Terk. However, his naturally crooked mouth looked more like a half-frown than a half-smile.

Jori focused his senses. A heaviness pressed down on him as J.D.'s despondency, worry, and fear doubled his own emotions. Something was wrong, but he didn't want to ask about it. If he did, the question might be turned around on him.

He left the matter alone and tried to get back to his reading as an overwhelming sense of uncertainty swelled like a dying star.

48
The Twig Snaps

3790:271:08:22. Ander Vizubi closed his eyes and counted his breaths. No matter what he did, though, apprehension and irritation clung to him like a junkie begging for a fix.

None of their escape plans had worked and their last brainstorming session turned into a ridiculous storyfest. Worse, Hesteben had just taken another dose of starhash. The man talked to himself while pacing the cell like a hyperactive pendulum.

Woolley clenched his fists and snarled. "Will you sit the fuck down already! Or at least quit the damned muttering."

Hesteben halted. "Screw you, man. I didn't complain when you all did that martial crap earlier. I was having a pleasant dream until someone knocked Bari onto my bed."

Vizubi ground his teeth. If these two weren't bickering, it'd be Bari and Fung. While Quigley seemed to take it all in stride, Vizubi struggled to keep from strangling them all.

"What the hell do you have to complain about?" Woolley replied to Hesteben. "You chose to be here."

"I didn't choose this. They were supposed to let me out!"

Woolley sprang to his feet, planting them in a wide stance. A purple vein pulsed in his forehead as he sputtered. "What about us, you asshole? We shouldn't even be here!"

"Quit your whining, man. No one's being hurt."

Woolley roared and lunged. Bari caught him by the arm and jerked him back. Vizubi jumped between them.

Hesteben stepped back and laughed. "You can't touch me, man. Not when I got my big bro on my side."

Heat erupted in Vizubi's skull. He imagined his eyes spewed fire as he faced his brother with gritted teeth. "I'm not on your side, you dolt! Now sit your asses down, both of you, or I'll tie you up and make you stay in opposite corners."

Hesteben flinched. “Alright, alright, Andy. But he started it.”

Vizubi jabbed his finger. “Don’t you talk to me about who started it.” He paused, debating whether to say more about Steben’s starhash addiction.

He thought better of it and glowered silently until the two men found their cots. His blood cooled, leaving him with a grating headache.

He fell onto his bed and cradled his forehead in his palm. *Please, God. Get us out of this mess before we kill one another.*

*****

3790:271:15:32. Jori rested on the bench with his hands behind his head. Birds twittered above within the canopy of trees. The red-capped bird was among them—the same one as before. It fascinated him how some animals had a distinct essence the way people did, though creatures were less complicated.

His gaze flicked to three nearby squirrels. The chitter-chatter of one echoed from the branches of a tree while the other two foraged below. This noisy rodent could be the father-squirrel cursing at the younger ones. The two on the ground might be brothers, each doing their own thing, ignoring the other. Did squirrel families grow apart as they aged?

An ache swelled in Jori’s throat. Terk hadn’t made more than a few perfunctory remarks today. Had their argument set him off? Maybe J.D.’s despondent mood influenced him.

How much worse could this ordeal get? This mission had started out so well. The time he and Terk had spent at the outpost was the best they’d had together since Dokuri died. Neither had been to a station outside of Toradon territory before, so they both enjoyed exploring and watching all the strange people. They’d laughed, wrestled, and talked on about both important things and the mundane.

Now they either argued or didn’t speak at all. He wanted to blame the Grapnes, and even the Cooperative. The more he tried, though, the less sense it made. He and Terk had been growing apart for some time. Their fun together at the outpost was nothing more than a false hope.

The bird hopped about and the squirrels romped. Jori sighed. There must be a way to mend their relationship. However, the idea of going along with Terk's plan sent his stomach galloping. Ever since Gonoro, he hated hurting people. Even the thought of harming these creatures bothered him. To hurt J.D. would be much worse.

The tree canopy blurred as his eyes watered. Betraying J.D. by taking the device troubled him too. He had to find a way out of this.

Sensei Jeruko had instructed him to memorize the layouts of various starships, including ones like the *Odyssey*. Now it paid off. He had figured out the most likely location of the device by using his ability to locate a taint of guardedness.

He hadn't told Terk yet and considered telling him he couldn't find it. Lying didn't sit well, though. Sensei Jeruko always said it was cowardly. Jori should just face up to his brother and tell him he wouldn't do it. But then it'd drive them even further apart. Then Terk might act on his own and get caught.

Damn. The consequences would hurt no matter what he chose.

A foulness permeated his brooding. An image of a dirty blackbeast cage flashed in his mind.

Chusho. Calloway was here.

Jori usually slept during his shift, but time had gotten away from him. He sat up, not wanting to leave but reluctant to stay with that man's presence marring the arboretum's tranquility.

He swung his feet to the ground just as an ugly head poked around the bushes.

Calloway smirked. "Well, well, well." He stepped into Jori's full view. "If it isn't the little dragon spawn."

Three other guards slid in behind him.

Jori tensed. "What do you want?"

Calloway swelled with giddiness and loathing. Hostility surged from the other men. The one called Hammer also carried a touch of nervousness.

"I see you've got nowhere to run this time," Calloway said, his tone full of menace.

Jori's skin crawled. The confrontation had come, but the odds were against him. He kept his eyes locked on the foul man while searching the corner of his eye for options. He could either flee by jumping through a tangle of bushes and screaming for help or face his enemy. He doubted anyone would come to his aid, so he rose with his fists at his sides. "What's with your friends there? Are you too frightened to come at me alone?"

Calloway's eyes gleamed. "Aw, them? They're only here to make sure everyone knows you started it and that I kicked your backside in self-defense."

"Coward!"

"I'm not the cowardly one. You murdered my family. You ravaged my sister to death. She was just a girl and you dirty taipans took her like the animals you are."

Jori suppressed a shiver as an iciness bit into him. "I did no such thing."

Calloway barked a laugh. "You're a Tredon. That makes you culpable. You and all your people should be exterminated."

Jori could practically feel the heat from the man's eyes as they burned with battle-lust and malevolence. He wet the dryness of his mouth. *I can beat him.* Yet he'd rather face his father's anger than this righteous wrath.

Calloway charged him like an angry blackbeast. Jori leapt out of the way. The space was so small that he came within reach of Sergeant Addams who seized his arms. He twisted his body, breaking the hold.

Before he could straighten, the palm of Calloway's hand slammed into his chest, knocking the air out of him. He flew backward, landing with a hard thud. Sensei Jeruko had taught him how to recover from a fall but catching his breath after such a blow took longer.

He regained his feet in time to duck under Calloway's swing. Two more punches came at him and both missed. He balled his fist and slammed into his opponent's kidney. The feebleness of his attack did nothing. He opened his mouth with an insult ready on his tongue but Terk appeared.

His older brother's elbow drew back, then a loud pop echoed as he struck Calloway in the center of his ugly face. "Chima! Don't touch my brother."

The foul man landed with a grunt.

The guards closed in, surrounding them. He and Terk fell into a battle crouch and stood back-to-back, ready to fight them off.

"Evade!"

His brother's command in their Toradon tongue spurred him to duck. The air crackled above him as stun fire zipped past. A yell cut short, indicating one guard had shot another by mistake. Jori grabbed the wrist of the man holding the phaser and flipped, twisting it. The weapon dropped with a clatter.

A loud thump sounded behind him and a shock of pain entered his senses. He glanced back to see Terk had knocked Calloway down.

"Stop!" a female voice yelled. "Stop, damn it! That's an order!"

Addams grasped Jori by the shoulder. He turned his arm about, breaking away once again. His heart pounded wildly while the heat of his brother standing behind him provided comfort.

Addams and another man both lunged at him at once. His smallness came in handy, but he had to separate from Terk by twisting and ducking, then darting under their legs.

"Get off me, you chima!" Terk yelled as new arrivals tackled him.

Jori rolled to a halt and found himself at Gresher's feet. He moved to rise, but the lieutenant pressed his shoulders as he squatted to his level.

"Stop," Gresher said, radiating a quietude that stilled Jori's energy.

He considered using the nanites in his hand as a weapon, but Gresher emitted no hostility. The man didn't have any emotions he associated with violence, so he stayed put.

Another loud pop grabbed Jori's attention. Addams sprawled on the floor. Calloway retaliated by plunging his fist into Terk's gut. His brother grunted, but the blazing inferno burning in his eyes indicated it wasn't enough to stop him.

The distinct buzz of a phaser discharged and Terk halted mid-strike. He fell, folding into a heap.

Jori tried to push himself up. "No!"

Gresher clasped Jori's upper arms. "He's okay."

Jori swallowed down his panic and focused his senses. Terk was unconscious but fine, although surrounded by armed guards.

They all turned to him at once. Gresher rose and helped Jori to his feet as well. He wrapped his arm around him as though protecting him.

"What in God's name is going on?" a man yelled.

J.D.

A fiery rage filled the commander's features. A vein on his forehead pulsed and his lips twisted, making his usual half-smile look like a snarl.

Everyone stiffened, including Gresher.

Sharkey pushed her way through the gathered crowd. "I told you all to stand down!" Her red face contrasted with her cold and hard eyes.

The guards tucked their weapons away and stepped back. Some bowed their heads in shame, but others matched her dark look.

Jori's limbs trembled and a wave of dizziness snuck in as adrenaline coursed out. He gulped, each intake of air sending a spasm of ever-increasing pain over his chest.

He endured it stoically and hoped his face reflected the same indignant outrage as J.D.'s and Sharkey's.

"What the heck happened?" J.D. demanded no one in particular.

"He broke my nose." Calloway pointed at Terk's unconscious form as blood gushed from between his fingers.

The commander peered at Terk and shook his head. Jori sensed his disappointment and it inflamed him. He jabbed his finger at Calloway. "He. Hit. Me!"

J.D. met Jori with eyes less heated.

"You attacked me," the foul man replied, his voice nasal from pinching his nose.

"Liar!" Jori pushed forward against Gresher's grip. The lieutenant held firm, so he ducked out of it.

J.D. lifted his hand. "Stop!"

Jori halted with a growl. He thrust his finger at Calloway's stupid face. "He cornered me here. Then he and his cronies attacked me. Terkeshi was only protecting me from this koshinuke." *Terk came to my rescue.* A brief spark of elation ripped through his temper.

"No." Calloway shook his head. "It was him. He charged me. I was only defending myself."

"You liar!" He marched to the man with a snarl.

The commander pulled him back. "Stop, Jori!"

Jori jerked out of the grip.

J.D. knelt close enough for Jori to feel his breath. "I believe you," he said in a calm tone.

Jori's growl died. He sensed the commander's truthfulness and noted the earnestness in his eyes. Those same eyes darkened when they turned to Calloway. Calloway's face twisted, undoubtedly offended that the commander sided against him.

"Are you alright?" J.D. asked Jori.

He nodded. The pounding of his heart subsided.

"Let's get you and your brother to the medical bay, alright?"

The commander gave Gresher and Sharkey a look. They acknowledged and retrieved Terk.

"What about me?" Calloway said.

J.D. scowled. "You want us to carry you out too?"

Calloway's face tightened and turned scarlet.

Addams stepped before the commander. "Aren't you going to arrest them?"

"Let's see who struck who first and go from there," J.D. replied. "Report to Major Bracht immediately, all of you."

Eyes darted about with unease, except Calloway's. His darkened, especially when he looked at Hammer who winced under the scrutiny.

J.D. nudged Jori, but he waited. Terk's head bobbed about as the two lieutenants carried him out.

Jori glowered at Calloway who staggered behind. *Chima.*

49
The Rat

3790:271:16:27. A team of medics met J.D. Hapker and the others in the corridor just before they reached the medical bay. Sharkey and Gresher set the unconscious prince on a gurney.

Terkeshi wore his night clothes, as did Hapker, only the light colors and soft material did nothing to deter from Terkeshi's hard appearance of a warrior. Despite his current peaceful state, his jaw still clenched, and his brow remained tight. The short sleeves of the shirt revealed the taut muscles of his arms. No wonder Calloway's face was such a mess.

Medic Shera did a quick scan before letting the other team members roll Terkeshi away. Hapker allowed Jori to follow his brother while he stayed with Sharkey and Gresher.

"The prince and I were getting ready for bed when he rushed out yelling that Jori was in trouble. I let him run ahead as I retrieved my comm and called for security. By the I time arrived, it was mostly over. You were there before me. What did you see?"

Sharkey's forehead wrinkled. "We didn't see how it started either. When we arrived, our security officers had the two boys surrounded."

"They were all fighting," Gresher added.

Hapker rubbed his brow. Considering Calloway's previous behavior, the officers might have been the instigators. He had a hard time believing an officer with Addams' rank would act this way, though. "Alright. Report to Bracht. Tell him what I told you as well."

"You're not coming?" Gresher asked.

"Not yet. Everyone knows how biased I am. It would be better if you gave your objective views first."

Hapker dismissed them and headed to the medical bay. He found Jori's examination room and entered. He crossed his arms and leaned against the counter as Doctor Gregson ran a scanner over the boy's body.

"Does that hurt?" the doctor asked as he pressed his hand onto Jori's sternum.

The boy didn't even flinch. "A little."

The doctor reviewed his findings and faced Hapker. "He's definitely been struck recently. And hard, too."

Hapker straightened. "How hard?"

"Not enough to fracture anything, fortunately, but enough to leave a remarkably large and painful bruise if I don't treat it."

"No treatment," Jori replied.

The doctor looked down at the boy and rested his hand on his shoulder. "You are very brave, but there's no reason for you to be in pain if we can ease it."

Jori frowned. "I said no."

Doctor Gregson sighed and patted Jori's arm. "Alright, then. Let me know if you change your mind."

Hapker peeked over to where Terkeshi lay silent. The elder prince looked so peaceful, but he doubted the peace would last when he woke.

He massaged the pulsing ache in his forehead.

"Commander."

Hapker's head popped up. "Captain." He pulled back his shoulders.

Captain Arden gestured, indicating he wanted him to step out. Hapker gave Jori what he hoped was a reassuring expression, then met with him.

"What happened?" Though the captain's flat tone held no hint of anger or accusation, his eyes tightened.

Hapker closed the privacy curtain behind him, and they moved out of earshot. He stood erect, maintaining an outward confidence while suppressing the urge to fidget under the intensity of the man's steely gaze. "The elder prince rushed out of my quarters saying his brother was in trouble. It was over by the time I arrived but Gresher and Sharkey had arrived before me. They stated they saw several officers surrounding the two boys. Jori claimed Calloway struck him and Calloway said it was self-defense. The doctor says Jori has been punched in the chest. Calloway has a broken nose, and someone stunned the elder prince. Those are the only facts I have so far."

He clamped his mouth closed, realizing everything had come out in a jumble.

The captain's lips pressed into a thin line. "I won't even ask what your opinion is."

The hint of reprove in the man's voice prompted Hapker to justify his stance. "Calloway's tried to start trouble before."

The captain made an almost imperceptible shake of his head. "You're not making any friends by constantly siding with this child."

Hapker cleared the dryness from his throat. "I'm doing what I feel is right, Sir."

The captain's eyes narrowed.

"Not that I'm going against you, Sir," Hapker added hastily. "I'll do what I must." *Even though it's wrong.*

Captain Arden exhaled noisily. "I've been considering things, Commander."

Hapker held his breath.

"I want you to go with them when the admiral takes them."

"Sir?" This wasn't what Hapker expected him to say—or what he'd hoped.

"You said yourself once that these children need an advocate. I realize you and Rear Admiral Zimmer don't get along, but this might go better if the princes know they're not in this alone."

"And if there's someone to remind the admiral of his moral obligations."

The captain raised an eyebrow. "I doubt he would do something immoral."

Hapker cleared his throat. He could debate that taking them in the first place was wrong but thought better of it. "Thank you, Sir, for the assignment."

The captain's blue eyes seemed to turn grey. "I believe you are the best one for the job," he replied in a dull tone.

A cold, heavy feeling filled Hapker's gut. Was this Captain Arden's way of saying he wouldn't keep him as his second-in-command? The man veiled his disappointment too well with the compliment.

"In the meantime, though," the captain continued, "we will place these two in a cell until this gets sorted out."

Hapker's heart leapt to his throat. "Sir, we don't even know if they caused it yet."

"There has been violence on my ship, Commander." The captain's blue eyes darkened. "And when you side with this child, you neglect your duty to this crew."

Hapker stood stunned, as though the man had slapped him. "Yes, Sir," he said. "You're right, Sir."

He hung his head, crestfallen. It was over. He had failed for the last time.

*****

3790:271:17:19. Silas Arden left the medical bay with a hardness in his gut. No one ever claimed being a captain was easy. He wanted to trust in Commander Hapker but opposed his blind faith in these children. His old commander, Commander Frida Findlay, had divided his crew with her harshness. Now Hapker created dissonance of his own, albeit unintentionally.

Arden frowned. His wife had pointed out that Hapker's tendency to see the good in everyone was a promising trait. He agreed. This quality of his could do very well when they returned to the center of Cooperative territory and performed more diplomatic functions. In this current situation, though, the commander came across as being naïve.

"Pardon me, Captain."

Arden stopped short. He'd been so lost in thought that he almost ran into the officer stepping out of the conveyor. "My apologies," he said with a small smile.

The officer moved on and Arden took his place in the conveyor. "Main Security." An almost imperceptible jolt indicated its movement.

Locking the children in a cell didn't sit well with him, but it must be done. That he'd allowed things to go this far by continuing to give Hapker the benefit of the doubt was inexcusable. Someone could have been killed.

The conveyor let him off at the main security hall. Arden stalked into the meeting room. Four officers stood in the center with feet planted wide and hands behind their backs. They glanced up when he entered but quickly looked away again.

Bracht turned his back on them. "Captain."

Before Arden could ask for a report, the Rabnoshk warrior tilted his head toward his office. Arden followed him inside. Despite his mood, the cluttered room captured his interest with its various old-fashioned weapons and other memorabilia from Bracht's homeworld. Where most people kept such things hanging on a wall or sitting on a shelf, the major had them out as though for playing.

"Captain," Bracht said again when the office doors closed. "I haven't sorted this out yet, but I've interviewed them separately and there are discrepancies in their stories."

"What sort of discrepancies?"

"Discrepancies with how it started, Sir. All say the boy instigated it, but when pressed for details, they hesitated. That is, everyone except Calloway. He seemed to have a story already prepared. If I didn't know any better, I'd say they rehearsed this."

Arden stared at him with incredulity. "Are you telling me you suspect our people started it?"

Bracht let out a growl directed at the officers outside. "I hate being wrong, Sir, but…" The warrior pressed his lips together.

Arden waited.

The major flushed and glanced around as though looking for the proper words. "But Hapker may have been right in his arguments against Calloway."

"And right about the children, it seems."

Bracht darkened. "I wouldn't take it that far, Sir."

Arden let the comment go. "So, what do you suggest?"

The major puffed out his chest. "I believe Private Jacques Harmel is the weak link. I haven't pressed him too hard yet, but I bet with both of us here we can break him."

The major's words almost sounded like he intended torture, but Arden knew better. "Bring him in."

Bracht stepped out and barked for Harmel. The man's face turned white as he entered. However, he placed himself in full attention before them with no other sign of nervousness.

The major bared his teeth as though ready to rip the man to pieces. Arden decided on a subtler approach. He paced while looking down and pinching his lip. The silence hung for a long while.

Harmel shifted in his weight several times. Arden let the quietness dwell a little longer.

He stopped mid-stride and planted himself in front of the man with a granite expression. The private flinched. Sweat formed on his upper lip.

Arden stared hard. “I heard you started it.”

Harmel’s eyes widened. “Me?” he said in a high-pitched tone.

“You,” Arden replied tersely.

Harmel wagged his head. “I didn’t start it. Not me. Whoever told you that was lying.”

“There seems to be a lot of that happening here lately and I’m utterly disgusted with it.” Arden maintained an unyielding scowl. He didn’t use this expression often, which was why it was so effective.

“No, not me. It was Corporal Calloway’s idea. He said they killed his sister. They deserve this.” Harmel’s eyes darted about as though searching for a way to escape.

Arden’s outward composure remained firm, but his surety shattered. Hapker was right.

“Major,” he said without turning to Bracht. “Tell Commander Hapker that he is not to lock up the children after all. I want these four taken there instead.”

“But, Sir!” Harmel tottered as he spoke, as though his legs turned to rubber. “Please, Sir. It wasn’t my idea. I only thought we were going to scare him. I didn’t know—”

“Enough!” Arden’s blood boiled. He held back a string of criticisms telling him how irresponsible, dangerous, immoral, devious, and just plain stupid this was. “Get this man out of my sight,” he said to Bracht instead.

With that, he turned and stomped out of the room and on out of the meeting area with a dark rumbling cloud of thunder and lightning following in his wake.

50
The Guilt Trip

3790:272:00:18. Jori yawned. He'd slept fitfully while the stun Terk received moved him from a state of unconsciousness on to the normal stages of sleep. He had stayed by his side the entire time, trying to make the best of an uncomfortable chair and the sensation of J.D.'s melancholy mood.

J.D. had gone to do his duties. Terk still rested, but his rising sense of wakefulness prompted Jori's own mental state to alertness. After a long stretch of his arms, he leaned onto Terk's bedside. Hoping to head off any residual agitation left over from Calloway's attack, he made sure his brother saw him first thing.

Terk blinked and frowned. "What the hell?"

Jori placed his hand on his chest. "You're fine. Just a little zap."

Terk bolted upright. "Those koshinuke!" His eyes darted about as though looking for someone to fight. However, the guards kept their distance outside the room. Jori had suggested everyone stay away until he talked to his brother, and J.D. agreed.

"Don't worry." He attempted to push Terk back down. "They got what they deserved."

His brother glowered. "So, they're dead."

Jori sighed. "Even Father doesn't do away with his own people for starting fights."

"He would if they fought *him* or tried to kill us."

Jori leaned in with a furrowed brow. "They weren't trying to kill us." He bit the inside of his cheek to keep from thinking about how calloused his brother was becoming.

Terk grunted. "That Calloway sure felt like he was."

"He's too cowardly to take it so far."

"He deserves to die," Terk replied. His dark mood kept him from catching Jori's half-lie. Calloway *was* a coward, but his rage over what his people had done to his sister had driven him beyond reason.

"His punishment is much longer-lasting," Jori said lightheartedly, trying to keep his tone from being argumentative. "You broke his nose in front of all his peers. Now he's the one sitting in a cell instead of us."

Terk cocked his head. "They locked him up?"

Jori smiled even though guilt gnawed at him regarding Calloway. If someone had murdered his sibling that way, there would be no stopping his vengeance.

The information didn't seem to appease Terk. He ground his teeth and rubbed his chest where the phaser stun had hit him. "We'll make sure he gets what's coming to him when we deliver this ship to General Sakon."

Jori sucked in his breath. "We can't let him have it." He kept his voice low, even though no person or no translating device could interpret their secret language.

Terk released an exasperated sigh. "Not this cursed argument again."

A sinking feeling sent Jori's gut rumbling. He hadn't meant for the issue to resurface, so he said nothing in hopes the conversation would end.

Terk's current frame of mind wouldn't let it pass, though. He leaned in with teeth clenched. "We will do whatever it takes to make up for this disaster."

Jori's chin dropped. "I don't want to," he muttered.

Terk darkened. "Fine. You can stay here, then."

Jori looked away. His brother couldn't have meant it, but his anger made the words sting with truthfulness.

"Have you found where they're keeping the device?" Terk asked.

"Yes, but I don't want to do this. I can't betray them after they saved our lives."

Terk growled as he threw his covers off and swung his feet to the floor. "Damn it, Jori! We're taking that thing back and we're helping Sakon capture this ship."

"We can't! You know what he will do to the crew. Calloway might deserve it, but J.D., the captain, and the women here certainly don't."

His brother emitted a wave of unease, but he was like a blackbeast over a fresh kill. “Why the hell are you being so stubborn? These people are not our friends.”

“Most aren’t, but some are.”

Terk’s face twisted. “The commander is *not* your friend.”

Jori crossed his arms. “He’s not my enemy either.”

Terk slammed his fist on the bed. “Idiot! You think that because he’s being nice to you, he won’t turn on you the moment he’s given the order? We are enemies, whether you like it or not. It’s just how it is.”

Jori looked away. His jaw worked in frustration. How could he argue against such stubbornness?

“You said you sent Sakon a message?” Terk asked.

Jori’s stomach rumbled. “He knows we are on a Cooperative ship and headed to the Chevert outpost.”

“No one here is aware you’ve contacted him?”

Jori shook his head.

“Good. If the captain told you we’re allowed to contact him when we get close to the station, then we will put this to the test—see if these people are friends or enemies.”

Jori folded his arms. “He was telling the truth.”

“Don’t be so naïve. We should be near enough to the station by now, yet has he offered to let us call him? No, he hasn’t. They’re not letting us go.”

“I don’t believe that,” Jori said with a certainty he didn’t quite feel.

Terk smacked him in the shoulder. “Well, then, why don’t you hack into the commander’s console while he sleeps to see how much they’re really trying to help us.”

Jori hung his head. He was running out of excuses. “I don’t want to.”

“Damn it, Jori!” Terk loomed over him with a heated glare. “Do you want me to fail? Do you want Father to kill me the way he killed Montaro?”

Jori averted his gaze. His courage failed. If only he was as brave as J.D. had been against the admiral and do what was right instead of what his father expected of him. “No.”

“Are you sure? Because if Father kills me, that means you will take my place. Is that what you want?”

Jori's mouth fell open. "No, of course not!"

"Then make up your mind on whose side you're on," Terk said with a bit of spittle flying. "You're either supporting me or fighting me. Which is it? Are you my brother or my *competition*?"

Jori crossed his arms as though his brother had punched him in the stomach. "I would never go against you," he mumbled.

"Look at me, Jori." Terk's tone softened but it still had a hard edge to it. "If I face Father empty-handed, he will see me as a failure. Don't think for one moment that I haven't noticed how much better you are at things than me."

Jori shook his head as he held back tears.

Terk raised his hand. "We both know it's true. All you need is a couple more years to gain strength and you'll beat me at *everything*. If I don't prove my worth in another way, Father will kill me."

Jori's chin quivered. "I'll hide it from him."

Terk's temper dropped. "Then he'll kill you," he said mildly. "Help me, Jori. Let's do this together, like we planned. Let's show Father we're better together than we are alone."

A tear trickled down Jori's face.

Terk touched his cheek. "I need you, little brother."

Jori's vision blurred as more tears washed down. Rivulets followed his jawline and dripped from his chin. The truth of his brother's words warmed him. They were close again, just like he'd wanted. It came at a cost, but at the moment that cost seemed trivial. "Fine, but on one condition."

Terk narrowed his eyes.

Jori squared up his shoulders and told him. Before Terk objected, he spilled out a scheme that would give them both what they wanted. His brother couldn't do any of this on his own. Jori was the one with the defensive nanites. He was also the one with the most knowledge of ship functions and computers. Terk could've pushed it, and Jori probably would have given in, but the plan was solid.

"Alright then. It's decided." Terk placed his arm over Jori's shoulder. "Now quit being such a baby," he said in mock sternness.

*****

3790:272:20:34. Jori sensed the deepness of the commander's slumber. Even though the man slept with his bedroom door closed, Jori tiptoed to the console in the living area where he and Terk were also supposed to be sleeping.

It was time. There was no going back now. Jori bolstered his resolve as he turned the machine on. "I'm in," he said.

Terk paced. "Hurry, damn it," he whispered.

"This isn't easy," Jori replied in the same quiet but annoyed tone.

Terk leaned over his shoulder. "You're in, aren't you? Just find out where we are."

Jori huffed. "I'm in the commander's console only. I must be careful with what information I look at or we'll get caught."

"Yeah, yeah, yeah. You have to sneak through a room full of snakes without getting bitten. I get it, but hurry before he wakes."

"I can do this much faster if you leave me alone," Jori said through his teeth.

Terk growled and resumed his pacing. Jori blocked his brother's frustration while keeping a thread of thought linked to J.D.

After a few moments of examining the interface, he found the access point to the ship's navigation information. Dare he click it?

He had to take each step with care. If he came upon an alarm system, it would all be over. It wasn't quite like tiptoeing through a room full of snakes, but it was the best analogy he could think of that his electronically illiterate brother would understand.

Several minutes ticked by and Terk's frustration broke through his thoughts. Jori let out an exasperated sigh. "Will you sit and focus on whether the commander is still sleeping?"

A hushed plop indicated Terk sat. Jori clicked the navigation icon and waited.

His heart leapt. "Got it," he said a little louder than intended. He wasn't sure if relief or disappointment jarred his emotions. A part of him wanted to get caught.

Terk bounded to his feet and hovered over him again. "Where are we?"

"Hold on." Jori mentally calculated the coordinates. A lump hardened in his throat. "We passed out of range of a communication hub yesterday."

Terk bolted upright. "I told you!"

Jori shushed him. "We'll reach the station in a few hours."

Terk's face darkened. "Why did we pass the hub? You said the captain promised to let us speak to General Sakon."

"Maybe he wants to wait until we're actually at the station," Jori replied with a confidence he didn't have.

"Why in the hell would he do that?"

"The same reason he wanted to wait until just before we reached the station—to give Sakon no time to plan anything."

"Check for transmissions from the captain," Terk said sourly. "Let's see if your *friend* has contacted the station and made arrangements."

Jori swallowed the hardness forming in his throat and did as his brother wanted. Opening the captain's communications proved challenging, but he succeeded without alerting the security system to the breach.

One message from an Admiral Zimmer glared at him. He poised his finger over it and held his breath. *Might as well get this over with.*

The image of an older man popped up on the screen. Admiral Zimmer had an ugly, high-bridged nose and a weak chin. The man's crisp and lofty tone made Jori twist his mouth in immediate dislike. Goosebumps formed on his arms as the captain tried to argue in his favor but kept getting cut off.

"I've heard enough, Captain," Admiral Zimmer said with a chop of his hand. "Bring the boys to me. I will be at Chevert in three days."

Jori's mouth fell open as frigidness radiated from his core.

Terk's face contorted in a volcanic expression. "I knew it!"

The heat radiating from him clashed into Jori's senses and sent him reeling. "He promised."

Terk slapped the side of his head. "You're an idiot! I told you they're not our friends. We move as planned."

A sensation of numbness replaced the heaviness in Jori's chest. He had held on to the small hope of Terk changing his mind if the captain kept his word, but that hope crashed and burned like their ship.

He forced back his tears. "We should wait until we're a little closer to the station so General Sakon can find us."

"How long?"

"Three hours should be enough." Jori slouched and stared at the console.

"Let's finalize our plans and then get some rest." Terk's hard and resolute tone matched his emotions.

Jori nodded dumbly. This would happen whether he wanted it to or not. The symbolic ship hadn't crashed. It drifted lifelessly into a dark abyss.

51
Dragons Unleashed

3790:272:23:31. Jori bounced his feet while waiting for J.D. to dress. The time had come for the man to attend his duties and for them to stop him. He willed himself to still and tried not to dwell on what he was about to do.

Terk lounged in the chair with his arms crossed as though he hadn't a care in the world, but Jori sensed his internal tension. Where his own nervousness carried dread, Terk's was peppered with determination.

So far, the nanite defense functions in Jori's hand worked well. Bio-reader information had been gathered from the commander and guards. If all went smoothly, his nanites would replay the steady recorded signals as though the readers still operated.

He nearly jumped when J.D. exited his room.

"You two are up early," the man said with a smile that didn't touch his eyes.

Terk stood in a stiff at-ease stance. "Why haven't we been able to talk to General Sakon?"

J.D.'s jaw dropped and Jori sensed a barrage of apprehension bespeckled with guilt.

"You betrayed us?" Jori quivered as his body swelled with heat. This explained why the commander had been downcast, but he still couldn't believe it.

The man moved his mouth, but no sound came out. The heaviness of his emotions contended Jori's own.

Terk emitted a sense of vindication. He planted himself in front of the commander. Muscles corded in his neck. "Speak!"

J.D. hung his head. "The admiral ordered us to bring you to the Chevert outpost."

Terk's face reddened. "And do what with us?"

"Turn you over to him," J.D. said in a pained voice.

Terk's arm shot out and his fist slammed into J.D.'s temple. The man crumpled to the floor Terk kicked, pummeling his rib cage.

Jori rushed in. "Terk! Stop!"

His brother halted with his knuckles poised to strike. His mouth contorted into a snarl. "Liar!"

The commander lay on the floor like a beetle on his back. His elbows drew to his sides and his arms protected his chest. "I didn't lie. The admiral gave an order. I had no choice."

Terk snarled. "You betrayed us."

Jori leaned in, trying to placed himself between them. "We are betraying him too," he said in their secret language.

J.D. rolled to his side as though to rise. Terk growled and raised his fist again.

The commander stayed on the floor with one arm hugging his ribs. "Look, it will be alright. The captain has allowed me to go with you to act as your advocate."

Terk barked a laugh. "What good will that do?"

"Tredon or no, you have rights. The admiral won't hurt you." J.D. panted.

Jori took in a breath that trembled through his body. A numbness fell over him like a crashing wave. "You should have told us." He sensed the man's trepidation, but it paled compared to the intensity of his regret.

"You can just tell the admiral to go stick his head up a blackbeast's ass," Terk said. "We're leaving."

"Don't do this." J.D. pleaded with Jori.

"I made a choice to do my duty, J—Commander." Jori's voice cracked, his betrayal making him unable to use the man's common name. "As did you." Something swelled deep inside him and he struggled to keep it down. This was no time for sentiment.

"Oh, Jori. I'm so sorry, but we can get through this. You don't—"

"Shut up!" Terk threatened to strike him again. When Hapker didn't move or speak, he turned to Jori. "If you don't want me to kill him, then I suggest you tie him up."

Jori nodded. He ducked behind the chair where they'd hidden the linen bonds made from sheets. As Terk stood guard, ready to strike, he bound Hapker's feet first, being careful not to meet the man's eyes. His fingers tingled with numbness as he drifted mindlessly about his task.

"You don't need to do this," the commander pleaded.

The man's guilt tugged at Jori's heart, but he shoved it into a deep well of emptiness instead. "I do."

"Jori, please."

"You should just use that nanite weapon you have in your hand," Terk said in their secret language. "That way he'll shut the hell up."

"I'll gag him," Jori replied. The nanite shock might do too much or not enough. It could also deplete its energy.

He finished binding the man's hands behind his back and grabbed a wide piece of linen. As he wrapped it over Hapker's mouth, their eyes met. He froze. His anguish threatened to overwhelm him. "I'm sorry."

He clenched his teeth to keep his chin from quivering and stood. Although this wasn't the commander's fault, he and his brother couldn't allow themselves to be kept as prisoners. He balled his fists in resolve and pushed his emotions away, letting the emptiness return once again.

Terk checked Hapker's bonds. "You ready?" he asked Jori.

He nodded. They headed to the exit but paused before the door sensor activated and concentrated their sensing ability.

"I sense four people on either side," Terk said.

"Me, too." Jori recognized them all by their essence but tried not to think of them as anything other than the enemy.

"You take the ones on the left." Terk grabbed the foot-high statue of a water bird from the table. "I'll handle those on the right. Get their weapons as soon as you can and reset the bio-sensor."

Jori flexed his hand. Once they confiscated the phasers, his nanites would defeat their security and allow them to use them.

He inhaled and grabbed the decoratively carved stick from Hapker's wall. He twirled it and tested its weight and balance. Exhilaration flushed through him. All his senses intensified as a familiar thrill of battle came over him. This was what he'd trained for, what he'd been born to do.

He and Terk rushed through the opening door together but split as soon as they were out. Jori swung the stick into the gut of the closest guard on his left. At the same time, he used his other hand to snap open the man's holster. As the guard fell, he snagged the phaser and discarded the wood carving. His nanites instantly disabled the bio-sensors, enabling him to shoot. A guard dropped. With a quick somersault, he rolled up beside him and snatched his weapon too. A half second was all his specialized nanites needed. He tossed it to Terk.

A female guard jumped aside, avoided his next shot. The man behind her pulled out his phaser. Jori fired, stunning him to unconsciousness. Then he dived away as the woman blasted her weapon. A flare of power crackled through his hair but missed his head. He rolled to his knees and shot her.

Jori rose and swept his gaze over their handiwork. All eight guards were down. No one moved.

"Gather their phasers," Terk said as he grabbed a guard by the legs and pulled him into the commander's quarters.

Jori confiscated weapons and comms. His clothes didn't allow any place to carry all the phasers, so he dumped four into the recycle chute, being careful not to look at Hapker as he lay helpless on the floor. Using the heel of his boot, he destroyed the comms and threw the resulting scraps away.

Terk brought the last guard inside just as Jori finished. He handed two of the four remaining phasers to his brother. "The bio-sensors have been reset. You have ten stun shots in each."

Terk palmed the weapons in each hand and planted himself in the center of the corridor. "Lock the door." He swiveled his head, checking both directions with his eyes and sensing ability.

Jori popped off the outside door panel with ease. It shouldn't be effortless, but the intensity of his training made it so for him. With it open, he aimed his phaser and disabled the mechanism.

He closed the panel, hiding any evidence that something was amiss. "Let's go."

Since his ability was more acute than Terk's, he led the way. He paused at the first intersection. "Three people coming."

They ducked behind the corner. Jori held his breath and focused. He sensed the hilarity of the unaware trio before he heard their echoing laughter. So far, no one had raised an alarm.

"The fewer people we have to shoot, the better," Jori whispered.

Terk's jaw twitched as the trio approached the intersection. Jori laid his finger over the trigger but otherwise remained still.

The people turned to the opposite corridor without noticing them. Jori breathed again and they prowled the hallway the others had just exited until they reached the conveyor.

Jori focused his senses. "I think someone's in it." The car moved too fast for him to be certain.

The doors slid open. Terk fired at the man before he noticed them.

"Bridge peripheral," Jori said as the conveyor closed the three of them in. Security protocols didn't allow them to enter the bridge itself, but this stop brought them close.

Jori concentrated his senses on their destination. "Two guards outside."

Terk raised his weapon. "Left and right, as before."

The conveyor doors slid open. Jori jumped out and shot the guard on his side while Terk took out the other. As his brother pulled them into the car with the man, Jori tinkered with the conveyor's control panels.

With the three people shut inside, Jori glanced up and down the corridor, assessing the situation. "We must hurry. Disabling the conveyor will alert maintenance."

Before they moved on, a foulness crept into Jori's senses. "Calloway," he said with a rumble in his throat.

Terk's eyes lit like a torch. "I thought you told me they locked him up."

"They did." He concentrated. "He's being accompanied by two guards."

His brother's expression hardened. "He's mine."

They waited just out of sight in the curved corridor. Calloway emitted a smoldering sense of displeasure. Perhaps he'd requested the meeting so he could plead his case. He'd never get the chance.

The first guard appeared around the curve of the wall. Jori fired and the woman fell. Terk shot Calloway in the leg, causing him to crash to the floor with a yell. Jori struck the second guard.

Terk charged and smacked Calloway in the side of the head, cutting off his cry.

The foul man shielded his face with his hand and tried to rise. Terk and Jori stopped him with their weapons aimed at his chest. He reddened and his burst of fury assaulted Jori's senses.

"They let you out?" Terk said.

Calloway turned purple. "Yeah, but thanks to you I'm not wearing a uniform, you ugly taipan."

The man moved to stand again and Terk pointed his phaser at his forehead. "Don't even think about it, koshinuke."

Calloway remained on all fours. "I knew it. I was right about you all along, you little monsters." He displayed his teeth in a wide grin.

"Don't test me," Terk said. "You're part of the reason we're doing this. You think you're better than us, but you're the same."

"You fucking animals won't get away with this." Calloway huffed. "The Cooperative will hunt you down and end you and your entire race."

"I think you're the one who will be ended," Terk replied with a mocking smile.

"You monsters!" The man's rage did not move him to act. He stayed on the ground with them towering over him. "You murdered my sister. You have no right to live!"

Jori's hate for the man slipped as a stab of pity struck him. "I'm sorry about your sister. My brother and I had nothing to do with it, but I'm still sorry."

"Fuck you!" Calloway jabbed his finger at them and stood. "I hope you choke on your own—"

Terk shot him. Calloway folded to the floor. He fired the stun weapon again.

Jori slapped his arm away. "No!"

Terk glared at him.

Jori met his glower. "You promised."

His brother's eyes blazed with hate. "That coward attacked you. He must die."

"You promised," Jori said through his teeth. That was the deal. He'd help Terk but only if no one was hurt.

"You've got to be kidding me. You can't mean for that promise to apply to *him*."

Jori held his glare.

"You stayed too long with Mother." Terk's expression soured but he lowered his weapon. "Let's go. We're wasting time."

Jori stiffened as a sudden sensation hit him. "There's someone else coming."

Terk cocked his head, listening with his ability. Then he grabbed Calloway by the collar and dragged him. "Quick. Over here."

Jori forced the conference room doors open and Terk pulled the three people in. They waited as the person approached. At first, there was no hint of concern. Then a sense of curiosity seeped out. Her growing confusion indicated she was probably trying to use the conveyor.

"Let's take him," Terk said, apparently unable to recognize Director Sengupta's essence. "He knows there should be guards there and will call it in."

Jori opened the doors and they rushed out. Sengupta's eyes bulged, then closed as a phaser blast struck her. Terk grabbed her arm and pulled her into the conference room with the others.

They discarded their spent weapons and collected fresh ones from the guards.

"Alright. Let's go," Terk said.

They darted out and took cover before the corner to the bridge entrance. Jori sensed four guards on the outside and several people on the inside.

"Can you tell who's in there?" Terk asked. "We must get that Rabnoshk warrior first."

Jori concentrated his senses. "He's there. At the tactical station, I think. Captain Arden, too. His chair."

"I'll take the Rabni," Terk said. "You take the captain, and we'll go from there. Move fast before they lock down the ship."

Jori nodded. If someone did that, the plan would fall apart.

They shot down the four guards with ease and entered the bridge. Jori struck the captain in the back. He darted around the platform and blasted the helmsman. A woman yelled. He fired his stun weapon, cutting off her cry for help. The communications officer tapped on his console. He stunned him too.

Silence cut through the command center. Jori panted, glancing about the room in disbelief. Men and women sprawled on the floor or slumped over their consoles. Except for the odd angles of their limbs, they could have been sleeping.

"The ship is ours." Terk clapped Jori on the back.

Taking the bridge had been easy, but they had more to do.

Terk brought in the four guards from outside. Jori jolted into motion, locking the door then hastening to the communications console. He moved the officer out of the way and tapped at the controls.

His brother gathered weapons and removed devices from all the officers, then slapped two bio-readers onto Jori's workstation. "Here. Fix these. I'll contact the general."

Terk took his place while Jori executed the scanning function of his nanites. Within moments, the red glow of digits illuminated on his hand.

"General Sakon," Terk said in their native tongue into the comm console. "First Prince Mizuki here. Respond."

Jori memorized the bio-readers' identification codes. He handed one to Terk and put the other in his pocket. If they succeeded, Sakon could use these to lock onto their location anywhere on this ship and beam them both away.

"Authenticate," a rough voice transmitted.

"One-seven-zero-one-dash-four-seven-ro," Terk replied.

Jori used another console to lock down all the conveyors. His brother tapped his fingers as he waited for the reply.

"First Prince Mizuki," a new voice broadcasted. Jori recognized the guttural slur of General Sakon himself. "How are you able to contact me from a Cooperative ship?"

"We've taken it over."

Jori reached over Terk's station to lock out the ship's internal communications, then analyzed their location and trajectory at the helm. *Not far from Chevert.* His shoulders fell. If the admiral had ordered the captain to meet somewhere other than this station, Sakon would have been too far.

"How do I know this isn't some trick?" the general said.

Terk scowled. "You have my authentication code. The Cooperative is too weak to force that information from me."

General Sakon grunted. "Of course, my Lord. Will you need escort into Toradon territory, then?"

"No. You must come here. There have been… Complications." Terk shot Jori a side-eyed glower. "We won't have control of the ship for long, so get here as soon as you can and beam us off."

"Yes, my Lord. Your coordinates?"

Jori gave his brother the information plus the identification codes for the bio-readers. Terk rattled them off to Sakon.

"We've had our own complications, but we'll be there in thirty-three minutes," the general replied.

"We can cut that time down and meet you part way. Your heading?"

After they coordinated, Jori showed Terk how the helm of this vessel differed from their own. His brother wasn't as familiar with foreign ship controls, but his pilot skills enabled him to catch on quickly.

"Go do your thing," Terk said.

Jori replaced his phasers with fully loaded ones. He sensed two people outside with emotions indicating confusion. With communications and automated systems down, more would gravitate toward the bridge.

He unlocked the entrance and ducked aside. As soon as the doors slid open, he shot the closest. The other drew back and Jori stormed after her. The woman raised her arms as though she could deflect his phaser blast, and fell with a thud.

Terk left his station to help as Jori grabbed her sleeve and pulled her in.

"Lock the door like I showed you," Jori said.

Terk nodded. The bridge doors closed him in. Jori leaned against the wall to catch his breath and gather his wits. Since Terk's senses weren't as acute as his own, he was the logical choice for carrying out this second-hardest part of the plan.

He jogged past the captain's office. He found the emergency box and retrieved some maintenance tools. Finding a vent and removing the panel was just as easy. Inside was a tunnel with various electronic components on either side.

With ship transportation shut down, the only way to move about was to walk, climb emergency ladders, or crawl through maintenance tunnels. This was the route least likely to have traffic. He slid backward inside and pulled the panel up behind him.

52
Friends or Enemies

3790:272:23:48. J.D. Hapker watched with saddened eyes as the boys moved with determined efficiency. They took the eight officers down and out so quickly that no one had time to call for help.

Their bio-readers should have alerted main security and they'd come soon. With what he'd just seen, Jori and Terkeshi might be able to fight them off. Either way, this would end badly.

Anxiety burned in his chest as Terkeshi dragged the officers inside. Were they dead? Private Lang's head wobbled lifelessly as they moved him. Fresh blood trickled over his temple. Hapker focused on the man's rib cage. A fleeting twinge of relief washed through him as it rose and fell in rhythm.

His heart sank back to despair as Jori tampered with the weapon settings. Somehow, he had bypassed their bio-sensors and authentications. It shouldn't be possible but Hapker couldn't deny what they had done.

Jori gave Terkeshi two weapons and kept two for himself. His stone expression indicated his determination to go through with this. Hapker had hoped the glistening in his eyes when he tied him up meant he would rethink what he was doing, but he showed no hint of hesitation now as he moved with quick purpose.

They must have planned this all along. How had he been so gullible? The captain was right. Hapker had let his faith in Jori blind him from his duty to his crew. *Stupid, stupid, stupid.* He knocked his head against the floor, ignoring the jarring pain from where the elder prince had struck him.

Terkeshi shot him a fiery glare. Hapker attempted to return the look, but he had no enmity in him—only regret, and perhaps a little pity. These boys were the product of their environment. How could they not act this way, especially with the admiral's orders setting them up for failure?

They disappeared as his door slid closed. Hapker slumped. He coughed at the rising despair. A sharp pain shot up from his wrists and ankles as he wiggled against the tight bindings.

He rolled to his knees. Another spike of hurt jabbed him in the side where Terkeshi had kicked him. After inching his way to a table, he attempted to hook the tie around his mouth on the corner. Several attempts later, nothing had changed.

This time, he tugged downward. He pulled his jaw in at the same moment and almost had it. He tried again. The gag slipped off.

"Security," he called out to the intercom. Nothing. "Security!" Still no response.

He panted. They must've disabled the room's comm. "Computer!" No reply. He dropped his head to the floor. *Now what?*

With an effort, he inched his way to the console and teetered to his feet. He bent to let the biometric scanner read his retina. Nothing happened. He turned around. His neck arched over his shoulder as he looked back at the screen and tried to stretch his restricted hands to the comm key.

By scooting partway on top, he finally reached and pressed it. The screen still didn't come on. His shoulders fell.

"Security!" Nothing.

He tilted his head up and groaned. Jori had disabled the console. Without knowing what he'd done, he had no idea how to reactivate it.

He swallowed hard and closed his eyes. No doubt the armed boys were headed to the bridge. Since he couldn't alert anyone, they had the element of surprise on their side.

He slid to the floor and rested his head between his knees. His heart drubbed as he stared dully at the carpet. He could try removing his bindings, but what was the point? He couldn't do anything. He'd doomed everyone on the ship.

"*You don't belong with the Cooperative*," his father had said. "*They think you're weak and naïve*," Sharkey had told him of the personnel. "*And when you side with this child, you neglect your duty to this crew*." Captain Arden spoke in his head this time. "*The Kimpke incident changed you*," Sharkey's voice added.

Changed for the worse. What had happened to him? He had been the best strategist at the PG Institute. He'd risen quickly in the ranks. People had told him he had the makings of a great leader. The legendary Captain Richforth himself had recommended him to the rear admiral.

He could have become one of the youngest captains of the fleet and showed his father once and for all that he could succeed on his own merits. Sharkey was right, though. The Kimpke incident had changed him. He'd lost his confidence.

Could Rear Admiral Zimmer's orders have been sound? Hapker didn't fire on the ship Kimpke occupied because he feared for the lives of innocent people. After the man's escape, those innocents had died anyway.

What about Zimmer's plan regarding the princes? It made sense to exchange them for Cooperative citizens taken as slaves. At the expense of children, though?

Hapker wanted to say the admiral's commandment had spurred the boys to action, but something told him they would've done it anyway. So maybe the admiral had been right, along with everyone else. How many lives did his gullibility risk by not doing what he should have done in the first place?

Jori's words rang in his head. "*That's the biggest difference between you and me, Commander. If I want something, I will fight for it no matter what the cost. While you, on the other hand, are so worried about what will be lost that nothing is ever gained.*"

Initially, Hapker had interpreted Jori's meaning at face value. Another interpretation came to mind. He'd been too much inside his own head—too concerned with what the captain thought, too unsure of whether he even belonged with the Cooperative, and now, too uncertain to act.

Although siding with Jori still resonated as right, it would be wrong to let the betrayal cripple him. He must quit dwelling on his mistakes and fight to protect his crew.

A new energy sizzled through him. He twisted his hands against the bonds. A sharpness ran up his arms like a blade as the bindings cinched around his wrists. They didn't loosen. He glanced about for something to use and the kitchenette caught his eye. *A knife.*

He leaned over and used his elbow and hip to crawl over. After standing, he opened the utensil drawer and shuffled through until he found it. The simple serrated blade had a dull edge but would do well enough.

He sawed through the bindings. A quick review of his console told him he'd be better off getting out of here than staying to fix it. He checked the unconscious officers, hoping Jori had missed something. He hadn't, but at least these people were alive. The boys had only stunned them.

The exit didn't open. Jori must have locked it. Hapker opened the panel and manually released it. With effort, he pulled the door ajar, jammed his foot in the gap, and levered himself until the opening widened.

He squeezed through to find an empty hall. Adrenaline shot through him as he sprinted to the conveyor. The summoning button didn't react. He pressed it again. Nothing. Desperation spurred him to jab the operating and comm buttons several more times. Still, nothing happened.

"Darn it!" He slammed his palm against the wall. The boys must have reached the bridge and disabled everything.

A pang of despair clutched his chest. He sucked in air and raced down the hall to find another way to the command center.

*****

3790:273:00:18. Jori held his breath as he waited behind the maintenance panel. The pulsing sensation in his ears increased as his lungs demanded oxygen. Two people passed by. Their emotions radiated concern but no indication of organized action—yet. Others would gather soon enough and organize face-to-face.

Jori exhaled. His heart throbbed wildly as he opened the panel and slid out into the bright expanse of the docking bay. A handful of officers in grey jumpsuits bustled about with their mechanic work, but no one noticed him. He replaced the covering in such a way that he could quickly access it again, then ducked behind an idle tool bot.

He wiped the sweat from his brow and concentrated his senses. Distinguishing between guards and mechanical engineers proved easy. The emotions of the guards discharged vigilance while mechanics exuded concentration. The alertness of those guarding the device meant they'd be difficult to overcome.

He had to reach them without anyone seeing him or his advantage of surprise would vanish. He peeked beyond the tool bot, looking for more cover.

Hunching low, he darted to a hand truck, then to a diagnostic machine. He stopped, puffing for air. Four guards gathered in or near a work room. Although their voice reached his ears, he doubted they heard him.

He dried his palms and re-gripped his weapons. Two guards spoke in hard tones. The strength of their emotions told Jori they argued. The other two stood by, radiating anticipation.

One pointed through the room door at the main cargo entrance. "—should go tell someone."

"—stay here." The other said.

Jori tensed, ready to take advantage of their distraction. He leapt from his hiding place with a phaser in each hand. A blast from each dispatched the ones arguing. He shot at the third but missed as the man dived away. He fired again and caught him just as he rolled to his knees with his weapon aimed.

Jori zeroed in on the fourth officer. Both shots flew beyond her as she dodged. She used a bot as a shield and fired, forcing him to take cover. *Damn it!* Even though only one guard remained, several workers labored nearby. He doubted they had weapons, but this didn't make them harmless.

He spread out with his senses. The workers had shifted to alert mode. Two radiated a resolve that indicated they intended to move against him.

Now or never. He jumped from his hiding place and rolled toward the remaining guard. The crackling of firepower erupted around him, but nothing struck him. He hit the floor flat and fired at the officer behind the bot. She collapsed.

He spun to his side and aimed at the two workers rushing at him. One wielded a large metal scrap piece that acted as cover, the other a heavy tool. Jori caught the unshielded man in the breast and clipped the other in the shoulder. The shield lowered and he shot him in the chest. Both fell with their tooled weapons clattering to the floor.

Jori rolled to his knees with his phasers ready. He scanned the area. The remaining workers hid, so he lurched to his feet and darted into the once-guarded room.

Relief struck him. Despite all the mechanical instruments and other items littering the counter, he spotted the perantium right away. It sat in a glass container at the rear of the table. He grabbed something to break the glass but found it open. He snatched the yellow crystal and the device parts laying nearby.

Three sneaking people wriggled into his senses. He set everything down and hid behind the doorjamb. As they crept toward the room, he remained still and silent.

A worker spun around the corner wielding a hefty wrench. Jori flew back as the tool struck where his head had been. He fired and the man fell. A woman dashed in with a hand-held laser saw. He took her out too.

With that phaser's energy spent, he discarded it. He only had six shots left from his remaining weapon, so grabbed another from an unconscious guard, giving him two again.

"Chusho," he cursed. This phaser was on the highest setting. These guards had been firing at him with kill weapons. He pocketed the implication in the back of his mind.

With no time to change it to stun, he readied for the third worker who huddled around the corner. More closed in. He had to get the hell out of here before he ran out of firepower.

The person hiding emitted nervousness and hesitation, so Jori retrieved the perantium device. He emptied a tool bag, wincing as the sound of clanging metal pierced his ears. After sweeping the pieces into it, he rushed out of the room to the tool bot. No one fired at him, meaning he'd likely taken out everyone armed with a phaser.

He pushed the wheeled bot with a grunt, blocking the line of sight of his enemies. Despite its heft, it rolled with ease. With the machine providing cover, he removed the hatch and shoved the bag in.

After sliding in, he resecured the cover with the tool, then scooted away as fast as the narrowness of the passageway allowed.

Muffled voices approached his location. The clacking of someone trying to open it reverberated in the tunnel. Jori huffed as he scuttled off, hoping to reach the intersection and turn out of their line of sight.

A clack indicated the panel opened. He scrambled around the edge. A fire flash swept by. He fired his own weapon blindly in their direction. A mental tally told him he had only four stuns remaining from his first phaser and three kill shots from the other.

This wider passageway enabled him to move quickly before taking another corner. He left his pursuers behind, moving level by level to get back to Terk. It might have been smarter for him to hide and wait for General Sakon to arrive and beam him off. That's what the bio-reader was for. However, he didn't want to leave his brother to defend the bridge all by himself.

He reached a ladder shaft leading to the command level. His sweaty palms hindered his climbing speed. Voices echoed from below, indicating others were using the ship's maintenance tunnels to get around.

His hands almost slipped from the last rung and he grabbed on with the crook of his arm. He dared not pause to catch his breath. He swung over the rail and hopped into a wide niche where a paneled exit awaited. The voices came closer, but they weren't looking for him.

He worked with haste. His senses didn't detect anyone on the other side, so he exited the maintenance tunnel and entered the corridor. He clutched the tool bag in his arm as he sprinted down the hall.

Using his ability, he found a group of three people. They had no time to react with more than a cry as he ran up and shot them. The lifeforce of another person sent him stumbling. *Hapker.* A small piece from the device fell from his bag with a clatter. He skidded to a halt and lurched back to pick it up. His stun phaser slipped out of his sweaty hand and bounced out of reach.

Hapker appeared from around the corner. Jori pointed his kill weapon with his heart in his throat.

*****

3790:273:01:07. J.D. Hapker pulled up with a jerk. "Jori!"

The boy's feet planted wide. He stood sideways to present a smaller target. Hapker swallowed the lump in his throat as the muzzle and Jori's dark piercing eyes aimed at him, just like on the day they'd first met.

Hapker raised his hands and stepped forward.

"Stop!" Jori's lips pressed in a thin line. His chin trembled.

Hapker moved by another foot. "Don't do this, Jori. We're friends, remember?"

"We're not friends," the boy replied. The pained expression on his face revealed his lie.

Hapker stepped again.

"Damn it, Commander! I said stop. I don't want to hurt you."

"Because we're friends."

Jori furrowed his brow as though in anger but the wetness in his eyes gave him away. His hand shook, but the phaser point didn't waver.

Hapker stopped. The boy might not want to shoot, but he held no doubt that he would if he had to. "Why are you doing this?"

"I told you—duty."

Hapker nodded. "You understand, I also have a duty. I can't let you go through with it."

"You can't stop me," Jori replied in a low tone. "It's too late."

Hapker shook his head. "No it's not. I'm on your side, remember? I won't let anything happen to you."

"You don't understand what's at stake." Though Jori's eyes still glistened, his voice held steady. "I *must* do this."

"Oh, Jori. I'm so sorry. I wish things were different. If only we lived in a universe where our people weren't enemies."

Tears trickled down Jori's cheek, but he didn't lower his weapon. "Me too."

They remained frozen. Neither wanted to make the first move.

The sound of footsteps broke the moment.

Hapker eased forward. "It's over. Put the phaser—"

Jori fired. Hapker ducked unnecessarily. The shot zipped well over his head. The boy intended it as a distraction, then ran. Hapker gave chase.

"Commander!" a woman's voice called from behind.

He halted and turned. "Sharkey. We've got trouble."

"I know. I believe someone's taken over the bridge."

The bridge. Hapker glanced over his shoulder in the direction Jori had gone. The boy would have to wait. They must retake the command center.

Hapker counted five people plus Sharkey. Only she and Gresher had phasers. The others, which included Doctor Canthidius, were non-combatant personnel. It had to be enough.

"It's those Tredon brats, isn't it?" Canthidius asked. "I knew they were trouble, but no one listens to me."

"Jori just went that way," Hapker said to his lieutenants as he pointed over his shoulder. "So, it's only the elder prince on the bridge, but I'm sure he's armed."

Sharkey glanced behind him, though Jori was long gone. "Why isn't he in there with his brother?"

"I believe he has the perantium."

"What?" Canthidius growled. "We can't let them have that."

Hapker ignored the man. "Let's go," he said, motioning for them to follow.

His group met two more security officers on the way. Before long, they reached the bridge and congregated around the entrance.

A young engineer opened its control panel and messed with its guts. "My goodness. It's locked tight."

"What do you mean? How tight?" Hapker asked.

"I'll need some tools. He's not only disabled the electrical components but also jammed the manual gears."

Hapker ran his hand down his face, then wiped his wet palm on his thigh. "Sharkey, check an emergency box."

She nodded and rushed down the hall, weapon ready.

"I warned you this would happen," Canthidius muttered. "Letting Tredons run about this ship was stupid."

"This isn't the time, Doctor," Hapker said.

"Well, when is? After we're all—"

"Shut up." The glower Hapker gave the science officer kept him quiet but didn't remove the I-told-you-so look from his face.

Sharkey returned with a small silver box. His heart pounded as the engineer grabbed a tool and set to work.

The young man bared his teeth and grunted while prying at something inside the panel. "I almost got it… Almost got it… Ow!" He pulled his hand away and shook it.

Hapker clapped him on the shoulder. "You can do this."

The engineer resumed his work. "Got it!"

Hapker's heart jumped. "Alright. Those of you with weapons, get on either side of the door." He dipped his head to the young man. "We're ready when you are."

The doors slid open. Phaser blasts erupted from inside. Sharkey and the others pivoted toward the opening and laid fire. More return fire sent them back.

"He's taken cover behind the captain's chair," she said breathlessly.

Hapker ran his hand down his face again. "Alright. He can't have much firepower in there. Let's get him to run out."

Gresher frowned. "We don't have a lot of firepower either, Sir."

"I'm sure more officers will turn up here," Hapker replied and the lieutenant nodded. "Let me try something else, though.

"First Prince Mizuki," he called out. "This won't work. You can't stay in there forever. Eventually, you'll run out of ammo."

"I don't need to worry about that, Commander."

A chill plunged down Hapker's spine. How many weapons could the boy possibly have? "It's over," he replied, trying to sound confident. "The sooner you give up, the better it will be for both you and your brother."

Terkeshi laughed. "You're the one in trouble. You just don't know it yet."

Sharkey's brow furrowed. "What the hell is he going to do?" she whispered.

Hapker tried to swallow but his dry throat didn't let him. The prince could win this in several ways. He had control of the bridge, after all, and this meant control over everything from the ship's air supply to its fire suppression systems.

A beep sounded from inside. "Time's up, Commander," Terkeshi said.

Hapker jolted. "Fire now!"

The three officers with weapons all turned in and blasted. Several shots from the officers struck the back of the captain's chair. Some flew over and into the workstations, others off to the side. All landed pointlessly.

"Stop!" Hapker commanded them.

They stopped. He glanced in. The stillness raised the hairs on the nape of his neck. Had they hit him? It couldn't be that easy. He crept inside. Sharkey pressed her weapon into his hand. He grasped it and stalked forward.

A glance around the room revealed several officers sprawled on the ground, but no Terkeshi. He swallowed hard. The captain lay flat on his back and his arms splayed out. His eyes were closed and his mouth open. Hapker wanted to check if he lived, but he still had the pressing matter of the prince to deal with.

He darted around the captain's chair and aimed… At nothing. He sidestepped to the workstations, holding his weapon high. *Where is he?* The openness of the bridge meant he should see the boy somewhere—a shoulder sticking out from behind a chair or a leg from under a console.

He circled the room. Nothing. "He's gone?"

"Where? How?" Sharkey asked.

The floor lurched and Hapker tumbled. He scrambled to his feet. "We're being fired upon! Everyone take a station. Someone activate our shields."

What have those boys done?

53
Enforcer and Pholatian Protector

3790:273:01:46. Ander Vizubi pushed himself up as the gloom of an invisible load pressed him down. The Grapnes hadn't harmed him or his crew, but all this time with nothing to do fed his regrets until they festered.

His team had brainstormed several options for escape, but every scenario ended with these machines killing them all. They had one viable plan—take a Grapne hostage at the first opportunity. That moment had finally come.

As the main cell-block door opened with a creak, Vizubi wet his lips in anticipation. The Overseer entered. *Perfect.*

A cluster of guard bots followed in the Grapne's wake and Vizubi's shoulders sank. No way could he move fast enough.

"Let's go," the Overseer said with a gloating grin. "Your ship is waiting."

Vizubi sighed and approached the cell exit. Woolley tensed as though to rise.

The Overseer flicked his index finger. "Eh-eh. Everyone else stay down or my bots will shoot you."

The machines remained cold and motionless. Disabling the AATA-bot 120 would take a matter of seconds. Even so, Vizubi dared not risk it. The nearby RRAB-bot had a reputation for shredding its target into mincemeat.

He exited the cell and allowed a Grapne to put restraints on his wrists. All his fight left him as he succumbed to the inevitable.

"Come, come." The Overseer motioned him forward.

Vizubi peeked over his shoulder, taking in the forlorn features of his crew. *Please, God, keep them safe.*

The Overseer led him away and down a grey-walled corridor. Vizubi trudged along with his head hanging. Soon he'd be back on his own ship. However, he'd return on his knees and plead with

Captain Arden to exchange the children for his people. His gut tumbled at the thought, but it writhed when he considered the fate of his crew.

The Overseer halted. His hand poised over the comm taped behind his ear and his smile contorted into a frown. "What do you mean the Tredons are there?"

Vizubi's head snapped up.

"They're attacking the *Odyssey*!" The Overseer stomped his foot and Vizubi's heart jumped. "No! This can't be happening. Those children are mine!"

Vizubi imagined a Tredon warship demolishing his beloved home. *Damn it.*

The Overseer gestured with his fist. "Yes! Of course leave. Get out of here now."

Vizubi's heart leapt to his throat. "Wait!"

The Overseer glowered at him.

"Wait," Vizubi said again as energy surged through his veins. "We can help you. I have a pilot who's excellent at evasive maneuvering during combat. My Corporal can handle your operations and I will do tactical. You have weapons on this ship, don't you? Let us help the *Odyssey* fight off the Tredons and maybe you can still make your trade."

The Overseer's eyes brightened with every word, but he hesitated. "Hold on," he said into the comm. "Stay right here. We may have help." He narrowed his eyes at Vizubi. "Why should you help me?"

"I want to save my ship. You should want to help them too. It's the only way you'll get the princes." Vizubi leaned in. "Look. I know you've lost a lot of money on this venture. This is the only way you can make up for it. Don't give up now."

The Overseer moved his mouth from side-to-side as though thinking.

"It's two ships against one," Vizubi added. "We have a chance to defeat them. That way, both of us get what we want."

"You are a good tactical officer?"

"Yes. My team and I go on missions all the time. My brother can help, too," Vizubi said as another idea came to him. "He is excellent with machines. He can monitor the engine functions as we fight, make sure they keep up with the task."

The Overseer called out orders as he ushered Vizubi to the bridge. Artillery bots discouraged him from attacking the man or any other Grapnes, but he had more pressing concerns anyway.

With the cuffs removed, he reviewed the stats on the viewscreen and weighed the situation. "We'll be in firing range in two minutes." *Too long*. Moving to the tactical station, he checked the weapons cache. "I'm loading torpedoes and prepping the energy cannons."

Once Woolley, Quigley, and his brother arrived, Vizubi faced them. "We have an opportunity here. The *Odyssey* is being attacked by a Tredon warship and the Overseer is permitting us to defend them. Woolley, helm. Quigley, operations. Hesteben, engineering." He turned to the Overseer. "Can he handle it from here or does he need to go to the engineering room?"

"We have access here."

Woolley scowled at Hesteben before dashing off to the helm. He elbowed the Grapne already sitting there, making the skinny little man cower and scamper away. Quigley rushed to operations.

Vizubi stopped his brother and leaned in. "Help us out here, then see what you can do to convince the Grapnes to let us go."

Hesteben's dark eyes brightened as a wide grin spread across his face. Thanks to the fix he'd taken earlier, he rode the upside of the drug's reaction. His most cunning ideas came in this state.

Vizubi returned to his station in time to fire the energy cannons. His gut wrung as a mixture of anxiety and hope fought for control. He had one chance at this and determined to make it count.

*****

3790:273:01:53. J.D. Hapker leapt onto the platform at the center of the bridge and activated the tactical console. He expected the boys had disabled it, but it brightened to life. The others rushed in with only minor scrambling over who would operate which station. They jumped to work right away, which meant their stations hadn't been locked out either. Why, if Jori and Terkeshi had deactivated communications and other ship functions, did they leave these operations open?

Another blast struck the *Odyssey*. Hapker grasped the edge of the console. "Get those shields up!"

"Up, Sir!" an officer said.

"Activate red alert," he called.

"Trying, Sir," another officer replied. "Communications are still down."

The viewscreen blinked on. Hapker glanced over the information. The *Brimstone*.

In a flash of insight, he understood what had happened to Terkeshi. General Sakon had beamed him off. Jori, too, and he had the perantium.

Hapker launched the energy cannons, hoping his quick aiming calculations would hit the moving enemy ship between its port and forward shields. Analysts suspected this to be the most vulnerable point of a Tredon warship and if he could weaken their defenses before they weakened his, he'd have the advantage.

"Jensin, delta maneuver," Hapker said to the young man at the helm. Officer Jensin was new at his job, but he was the only one available right now.

"Sir!" an officer called out. "They've launched their asps."

Hapker's thoughts whirred. Those smaller Tredon space fighters could be a problem. He continued firing the energy cannons at the ship and readied the projectile weapons for the oncoming asps. It might not be enough since this expedition vessel had little firepower. Maybe they would buy him time, though. "Sharkey, call for the PG-Force as soon as communications are open."

"On it, Commander."

He tried not to think about his limited options. Run or fight, that's it. He couldn't let them have the perantium prototype, so opted to fight for as long as possible.

"Comms are up."

"I need all bridge crew here now," Hapker transmitted. "Red alert. All other personnel to the safety depots."

"Sir, another ship is approaching!"

Hapker's chest constricted. "Get us out—"

"Sir, it's the Cougar and they just fired at the *Brimstone*."

"Sir," Sharkey said from the communication station. "Sergeant Ander Vizubi is calling from that ship. He says the Grapnes are allowing him to help us."

Hapker held in his surprise. "Open the channel."

"Done."

"Sergeant Vizubi, this is Commander Hapker. Target the *Brimstone* while we take care of the approaching asps."

"On it, Commander," the man's voice said through the transmission.

Hapker launched the slower projectile weapons at the oncoming asps. His targeting systems meant he didn't need to aim, but no doubt those vessels had their own defenses.

He fired two cannons in quick succession. "Jensin, zeta maneuver with a thirty percent alteration on dive two."

He fired more weapons just as the viewscreen showed his ship turning into its deviation. Another section of the screen showed a shot from the *Brimstone* had missed, but Hapker and Vizubi both struck their target.

He aimed again, taking care not to waste the depleting energy store, and fired. A moment later, the data indicated enemy fore and port shields had fallen to fifty percent.

"Sir!" Sharkey said. "The PG-Destroyer has already suffered an attack. They can't come."

The *Brimstone* had probably encountered them. It explained their weakened shields.

"Commander. Our starboard shields are at thirty-seven percent," an officer called out.

"Auxiliary power to starboard shields," Hapker replied. "How have we lost those defenses so quickly?"

"Sir, I think their asps are releasing energy bursts right up against us."

Hapker shook his head at their crazy tactics. Doing that so close to a shield was as effective as it was dangerous. He had no idea the Tredons had that in them. Then he recalled Jori's sacrificial strategies when they'd played games, and how the boy had said he'd learned from General Sakon himself.

This was how it would be then. Schemster—the game he kept losing because he wouldn't make sacrifices. *Well, I won't lose this one.*

He fired two more weapons at the enemy's fore-port. He received more hits than he gave. Shield levels fell but he wasn't ready to run. Not yet.

Officer Wilshire stepped beside him. Hapker let him take over the tactical station and moved to the captain's chair. "Jensin, theta maneuver. Then halfway through, I want you to alter to omega."

"Omega?" someone asked with disbelief in their tone.

Hapker ignored them. Few used this tactic except as a last resort. Even with Vizubi's help, they were no match for the *Brimstone*. He must get back that perantium. Taking this terrible chance was a small price for protecting humanity from the Tredons.

"Evacuate fore section all levels," he announced through the ship-wide comm.

A senior officer entered to take Jensin's place. "No," Hapker told him. "Jensin stays." The man didn't need interruption when he was doing so well.

He allowed another officer to replace Canthidius.

"Doctor, buckle in," he said, indicating the row of safety seats in the back.

The man frowned. "Sir, I'm qualified for bridge duty."

Hapker thumbed behind him. "Sit!" He'd never seen Canthidius in action, while he appreciated Doctor Choi's competence and experience.

Other crew members arrived and either took over stations or carried the bodies of the unconscious or dead officers to the safety depots.

Hapker's chest tightened at the sight of the captain. If the boys had killed him, he was to blame.

He pushed the idea out of his head and focused.

"Sir, auxiliary power failed," an officer reported. "Starboard shields are down to thirty percent. Forward shields at fifty."

"Enemy fore and port shields at forty-four percent, Sir," another officer added.

Hapker's breath hitched. "Wilshire, Vizubi, fire all remaining weapons between the fore and port on my mark. Canthidius, are you still here?"

"Here, Sir," the man said sourly from behind.

“Simmonds had mentioned certain waves can destroy perantium. Can we adjust this ship’s wave emitter in time to damage what they have on the *Brimstone*?”

“Not with her at the controls,” he replied. “It takes special—”

“You’re part of a team, Canthidius! I suggest you act like it. Can it be done and done quickly or not?”

“Yes,” the doctor said sullenly.

“Then help Doctor Choi. Tell her the frequency and give her your support, not your attitude.”

Canthidius helped but in a petulant voice. Hapker shoved aside his annoyance and eyed the *Odyssey*’s heading on the viewscreen. Five more seconds and the helmsman should change course. He counted in his head.

Jensin moved right on target. The ship turned about and charged the *Brimstone* at full impulse.

“Fire!”

A barrage of blasts peppered the enemy’s shields like hail. Hapker gripped his armrests as their heading closed in.

“Sir, the *Brimstone*’s taking evasive maneuvers.”

“Stay on him, Jensin,” Hapker said.

“One minute to impact!”

*****

3790:273:02:29. Ander Vizubi’s jaw dropped. *What the hell is he doing?*

The *Odyssey* charged toward the enemy warship like crazed drug addict. It was risky, but mad enough to work. The *Brimstone* was not an immoveable force. That meant, despite the *Odyssey*’s velocity, it stopping time would be spread out and much of the impact energy would be transferred to the enemy. Vizubi could lessen the effect on the *Odyssey* even more by making sure the Tredons ran away.

“Stay on the enemy’s tail!” he called out to Woolley.

He released a barrage of weapons from the Grapnes’ dwindling arsenal.

*****

3790:273:02:30. "Ten seconds! Nine… Eight…"

Hapker double-checked his harness. Hopefully, everyone else on the ship was strapped in or had made it to a safety depot. If Captain Arden still lived, he'd never forgive him for risking the crew with this crazy maneuver. "Brace for impact," he called into the comm.

Three... Two... One. The *Odyssey* rocked violently as the shielding of the two ships collided. If not for the inertial dampeners, they'd all be pancaked against the walls. Still, his head felt as if someone pounded it with stones. A violent bout of sickness came over him.

"Report," he managed to say.

"Their shields are down, Sir."

"As are ours," another officer said.

"The Cougar's defenses are still operational," the first officer added.

Hapker straightened. "Choi, aim that wave emitter in the general area of the fore-port. Look for the appropriate electromagnetic disturbance. Jensin, as soon as that's reported, get us the heck out of here as fast as you can. Sergeant Vizubi, cover us for a few moments, then fall back to the rendezvous point I'm transmitting."

"Will do, Sir."

"Sir," the operations officer called out. "I think the *Brimstone* is preparing to leave."

They must have known what he intended. *Good*. They couldn't go with that perantium, though. Hapker prepared to ram them again if Choi didn't strike the target soon. Better to take the risk than allow the Tredons to get their hands on a potentially dangerous weapon.

His nails dug into his palm as he monitored the screen. Seconds passed, but they seemed longer as sweat dripped from his brow.

"I'm sorry, Jori," he whispered. If the boy still held onto the device or if he were anywhere near it, the exploding perantium might kill him. The thought turned his insides, but they both had chosen duty.

He wiped his sweaty palms down his thigh. Every second that ticked by increased the patter of his heart.

"A hit, Sir!" the operations officer said of the perantium.

"Go!" Hapker slammed his fist onto the chair arm. "Get us out of here, Jensin. Now."

54
The End?

3790:273:03:05. The *Odyssey* shuddered after it reached the distance required for arc drive initiation. J.D. Hapker plopped back into the chair and puffed out his cheeks with an exhale. A million thoughts ran through his head, and he couldn't grasp onto a single one. He wiped his sweaty hands down the front of his shirt only to find it soaked through.

"Damage report," he said weakly.

The operations officer rattled off several downed and critical systems. Hapker barely heard. None seemed too concerning.

He leaned forward and rested his forehead in his palm as a ripple of dizziness ran through him. "Casualties."

The officer paused to review the bio-readers and reports. In that silence, the pace of Hapker's heart battered his eardrums.

"None reported, Sir."

Hapker sat up. The abruptness sent his head spinning, but he remained upright. "None?"

"None, Sir."

"The captain?" He was sure the man had been dead.

"Just stunned, Sir."

A tremendous weight lifted. "What about where our ships collided?"

"So far, all reports indicate personnel were safe at their battle stations or safety depots, Sir. Even our pets are reported as okay."

Hapker fell back into his chair again. It shouldn't surprise him, though. Most people who traveled a Prontaean ship had to undergo emergency training, and personal bots ensured pets were secured.

"Review the SRS history," he ordered. "I want confirmation the perantium was destroyed."

The viewscreen flicked to a new image. "The wave signature is there," Choi replied.

Hapker leaned forward. "How can we be sure it was the perantium?"

"I believe it's about the right size."

"You believe?" Canthidius said snidely from behind. "One would think—"

Hapker snapped his head around and glowered. "One would think, Doctor, that as a professional you'd act more like an adult and less like a petulant child."

The corners of Choi's mouth curled up.

A few others held a half-hidden smirk. Perhaps he hadn't been the only one tired of Canthidius' pompous attitude.

"I want a full report as soon as possible," Hapker said to Choi.

"Yes, Sir. And thank you, Sir." She gave him a respectful nod and went to work.

Hapker glanced at his crew. They seemed to look at him differently. Their expressions made him feel less like an interloper and more like a team member.

He wanted to relish the moment, but that explosion could have killed Jori. Everything they had been through together these past several days had been all for nothing. The Tredons were still their enemies and the future spelled war.

*****

3790:273:03:06. Ander Vizubi huffed. He dropped his weight on his palms, leaning on the edge of the tactical station. "We did it." *Thank you, God.*

Quigley turned to him with a light in her eyes. "Wow, Sir. We fought off a Tredon warship."

Woolley wiped his brow. "We'll rendezvous with the *Odyssey* in twenty minutes. We're still in deep shit, though, Sir."

"Maybe not," Hesteben said as he stood with a smug expression.

Vizubi straightened. "What's the plan?"

Steben clasped his hands behind his back. "You won't like this, but neither will our friends." He jutted his chin at the Overseer.

The Grapne curled his lip. "Like what?"

Hesteben showed his teeth. "The arc reactor is running on overdrive and unless you let us go, your ship will explode."

"What?" the Overseer screeched and pointed to his people. "Fix this!"

The Grapne scrambled to the station and tapped the console.

Vizubi crossed his arms and raised his brow at his brother. "That's your idea? Kill us all?"

"It's a game of chicken, and we all know who the chickens of the galaxy are."

"I can't fix it, Overseer," the Grapne said. "He locked us out."

The Overseer faced Hesteben with a scarlet hue. "Stop this!"

"We'll come out of arc once we reach the *Odyssey*, but that won't stop the reactor from overheating."

The Overseer jabbed his finger. "Arrest him!"

Two Grapnes approached with hesitation. Hesteben laughed. "Go right ahead. It won't do any good."

"If you do this, you die too!"

Hesteben shrugged. "The expiration date of my life is coming up anyway."

Vizubi rubbed his jaw. He never liked this game, but by the looks of the wide-eyed Grapnes, it could work. "We'd rather die than be your prisoners. I suggest you agree to let us go."

Hesteben bounced on his heels. "Give us bio-readers, contact the *Odyssey*, tell them to transport us off. When we're there, I'll walk your people through the reactor shutdown process."

The Overseer clenched his fists at his sides. "You can't do this. I have invested too much to lose now. Those children are mine!"

Vizubi stabbed his index finger at him. "This is what you get for messing with the PG-Force." He planted his hands on his hips. "Your actions against us have left you with two options. Let us go and beg to be arrested, or die as the Cooperative blows your ship to dust."

The Overseer pulled back with a scowl. "Beg you to arrest me?"

"Beg," Vizubi said with a snarl. "Because your other option is to run and hide while we hunt you down. It's over. You fucked up by taking us."

The overseer paled. Vizubi hid his satisfaction as his faith renewed. Hesteben would face charges for getting them captured, but he'd get drug treatment out of the deal. Besides, PG-Force holding facilities were sunny beaches compared to the Depnaugh space station. Maybe this would prompt his brother to turn his life around. Miracles happened.

*****

3790:274:00:21. J.D. Hapker rubbed his eyes. After securing the Grapne Overseer and discussing the arrest of Hesteben with Sergeant Vizubi, he'd finally made it to bed. He'd slept fitfully, though, as the anticipation of facing Captain Arden plagued his thoughts.

Sharkey caught up to him and flashed a beaming smile. "You're back."

"Back?" Something about the way she gazed at him said she didn't mean back to his duties.

"Your confidence," she replied. "I saw it there on the bridge. You handled everything like a master schemster player."

Now her glittering features made sense, but he didn't share her joy. He shrugged his shoulders. "It's not how I wanted things to end. General Sakon killed a lot of good people when he attacked our Destroyer."

"That's not on you. Records confirm this happened prior to his contact with the princes."

True. Those deaths should be on Zimmer's hands for trying to keep the princes from going home in the first place, but guilt still plagued him. "I was so sure of them, especially Jori."

"They made their choice," she replied. "Besides, something good came out of it."

He frowned. "You mean my confidence?"

"No," she said in a drawn-out tone. "Though that's good too. I mean they didn't kill anyone."

"Oh." She was right. "Thanks, Sharkey."

"Sure thing, Commander." Her eyes sparkled as she nudged his shoulder, then turned about and left with a spring in her step.

Hapker stared at her hips, then shook his thoughts to the task at hand. He pulled back his shoulders and entered the conference room.

His newfound surety faltered. Bracht glared at him. Sengupta didn't meet his eyes. Captain Arden held an unreadable expression, but a coolness permeated the air, telling him all he needed to know.

He sat and faced the captain. "Sir, it's good to see you're well."

"No thanks to those children," the man replied in an abrasive tone.

"Actually, Sir. I believe they *chose* not to kill you."

"They hijacked my ship, Commander." The captain's nostrils flared, and the knuckles of his clasped hands whitened.

"If I may, Sir. We didn't give them much choice. They found out we broke our promise to get them home."

"How in the hell did they find that out?"

"I suspect their sentio-animi ability told them something was wrong. When they asked me straight out, I couldn't lie without them knowing."

The captain's hard demeanor didn't change, so Hapker pushed on. "Their reaction was swift, and they overwhelmed me. That shouldn't be a surprise to anyone here, considering their abilities. What is surprising, though, is they didn't kill me. They could have, but they didn't. They had plenty of other opportunities to kill. Again, they didn't. Despite all the hate the crew threw their way, they didn't kill anyone. Not even Calloway."

The captain leaned back in his chair with a less hardened expression. Hapker held the captain's eyes and continued. "After I escaped from my room, I ran into Jori again. This time, I suspect he had a kill weapon since a security officer guarding the perantium is missing his. Jori wouldn't shoot me, though. You should have seen his face, Captain. He acted out of desperation. He did what he had to, but he still wouldn't kill me."

"They had control of our bridge, Commander," the captain said in a subdued tone. "They had control over our entire ship. Not only would they have taken us captive, but they'd also have the prototype of a planet killing device."

Hapker leaned in. "Did you know they left the tactical station and all the other stations on the bridge open before they beamed away? I'm not sure how they manipulated any of our secure systems, but it's obvious they did. It's obvious they knew what they were doing, too. They probably could have locked us out, yet they left a way for us to fight back."

"That's merely speculation," Captain Arden said.

Hapker shook his head. "Perhaps, but we acted justly, beginning with the decision to not treat the boys like criminals. If we had, how many people would be dead now?

"If I made any mistakes, Captain, it was in not understanding Jori's sense of duty," he continued. "What he did… What he and his brother did wasn't personal. They had a difficult choice to make, and we can't blame them for making the one that would appease their father. Besides, wouldn't we have done the same if we had been captured?"

He sat back to let the information sink in. The weight he had been carrying these past months lifted as Captain Arden's expression lost its hardness. He still had one regret, though. Jori might have died when he destroyed the perantium. This was Jori's doing, though, not his. If he had to do it all over again, he'd do everything the same way.

The captain sat forward with his chin resting on his index fingers. He glanced at Sengupta.

She nodded in reply. "I agree with Commander Hapker."

The captain looked to Bracht next. The big warrior frowned. "I don't like what happened. I should have had a better security plan. My people should have been more vigilant." He took a deep breath. "The Commander is right, though, and his actions in fighting off the *Brimstone* and destroying the perantium were first rate."

Hapker gave the Rabnoshk warrior a thankful nod.

Captain Arden stroked his beard. "You've given me some things to consider, Commander. Perhaps this all didn't play out the way we wanted it to, but the situation was complex."

This wasn't approval, exactly, but neither was it the caustic accusations the captain had expressed earlier. That the man considered changing his standpoint was more than he ever would have gotten from Zimmer.

"You made a judgment call," Captain Arden continued with a thoughtful look. "One that put us in harm's way. However, I supported your judgment." He spread out his arms. "We're all here. Despite what those children did, they didn't do everything they could have done. I believe it's because of you. Even though you sided with the young prince when everyone else was sure it was a mistake, you protected the crew in the end."

The tension in Hapker's shoulders relaxed. "Thank you, Captain."

"Now down to business," the man replied. "With the perantium device destroyed, we can pretty much count on the emperor attacking Thendi where the larger emitter is located. So we must prepare for battle… And possibly for war."

*****

3790:275:10:15. "Mom," J.D. Hapker said as soon as his mother appeared on the screen. "I have some great news."

"J.D. Good to see you. Are you coming home, dear?"

"No, Mom. Captain Arden has fully accepted me as his second-in-command. I'll be staying onboard for the foreseeable future."

Neither Mom's frown nor the prospect of war with the Tredons kept the grin off his face. He wouldn't need to go back to Pholatia after all. He'd met tough challenges, and, in the end, made a difference. He was ready to deal with anything now. The marrow of his bones told him he belonged here. The Cooperative was where he wanted to be, and Captain Arden was the man he wished to serve.

Did you enjoy this novel? Leave a review. Authors love reviews!

Next:
At the end of Book One, both Jori and Commander Hapker chose duty. But what happens when the emperor wages war and roles are reversed? Will Jori uphold his familial duties while his new friend is being treated as a slave? Find out in Dragon Emperor: Book Two.

Sign up for my newsletter by visiting my website, DawnRossAuthor.com, and get great deals!

The first thing you'll receive is an exclusive Prequel to Book One. You'll also get access to the first few chapters of the current books plus upcoming books. There may also be more free short stories related to the main story.

Connect with Dawn Ross online:
DawnRossAuthor.com
Twitter.com/DawnRossAuthor
Goodreads.com/author/Dawn_Ross

Glossary

AATA-bot 120 – An outdated artillery bot.

Addams – Sergeant Siven Addams is a PG-Force officer on the *Odyssey*.

Adosela – A place on Hapker's homeworld with crystal clear waters.

Agni – Private Agni, a PG-Force officer on the *Odyssey*, is Calloway's roommate.

Alkon – A scientist who formed theories on quantum mechanics.

Ander – Sergeant Ander Vizubi, a PG-Force officer on the *Odyssey*.

Angolan – A proper adjective used to describe something or someone from Angola. In this case, the Angolan Cougar is a type of ship from Angola, a continent on one of the Cooperative planets.

Animus – A word that encompasses a person's emotions, spirit, consciousness, and soul. Liam Garner says that only people who are in touch with their animus can be readers or can block readers. The plural version of this word is animi and is used in combination with sentio-animi, extraho-animi, and imperium animi, for the three levels of readers.

Anpan – A Toradon dish described as a bread filled with bean paste or other types of foods.

Arashi – A planet that has swirling storms.

Arc drive or Arc reactor – This is one of the largest components of a spaceship. It is the engine that allows a ship to travel many light years away without violating the speed of light by bending space-time.

Arden – Captain Silas Arden is the captain of the *Odyssey*.

Aronson – Lieutenant Aronson is a man Hapker had worked with when he was a Pholatian Protector.

Aurichian – To play with an Aurichian warhead is to meddle with something that is dangerous. The saying is coined from its namesake city where a warhead manufacturing facility blew up.

Bantam – A small ship used primarily for hauling small loads of cargo.

Bari – Private Ishaq Bari is a PG-Force officer on the *Odyssey*. He serves under Sergeant Ander Vizubi.

Barson-hop – A kid's game.

Bastion – A small ship used for transport. It has decent firing capabilities for its size but isn't as fast as a Swift-class ship.

Beck – Doctor Beck Jerom is one of the primary doctors on the *Odyssey*.

Biometric authentication – A security measure that uses retina scans, fingerprint identification, voice recognition or other unique biological characteristics to keep anyone but the authorized persons from using certain devices.

Bio-reader – A small device carried or adhered to the body that keeps track of and transmits vitals. It also has a unique embedded signal used to allow the transport to beam the carrier from one place to another.

Bio-sensor – The biometric authentication part of a weapon that allows only certain people to use it. It verifies both the fingerprint and the vascular pattern of the intended users.

Bjornicibus – Major Bjornicibus Bracht is a Rabnoshk warrior who is the commanding officer of the PG-Force stationed on the *Odyssey*.

Blackbeast – An animal that Jori often refers to. It is never described but it is hinted that it might be dog or wolf-like.

Blue Blight – A planet in the Hellana system that is in the process of being terraformed. It is the planet that Jori and Terk crashed on.

Bok – A Toradon senshi whose bragging caused Jori and Terk's ship to be attacked by the Grapnes.

Bracht – Major Bjornicibus Bracht is a Rabnoshk warrior who is the commanding officer of the PG-Force stationed on the *Odyssey*.

Brenson – Officer Brenson is a communications officer on the bridge of the *Odyssey.*

Bret – Corporal Bret is a PG-Force officer serving on the *Odyssey.* Calloway calls him a primed-up know-it-all.

Brimstone – A Toradon warship captained by General Sakon.

Brinar's bluff – When J.D. Hapker says he must wait on Brinar's bluff, he is implying that he's waiting anxiously or precariously.

Cad deck – It houses a recording-type device in the cockpit of small ships.

Calloway – Corporal Mik Calloway is a hateful and bitter man who serves as a PG-Force officer on the *Odyssey.*

Canthidius – Doctor Holgarth Canthidius is a lead science officer on the *Odyssey.* He is a haughty man who reminds Hapker of a fish.

Capsian pirates – A sub-race of people known for attacking other spaceships and stealing their cargo.

Celenia – A woman briefly mentioned by Calloway.

Chandly – Officer Chandly is the head operations officer on the bridge of the *Odyssey.*

Chevert outpost – A space station situated between Cooperative and Tredon territory. It has many of the same amenities as a town or city.

Chima – Means vile one or hated enemy in Jori and Terk's language.

Choi – Doctor Choi is a science officer who serves on the bridge of the *Odyssey.*

Chokuto sword – A narrow sword.

Chusho – Means shit in Jori and Terk's language.

Ciculata – A poisonous plant variety that has undetectable properties when it comes to medical scanners.

Clyde – The name of one of the Grapnes.

Comm – A communication device.

Communication hub – A form of communication that uses quantum entanglement technology for an instantaneous exchange.

Conveyor – An elevator-like car on a spaceship that moves vertically and horizontally.

Cooperative – The agency that governs space. It has numerous treaties with various worlds that provides its charter to keep space safe, ensure peace, regulate fair trade, and colonize new worlds. Its powers are granted by several planets, and the number of planets that are part of the Cooperative continues to grow. The Prontaean Cooperative has two aspects to it. The first is the Prontaean Colonial Cooperative (PCC). This sub-organization handles intergalactic relations, conducts space exploration, performs space-based scientific endeavors, assists travelers, and sometimes provides transportation. The second aspect is the Prontaean Galactic Force (PG-Force). This sub-organization polices space.

Cougar – A large carrier ship. It's smaller than the *Odyssey* but many times larger than a Serpent.

Crash pod – Smaller ships generally have one pod for every authorized passenger. It is intended to protect them if their spacecraft crashes. They can also be injected into space and emit a distress signal.

Cycle – A cycle is the universal standard for a year of 360 days. A day-cycle is approximate to one Earth 24-hour period. While each planet might have its own unique standard, anyone who conducts business off-world used the universal standard.

Damark – Jairo Damark is J.D. Hapker's formal given name.

Davin – Someone mentioned by Ander Vizubi.

Defuser – A device that keeps someone's phaser from working.

Depnaugh space station – A large space station located outside of Cooperative territory. It has many of the same amenities as a town or city. This station is known for harboring lawless activities and attracting unsavory characters.

Deskview – A desktop computer.

Diptera – The name of a drug addled resident of the Depnaugh space station. He is also good at eavesdropping. Incidentally, diptera is the name for the scientific order of flies.

Dokuri – Jori and Terk's older half-brother who was killed by a rebellious Toradon lord nearly a year ago.

Dragon Emperor - Emperor Mizuki is the ruthless ruler of the Toradon Nohibito/Dragon People, aka Tredons. He is often referred to as the Dragon Emperor.

Enviro-suit – A form-fitting spacesuit that uses nanites to regulate body temperature and protect the wearer from just about any environment, including the void of space.

Expedition-class – The largest of the Prontaean Colonial Cooperative (PCC) spaceships. Though the officers who run this ship are formal personnel of the Cooperative, they are sometimes considered civilians because they are mostly doctors, engineers, and technicians. This ship has a small presence of Prontaean Galactic Force (PG-Force) officers for security. Expedition-class starships have the broadest scope of responsibilities. They are the ships most often used for exploration and scientific endeavors, but they also provide transport, medical and mechanical assistance, and are used for diplomatic missions.

Extraho-animi – A reader who can pull thoughts from others. It is the second level of a reader. The Cooperative requires any of their personnel with this ability to register it.

Fabricor – A replicating machine. There are various types such as a food fabricor, a clothing fabricor, and a parts fabricor. Fabricors work much like our digital printers of today but the types of things that can be made has expanded greatly.

Fargoza – The bounty hunter captain of the Bantam C.T.V. *Spike* ship.

Feast of Sato – A festival held in the Nagra Province of Toradon.

Felissa – Addams's girlfriend mentioned by Calloway.

Findlay – Commander Frida Findlay was the strict Vice Executive Commander of the *Odyssey* before J.D. Hapker. She is mentioned by Arden as being an instigator of dissention amongst his crew.

Fisher – Officer Sara Fisher is an engineering officer on the *Odyssey.*

Fortification – The name of Ander Vizubi's Bastion-class ship.

Frebt – Private Frebt is a PG-Force officer serving on the *Odyssey.*

Frida – Commander Frida Findlay was the strict Vice Executive Commander of the *Odyssey* before J.D. Hapker. She is mentioned by Arden as being an instigator of dissention amongst his crew.

Fung – Private Mei Fung is a PG-Force officer on the *Odyssey.* She serves under Sergeant Ander Vizubi.

Galunta system – A star system close to but outside of Toradon territory.

Garner – Officer Liam Garner is an extraho-animi on the *Odyssey*.

Genevian – A proper adjective used to describe a type of food. It is not stated in the story but is named from a place called New Geneva.

Gonoro – A small outpost attacked by Jori's father. Laren's family was stationed there and were killed in the attack.

Grapnes – A race of people known for being scavengers. They are described as thin and wiry, and they speak with a lot of s-sounds.

Gregson – Doctor Gregson is one of the primary doctors on the *Odyssey*.

Grendork – The Battle of Grendork was a terrible battle fought between the Cooperative and the Rabnoshk several years back. This was the battle that ended the war and inspired peace.

Gresher – Second Lieutenant Rik Gresher is one of two lieutenants serving under Major Bracht on the *Odyssey*.

Guillermo – He is one of the leading figures on the Depnaugh space station.

Guniku – A meat mentioned by Jori. It is sometimes seasoned with yakume, a type of spice.

Hae fly – A type of stinging fly mentioned by Jori.

Hanna – First Lieutenant Hanna Sharkey is one of two lieutenants serving under major Bracht on the *Odyssey*.

Hapker – Vice Executive Commander J.D. Hapker is second-in-command of the *Odyssey*.

Harbon – A race of people known for their strategic ability. Hapker mentions one as being a great schemster player.

Hardimen – A type of tree described by Jori as having broad leaves and as being strong.

Harmel - Private Jacques Harmel is a PG-Force officer serving on the *Odyssey*. His nickname is Jack Hammer, though he has a rather weak personality.

Hellana – The Hellana star system contains the planet known as the Blue Blight where Jori and Terk's ship crashed.

Heracu – A type of owl mentioned by Hapker.

Hesteben – The younger brother of Sergeant Ander Vizubi. He lives on the Depnaugh space station.

Hippoceretine – A healing drug used by medics.

Holgarth – Doctor Holgarth Canthidius is a lead science officer on the *Odyssey*. He is a haughty man who reminds Hapker of a fish.

Holo-man – A projected image of a person. This projection uses haptic technology that allows it to be touched and felt. It is used for various functions including as a visual instructor for dancing, exercise, and martial arts. It isn't always a man. It can be programmed to look like just about anything, including animals and objects. There is a more technical term for this, but it is not mentioned in this story.

Hurvans – A race of people who were mentioned by Jori as transporting laverjack beasts at the Depnaugh outpost.

Hypospray – Used by medics to inject medicine or nanites.

Imperium-animi – The strongest and most dangerous type of reader. They can wipe memories or implant thoughts into another person. The Cooperative strongly regulates people with this ability.

Inertial dampeners – A device on starships that keeps inertia from throwing and smashing the crew when the starship is being maneuvered or when it is struck.

Ishaq – Private Ishaq Bari is a PG-Force officer on the *Odyssey*. He serves under Sergeant Ander Vizubi.

Ivory – A prominent prostitute who lives on the Depnaugh space station.

Jairo Damark – The full given name of Commander J.D. Hapker.

J.D. – Vice Executive Commander J.D. Hapker is second-in-command of the *Odyssey*.

Jensin – A relatively new and adept helmsman on the *Odyssey*.

Jerom – Doctor Beck Jerom is one of the primary doctors on the *Odyssey*.

Jeruko – Sensei Jeruko is one of Jori's primary martial instructors.

Jeyana – Director Jeyana Sengupta is chief director of intelligence on the *Odyssey*.

Jintal – A Jintal master is a master that teaches people how to endure pain.

Jokko – Jokko Kimpke was an outlaw who killed many people.

Jori – A ten-year-old warrior from a race of people the Cooperative calls Tredons. Jori refers to his people as Toradon or Toradon Nohibito/Dragon People.

Kimpke – Jokko Kimpke was an outlaw who killed many people.

Kochuru – The desert-like planet where Sengupta is from.

Koshinuke – Means coward in Jori and Terk's language.

Lang – A private of the PG-Force who serves on the *Odyssey*.

Laren – A medic on the *Odyssey*.

Laverjack – The laverjack beasts are beasts mentioned by Jori as being transported by the Hurvans. They are not described.

Lazarus shield – A shield within a shield where the depletion of one initiates the other as it regenerates.

Liam – Officer Liam Garner is an extraho-animi on the *Odyssey*.

LRS – Long-range sensors.

Maderu – The name of an officer mentioned on the ship attacked by *Brimstone*.

Makala – The name of Sergeant Ander Vizubi's cat.

Mark – Someone mentioned by Ander Vizubi.

MDS – This is a read-only device used to access the Main Data Stream, which is a digital public library. Media can only be accessed via a direct-connection port and must be uploaded onto it.

Med-scanner – A medical scanning device that can detect heartbeats and a range of other physiological functions.

MEGA – Stands for mechanically enhanced genetically altered.

MEGA hunter – A slang word for a MEGA Inspection Officer.

MEGA Injunction – Some decades ago, it was popular for rich people to get genetic and biometric enhancements. Common people felt such enhancements were unfair, especially since these enhanced people considered themselves superior and tended to seek positions of power. Protests became violent. As such, governments all over the galaxy stepped up. People with unnatural abilities were ejected from positions of power and strict laws were made to protect future generations.

MEGA Inspection Officer – This officer works for an organization that roots out MEGAs and makes sure they get filed in the intergalactic database. Many officers are fanatic about their work as they strongly believe that alterations to the human body is immoral.

Mei – Private Mei Fung is a PG-Force officer on the *Odyssey*. She serves under Sergeant Ander Vizubi.

Melna – A police station in space operated by the PG-Force.

Merele – A woman mentioned by Hapker's mother.

Mierda – A curse word that means shit in Guillermo's language.

Mik – Corporal Mik Calloway is a hateful and bitter man who serves as a PG-Force officer on the *Odyssey*.

Minski – A professor at the PG Institute briefly mentioned by Hapker.

Mizuki – Emperor Mizuki is the ruthless ruler of the Toradon Nohibito/Dragon People, aka Tredons. He is often referred to as the Dragon Emperor.

MM – Stands for Mini Machine. It is a computer that is most often worn around the wrist like a brace but can be flattened and held like a tablet.

Montaro – Jori and Terk's incompetent brother who was killed by their father for being grossly incompetent.

Munchani – A race of people known for their diminutive height. Munchani is a derogatory manipulation of their actual name as it sounds like munchkin.

Nagra – The Nagra Province in Toradon hosts the Feast of Sato.

Nanites – Microscopic machines with various capabilities. The Cooperative uses them in their healing beds, enviro-suits, and more. The nanites in Jori's body can replicate into various properties. Some specialize in helping him heal while others create electronic functions that record, emit signals, or send out pulses. The Cooperative highly regulates the use of nanites since they can be used as weapons and can be dangerous if there is a flaw in their programming.

Naran – Sergeant Naran is a friend of Private Agni. He is a PG-Force officer serving on the *Odyssey*.

Nohibito – Means people in Jori and Terk's language. It is often used together with Toradon Nohibito, as in Dragon People.

Nomare – The ocean planet where Canthidius is from.

Odyssey – The name of a PCC Expedition-class vessel captained by Silas Arden. This vessel is the largest type of vessel in the PCC. It has some firepower for protection, but it is a non-military ship. The ship houses hundreds of people and their families. Families are permitted on this vessel because of its non-military nature. There are military personnel serving on this type of ship, but they act more as security than as a military force.

Office – The captain's private office located near the bridge.

Ornman Treaty – A treaty that regulates the use of weapons in Cooperative space.

Oscar – Staff Sergeant Oscar Woolley is a PG-Force officer on the *Odyssey*. He serves directly under Sergeant Ander Vizubi.

Overseer – What prominent leaders of the Grapne race call themselves. Ever since the Grapnes destroyed their homeworld with pollution, their race has spread to the stars. Many work as cargo haulers or scavengers. Overseers coordinate multiple vessels and consider themselves nobles.

P-Cam Compromise – Since different cultures have a different level of comfort regarding surveillance, the P-Cam Compromise id a way to appease the various cultures within the Cooperative. The compromise prohibits surveillance on PCC ships but permits them on PG-Force ships.

Palimyogenesis – A medical treatment that rebuilds atrophied muscles.

PCC – The Prontaean Colonial Cooperative is the sub-organization that handles intergalactic relations, conducts space exploration, performs space-based scientific endeavors, assists travelers, and sometimes provides transportation.

Perantium – A hardy type of crystal.

Period – A period is 30 days. This term is often interchangeably used with the word month.

Pershornian warfare – A source of media that describes a style of waging war.

PG-Force – The Prontaean Galactic Force is the sub-organization that polices Cooperative space.

PG Institute – The Prontaean Galactic Institute is a training facility for anyone who wants to work for the Prontaean Cooperative. The institute trains both PCC and PG-Force officers.

Pholatia – Hapker's homeworld.

Pholatian – A proper adjective defining people or things from Pholatia.

Pholatian Protector – A service-oriented military force from Pholatia.

Privy – A derogatory term for a PG-Force officer with the rank of private.

Prontaean – It is a word that describes the known galaxy. It is believed the word derived from an ancient Earthen Indo-European language where the prefix pro- means advanced or forward and the suffix -anean means relating to.

Prontaean Colonial Cooperative – The PCC is the sub-organization that handles intergalactic relations, conducts space exploration, performs space-based scientific endeavors, assists travelers, and sometimes provides transportation.

Prontaean Cooperative – The agency that governs space. It has numerous treaties with various worlds that provides its charter to keep space safe, ensure peace, regulate fair trade, and colonize new worlds. Its powers are granted by several planets, and the number of planets that are part of the Cooperative continues to grow. The Prontaean Cooperative has two aspects to it. The first is the Prontaean Colonial Cooperative (PCC). This sub-organization handles intergalactic relations, conducts space exploration, performs space-based scientific endeavors, assists travelers, and sometimes provides transportation. The second aspect is the Prontaean Galactic Force (PG-Force). This sub-organization polices space.

Prontaean Council – The Prontaean Cooperative is ruled by an elected council.

Prontaean Galactic Force – The PG-Force is the sub-organization that polices Cooperative space.

Prontaean Galactic Institute – The PG Institute is a training facility for anyone who wants to work for the Prontaean Cooperative. The institute trains both PCC and PG-Force officers.

Prontaean Games – Similar to the Olympics from ancient Earth.

Quavian baroque – A style of music.

Quigley – Corporal Rona Quigley is a PG-Force officer on the *Odyssey*. She serves under Sergeant Ander Vizubi.

Rabni – A derogatory word for a Rabnoshk warrior.

Rabnoshk – Major Bracht is from the Rabnoshk race. The culture of this race is dominated by warriors. They were once enemies of the Cooperative.

Reader – The generic term for someone who uses the power of their mind to sense emotions or to read or manipulate thoughts.

Richforth – Captain Richforth is the captain of a PG-Force ship. He recommended Hapker to Rear Admiral Zimmer. Calloway served briefly under his command.
Rik – Second Lieutenant Rik Gresher is one of two lieutenants serving under Major Bracht on the *Odyssey*.
Rocky – Rocky is an enforcer who works for Guillermo and Ander Vizubi's brother, Hesteben.
Rona – Corporal Rona Quigley is a PG-Force officer on the *Odyssey*. She serves under Sergeant Ander Vizubi.
Rosta – Doctor Rosta is a science officer serving on the *Odyssey* who can read lips. This implies she may be a linguist.
RR-5 rifle – A phaser rifle with multiple settings and functionalities.
RRAB-bot – A rapid fire artillery bot.
Safety Depot – When a ship is in danger, non-essential personnel go to one of these many designated areas to strap in. Many safety depots double as escape pods when needed.
Sakon – General Sakon is the captain of a Toradon vessel called the *Brimstone*. He is known for great violence.
Sam – Chief Sam Simmonds is the chief engineer on the *Odyssey*.
Sara – Officer Sara Fisher is an engineering officer on the *Odyssey*.
Sardeer – An ice planet mentioned by Hapker.
Sasha – Someone mentioned by Ander Vizubi. He was close to her when he lived on the Depnaugh space station.
Sato – The Feast of Sato is held in the Nagra Province of Toradon.
Scheisse – A curse word that means shit in Gresher's language.
Schemster – A complex strategic game.
Sengupta – Director Jeyana Sengupta is chief director of intelligence on the *Odyssey*.
Senshi – Means warrior in Jori and Terk's language.
Sentio-animi – The lowest level of reader. They can sense emotions only. Their ability does not force anything out or in and so people with this ability are not required to register with the Cooperative.
Serpent – A small transport ship with some firing capabilities. It is often used by the Tredons for raids or pirating.
Seth – Captain Seth is the Grapne who captains the Angolan Cougar.
Shannah – The woman Hapker was supposed to marry.

Sharkey – First Lieutenant Hanna Sharkey is one of two lieutenants serving under major Bracht on the *Odyssey.*

Shekaka – A black-market dealer at the Depnaugh outpost.

Shera – Medic Shera is a lean and exotic medical doctor serving on the *Odyssey.*

Shika – A type of deer in Toradon.

Shrana – She acts as a hostess in the lounge on the *Odyssey.*

Shuku – The name for a particular nebula that Jori is familiar with.

Silas – Captain Silas Arden is the captain of the *Odyssey.*

Simmonds – Chief Sam Simmonds is the chief engineer on the *Odyssey.*

Sindy – Private Sindy is a PG-Force officer on the *Odyssey.*

Siven – Sergeant Siven Addams is a PG-Force officer on the *Odyssey.*

Snyder – The name of one of the Grapnes.

Sonometer – Used to monitor vitals while exercising.

Spiffle the Kooky Alien – A funny cartoon character. It's funny because everyone knows there's no such thing as aliens, at least not intelligent ones.

Spike – The *C.T.V. Spike* is the name of the Bantam model ship captained by Fargoza.

SRS – Short-range sensors.

StarFire – A starfire is a type of phaser weapon with no stun setting, only kill. The *StarFire* is the name of Jori and Terk's Serpent ship.

Starhash – An addictive drug used to get high. It is not mentioned how it is ingested but assume a hypospray or other form of injection. Sometimes a stub can be laced with it, but its effects are not as strong.

Steben – Steben or Hesteben is Ander Vizubi's younger brother.

Stever – Officer Triss Stever is the bridge chief on the *Odyssey.*

Stub – Similar to a cigarette from ancient Earth.

Swift – A small ship used for transport. It is fast but has minimal firing capability.

Symphonia – Symphonia Arden is Captain Arden's wife and Steward of Entertainments on the *Odyssey.*

Tablet – A small hand-held computer device much like the tablets of the 21st century, but with more functionality. Some tablets can be folded around the wrist, and are then called an MM.

Taipan – A type of snake.

Tan – The name of one of the Grapnes.

Tanaka – Lord Tanaka is a lord in Tredon. The district he rules is not as bad as most.

Terk – Terk or Terkeshi is Jori's older brother.

Terraforming – A process of converting a planet so that it can sustain human life. This process is expensive and takes many decades, so it is only done on planets that meet a very narrow set of criteria.

Thendi – A planet that is having trouble with plate tectonics.

Tirad – The name of one of the Grapnes.

Toradon – Means dragon in Jori and Terk's language. It is often spoken as Toradon Nohibito, which means Dragon People.

Translator – A device that can translate over a thousand spoken languages across the known universe.

Transport – A device that teleports people or objects from a ship to another ship or to a planet's surface. The person or object transported must have a bio-reader.

Transport-blocker – A device that keeps the transport from working. Since the shields on a ship work the same way, transport-blockers are usually used on planets or other bodies.

Tredon – This is what everyone outside Toradon calls this race of people. It sounds like the words tread on, which is what the Toradons are known to do to people.

Triss – Officer Triss Stever is the bridge chief on the *Odyssey*.

U-Bank – One of the most prominent banks in the known universe. Each world has their own currency, but the U-Bank helps with the exchange of currency.

Universal language – This is the language of commerce. Most tradesmen and leaders of advanced worlds speak this language.

Vandoran – The Vandoran sand dunes are part of a desert on one of the planets in Toradon territory.

Veda – A Toradon senshi with the rank of second lieutenant who was killed when Jori and Terk's ship crashed.

Viewport – A large screen that shows the view from outside. Ships don't have windows, but a viewport simulates a window.

Viewsceen – A large computer screen.

Vigan – Private Vigan is a PG-Officer on the *Odyssey*. He is short and creepy looking.

Virlini – A type of non-alcoholic drink that resembles alcohol.

Virtuous Dealings – The name of the Angolan Cougar spaceship run by the Grapnes.

Vizubi – Sergeant Ander Vizubi, a PG-Force officer on the *Odyssey*.

Wendar – An uninhabited planet in the Xenar system that is known to be a good source of perantium.

Woolley – Staff Sergeant Oscar Woolley is a PG-Force officer on the *Odyssey*. He serves directly under Sergeant Ander Vizubi.

Wyndhill – A brand name of ale.

Xenar – A star system that contains the planet Wendar.

Xien Zhang – The author of *Treatise on Humankind.*

Yakume – A spice commonly used by Toradons to season steak.

Yendunian – A race of people whose dignitaries tried to blackmail Hapker.

Zervians – A race of people. A small band of them were thought to have stolen a prototype wave-emitting device from the Thendi.

Zhang – As in Xien Zhang, pronounced Shien Jang, who is the author of *Treatise on Humankind.*

Zimmer – Rear Admiral Zimmer presides over both the PCC and PG-Force. He commanded over Hapker during the Kimpke incident.

Zraben – A race of people known to be well organized, especially their arms dealers.

Zurenian – A race of people. Hapker mentions a Zurenian monk who liked to drink.

Books by Dawn Ross:

The Dragon Spawn Chronicles

StarFire Dragons
Dragon Emperor
Dragon's Fall
Isle of Hogs (a novella)
Warrior Outcast

Connect with Dawn Ross online:
DawnRossAuthor.com
Twitter.com/DawnRossAuthor
Goodreads.com/author/Dawn_Ross

About the Author

Dawn Ross currently resides in the wonderful state of Kansas where sunflowers abound. She has also lived in the beautiful Willamette Valley of Oregon and the scenic Hill Country of Texas. Dawn completed her bachelor's degree in 2017. Although the degree is in finance, most of her electives were in fine art and creative writing. Dawn is married to a wonderful man and adopted two children in 2017. Her current occupation is part time at the Meals on Wheels division of a senior service nonprofit organization. She is also a mom, homemaker, volunteer, wildlife artist, and a sci-fi/fantasy writer. Her first novel was written in 2001 and she's published several others since. She participates in the NaNoWriMo event every year and is a part of her local writers' group.

Made in the USA
Monee, IL
14 September 2024